Of Apples And Trees

RENATE ROWLAND

Runik Press

ISBN: 979-8-9883406-1-4

Author's Note

Dear reader,

Thank you for picking up my book. Before you dive into the story, I would like to warn you about certain triggers. My novel is intended for an audience of 18+ and contains explicit sexual scenes as well as mentions of domestic violence and sexual assault. If these are subjects you feel sensitive about, don't read this book.

If you do decide to give my novel a try, I hope you will enjoy the journey of my characters as much as I do.

Thank you.
Renate Rowland

Playlist

Screaming Bloody Murder – Sum 41

One Track Mind – Papa Roach

I'm Not Okay – Citizen Soldier

Just One Yesterday – Fall Out Boy

FELL IN LOVE – blink-182

Lifestyle of the Rich & Famous – Good Charlotte

Blank Space – I Prevail

The Calendar – Panic At The Disco

Wondering – Good Charlotte

Like I Roll (Jamie's Theme – Teenager)

Die Rockin (Jamie's Theme – Adult)

Next 2 You – Buckcherry

Stuck – Thirty Seconds To Mars

Shape of You – Fame on Fire

Say Fuck It – Buckcherry

Shivers – Ed Sheeran

Sin So Sweet – Warren Zeiders

Mine – Sleep Token

Say You'll Haunt Me – Stone Sour

Manic – Wage War

Enemy – Papa roach

Deep End – I Prevail

IS IT ME – Loveless

Let the Sparks Fly – Thousand Foot Krutch

bloody valentine – Machine Gun Kelly

Liar – Papa Roach

Bad Habits (Book Theme) – Ed Sheeran (feat. Bring Me The Horizon)

Wait For Me (Hayley's Theme) – From Ashes To New

Wicked Game – Theory Of A Deadman

The Jester – Badflower

Loving and Hating You – Warren Zeiders

Dynamite – Any Given Sin

forget me too – Machine Gun Kelly & Halsey

All or Nothing – Theory Of A Deadman

Perfect – Ed Sheeran

Hayley

Her life is not as blissful as it seems. Everything you see is a lie, a mask she is forced to wear in public. But there's a light at the end—Jamie, the beacon that calls her back to him each summer.

He is her escape. Her freedom. And although she knows their days are numbered, she can't resist the temptation. Each touch, each kiss, sears her to the bone. He's the one she always wanted.

2023

1

Her ponytail bounced impatiently from side to side. Hayley was on the home stretch now. One minute to go.

Her grip tightened around the rubber handles as she pushed more speed into the long, up-and-down striding motion for the final interval. The resistance increased as well. Her quads and glutes burned.

Her body had been aching to the bone prior to her workout, but she'd decided to go to the gym anyway. She needed to get out of the house. Needed the hour of freedom from her golden cage.

The guy in the free-weights section to the left was still there. She could see him from the corner of her eye, watching her. He'd arrogantly given her his unsolicited advice, offering to spot her form.

Yeah, right! On her squats, no doubt.

That was how she'd ended up on the cardio equipment. All she could think of was someone watching them together and assuming the wrong thing. There were always eyes on her, judging every move, disapproving of her going out alone to begin with.

And she wasn't even alone. Not technically. Mateo was waiting in the gym's parking lot. He was supposed to always keep her in his sight, but his ever-stoic expression was so irritating, she'd told him to wait in the car instead of making it like an Easter Island statue by the juice bar. He was intimidating the staff with his wide build and silent demeanor. Honestly, he could've been the gym's official poster boy if it weren't for his suit-and-tie outfit.

Hayley started the countdown in her head, watching the last seconds go. Sweat left a trail from the hairline at her neck down to where her leggings cinched her waist, not to mention her armpits, making her long-sleeved shirt stick uncomfortably to her skin. She couldn't wait to get it off. The sports bra was always the worst. A pool had gathered in between her boobs, and the band felt tighter now than it had thirty minutes ago.

3…

2…

1…

Done!

Hayley slowed her stride gradually before jumping off the elliptical. Her knees went soft for a second with the abrupt change, and her legs felt like cooked spaghetti. She would probably regret this tomorrow morning when she tumbled out of bed.

Her shoulders felt a little stiff too, and all she wanted to do was soak her sore muscles in a hot bath, but she didn't even have time to stretch. She'd barely squeezed the workout into her full schedule for today. Not that she'd be doing much other than parade around and look pretty with her mouth shut.

She gave the machine a quick wipe-down, then veered toward the locker rooms to wrangle herself free of the black spandex contraption around her chest.

Her hair was still damp when she arrived at the salon for her appointment. She'd be tormented in the chair for two hours before the real torture started.

Anthony kept eying her expectantly in the mirror up ahead to gauge her opinion on the makeup and hair. He was young, eager to please, and naturally looking to build a reputation with esteemed clients.

He had hopes. Dreams. A future.

There was freedom in that.

He added one more pin, then stepped back to give her a look from all angles with the hand-held mirror. It was, of course, flawless as ever. A work of art. After opening his own salon, he'd quickly made a name for himself as one of the best stylists in the state. And that was why she was here. To receive the best. But she hadn't *chosen* this. All decisions were made *for* her.

She had none of the freedom.

Still, he was probably the only one who actually cared whether Hayley liked her appearance or not. She gave him a polite smile and a nod of approval. It was the mask she wore in public.

How could no one see her screaming underneath it?

Hayley focused on her reflection. She felt dead inside. She didn't recognize the woman staring back at her. She was a beautiful shell.

A bright future indeed…

Unlike me.

Before the thought could consume her, she forced a slow blink, then glanced at the woman doing her French nails. She would've wanted them black to match the void inside her, but that wasn't an option.

Don't let them see you break.

Hayley endured. Silently.

Once the basics were done, Mateo took her home to get dressed. Hayley picked the piece herself, but her options tonight were limited. The only cocktail dress with long sleeves was the black Tom Ford turtleneck. It had a large asymmetrical cutout across her left shoulder that, if she shifted it right, would cover all the necessary areas.

An hour later, she stepped out of the car, all dolled up to be shown off like a prized pony.

That was her sole purpose. To be seen. Not heard.

And there were a lot of people watching. The crowd out front was huge. Both sides of the carpeted aisle were filled with Press and onlookers alike, shoving to get a better glimpse of the limos that pulled up. They were held back by a thick black rope.

Hayley drew up a smile, but not enough to show teeth. Cameras flashed in her eyes as she set one foot in front of the other. The grand opening tonight was reserved for the A-listers. No one without a personal invitation got to see the long-anticipated interior until tomorrow, but that didn't mean it wasn't already packed inside.

The entrance to the brand-new casino was striking. The attached hotel had undergone renovations last year, and it had been decided to build the addition to draw in more money through entertainment. Tourism was always booming, so everyone profited, but the 'Good Governor' had played a major role in the operation.

Hayley's attention was captured by the striking arches and high tray ceilings. It was something you'd find at the *Bellagio* in Vegas, and there was even a large, rectangular fountain basin in the center. But that was as far as the comparison went. Each cascading tier of the water feature was lit in a different color, from turquoise to blue to deep purple. It was a very modern, contemporary design, unlike anything she'd ever seen.

What else struck her was the sporadic application of copper. Where classic casino hotels like the *Bellagio* used gold, crystal chandeliers, and white marble tiles, the *Zion* set itself apart with the extravagant use of limestone. It really embodied the local personality.

Hayley lingered a little too long when the hand at her back nudged her onward.

A crystal champagne flute was roughly shoved into her hand, probably to keep her mouth occupied as a gentleman approached them, immediately falling into small talk that had the air of familiarity.

There was lots of gray in his brown hair and beard. He appeared to be her father's age, but she didn't recognize him or bother remembering his name when he introduced himself to her with a flaccid handshake.

Is there anything worse for a man than making a limp first impression? She was a woman, but her hands weren't delicate. Hayley preferred a firm grip on things.

Looking the other way, she tried to tune out the conversation going on beside her. Her eyes scanned the blinking lights and jingling machines. There was too much noise. She longed for the seclusion of her library… the silence under the stars… her haven…

A terse kiss was pressed to her cheek, which she hardly felt. It was a reflex. No affection. And as such, she disregarded it.

As her male company excused themselves to play poker in one of the private lounges, Hayley took to browsing on her own. Champagne in hand, she made her pass around the familiar faces. She only did the bare minimum of socializing—didn't feel like talking to anyone—but she sensed everyone's stares.

Instinctively, she tugged on the top of the sleeve at her upper arm to make sure it stayed where it needed to and also double-checked her cleavage. The cutout was so big that the left side above her chest as well as half her back were exposed in the snug bodycon midi.

She'd become one of them, hiding behind a fake smile. A mask. She couldn't wait to get away.

Just a few more weeks…

Ashley Townse spotted her in the crowd and gave her a high wave before making a move to stroll over.

Fuck!

Hayley downed the rest of her champagne, then quickly reached for another from a passing waiter. If she started swaying, she could blame it on the feeble heels.

She exchanged her empty glass for a full one on the tray as Ashley came up behind her in a vintage, dark purple petticoat dress that matched the color of the fountain. Lime green ruffles stuck out from under the hem. She had a very versatile fashion sense and could pull off anything from cowgirl to emo punk. Today, she was a cross between Audrey Hepburn and Maleficent.

"You've done an amazing job with the interior design," Hayley said, raising her drink in a toast.

"Thank you." She mimicked the gesture. "The new casino was quite an undertaking. A baptism by fire, if you will."

The mayor had thrown his daughter a bone by giving her full control of the casino's construction. She ran her own business and had done other jobs on a smaller scale before this.

"And you passed with flying colors." Sure, it was gorgeous, but Hayley couldn't shake her concern about all the taxpayer money that had gone into it. "What's going to be your next project?"

Ashley lowered her glass. A sly grin teased her bright red lips. She was no more than five feet tall, and Hayley had some significant height over the short female in her Louboutins, but the edge of deviance in her expression was unnerving.

"Nothing as ambitious." She shrugged innocently, giving her coffee-colored blowout a little bounce on her shoulders. "We're having a fashion show in a few weeks. You should come. I'll send you the e-vite."

Hayley cringed. She didn't mind the woman, they were about the same age, but she was a little too outgoing. Starting with her shoulder-length hair that she wore down as opposed to having it pinned into an elaborate chignon. Her own felt so tight, it was as though she'd gotten a free facelift with it.

Maybe the eccentric event was exactly what she needed.

"Alright," Hayley agreed gruffly.

"Yay! Awesome!" Her steel blue eyes gleamed at the prospect, and her hair did another bounce. "Then I'll at least have one friendly face in the crowd."

Hayley almost choked on a laugh. She wouldn't go as far as considering her expression *friendly*. The fake smile was hardly a step up from resting-bitch-face.

Ashley didn't notice. Her eyes caught on something over Hayley's shoulder that seemed to be a more pressing matter. She sputtered a quick excuse, her body already in motion to leave.

"Oh," she halted to touch her free hand to Hayley's arm in a warm gesture. "And there will be a theme. Dress accordingly." She winked, then whipped past.

Dress up? As in costumes? She felt as though she were already wearing one.

Hayley hoped she wasn't going to regret that. How much worse could it get?

Closing her eyes, she dragged in a long breath, and her mind slipped into that calm place that was her refuge. She pictured the light beaming through the lush green, the sunset painting the sky in a rainbow of colors over the mountains, and the bright blue she would never forget.

And then she felt at peace because there was one thing she had to look forward to. The one thing no one had managed to steal from her yet. That one trip she still took every year, granting her a little taste of freedom away from this pretentious crap.

Just a few more weeks…

"Bring it, you pussy. I can do this all fucking day."

White-hot rage blinded him. It fueled his blood with a fire he hadn't felt in a long time. And he gave in to it. Unleashed the fury building in his veins. One brutal, unrelenting hit after another collided with the guy's jaw, cheek, temple…

The violence in his blood resurfaced, drawn out by a careless remark. A stupid joke. But it was enough to get his temper going.

Jameson's vision flipped to red as he embraced the rush. Everything was a blur. Right… left… right. He kept pummeling his helpless victim. The man on the ground beneath him had stopped fighting back the moment he'd straddled him, but he couldn't contain the blows that exploded out of him like bullets from a machine gun.

And there was blood. Lots of it. He'd probably broken his nose. Knocked out a tooth or two.

Someone yanked him off by his shoulders. It wasn't easy. Whoever tried to peel him off was below his weight class.

But he submitted to the pull, knowing if he didn't stop now, he'd end up killing the guy. And he was still trying to avoid hard prison time.

A sharp burn traveled through his cracked knuckles. The skin had burst open, leaving deep gashes.

Jameson lifted his fist, letting the fresh blood trickle down his forearm. He hadn't even felt the pain through the adrenaline rush. The left side of his face ached too, around the eye socket. The bastard must've gotten a hit in himself. He had no recollection of that. He'd been in a frenzy. And damn him, but it had felt good to let it all out.

Staring at his own injuries, a different scene replayed before his eyes. The night that had landed his ass in jail. He had been on a downward spiral with no bottom.

Jameson didn't need a reminder of how he had gotten there. The wound remained a gaping hole in his chest.

He worked his fingers, clenching and unclenching them to coax the mobility back. The fight had ended his clean streak. Just when he thought his life was finally on a good track and things were looking up.

His head protested every time the hammer struck a nail. Jameson felt the massive hangover the next morning as the sun beat down on his neck. He thought about the social obligations everybody had, like finishing high school and getting a job. But then what?

His chest dropped with a sigh while watching Elliot chase after his big sister. The strides of the seven-year-old were much too long for his little legs to keep up with. Nevertheless, his pitter-patter followed her like an echo, never relenting.

Their laughter rang in his ears, tugging at something inside him.

Why was he running from this? The chance of a future filled with more than the need for a steady paycheck finally presented itself. A good paying job, a wife and kids. He could have that with Amber. Why wasn't he fucking content with that?

Deep down, he knew the answer. His heart yearned for a passion he'd once known. A good kind. Not the one that made him violent.

A heavy thud was followed by a cry that pierced his eardrums.

Shit!

Jameson kicked off a sprint down the lawn. He was on Elliot in a flash, cradling his body to his chest to take him to the house. Tiny fingers gripped the shirt as he buried his face in the fabric. His warm breath seeped through the cotton fibers, heating the skin underneath.

"Mommy! Mommy!" His sobbing voice broke out the moment they stepped onto the back deck.

The doors were open, and she must've heard Elliot's scream because she came rushing toward them before they made it inside.

Her hands shot out to take her boy away, her eyes never lifting to meet Jameson's. She took one look at the scrapes along his knuckles and knew they weren't from working outside.

"Thank you. You can leave," she said in an abrasive manner.

Jameson stalled. He didn't want to let go.

2

Hayley packed up her car and left home early in the morning, as soon as the coast was clear. For once, there would be no one on her tail. Even Mateo had the three-day weekend off, and she got to do the driving herself. Which was nice. She rarely had the chance.

She drove the whole way with a lead foot, keeping an eye out for troopers on the road and only stopping twice to go pee. Traffic wasn't too bad either.

It was a little past noon when she arrived at the Airbnb. She unloaded the small suitcase that only held the bare necessities and unlocked the tiny cabin.

The inside was no bigger than a tree house: a minimalistic kitchen, a seating corner, and a loft bed she had to climb a ladder to reach. Somehow they'd also managed to squeeze a full-size bathroom into the confined space.

Every nook and cranny was utilized. Hayley thought of it as a house fit for a fairy. It was freakin' adorable.

She flung her suitcase onto the loveseat and unlatched it. She was ecstatic as she dug through the few layers. Come Monday morning, things were back to their usual pattern, but for three days, she was free, nobody telling her what to do, what to wear, or how to act.

Three days. That was all she had. So she'd better make the most of it.

After a change of clothes, Hayley went back to her car for her shoes. She couldn't wait to break in the new Merrells. She'd splurged on the ones with extra ankle support. They were better suited for the rough terrain than the low sneaker style.

A woodpecker was going at it with a tree somewhere in the distance, telling her to get a move on already. She hopped out of the SUV's trunk space with her ponytail pulled through the back of her cap and her hood raised. The August sun was hot, so she left the zipper of her athletic jacket halfway down to catch a breeze. The smell of earth and pine tingled through her nose as she inflated her lungs.

She grabbed a light lunch at the lodge nearby before embarking on her first hike for the weekend. Soaring mountain tops awaited her right around back with the familiar thousand-foot drop to the crystal-clear lake below.

The sweeping view at the summit was as thrilling as she remembered. The switchbacks down the steep mountainside had lost none of their horror over the years. Her stomach twisted into knots the same way it had done the first time she'd laid eyes on it, but the wind called to her, welcoming her home.

On her steady descent, she weaved through the huckleberry bushes that cluttered the trail. They were full and overgrown this season. She presumed that not too many tourists were sampling the goods these days. People kept their distance, as though the place were haunted.

She slowed her pace to let her fingers dance across the tops. Twigs pricked her fingers and snagged on the nylon of her long sleeves. The rough contact startled her. It felt so foreign.

Smooth, delicate textures were more common in her world. Clothing, as well as furniture, were all high-end quality with ridiculous price tags. Everything had to be glazed or polished to perfection to hide the flaws underneath. It made her miss the raw savageness of nature.

As she picked a few berries off the branches to put in her mouth, she reminisced about her date with Jamie. For a moment, the sweet taste transported her back to the naïve girl she'd once been, chasing dreams. She was herself a porcelain doll, glued back together more times than she could count.

Hayley followed the small path along the cascading waterfall, taking in the force plummeting down the mountain. The boardwalk she was standing on trembled from the power of the rushing flood, and the fresh scent of water and rock sent more ripples down her spine.

She dropped the hood of her jacket to feel the spray on her skin. Wearing it up was a force of habit. It created a sort of safe place for her to hide. She hated being on display. Always exposed.

Ducking back into her shell, Hayley continued on the trail. It wasn't difficult to pick the right one out of the various options in the woods. The winding course of the creek led the way to her ultimate destination. There'd be no turning back until she reached it. Her feet moved on their own.

She snubbed the planked walkway, skipping from boulder to boulder instead. The traction of the outsole on her shoes worked like magic.

Until the rock itself lost its grip on the creek bed.

Her pulse kicked into gear. The momentum from her jump knocked one of the supports loose, and she went tumbling with it. Water splashed into her vision. Hands splayed, she braced her fall in the ice-cold stream, her face inches from smashing into the next boulder.

Close call! She should probably leave the shenanigans up to the professionals. Her day job consisted of little more than prancing around in high heels. She wasn't exactly moonlighting as a free runner.

Hayley pushed herself to a stand and looked down. The Gore-Tex membrane on her Sedona Sage Moab 3 had been worth every penny. Four inches deep in water, her feet were dry. Unfortunately, her hands hadn't been that lucky. Her right palm was cut, and sharp pain raced up her arm. There was a small tear on her lower leg as well. The rocks had sliced right through her leggings.

What was it with this mountain trying to eat her alive?

She wiped her hands down her thighs and kept going, ignoring the minor setback. When she reached the last clearing before crossing into the restricted perimeter, she pushed through the ache in her leg and went into an all-out sprint, holding nothing back.

She wanted to feel the wind on her face. Wanted to feel the blood pumping in her veins. But most of all… she wanted to feel alive.

Hayley came to a stop in the middle of the old-growth forest, panting for air. She hunched over, hands on her knees. Her lungs were on fire. Her heart battered the inside of her chest. It felt wrong to step foot on the premises. If she got caught and the cops were called, she was screwed. There would be no more hiding her annual adventure. She would get arrested, and that was as good as a death sentence in her situation.

Despite being abandoned, the property still appeared well-maintained. She'd always wondered if there was a groundskeeper taking care of it. She'd never encountered anyone on her sporadic trips here, but she knew the resort hadn't gone bankrupt. It had been shut down years ago, and according to her inquiries in town, no one had seen the heir of

Bishop Park, as Jamie was known to the locals, in as long. She'd asked around without making her inquiry too obvious. It was as if the ground had swallowed him up. Or maybe the lake?

Hayley straightened and took no more than one step forward when she caught the distinctive *click* of a rifle being cocked behind her.

2012

3

'*Y*ou'll *make friends… forge bonds for life*,' Dad's words mocked her when the doors sprang open to launch them into summer camp.

Like the kids on the bus weren't the same bunch, she was forced to tolerate every single day of the year locked up in that school. At least the scenery here was a lot better than in the old, stuffy classrooms. The best part, though, was that she'd have a cabin to herself. In the dorms at school, she shared a room with Heather. It was torture.

Hayley stepped off the bus, clutching her notebook close to her chest. Her eyes immediately scanned her surroundings for an escape route. Four hours on the cramped bus with Satan's spawn had been overkill.

She wanted to hide. Crawl into a small, dark space and get lost for the next three weeks.

"Hey, Carter! Wait up."

Speaking of the devil. Hayley's dorm mate brushed past her to meet up with the rest of the popular crowd, leaving the delinquents behind. To make a point of her disdain, Heather rammed her shoulder into Hayley's back, knocking the books out of her hands in the process. Carter and Joey laughed as the vile girl caught up to them, throwing one last spiteful glance her way. Long, blonde hair styled to perfection framed her head; no roots showed to make it appear natural, but Hayley knew better. The color was as fake as her extended eyelashes and full lips. Barely fifteen, and she was already dabbling with Botox. Well, the apple never fell far from the tree, did it?

Hayley dialed her laser beam glare down a notch and started picking up her notebooks. Good thing her Kindle was safely stored in the backpack slung over her shoulder. By the time she'd gathered them, she was alone in the parking lot.

It was just as well. She never felt like she belonged. She was the ugly duckling no one paid much attention to, with ash brown hair, eyes that were more gray than green and lacked any form of vibrancy compared to Heather's cornflower blues. They were also hidden behind a pair of plain black frames that did nothing to attract boys her age.

She pushed her glasses up the bridge of her nose and made her way to the common room. Once she made it through the check-in process, she was home free. It was only a matter of minutes—

Hayley's heart sank when her eyes landed on the crowd. Other buses must have arrived minutes prior, and the room was packed full. It would take probably an hour to get to her cabin. She couldn't even see the walls from her low vantage point of five-foot-two. Everyone was shoving and yelling well over the indoor level. She couldn't breathe in the mayhem.

Hayley backed out of the main building, keeping her head down and clutching her books tighter to her chest. She hung a right, which led her toward a larger log cabin that had no number on it. It appeared to be a homestead. The windows were open, and she could hear voices inside.

Plopping down on the low stone wall, she finally took a deep breath. The sweet smell of freshly baked chocolate chip cookies wafted her way, and she inhaled more deeply, letting the aroma settle her anxiety.

"Be careful. They're piping hot," a woman's voice called out.

But the warning came too late for the poor soul reaching for them. A man's bellowing wince was followed by a curse.

Melodious laughter burst from inside. "Told ya."

Hayley caught the sound of footsteps coming her way too late, and the back door beside her swung open, making her flinch.

"Oh! Sorry, honey, didn't mean to scare you. Are you lost?"

Hayley looked up at the woman standing in the frame and was immediately struck by her stunning blue eyes. They were simply captivating. She flashed a warm smile that came off as more than the polite gesture she was used to at school or her father's residence. It was open. And welcoming. And honest.

"Um, no. I just... I was going to check-in, but it's too crowded in there," Hayley stammered, thumbing over her shoulder toward the common building. "I was waiting for it to clear out a bit."

"No worries. Come on in," the woman said, stepping back and opening the door wider. "Would you like a cookie? They're fresh."

"Don't touch those, they're hot."

Hayley's eyes found the burn victim half-standing, half-sitting on a stool at the island. He pointed at the oven rack in front of him, which had an empty space where a cookie should have been.

"Yeah. I've heard," she giggled.

The dark-skinned young man tossed the last bite into his mouth and raised both hands in a shrug, head cocked to the side. "Worth it."

He swiped some crumbs off the counter and rose to leave the kitchen through the open archway on the opposite side. Hayley couldn't see where it led. He nearly filled the entire frame with his massive upper body.

"Don't mind Carl. He's a bad role model," the woman laughed. "Have a seat."

She pointed toward the closest stool and went around to the cabinet for a plate. Her dark curls fell back from her face as she reached up. "Is this your first time here?"

"Yes," Hayley replied. "My father insisted. He used to come here when he was a teenager and was very fond of the place." *'Lots of great memories,'* he'd always said. Though he'd never actually elaborated on them. But then he'd been a lot more outgoing than his daughter, too, hadn't he? She didn't have any great expectations for summer camp. It was merely an escape.

Carl's deep, hushed voice talking to someone else in the back drew Hayley's attention toward the archway, but her host didn't notice. A soft snicker trailed his remark, and then came the slam of a door.

"The first day can be quite overwhelming." The woman stepped into her view, snapping her focus back. "I promise it'll get better."

"Thanks," Hayley said, taking the plate she held out to her.

Her fingers were bare of jewelry. The only piece Hayley could see was a thin silver chain around her neck with a simple cross pendant.

Her host lowered herself down on the kitchen island, leaning into her elbows, hands clasped. "What kind of things are you into? We have lifeguards, in case you're not a strong swimmer."

Swimming?!

No way was she going to get into a swimsuit. Fourteen and underdeveloped… boys weren't exactly tripping over themselves for her. She'd rather be caught dead than stand next to Heather.

"We offer all kinds of outdoor activities around the lake," she switched the topic, catching Hayley's discomfort with the first suggestion. "And the common room has sign-up sheets for other stuff too."

Hayley took one of the cookies that had now cooled to a safe temperature and raised it to her mouth. She didn't want to offend the woman, but she'd be happy to spend the entire time locked up in her cabin.

"I haven't really thought about anything," she admitted sheepishly, sinking into her bite—

Oh. My. God.

Her taste buds exploded in a whirl of euphoria. She couldn't contain her moan. The chocolate chips melted on her tongue. It was heaven.

"*Mmmm…* this is *soooo* good."

"I'm glad you like it," she chuckled. "My name's Beth, by the way. Feel free to call me that."

"Uh, Hayley. Hayley Wilkins."

"Wilkins, huh?" Beth propped her chin on her hand and tipped her head as if she were studying Hayley's face. But maybe she was simply making a mental note.

"Okay, then. Nice to meet you, Hayley." Her eyes crinkled with a deeper, even more profound smile than seemed humanly possible. Beth had a spark about her that reached right into Hayley's soul. She was the most beautiful woman she'd ever seen.

A sharp pain erupted in the center of her chest. Hayley hardly knew her mother. She'd passed away when she was only two years old, and her father had raised her all on his own.

Well, that wasn't exactly true. There'd been plenty of nannies over the years.

"May I have another?" Hayley asked, eyeing the addiction-worthy baked goods in front of her to deflect from her sudden unease. Carl was totally right. The cookies were worth the pain of a second-degree burn. They were like crack… she presumed.

Beth beamed. "Of course, honey. Have as many as you like."

"You make the best cookies I've ever had."

"Oh, I didn't make them," she laughed, waving her hand dismissively. "I just pulled them out of the oven."

Beth's eye caught on something over Hayley's shoulder, and she jerked up, her brows set in a subtle frown. Snatching a set of keys from the counter by the door, she reached for the handle and swung it wide.

"Hey, Jamie," she called out, tossing the keys. "Move the truck for me, will ya?"

They were caught in a hand with a soft *clank* and no verbal acknowledgment. Hayley couldn't see whom she was addressing.

"I'd better go," she said, picking up the books in her lap and rising from her seat. The crowd in the common room should've cleared out by now, and who knew where her luggage from the bus had been dumped.

"Here. Take some to go." Beth turned to grab four more cookies off the rack, then shoved them into Hayley's hands. "And my kitchen's always open," she tagged on with a wink.

Hayley didn't know if she meant for additional cookies or to talk, but she had a feeling Beth was offering both.

She pushed out of the kitchen's back door and locked onto the boy's profile in the Silverado's cabin as he put the truck into gear. The white reverse lights came on, and when he swung around to look over his shoulder, she caught a glimpse of his grin.

Too bad it wasn't directed at her. *Go figure*

4

J ameson brushed a hand through his hair, picking out another dried leaf. The dark mop on his head was never *not* tousled by the wind or from sleeping outside. Of course, Mom didn't approve of the latter, but he loved the outdoors. He knew the mountain like the back of his hand—knew the best places to hide and which ones had the best views.

Like the one he was currently enjoying.

The knee on his jeans was torn on his right leg, a patch of skin peeking through the fist-size hole as he propped it up; grass stains covered much of the rest of the blue denim. He didn't care about the remarks regarding his homeless look. The forest *was* his home, and he would rather stay outdoors all day. He only went home to change or grab a bite to eat. The insults about his appearance couldn't touch him.

Mom had insisted he switch to the local high school for his freshman year because she wanted him to make friends his age. He couldn't have cared less. As an only child, he'd grown up around the staff of the small resort and preferred the company of adults. The kids at school were alright, but he'd never clicked with any of them. He was a loner. And even after finishing his sophomore year, he was no closer to building any kind of lasting friendship.

The kids from summer camp were a different breed, though. The boys were pricks, and he couldn't stand the prissy girls with the 'Daddy's Little Princess' complex. Better to hang back and watch them tear each other apart. It was like a prison courtyard: you'd stick to your clique for protection, or you'd get eaten alive. Among their peers, there was no real friendship. They had everything they could ever ask for, yet envy and jealousy made them all bullies.

He hated the entitled kids. He had privileges too. The privilege of growing up here due to his family owning the place. For as long as he could remember, they'd offered this full-program summer camp where the rich could dump their offspring for three weeks every July.

"Hey, my man, how's it hanging?"

His head did a one-eighty to see Carl coming down the slanted hillside that led to the lake.

"Should've known I'd find you here. Watching the girls in their teeny bikinis?"

Jameson leaned back on his elbows, the incline of the slope providing the perfect angle. "Nothing wrong with enjoying the view."

"Got that right," he shot back, plopping down.

Jameson watched him stretch his six-foot-four body out next to him in the grass, folding his arms behind his head and crossing his ankles.

"Aren't they a bit young for you, *old man*?" he heckled.

Carl burst into a laugh. "For me? Sure. But I was expecting to find you with your dick in your hand. The rack on that blonde one… *goddamn*."

Jameson lifted his can of ginger ale in a salute. "Sorry to disappoint."

The soda was currently the only thing in his hand. He was technically on duty. He was the backup lifeguard. He'd met all the requirements to certify last year, but Mom wouldn't let him take over until he turned sixteen.

Buzzkill.

But she'd given him more responsibilities this year. So, he couldn't complain. Even let him take the truck to run errands as long as he stayed on the property.

Carl and he watched the new instructor at the canoes try to teach the group the basics. Jameson never bothered remembering their names. They were only here for summer camp and hardly ever returned the following year.

Mr. Canoe, in his bright orange shorts, had his work cut out for him. Though sign-up for the program was voluntary, the kids seemed to hardly care. *Barbie*, the tall blonde Carl was referring to, giggled through the whole introduction while *Ken* whispered in her ear. Off and on, their glances would dart toward *Mr. Canoe*, and they'd roll their eyes.

She was wearing a pink two-piece that matched her Latina twin's swimsuit in color but was far more revealing. Jameson couldn't argue with Carl. She was fine. Her friend, though, had smooth, caramel-colored skin that made him wonder what it would be like to touch her. He'd bet she smelled good too.

Jameson was itching to go down there. Not that he was hoping someone would get into trouble, but he wanted to do more than watch from the sidelines. Maybe *Barbie* could suffer a leg cramp…

Then again, he was merely a backup. What were the chances of him seeing any action?

28

5

As the weeks flew by too quickly, Hayley stopped by the homestead on numerous occasions, and it hadn't come as a surprise when Beth asked about her parents. Where she came from, people always wanted to know whose kid they were addressing. Whose parents they had to suck up to. Nobody wanted to get caught trash-talking to the wrong brat—Carter's, of course, had some of the biggest draw, with his father's political influences as governor.

Hayley's situation was the opposite. Sure, Dad running the family's pharmaceutical business was an easy enough answer, but the topic of her mother tended to steer the conversation into the usual morose territory.

She didn't like talking about her circumstances. Didn't like the pity in people's reactions.

But it was Beth's candid nature that made her company the only one worth seeking out.

Well… almost the only one.

During each one of her visits to Beth, Hayley hoped to catch another glimpse of the intriguing boy. To her disappointment, Jamie never seemed to be around the house when she was.

Perhaps it was for the best. What was the point?

Hayley enjoyed her free time any chance she could. Unlike her strict routine at school, none of the activities at Bishop Park were mandatory, leaving her to make her own schedule.

And the lack of a dress code was also a relief. Hayley stuck to wearing jeans and a t-shirt. Nothing flashy. Because there was nothing *to* flash anyway. The pleated skirt of the academy's standard uniform wasn't short, but it still granted easy access for uninvited touching.

It had taken her months to shake the sensation of Carter's hand on her every time she'd thought about it. As if it could've brushed up the bare skin of her thigh by accident.

Horseshit!

He could shove that lame apology up his ass. Hayley wasn't fooled by his fake smile and pretty features that wrapped everyone else around his finger. Deep down, he was vile.

Like his father.

Because that was the way of family. Sooner or later, you would follow in your parents' footsteps. Marriages were arrangements of convenience. The designated couples were easily identified at school. Heather had her match in Carter. Teresa was dating Joey. And Hayley? She would end up married to some influential prick of her father's choosing. Some preppy rich kid, working in his daddy's firm, looking to make him proud. A man she would no doubt despise. It didn't matter what she wanted. Her life would never be her own again.

A few weeks at summer camp were all she had. It was the closest she could come to tasting freedom.

Hayley was on her way back from lunch in the dining hall when Carter came up the hill, his arm slung around Heather's neck.

"Hay-Hay! Wait up!" he called out.

She didn't. She had no interest in the latest gossip about who'd gone to third base with whom over the summer. Nor did she want to become the object of that gossip. Best to avoid them at all costs.

Clutching her Kindle, she picked up her pace a little, but the flip-flopping behind her got gradually louder as her pursuers broke into a jog. They caught up to her right outside Beth's home.

"Slow down, will ya?" Carter's heavy hand landed on her shoulder, and he spun her around. "Where're you off to in such a hurry?"

"Back to your cabin to hide?" Heather chimed.

Carter ignored her mocking tone. "We're headed to the lake for a swim. Why don't you join us?"

Why? Because it was a trick to embarrass her in front of everyone. And it wouldn't be the first time they'd done it.

"Can't. Sorry. I already have plans," she lied to get away from them.

It wasn't *technically* a lie. She wanted to get a head start on packing so she could beat the crowd to the bus. They'd be leaving in the morning.

"She's probably going to touch herself while reading one of her smutty romance novels," her roommate laughed.

Like she read any of that garbage. The books Heather had flaunted back at school after supposedly finding them under Hayley's pillow had been her own. She'd used the false accusations as another way to embarrass her.

"Come on, Hayley. You don't even have a tan. You should come with us," Carter tried again. His finger hooked around the strap of her top, eyes wandering down her modest cleavage.

Was he attempting to coax her into a threesome?

Hayley swatted his hand away. "Don't touch me," she hissed.

His features turned hostile. "Prude bitch. We just want to have a little fun."

"You mean *you* want to have a little fun. I want no part of this." Hayley raised her chin with her jaw locked tight.

Carter huffed, glaring down at her, then opened his mouth—

The abrupt sound of footsteps approaching made them all flinch. He stepped back, making it appear as though they were engaged in casual conversation right as Beth's son rounded the corner. He was wearing a navy blue tee today with some kind of graphic she couldn't make out. He shot them a quick look of indifference before refocusing on the direction he was going. Kicking up loose gravel with his black military boots, he paid them no attention.

Heather grimaced in disgust. "Is that a hole in his shirt?"

She was referring to the long-sleeve plaid that was tied low around his hips.

"Fucking hobo," Carter said loud enough to overhear.

The boy ignored him. He ripped the rear door to the kitchen open and disappeared behind it.

That was fine. Hayley hadn't expected him to care.

Carter turned back, throwing her another disdainful glance, and then walked off, Heather in tow, swaying her ass.

Holding her head high, Hayley trotted back to her little sanctuary.

After tracking down her luggage that first day, she'd settled in the cabin that was the last one in a row of sixteen on this side of the resort. It was perfect. Right behind that lay an open stretch of grass, and past that… the woods.

It was mostly quiet since hardly anyone stayed in their cabin during the day. Other than taking part in various programs at the lake, the boys played football while the girls gathered on the beach volleyball field.

Hayley had refrained from signing up for any activities. Instead, she'd played the occasional game of chess in the common room and mostly hung out in her refuge to read during the three weeks.

With every item she packed into her little black suitcase, she dreaded her return to school. She couldn't wait to come back to Bishop Park. She had gotten a taste of freedom she'd never experienced before.

Thunk!

Something hit her wall with a dull sound, and a boy's laughter erupted outside of her window.

Hayley rose to her feet. Beyond the pane, Beth's son Jamie was goofing off with Carl, or *Mr. Fix-it* as he was called due to his habitual line of 'I'm on it' before anyone even asked. She guessed him to be in his early twenties. A lit cigarette dangled between his lips, and little puffs of smoke escaped as he shook his head and laughed.

She'd encountered Jamie only once in all the times she'd searched Beth out in her kitchen. He'd caught the car keys in his clasped hands, flashing a wide grin back at his mom. He looked older than herself by a year, at least. Maybe two. He was muscular for his age, too. She assumed it was from the resort's manual labor. But the best part?

He had his mother's eyes.

Even from a distance, Hayley had seen them clear as day, while he'd watched the other girls—Heather and Teresa being the center of his attention, much like anyone else's.

With his back toward her, she watched him bend down to pick up the football that had hit the side of her cabin. Taking aim, he drew his arm back and faked a throw, making Carl flinch in anticipation. Then, in one long, graceful stride, he sent it soaring like a rocket down the field.

Hayley stared in amazement. He had one hell of an arm.

But Jamie didn't stay still. He charged after it, long legs pumping like pistons, his open shirt billowing behind him.

Keeping his eyes on the ball, Carl shifted his weight and started sprinting. The ball went far and high before it made its descent. Tall as he was, he had to catch air to reach it and was promptly tackled to the ground. The kid was so fast. His shoulder hit the grown man square in the chest, plowing him over, and sending them both tumbling.

They wrestled in the grass for possession over the fumbled ball, boots digging into the ground for traction, kicking up dirt. Hayley couldn't see who had the upper hand. Carl didn't cut him any slack. Elbows flailed. It was an even match, neither of them holding back.

Somehow, during their scramble, the ball bounced free. Jamie lunged for it in a perfect combat roll that landed him in a crouch five feet away, cradling the valuable egg.

Howling in triumph, he pushed off first. He spiked the ball and threw his hands up. "Suck it, old man."

Carl sat up three long seconds later with a grunt, his cigarette still pinned in his mouth. His hand lifted to it, and his cheeks hollowed as he took a slow drag. He let his shoulders sag in resignation. Taking his time getting to his feet, he brushed loose dirt off the seat of his jeans.

The boy's unrestrained laughter was infectious. Hayley hadn't even noticed her mouth curving into a smile while she watched him until she caught her reflection in the glass in front of her.

Blowing the smoke of his cigarette up in the air, Carl suddenly stiffened when his eyes connected with Hayley's.

She'd been made.

His lips moved, speaking to the boy whose back was turned toward her, he pivoted his stance to look over his shoulder.

On a gasp, she ducked under the window, hiding out of view, her heart pounding against her ribcage.

Had he seen her?

6

Don't do it. You can't punch him.

Jameson took a deep breath, inflating his lungs to the max. Clenching his fist tights at the same time, he focused on his body's response to the boy's remarks. The burn from the adrenaline rushed through him, igniting a fire inside as it flooded every cell. But he didn't close his eyes. He kept them level on the sandy-haired boy, in case he was contemplating kicking up his verbal assault to battery.

He stared off at *Ken*, the ringleader of the boys. He and his two friends had cornered him behind the dining hall, giving it one last try to provoke him before getting on their bus out of here.

'Don't let him get to you, Jamie,' Mom had told him. *'You're better than him.'*

But what she meant was, *'I raised you better than that.'*

He knew violence was in his blood—hardwired into him. Dad had hurt people. Killed even. Jameson wanted to break the cycle. Conquer the temper and anger issues he inherited from the man, because God knew there was no violent bone in Mom's body.

The question was, could her nurturing outweigh his father's nature?

They made fun of him for his clothes, yet his jeans were the only ones that hadn't come pre-torn. He usually ripped them while climbing. And he'd ruined another shirt yesterday. There was blood on it too, where the tree branch had cut him on his fall. Mom had been pissed. Probably more at his fall, though.

It was the first time the boys had sought him out directly. He didn't even know their names. Didn't care. None of these entitled brats meant anything to him. They were no more than faces that passed through here every summer, interchangeable like rats. He tried to ignore them, but the insults kept coming.

He knew the mouthy little shit was afraid of him. Saw it in his shifty, hazel eyes. Jameson wasn't only taller. He was bigger, too. It wouldn't even be a fair fight.

So, that was why it was now three against one.

Am I allowed to defend myself?

Or was he expected to turn the other cheek to the rich folk?

His heart hammered behind his sternum, and a drop of water ran down his temple from his still-damp hair. He'd taken a dip in the lake before sunrise. The cool water was a thrill he never grew tired of. The thrill of getting knocked out, on the other hand… not so much fun.

But even if he didn't take the first punch, he couldn't do that to his mom. Couldn't bear the look of disappointment on her beautiful face. She already worried too much about him. July was hard on her, too; that was when Dad had been killed in action. Though nothing was as bad as Christmas when they had to watch the other families gather in the great room in front of the tree. They'd be whole, while the two of them remained one short.

Last Christmas had been especially hard on her for some reason. She'd put on a cheery face to hide it from him, but he'd found out through the staff. The new manager was extremely chatty, but not in an intrusive way. She'd told him because she cared.

Mom was a tough woman. Elizabeth Davis wouldn't let anyone knock her down. She held her head high and took on whatever fate threw at her. She'd take on the world if she had to.

Yet knowing that was no excuse. He'd beaten himself up about it for days.

How could I have missed the little signs?

He'd selfishly locked himself away in his room most of the time, not interacting with any of the guests.

That's how!

He had to do better by her. She deserved better than the cards life had dealt her, and he wanted her to be proud of him.

Jameson unclenched his fists and dropped his guard, tilting on his heel to walk away from his aggressor.

"Homeschooled inbred," the boy's voice grated out. "Your daddy took off because your mom's a whore."

That was it. Jameson lunged at the scrawny prick. It was one thing to harass him personally, but it became a whole other ballgame if he dragged his mother into this. *Ken* was going down.

His knuckles never made contact with Dipshit's face. Four hands grabbed him by the shoulders and ripped him backward.

Flanking him, *Tweedle Dee* and *Tweedle Dum* held tight, so *Ken* could use him as a punching bag. The hits to his temple and stomach didn't hurt that much; adrenaline numbed the impact, but the punches pissed him off.

Jameson's lips curled away from his teeth. Like a rabid dog off its leash, all but foaming at the mouth, he overpowered the two holding him back and finally got a swing at their leader.

With a sharp *crack!* *Ken* crumbled to the ground. His friends took off on a dead run, rocks popping beneath their shoes.

"You're dead, man," Dipshit sputtered, eyes wide in fear now that it was one-on-one. He kicked the heels of his fancy sneakers into the gravel, scrambling backward. "My father's going to shut this fucking place down. You and your mom are done, you hear me?" he threatened, clutching his cheek where a dark bruise was starting to swell.

Panic closed around Jameson's throat like a fist, his knuckles burning. *What have I done?*

"You're not going to tell anyone shit, Carter," the girl said from behind Jameson.

'The hell did she come from?

His head snapped around, staring at the girl cradling a book to her chest. Her other hand hung down by her side, clutching the handle of a black rolling suitcase.

He recognized her. It was the snobby one who thought she was above them because of her intellect. He'd noticed her before, always walking around with a book, using it like a shield. She might not have mingled much with the rest of the clucking hens, but she carried her nose just as high, and if she were any taller, she'd look down on the staff, too.

There were always two groups: the ones who got by on their looks and the ones who believed they were smarter than anyone else. He didn't want anything to do with her, either. She probably thought he'd never picked up a book in his life.

Her sharp eyes focused on the boy on the ground. "You're going to keep your mouth shut, or I will tell everyone how you pissed your pants."

Jameson's lips twitched, suppressing a laugh. Rumors spread like wildfire. True or not.

"You're defending him? He fucking hit me."

"I don't need your help," Jameson snapped at her. "Or your pity," he tagged on. He wasn't falling for her sympathy act. They were all the same. *Fucking rich kids.*

"This isn't about you," she said, shooting him only a glance, then shifting back to *Ken—Carter*. "This is about him being a bully. You take it out on others because you're weak, and you can't take it out on the one who's bullying *you*. You're pathetic, Carter. And you're an asshole."

Her shoulder-length hair whipped around as she spun on her heel without so much as acknowledging him with another look and marched toward the parking lot where the buses waited. The untamed waves bouncing behind her with each step were the last thing he saw of her.

Jameson took off in the other direction. Everyone would be busy with clean-up, and he wanted to avoid his mother seeing the cut on his brow. He was glad it wasn't a black eye. That would've been a lot harder to conceal, but how long until she found out he'd hurt one of the boys?

Could they lose the resort over his screw-up? How much truth was there behind Carter's threat? There were witnesses. Word would get out. There'd be consequences. He wasn't fooling himself into believing he could get away with this.

He'd let Mom down. Jameson was too scared to go home, but he couldn't hide out in the woods forever. Guilt sat heavy in his stomach, weighing him down like an anchor. He didn't even feel hungry. He felt sick.

He waited until sundown. The camp was quiet. Nobody was out looking for him as he passed by the final cabins. Maybe the drama could wait till morning. He was tired but doubted that his conscience would let him get any sleep.

"Hey! Jameson!"

Eileen, the housekeeping manager, was coming out of cabin one, making him jump with her stealthy presence. She'd been working at the resort since his grandparents had run the place. She was practically part of the establishment. They had hosted her 50th birthday party back in April. Big events were always set up on the north side of the park. Back in the day, when his grandparents ran the resort, they used to offer horseback riding. Their last horse had died over ten years ago, but the old barn and stables were still around. They'd converted into the perfect venue for large gatherings.

Jameson's hand darted up to his hair, teasing some of the rogue strands down over his brow to hide his injury. "Have you seen my mom?" he asked, averting his face as she turned to lock up.

She nudged her chin over her shoulder. "I think I saw her back at home."

Damn. He'd have to sneak past her.

Sure enough, through the open windows, his ears caught her melodious laughter coming from the kitchen. It tangled with Carl's much deeper, raspier tone.

Jameson went around to the front door and aimed straight down the hallway for his room before either of them could needle him about where he'd been all day. He wouldn't tell them about the fight until he had to. He didn't want to repeat what Carter had said. He wouldn't lie, though, if push came to shove. He'd own up to his mistake. He wasn't a coward. But for now, he just wanted to ignore it.

He grabbed his sketchbook off the desk and plugged his headphones into the jack of the brand-spanking new Galaxy S3 Mom had gotten him as an early birthday present—the amber-brown one. To his surprise, she'd sprung for the 32GB version and a microSD card along with it to expand media storage. She knew how much he hated July.

The rest of the year, the mountain resort was steadily occupied, easily enough to keep them afloat. Some of the regulars came around in December, too, meaning they wouldn't have to deal with the spawn but also with their breeders.

It was always the same families. Generation after generation came here, Mom had told him. Like it was some sort of rite of passage for them. Which was bullshit because the camp was *his* family's legacy, passed down from his grandparents to his mom and, one day, to him.

Jameson shut his emotions out and forced himself numb. He didn't want to feel anything anymore. Sprawled out on his bed, he turned up the volume. He'd made it through another summer. Forty-nine weeks before he had to repeat the torture.

2013

Hayley pressed her head against the glass, keeping her eyes peeled for the first sign of the camp through the trees. The view out of the window didn't reveal much, but she knew they were getting close. She'd timed the trip since leaving the school grounds. The rest stop had been at the halfway mark.

Heather had locked her in the bathroom stall by shoving a broomstick through the handle from the outside, and Hayley had been forced to crawl underneath the door to get out.

Who'd have thought her lack of boobs had a benefit?

But even after washing her hands and face, she still felt filthy from sliding along the gross floor. She wanted nothing more than to get out of these clothes—

There it was! BISHOP PARK.

Finally!

They passed beneath the wooden arch, and her tension left with a deep inhale. Hayley felt as though she were entering the gates of a haven. The resort represented freedom. A place where she could leave all her baggage behind and live a different life for a while. Like slipping into one of her adventure novels. The weight lifted off her shoulders, making her twenty pounds lighter. She'd longed for her refuge.

The summer camp, anyway.

Good thing they skipped the trip here last Christmas. The year before had been a nightmare. Carter's dad had acted like the freaking King of England, wanting to be personally served by Beth, hand and foot. The poor woman had endured the charades and played along, but Hayley had seen through her façade.

Carter's dad was big, like a pro football player, really intimidating, and sometimes she wondered if he beat his son. But she'd never seen any marks on him to prove her suspicion.

She wished Dad had spoken up. Roy was his best friend and business partner, and his unacceptable behavior reflected badly on both of them. Instead, Tom Wilkins had drowned his words in bourbon, rarely glancing over the rim of the Glencairn.

Hayley had felt superfluous. Per usual. She couldn't stand being around Carter, either. Watching Roy was like looking into the future. His son would become exactly like him—a boisterous, arrogant prick.

She had a hard time sitting still on her butt now. She had the urge to jump out of her seat and lunge at the door, prying it open with her bare hands.

But she waited.

Agonizing minutes went by as the bus wobbled through the bumpy parking lot, divot after divot making the vehicle tilt one way and then the other. And then finally, it stopped. The driver engaged the brake, killed the engine, and released the door.

Still, Hayley waited. Patiently.

The kids from the back rows always cleared out first, making their way to the front before it was her turn. She sat in the middle with a bench to herself, twiddling her thumbs in her lap while averting Heather's smug grin, followed by Carter, Joey, and Teresa. Aaron brought up the rear.

Hayley rose slowly, not letting her desperation show. It was all about maintaining appearances.

Stay aloof. Never let them see you break.

Which was hard when you wanted to cry yourself to sleep every night, but Satan's Spawn happened to be your roommate. Hayley bottled it up and put a lid on it.

Her feet met the gravel. Goosebumps immediately prickled across her skin. The air was different here, filled with a natural beauty that was almost magical. It was a fantasy world away from the torment at school, an escape from the dark stone walls that trapped her physically and emotionally.

Her eyes landed on the same manager from last year, greeting them with her polite smile and pointing them toward the main building with the common rooms and the check-in desks.

"Hayley! Over here."

Her head whipped in the direction of the voice calling her name, and her eyes went wide in surprise. The dark curls, the sapphire blues…

Beth was a mirage, beaming at her from the side of the bus, a set of keys dangling from her index finger. A golden charm with an engraved number sixteen hung from the ring.

"I got you all signed up, so you can skip the crowd. Come on," she tipped her head toward the luggage compartment, "Let's get your bag."

"How was the drive?" she asked as Hayley tugged her black suitcase free.

"Worth it." Because, to get to paradise, the four-hour trip cramped with society's worst of the worst brats really was.

Beth laughed, and the sound poured straight into Hayley's soul. It was the best thing she'd heard all year. It was as if she were sharing a piece of her majestic glow with the rest of the world.

"I'm glad you decided to return," she said, handing over the key. "It's the same as last time."

"Wouldn't have missed it for the world." Hayley's cheeks stretched with a grin from ear to ear while accepting the key to her new home for the next three weeks.

Before taking off, Beth pulled her into a one-armed squeeze. "It's good to see you again, sweetheart. Come by the house later, will ya? I'll whip something up." She winked and then headed across the parking lot.

Hayley watched her for another moment. The generous woman was exactly the mother she'd always wanted.

But then there would've been one strikingly handsome complication.

Jameson held the board in place with his knee and drove the bolt home. It was the last one. Taking his finger off the drill's trigger, he wiped the back of his hand across his forehead. The long-sleeved shirt was hot, but it kept the cuts and scrapes on his arms to a minimum.

He'd been spending a lot of time out here working on the tree house. It was only an eight-by-eight-foot platform around a single trunk for now, but it reduced the likelihood of him slipping off a branch while fast asleep. He'd eventually spread the entire structure out over multiple trees. He was thinking big. Operating power tools was nothing new to him. Even the circular saw had gotten more use in the past two weeks than it had gotten over the last four years combined.

He'd done all the work himself. The floor was about ten feet off the ground. He laid the two-by-fours across a few branches to get it level and fitted cantilever beams underneath to add diagonal bracing against the sturdy trunk. As for the roof and walls, he was considering a minimalistic A-frame.

He also had his mind set on solar rope lights, but catching enough sun through the dense leaves was questionable. The old storm lantern would have to do.

Jameson put the drill down and looked at his sketch again. The drawing had a spiral staircase wrapped around the tree. He was a long way from that. A simple ladder propped against the side was currently the only way up.

He kicked his legs over the edge of the loft and let them dangle. Leaning back on his hands, his eyes scanned the majestic grove. The yellow ponderosa pines were insanely tall. Probably 150 feet. He'd once scaled the branches to an approximate height of 50 without any kind of safety equipment. What a thrill that had been. And the view…

The alarm on his phone went off, killing his daydreaming.

He usually didn't bring it out here. *Yes*, he knew that was pretty reckless. *If there was ever an emergency or I was seriously injured, I had no way of calling for help…* blah, blah, blah…

Whatever.

Today, though, his phone's purpose was essential. He'd set the reminder for 9 a.m. He'd been at it for hours and usually lost track of time. The forest was like a black hole his mind got lost in.

Hence the alarm.

It would give him enough time to return the tools to the shed and casually stroll by the main house, like he just happened to be there by chance. Total coincidence. Because he hadn't been obsessing about her. At all.

Nothing ever happened after last summer. Every day he'd woken up expecting the bad news. They'd never come. Things had gone on as usual. He felt the urge to thank her. He *had* punched the kid after all. There should've been repercussions.

Jameson pulled the cell out of his back pocket and silenced the shrill noise. He pushed off to gather his sketch and the rest of his tools before taking the ladder down.

Lurking like a creep at the corner of the shed, he skimmed over the faces in the crowd.

Would he even recognize her?

The fuck was he thinking. He couldn't mingle with them. Not that he wanted to. Summer at the reception desk was much more his type.

But this girl is different… maybe.

He watched the herd spill out of the common hall after receiving the key to their assigned cabins. *She* wasn't among them.

He waited to make sure, but after the steady flow diminished to a trickle and then stopped entirely, it was obvious she wasn't there. No one else was left inside.

He didn't go in to verify. He wasn't *that* desperate! Jameson turned on his heel and walked away.

8

It was no big deal. So she hadn't liked it here. He didn't take it personally. The wild beauty of the Rocky Mountains wasn't for everyone. Especially not for someone as cultivated as her. She was the poster child for a fish out of water. They could've put a picture of her in the dictionary under the idiom.

Lying on his back, Jameson gazed up at the stars. It was a perfect night. The moon was full, and the sky was clear. He'd watched the sunset from up here. The continental divide that tore across the state made the scenery simply breathtaking. There were views of valleys, summits, crystal-clear emerald lakes, old-growth forests with magnificent trees, and extensive wildlife. The entire stretch of the northern Rockies was full of mountain lions and goats, bighorn sheep, grizzly bears, and black bears. And then there were the golden sunsets in flaming orange that made the sky appear on fire, or the deep reds and purples against the lingering blue backdrop…

He knew right then that he would never leave this place. Not even for a girl.

And that was how he'd fallen asleep in the woods. Again.

Sometime in the middle of the night, he'd been lucid enough to turn the music off, though, because it was the sound of chirping birds that woke him at dawn. He trotted home, while the camp was still quiet and sneaked into his room. Mom would start her day at eight, so he had a bit more time to crash.

When Carl's deep voice hollered through the kitchen, it was time to get a move on. Judging by the clanking sounds and the occasional swearing, he was fixing the sink again.

"Why is your hair wet?" she fired off before Jameson had barely taken two steps into the room.

"It's called a shower, Mom."

"As in bathroom or lake, smartmouth?"

Her comeback prompted a husky chuckle from below the kitchen sink.

She turned her attention back to the frying pan, putting the wooden spatula through unnecessary abuse. "When did you get home? I checked your room before I went to bed at one, and you weren't in."

She didn't wait for him to respond and drew the conclusion on her own, the crease between her brows deep as she scowled at him over her shoulder. "Did you sleep outside again?"

Jameson rolled his eyes in a high arch toward the wall. "Only until the sun came up." He'd gotten another hour and a half in his bed. What was the big deal?

She killed the stove, removing the pan from the heat. "Well, I hope you're rested because you're on lifeguard duty in thirty minutes. So sit down and have some breakfast, will ya?" she said, scraping the scrambled eggs onto a plate and pushing it toward him.

"Yes, ma'am." She didn't have to tell him twice. He'd skipped dinner and was starving.

He finished quickly and was out the door in fifteen, down by the lake in another five. Kicking off his boots, he sat down on the side of the dock. The wooden planks were already heated by the sun. A dip in the lake sounded honestly fantastic.

Rolling his pant legs up to his knees, he gave his toes a try. The intense chill sent a shockwave along his spine, which set his body on high alert. Every nerve ending prickled.

On the shore up ahead, a group of kids roughly his age were using the rope to swing into the water. The lake was much deeper over there. Around the boat dock, it was shallow enough for him to stand with his shoulders above water, and below the planks was an eighteen-inch gap to the surface, perfect for hiding.

Kids were welcome to use the lake whenever they pleased during daylight hours, but it was encouraged to stick to times with a lifeguard on duty. Jameson was assigned the morning shift from nine to eleven, which worked fine for him. He was an early riser anyway and preferred to have the rest of the day to himself.

A while into it, he was getting bored. None of the kids attempted any ambitious flips. The show was hardly entertaining. He should have brought his phone.

Barbie and *Ken*, aka Carter, took to making out in the water, while *Tweedle Dum* continued trying to impress the second female. It was the pretty Hispanic girl he'd seen around Blondie last year. They traveled in a pack. Always the same four.

Where's Tweedle Dee?

"I bet you five hundred bucks that I can do it," Carter yelled to his friend back at the shore.

Here we go. Jameson's eyes rolled skyward on cue.

There was always that one guy who thought he could manage the swim to the island. Jameson knew the problem wasn't the way out. It was the return. Everybody overestimated their endurance while at the same time underestimating the distance. Or the current. It appeared close, but the little patch of land was over a mile away.

He'd made the trip himself once, with Carl pacing him in a rowboat. They timed it at almost twenty minutes. He'd waited half an hour before attempting the swim back, and it had still taken every ounce of him. He would never do it again. He was reckless. Not stupid.

"You'll never make it." Jameson felt compelled to engage and warn him. "It's a two-mile round trip."

"Nobody's asking for your opinion."

"He's got a point. The buoy, then," *Tweedle Dum* shouted.

The buoy was a more reasonable challenge. It was a hundred yards out, and they kept track of the records at the camp for the fastest time to reach it.

"My father set the record when he was eighteen," Carter boasted to his friends as if it were *his* accomplishment. "He did it in under a minute."

Jameson couldn't contain the laugh that burst out of him.

"What's so funny, inbred?"

Besides the fact that he crushed the old record two years ago by ten seconds? "Nothin'."

Barbie leaned toward her boyfriend, mumbling something that didn't carry, and the diabolical foursome started laughing hysterically, their eyes focused on something up the hill behind him.

Jameson glanced over his shoulder and had to do a double-take.

It was *her*. She was here.

9

*D*amn. It was all about bad timing with her, wasn't it? He couldn't possibly go after her now. One, he was on babysitting duty, and two, he wasn't going to approach her in front of an audience.

Jameson watched her turn in the direction of the common hall. Maybe he could catch her on her way back.

The sun was beating down on the lake as it approached its eleven o'clock position, making the water glitter like gold. It was bright and hurt his eyes. The warmth spreading across his skin felt nice, but as the breeze died down, it got substantially hotter. It was torture not to jump in and cool off. The impulse was driving him nuts.

He needed a distraction. Needed to disassociate. *Mind over matter.*

Behind his closed lids, he pictured a different scene: the cool, silvery gleam in the full moonlight; a night so clear he could see the stars reflecting in the black mirror before him—

"Sup?"

Jameson squinted up at Carl, grinning underneath his bright red Kansas City Chief's hat. "You look hot," he pointed out, extending an ice-cold ginger ale.

The condensation that had formed on the outside of the can brought Jameson's attention back to the heat of the sun and how dry his throat suddenly felt. He was parched. He gratefully accepted the drink, cracking the seal and downing the much-needed relief. The chilled liquid was heaven on his tongue.

"You should wear a hat," Carl said, tapping a smug finger to his sun shield. "Keep your face in the shade."

"Thanks, *Captain Obvious*. I'll keep that in mind." Jameson could feel the flare of a sunburn on his nose and cheeks. That would suck later. He wasn't used to sitting around the lake like a statue, with the reflection of the sun frying him from all sides.

Hunched over, he lowered the can in between his thighs, holding it with both hands.

Carl dropped down next to him, crossing his legs. "So, how's babysitting going?"

"It's bullshit!" He blurted out the first thing that came to mind.

"Hey, now. That's some pretty colorful language you got there. Don't let your mother hear it. She'll threaten to wash your mouth out with soap."

"Yeah, she would," Jameson laughed, turning the drink in his hands to keep them busy. "That's your bad influence on me."

They had been hanging out since he started working here in oh-nine. Jameson had always wondered if he was hooking up with his mom but didn't have the balls to ask. Or maybe he didn't want to know. Carl was the closest thing he had to a friend, and having the truth out in the open would make things harder to ignore.

He offered him his smoke, and Jameson took a long drag before handing it back. It didn't even make him cough anymore. Carl *was* a bad role model.

"You going to hang around the watering hole all day?"

"Not planning on it. But it depends on *Loudmouth* over there. I'm afraid he's contemplating the island to prove me wrong." And he would stay until the group left to make sure that didn't happen. Even if it meant staying past the end of his official shift.

"So what do you have planned for the rest of the day?"

Jameson shrugged. "Don't know yet. Just don't wanna be responsible for this dumbass."

"You're worrying your mom, you know?"

"What does she have to worry about? That I'll get eaten by a bear?" Jameson joked.

Carl punched him in the shoulder. "She's your mom, asshole. Moms worry. And you never answer your phone. What's the point of having the damn thing?"

"I keep it in my room, where it's safe. What if I have to jump in to pull *Dumbass* out? The phone ain't waterproof. It would be a shame to ruin it." Or drop it out of a tree.

"And lose all the spicy pictures of naked chicks?"

"Is that what you think I do all day?"

"Come on, man, you're a teenager. What else would you be doing in the woods… by yourself?" He motioned suggestively toward Jameson's crotch with the cigarette, then lifted the butt back to his mouth.

Jameson wasn't taking the bait. It wasn't anyone's business whether he jerked off or not. "Who says I'm there alone?"

From below the curved, red bill, Carl shot him a skeptical look, blowing smoke out to the side. "You know your left hand doesn't count as a date, right?"

Jameson threw his head back and laughed. Carl joined in.

"But I can see why you wouldn't need a phone for inspiration. You got the live show right there." He gestured toward the girls in the water. "You taking a mental video for later? I saw you with your eyes closed. What were you picturing?"

True, his mind was on sex—A LOT—but he didn't always act on it. Even when he was alone. He had a thin sliver of self-control. He knew how to distract his thoughts.

"Something else," he replied vaguely into the mouth of the can.

Carl nudged his head toward the departing group. "Well, looks like you're off the clock."

He held the cigarette out to him again, but this time Jameson shook his head. Parking the smoke between his lips, Carl tugged the shield of his cap lower and leaned back on his hands.

Jameson pulled his legs from the water, scooting back a few inches to prop them on the edge. He gave them a minute to dry before going for his socks, then stuffed his feet into his boots. Picking up his can, he tipped it back one last time, finishing the rest of his ginger ale in one gulp, and pushed off the dock.

"I have to take care of something."

"Yeah, you do." Carl insinuated with a snicker.

Jameson stifled a grin, a slight flush rising to his cheeks. "Shut up."

Hayley didn't mean to eavesdrop, but when she passed by the homestead on her way back from breakfast, the windows were wide open, and she couldn't help overhearing the conversation inside.

"Any of the girls catch your eye?"

"Nah. You know me. What would I do with a girl like that?" His reply came out muffled; she guessed from food in his mouth, and there was also the sound of a fork stabbing a plate.

"Yeah, probably for the better. You should keep your distance from those girls. They'll only break your heart."

"What if I break theirs first?" he countered, and Hayley could hear the cheeky grin in his voice.

There was a short pause, and they both broke into laughter. "Now you sound like your dad," his mother chided him, no doubt pointing a wagging finger. "But I know I raised you better than that."

A soft sigh followed, and then the woman's tone turned stern. "He'd be so proud of you, Jamie. He was such a good man. Such a good father. Sometimes I think he was an angel sent to me right when I needed him."

"You are so cheesy, Mom," he said with a chuckle.

He dropped the fork onto the plate, and Hayley caught the shuffling of feet with the rustling of clothes as they presumably fell into a hug.

She had the urge to run. It was wrong to listen in on their private exchange.

Back at her cabin, she pulled her comfort book from her backpack. Sitting down on the bed, she brushed over the letters on the cover: *HATCHET*.

Corners bent and pages darkened, the old edition was worn from the dozens of times she'd read it. The spine was so cracked, it was hard to make out the title. The story, though, was timeless, and she'd considered it kind of fitting for her trip here. Not that she was planning on doing any kind of bushwhacking. The pages of her books were the only adventures she'd ever go on.

Hayley had always wondered whether she'd survived out in the wilderness like the boy did in the book; she wasn't brave and had zero survival skills. That hadn't mattered to him, though. He'd been a city kid too. He'd adapted. Yes, he'd broken down at times, but he'd come out stronger in the end. She admired the young boy's perseverance, as he'd faced his challenges all by himself. Every day at school, she was confronted by her own personal jungle, and yet she had survived. That must count for something? Would anyone consider her tough?

At the halfway point, Hayley flipped the book shut and set it down. She checked the time on her phone. It was almost eleven. She'd signed up for a chess match, so she'd better get going if she wanted to be on time.

She decided to take the scenic route past the lake, which turned out to be a huge mistake. She hadn't anticipated running into the squad from hell. She needed mental preparation for that to brace herself against their attacks. At meal times, she could avoid them altogether.

Her eyes located Heather first. She was hard to miss in her bright pink bikini. She was slung around Carter's neck. Naturally. The two deserved each other. They were a perfect match. His dad used to come here, too. Supposedly, he was a great swimmer. Teresa and Joey were floating nearby, and there were more kids at the shore, clutching a rope that was tied to a tree branch.

But there was someone else.

Sitting by himself on the boat dock, Jamie was watching the tacky display with eager attention.

A whole year later, Beth's son still only had eyes for Heather and Teresa. But who could blame him? There they were, half-naked, frolicking, all wet... *ugh!*

Hayley turned away and strode toward the main house. She pushed one side of the heavy oak doors open and stepped into the foyer. It was dark in here compared to the blinding sunlight outside. Her eyes took a few seconds to adjust to the drastic change as she scanned the hall. No one else was around.

Her gaze landed on the common board in front of her, on which students could pick courses or coordinate games like the chess match she'd signed up for. But she wasn't sure what exactly she was looking at. An icy sensation slithered up her nape, and she forced herself to blink, refocusing on the image before her. Something didn't belong there.

Her mouth fell open in utter disbelief, the shock rendering her paralyzed.

It couldn't be…

Hanging from the board was a bra, pale blue with white polka dots, and she knew exactly what size it was. Knew because it was her own, the one that had gone missing at the beginning of the school year.

And that wasn't the only thing pinned to the board. Next to the undergarment was a picture of her with a note attached to it that read 'Pop my Cherry'. Below that was her phone number.

HER ACTUAL PHONE NUMBER.

How many people have seen this?

Stomach acid rising in her throat, Hayley ripped it all down. The bra. The photo. The note. All of it. She tore it free from the corkboard, pins flying left and right, skipping on the tile floor.

Hands numb and shaking, she gathered the remainder of the foul prank in her hands and pushed it through the rectangular hole of the trash can. Then she stormed out the door, hauling right past Aaron, who was just coming through.

That evil bitch!

Hayley's feet thumped in long, heavy strides as she marched back to her cabin, hands balled into angry fists, looking for a target.

"Aaargh!" she roared, clenching them tighter at her sides.

Nasty, vile skank!

Keeping her head down, she stormed back the way she'd come, stomping through the grass, barely looking up to see where she was going, and muttering to herself like a mental patient.

But she would not cry. She would not break.

Thank God, she'd found it when she did. It could've been up all day.

Twisted, diabolical—

Holy shit!

Hayley did a skip mid-stride and almost tripped.

10

The girl took a wary step backward, eyes the size of golf balls.

Jameson pushed off the side of the cabin and straightened. "It's Hayley, right?"

Yeah, he did occasionally pay attention to names. *Whatever.* Sue him.

Noticing the subtle shift in the weight of her feet, like a doe ready to run, he approached slowly so as not to spook her.

Her vigilant eyes remained level on him, and for a moment they struck him dumb. He couldn't form the words he'd practiced in his head. Couldn't even form thoughts. His tongue felt heavy, moving sluggishly. There was no saliva to gather.

Damn.

Those eyes…

The first thing he thought of once his wheels resumed turning was the early morning fog rolling across the treetops, the luscious green peeking through the gray. That was how breathtaking they were. They made you want to stop and stare to admire their beauty. And he could hear the wind across the ridge calling his name, asking him to stick around, begging him to linger a while.

His body answered the call. He couldn't move. He was the one caught in the headlights.

"What do you want?"

Her stare narrowed as she appeared to close herself off on instinct, and that snapped him out of the trance. "Thank you."

"For what?"

Did she even remember? "For the lack of assault charges against me." He shouldn't have bothered bringing it up. He felt so stupid now.

"I told you, I didn't do it for you," she replied in that condescending tone he was all too familiar with hearing. It was the same tone these rich kids addressed the staff with. It was a trait passed down from their parents, and they carried that shit like second nature. It practically ran through their blood, engulfing them in a cloud to keep the riff-raff out and set them apart. And they let you know it, too.

He was wrong. She was no different.

"Carter's a jerk. His father always bosses him around, and he feels the need to take that out on others, so he can make himself feel stronger." She blew past him, charging up the steps of her cabin, then spun around to add, "It's nothing personal."

Nothing personal. Right. Got it. She'd defended him like she would've defended a raccoon scavenging through garbage for scraps. That was all he was to her. Trash. And she couldn't get away from him fast enough.

"Whatever. I just… I just needed to say that," he grumbled under his breath.

Get it out and move on. He shouldn't have expected anything else.

Jameson turned, watching her mouth plop open like a fish on dry land, but whatever else she had to say, she could damn well say it to his back.

He kept walking.

She kept quiet.

OF APPLES AND TREES

11

She'd damn near lunged at the door to get away from him. Well, he could do her one better. She wouldn't have to worry about him anymore. He had every intention of keeping his distance from now on.

Jameson's mood had taken a turn for the worse ever since that day. He had no business being so fucking pissed off. And yet he was. Every little thing was setting him off, like that bolt he'd stripped this morning by being distracted. His mind couldn't let it go. He'd kicked the toolbox in anger, sending its contents in a free fall to the ground below. Other than creating more work, it had brought him nothing.

To make matters worse, he saw her everywhere now. The more he tried to avoid her, the more he happened to notice her, whether walking to or from the common rooms, or popping up whenever he least expected it. Every time he turned his head, there she was. Hovering. Like he was freakin' haunted.

Jameson cleaned up his tools but left them at the tree house. He'd be back to work on it after his shift.

On his way to the lake, he caught her coming out of the dining hall. Breakfast was served until nine, and she was usually one of the last to leave.

So, there probably *was* a pattern to her habits. And somehow they seemed to be perfectly timed with his own. Go figure.

Jameson walked on with his head down, ignoring her.

He propped himself up on the slope, where he'd wasted two hours every morning over the past two weeks. He was already counting down the days until it was over.

During his 'watch' he kept his eyes mostly closed, focusing more on the sounds than the visuals. He had no interest in the shenanigans; his imagination was a bigger draw. Even *Barbie* left him cold.

Well, maybe not *completely* cold. At least not from the neck down. He hated to admit it, but he was developing a serious thing for brunettes.

The crowd at the lake dispersed slowly around eleven, and he trotted home to grab lunch before heading back to his project.

Aaaand there she was again…

…sitting near the group playing ultimate frisbee, a book opened in her lap.

He never saw her engaging with the other students. Weren't they all close? They lived together at that boarding school year-round, yet he always found her alone, or at the fringe of the cliques, the rejected animal that didn't belong with the herd for some reason he couldn't make out.

She was like a ghost, invisible to all but him, and Jameson's curiosity about the girl—about Hayley—was piqued.

12

Hayley plopped her food tray down on an empty table. There were plenty to choose from. Not all students from her school came to the camp; only the ones who could afford it. All in all, there were probably only thirty of them this year.

She usually went in late, knowing that Heather and her court had finished their meals already. Not today, though. Heather was still sitting at her table, her acrylic nails clacking in repetitive intervals against the top. She was alone. No sign of Carter or even Teresa.

Was the rest of the squad running late?

Odd.

Heather looked exasperated with her chin propped on her wrist. Hayley knew that expression well. There was a storm brewing.

She checked the board in the common room more frequently now—multiple times a day, actually—to make sure the bitch wouldn't repeat the prank. She'd received a few gross text messages from unknown senders on her phone after the unauthorized publication of her number. The dick pics had been among the worst. Texts she could delete without reading, but it was hard to unsee a picture. That shit tended to burn itself into your memory without your consent.

Maybe that was the point. She was afraid to even pick up her phone now. At first, she'd stuffed it under her pillow, but the idea of those pictures anywhere near where she put her head was almost worse.

The first thing she would do when she went home next week was get a new number. She didn't care what lie she had to come up with for her dad. She couldn't tell him the truth. He'd never taken an interest in her problems at school. They hardly talked at all. Her father wasn't a cold man. Or cruel. He simply didn't know how to interact with her. He'd shipped her off to boarding school the first chance he'd had and now dumped her here for three weeks every summer.

But, yeah, a new number was happening. And she wouldn't have to go through the hassle of informing her contacts; her phone was barely more than a paperweight. It was for emergency use. Dad had her number, of course, and school, too, but that was where the essential list ended.

None of her classmates had her contact information, either. Phone numbers were kept private at school. The only way Heather could've gotten it was by some illicit means. Maybe she'd flashed the guy in the office to get into the school records. Maybe she'd offered even more. Hayley wouldn't put it past her. Who knew what kind of information she'd gotten her hands on?

The thought ran like ice down Hayley's back as she glared a hole into Heather's forehead, visualizing the bullseye of a target. Her roommate's brows were knit tightly and trained toward the entrance to the dining hall.

Why did she have to bunk with her? Why couldn't Heather be paired up with Teresa? The two were attached at the hip anyway. And equally wicked.

70

Speaking of which, or more like *witch*, Heather's head snapped to attention as her partner in crime burst through the door, her attire slightly disheveled. Had she been running for her life?

Probably, considering what an insult it was to disregard the queen's invitation to breakfast. The punishment would be death.

'Off with their heads!' Hayley heard the voice screeching in her mind. It triggered a chuckle.

"What the fuck are you grinning at, freak?"

Hayley rolled her eyes and ignored the wrath that was quickly spreading like wildfire. It wasn't a question, and in her current state, Heather would lash out at anyone in her vicinity. Hayley didn't want to become the target again so soon.

In her periphery, Teresa shifted, quickly covering a very obvious hickey. The blotch on her neck was a dark shade of purple.

Was it Joey's?

Or maybe Carter's, judging by the way she was trying to hide it from Heather. What a scandal that would be. Too bad Hayley wasn't into starting gossip.

Her cell vibrated against her butt. She knew what that meant. Dad never texted her, so it had to be one of her not-so-secret admirers. Thus, the prank was still on. *Joy!*

Hayley choked the last bite of her bagel down, having lost her appetite. It tasted like cardboard, but she knew it wasn't the meal's fault. The food was actually really good here. The breakfast buffet was her favorite. If it were up to her, she'd have it three times a day. Sometimes she ate enough to last her till dinner. That way, she could skip the crowd at lunch.

Maybe she'd grab an apple to go. She'd had her eye on one of the Granny Smiths on her way in. Her appetite was bound to come back at some point.

She watched the girls push out of their seats and take off, then lingered a few more minutes to give them a head start.

When she finally left, she found Carter out front. In her shock, she almost dropped the apple in her hand. He was leaning back against the tree closest to the trail, one foot propped up by the trunk. Joey stood flanking his right.

Clutching the round piece of fruit tighter, her nails cut into the skin, leaving small crescent-shaped indentations. It wasn't a softball, but maybe if her aim was on point, she could hit one of them in the temple.

Wishful thinking. Her aim was shit. She'd have to be close to make contact.

"Sup, Hay-Hay?" Carter lifted a fat smoke to his mouth and took a drag. It didn't look like a normal cigarette. It appeared hand-rolled.

"You look tense. Wanna chill with us?" He blew a gray cloud into the air, then passed the joint along to Joey.

Hayley cocked her chin, ready to fire. "Gee, I wish, but I already made plans to swallow razor blades instead."

"Careful. She has a weapon," Joey snickered, handing the joint back to Carter.

Kill two morons with one apple? Unlikely.

Tongues licking across their lips, they watched her get closer like two drooling hyenas.

There was no other way to get back to her cabin. She was forced to walk past them and caught a noseful of the skunky stench.

Carter flicked the hand-rolled into the brush, and kicked off the tree as she went by. His grip closed around her upper arm, and he spun her back toward him. The abrupt shift in direction made her drop the apple.

Joey stepped around, closing in behind her before she had a chance to get away. Their clothes reeked, and their eyes were bloodshot, too.

Yep, they were definitely high.

"Don't you ever get bored with your books? You should live a little," Carter suggested.

Hovering so close, he smelled as though something had crawled into his mouth and died there. Her breakfast started churning in her stomach. The bagel was about to make a second appearance. If she puked on his new Ferragamo High-Tops, would he let go of her? The idea was appealing.

"I'd rather die than share breathing space with you. You should apologize to the trees for wasting all the oxygen they produce with your existence."

Carter relaxed his hold on her arm, raising her hope that he wasn't serious about keeping her here. He was all bark. No bite.

Hayley was done indulging them. She pivoted to leave, but then his left hand snapped to her chin. Pinching it between his fingers, he tilted it up, his hazel eyes studying her.

"You have that perfect mouth, begging to be filled," he said, rubbing his thumb across her lower lip. "Doesn't she, Joey?"

The coarse chuckle behind her agreed.

She jerked her chin away, wishing that looks really could kill. "You'll regret the day you try," she threatened.

"I have to remember to watch those sharp teeth of yours."

Joey's fingers gripped the sides of her hips and gave her a sharp pull, pressing her ass up against him. "You can have her mouth." His voice grated in her ear. "I have my eyes on something else... and my hands, too. Something without fangs."

Hayley struggled only for a second. Realizing she was making things worse by rubbing against Joey, she stopped squirming.

Carter stepped into her face again. "Now why do you have to be like that? I'll be happy to pop your cherry after... make sure you get off, too." He raised his index finger to the front of her modest neckline and dragged it down the crease between her breasts. "Why not get it over with?"

Honestly, she'd been asking herself that same question. Maybe he'd lose interest.

"Or you can keep your virginity if it's so important to you," he shrugged, removing his hand. "We'll work around it. Doesn't mean the three of us can't still have fun together." He chased his offer with sadistic laughter.

Hayley didn't find it funny at all. She jerked her elbow back and rammed it into Joey's ribs. He let go of her immediately. Carter made no motion to stop her, either.

"Come on, Hayls, you know we're just playin'," he called after her.

Jaw locked, Hayley was holding back tears while darting for her refuge.

Jameson was in a slightly better mood today. He'd made out with *Barbie's* friend behind the tool shed this morning. Even left his mark on her as she'd worked him in her palm. He'd made sure the hickey was hard to hide. It had pissed her off, too, so it was worth the effort. And yet he still couldn't remember her name.

Whatever.

"Have you decided on what you want for your birthday this year?"

Jameson shook his head. "I don't need anything, Mom."

He'd be seventeen in less than a week and a senior in high school in less than a month.

"Maybe it's time to start planning your graduation. We should make it big."

He burst into a laugh. "Make it big? I'm not close with anyone at school."

Having been homeschooled until ninth grade hadn't exactly helped him build significant relationships. He didn't care about a party with pretend friends that were little more than classmates to him, and he wasn't looking to win a popularity contest in his final year. It was merely a stepping stone. Though to what, he wasn't quite sure yet. He had no intention of applying to any colleges. Most likely, he'd stay at the resort after graduating.

"You know, you still have your dad's GI bill," Mom said as if reading his mind.

"No." Jameson shook his head more vehemently this time. Ditching his mom was out of the question. No matter how much staff they had.

He swiped the ginger ale off the counter and stuffed the second half of his ham-on-rye between his teeth, heading for the door. In the driveway, he caught sight of Hayley flying past him, her chin tilted high as usual. But what was *un*usual were the tears in her eyes.

And why did that suddenly bother him?

13

The only downside of having a cabin all to yourself at the furthest end of the resort was the walking distance to the showers. Tote slung over one side, Hayley made her long way back. Her hair was still damp and draped over her other shoulder. She preferred to let it air dry rather than fry it with the brutal heat of a blower.

She'd taken her time too, turning the whole spiel into a kind of spa treatment. She didn't have much else planned for tonight. Thinking about dinner made her queasy. She had, of course, skipped lunch and didn't want a repeat of this morning.

Her phone whirred inside her bag. She reached in to pull it out, her legs never slowing in their gait. The text came from an unsuppressed number this time, but one she didn't recognize.

God only knew why she clicked to open it. It read:

'If you change your mind, you've got my number. We can keep it between us. No one needs to know—C.'

Carter.

And by 'no one', he was referring to Heather. His girlfriend. Her roommate.

On a sigh, Hayley slipped the phone back into the tote. She hadn't pressed delete yet. She would do that later.

Probably.

No! Definitely.

Yes, definitely. She would delete his number.

Her steps faltered as she approached Beth's house. The back door was propped open, and she caught a glimpse of the woman buzzing around the kitchen in her sneakers. She seemed tall, but Hayley was used to everyone being taller than her. Her father was barely over six feet, and the ladies on his arm usually wore high-heeled shoes.

She took a glance over her shoulder. The walkways were deserted beneath the warm yellow glow of the pole lights. Everyone else was still at dinner, which was why she'd taken the chance to shower; it was more privacy than she got showering at school.

Her eyes shifted through the trees. The metal poles blended into the environment, making them nearly impossible to see if it weren't for the light they imparted in the dark. The bulbs were just coming on now. It wasn't as late as it seemed. It got dark quickly in the woods once the sun hid behind the mountain ridge.

Hayley swung her field of vision back around to the house and contemplated knocking on the doorjamb. The urge to talk to someone burned a hole through her chest, and Beth's door was literally always open.

"Looking for something?"

Her eyes shot to the left side of the house, where Jamie stood. Lurking. Arms folded in front of his chest, one black boot crossed over the other, he leaned into the corner. His hair appeared wind-tousled, and another plaid shirt was tied around his hip. He had that grungy bad-boy look girls found naturally irresistible.

How long had he been standing there?

He must've come out of the front door from the other side. He was wearing that shirt again. The black one with the Spartan helmet in the colors of the American Flag. It even had stars in the blue space. The way he was facing her, she could somewhat make out the brand's logo, stretched across his left shoulder. It appeared to be two crossed muskets with the letters GS below. He'd been wearing the shirt the day he'd come by her cabin to thank her. She'd been about to tell him that she liked it when he turned to leave.

"Um… uh, no," she stammered like a moron after an eternity of ogling him. "I-I was just leaving." Ducking her head, she clutched the strap of her tote with both hands and pivoted toward the trail.

"Hold on."

She expected him to grab her arm and pull her back the way Carter always did, but instead of touching without permission, Jamie took two long strides and planted himself in her path like a wall, obstructing the direction she was headed. They both skidded to a halt in the gravel.

He *was* fast.

And now she found herself face-to-chest with his formidable proportions. The stunning view sapped the moisture straight from her mouth. Which she noticed was hanging slightly agape as her heart pounded away behind her ribs.

Keeping his hands to himself, he gave her a quick once-over. His expression showed concern. "What did they do to you?"

Oh, great! So she didn't only feel like a wreck; she also looked like one. Or did his bloodhound sense tell him that something about her emotional state was off? "Nothing they don't already do on a daily basis at school," she told him, giving herself a shake to rein in her composure.

Yeah, she was used to being treated like a joke. She handled that shit like a pro.

He put his hands on his hips, and his sharp, blue eyes narrowed. "They pick on you? Why?"

"Oh, you know, boredom probably being the main reason." She added some sarcasm to her tone to lighten the mood while he held her under his microscope.

His mouth parted slightly, as though he were still figuring out what to say. "I'm Jame—"

"Jamie! I know. I hear your mom calling your name a lot."

Shit! Now it sounded like she'd been eavesdropping because he'd never actually introduced himself to her. They'd totally gotten off on the wrong foot, hadn't they?

He stayed quiet for a few moments, pursing his lips. "I read books too, you know? I'm not stupid."

"Uh, I never thought you were," she muttered, caught off guard by the out-of-the-blue statement.

"I got a four-point-oh GPA. Eh, three-point-nine, technically," he corrected, grimacing. "I graze in the ninety-six percentile."

"Wow! Impressive." She couldn't help but giggle at his easygoing attitude. She'd never met anyone like him. Besides his mom.

"Let me guess… a hundred." He flicked his pointer toward her, assuming he was right.

Hayley's cheeks flushed. "Ninety-nine."

"You headed to dinner?"

"No. Um, actually, I feel like skipping. I'm going back to my cabin."

"I'll walk you," he offered, turning around to lead the way.

He didn't give her a chance to refuse, and honestly, she was grateful for his company. Luckily, he wasn't in a hurry, and she kept pace with his long strides. Hands in his pockets, he strolled beside her.

"But don't eat the fruit of the shrubs if you get hungry later," he said, breaking the awkward silence. "The white ones are snowberries, and the red ones are chokecherries. Both are toxic."

"Chokecherries, huh? So that's what they look like." Hayley vividly remembered their description in her book. They had made the boy miserable. "I bet you know a lot about the flora and fauna around here."

"I should. I grew up here," he replied. "You like to hike?"

"I've never been."

"I know a trail that's not too challenging. It's about four miles roundtrip. We can do it in a few hours." He threw her a sideways glance, brows raised in an enticing arch.

"Not too challenging?"

The dread in her tone made him chuckle. "No bushwhacking, I swear. But the ascent will take us a few hundred feet up. The view at the summit is spectacular. It'll be worth it. The trails on the west and south-facing slopes lose their snow fairly early in the season, but some tops have snow almost until July."

"That sounds amazing. I'd love to go." The words were pouring from her mouth without a filter. Had she just agreed to venture through the wilderness with him? Alone? For hours?

Eh, what the hell? Carter had recommended she live a little. She would finally go on an adventure. And with her personal tour guide, nonetheless.

As they came up to her cabin, Hayley took the steps to the door. Jamie stopped at the bottom. "I got lifeguard watch in the morning. We can go after that," he proposed.

Lifeguard duty! That was why he'd watched the group so intently the other day.

"I'll pick you up at noon."

Again, without waiting for a response, he spun on his heel and walked off. He was kind of presumptuous, wasn't he?

Hayley felt compelled to look after him before digging her key from her tote and unlocking the door. She'd very much enjoyed his company. He was easy to talk to, and she had to admit she was smitten. Which was bad. It could only end in misery.

At noon sharp, Jamie knocked on her door. He was punctual for someone who didn't wear a watch. She'd never seen a phone in his hand, either.

She was glad that she'd picked an athletic shirt with long sleeves when her eyes fell on his maroon button-down. It hung open in the front, and his sleeves were pushed up his forearms, but surely the extra material over the black cotton tank had its purpose in something other than trapping heat. It was in the low eighties today. He'd promised her no bushwhacking, yet scrapes were still likely. Hayley had also chosen leggings in preparation for her adventure. There wasn't much skin exposed.

Swiping her tattered baseball hat off the dresser and pulling her ponytail out the back, she could hardly contain her excitement. She had a good pair of trail runners that held up well, compared to the heavy-duty military boots he always wore. He had on a dark pair of straight-cut jeans with a few rips here and there that she didn't consider appropriate hiking attire. They looked damn good on him, though.

So did the crooked grin he flaunted. It spelled trouble.

Her heartbeat fluttered, and she wasn't surprised if he caught the hint of a blush on her face. If he did, he didn't acknowledge it when she fell into step beside him.

He had a small, black-camo tactical bag strapped across his chest. She herself had a sling bag too, which held nothing besides water and her phone with the case that fit her ID and credit card. For emergencies.

She was curious as to what kinds of items he carried in his little survival pack, besides water.

"Since it's an easy hike, I went with the bare necessities," he answered her question. "Knife, tourniquet, first aid. Heads up: I don't have a CPR mask, so if resuscitation becomes necessary, I will kiss you," he stated boldly without so much as a blink. "If that's a deal-breaker, you better tell me now while you're still conscious."

Hayley's teeth tugged on her bottom lip to keep from grinning. "Hmm, I think I can live with that."

Her heart did a little jump as she agreed to his terms, and she redirected her thoughts. "No compass, though, *Boy Scout*? What if we get lost?"

He tipped his head back, breaking his intense eye contact, and let out the most beautiful laugh she'd ever heard. "We're not gonna get lost," he promised, his eyes and nose scrunching. "I have a phone too, and we're still in range of service."

Every time she took a glance, she discovered something new about him. For example, he wore a multi-functional paracord bracelet. If she didn't know any better, she'd guess he had some sort of military training.

And he smelled nice. A mix of sandalwood and something darker she couldn't pin down. None of that Gucci crap Carter used.

Most of the winding path he steered them through consisted of lush, green, old-growth forest that kept the trail shady, but there were a few spots that opened up to lovely scenic views. The low babbling water accompanied the serene sound of birds around them, and they had to cross the passing creek several times. She watched Jamie hop across boulders with a devil-may-care attitude while she stuck to the boardwalks. It was his confidence that made her feel safe with him, and she noticed how the excitement in his tone rose when he spoke of the region's topography and the wildlife. His love for nature was evident.

Off the main trail, they came up on several smaller paths that each led down to different vantage points along a cascading waterfall. A spur trail took them right up to the basin, where she could feel the power of the water plummeting hundreds of feet down the mountain.

Jamie reminded her to keep her eyes peeled, and Hayley spotted the bighorn sheep on the cliffs above before he did.

"You'll see the occasional beaver and otter here, too."

"What's the worst thing you've encountered?" she asked.

"There was this huge black bear once at the bottom of the tree I'd climbed. He walked right by. Never made a sound. That was kinda humbling."

"Have you ever seen a wolverine or mountain lion up close?"

"Not real close. Don't forget about moose. They like to hang out near lakes or the marshy area around and can be real dicks."

"Yeah, so I've heard," Hayley chuckled.

The two of them laughed about the most banal things they could think of and the little quirks they observed in people. It turned out, they shared the same sense of humor. They also talked about books. Hayley couldn't help but notice the similarities between him and the boy from her favorite story. Jamie was the more mature version of Brian Robeson.

"The kid from the Hatchet book?" He laughed at the comparison.

"Oh my God, you know the book? I've read it a million times."

"Got it from my mom as a birthday present one year."

Hayley pictured Jamie facing similar dangers without flinching. He had this resolute, courageous air about him. He seemed fearless. Invulnerable to intimidation.

Hayley found herself conflicted. She liked Jamie. A lot. He embodied everything she admired in a boy, but she couldn't let herself get attached.

As the trail veered and began to climb up the side of the mountain, they gained elevation more rapidly. Vivid blooms of wildflowers on the hillside added splashes of color, and Jamie pointed out the huckleberries littering the bushes.

But it was the sweeping view at the summit that had her in awe, as promised. Soaring peaks surrounded the turquoise lake and provided a stunning backdrop to the crystal-clear water below.

Letting her eyes drift, Hayley took it all in. She couldn't get her fill. The lakeshore, roughly one thousand feet down, was reachable by daunting switchbacks that had her stomach tied in knots. She also noticed an avalanche path about halfway to the lake.

They used the facilities at the lodge nearby and stopped in for a caffeine pick-me-up, which Hayley insisted was her treat to thank him for showing her around. After she'd finished her iced vanilla latte, they embarked on the 1.8-mile return.

She'd put on sunblock before heading out, but the ridge of Jamie's nose was starting to show a little bit of red from too much exposure.

"You should wear a hat, you know?"

"So people keep telling me," he countered in a huff.

On the way down the steep mountainside, they passed the huckleberry bushes again, and this time he picked two.

"Much better than chokecherries," he claimed, lobbing one her way in a high arc before popping the other one into his mouth.

Ten feet away, she caught it in her hands and copied his motion. Eyes on him, she smashed the dark berry between the roof of her mouth and her tongue.

The sweet juice hit the back of her throat, and instantly, an image of kissing him popped into her mind. She wondered what it would be like… his lips pressing to hers… to savor the sweetness mixed with the traces of him.

Would his kiss be as modest as the palate of the fruit, or would it be bold? And fierce?

Flustered by her fantasy, Hayley took a careless step to the side and lost her footing. One second she had solid ground beneath her feet, and the next it was gone. It happened so fast that she had no time to make a sound. Her shoe slipped off the edge of the narrow trail and took the rest of her body with it.

Her butt scraped along the rocks, taking the brunt of her painful slip-and-slide when Jamie's hand closed tightly around her forearm. His lightning reflexes had saved her from tumbling down the steep hillside.

She looked up, and his startling blue eyes cut into her vision as he hoisted her back onto the solid path without any effort. Hayley winced, getting to her feet and catching a breeze in an unexpected spot.

"You hurt?"

"I tore my pants," she replied, half whining, half laughing.

Damn. She'd ripped her leggings right down one cheek, exposing part of her rear. But she figured it could have been worse. She could've ended up at the bottom of the cliff. Or, God forbid, bare her ENTIRE backside to him.

Now her face really flared from embarrassment. It was not the kind of 'first outing' she'd expected.

Jamie shrugged out of his shirt and held it out for her with a sheepish grin. She vaguely noticed her fingers gripping the soft fabric, but she couldn't pry her eyes away from the ribbed, black tank he was wearing. Or rather, from the goods underneath it. His shoulders bulged out from the sides like branches of a tree. A very strong, very firm tree. Like an oak.

Alright, girl. Reel in the hormones.

Her cheeks—the ones on her face—were blazing.

"So, how many times have you ripped *your* pants?" Hayley asked to deflect from her embarrassment. He habitually tied his shirt around his waist in the same manner. Was he hiding any holes?

Jamie squeezed out a little laugh. "I usually tear out the knees. Not the back."

"Well, I think I know what I'll add to my emergency kit for next time," she joked, referring to her torn leggings. "Assuming there's going to be a *next time*." She shot him a hopeful glance over her shoulder.

"If there's a chance of you stripping in the woods… definitely," he replied with a smirk.

"You can wipe that cheeky grin off your face. I'll just pull the second pair over the other. No indecent exposure."

He kept giggling like that one kid in class who couldn't stop. Hayley felt left out.

"What?"

"You said 'cheeky'," he clarified, emphasizing the pun she'd missed. "As in 'your butt', if you catch my drift."

"Yeah, it's subtle, but I think I got it." Hayley kept her tone collected, though on the inside, she was laughing along with him. "I caught the *wind's* drift too," she tagged on.

Neither of them could contain their laughter anymore. It was the best date she'd ever been on.

The *only* date she'd ever been on.

Closing in on her cabin, she pulled off her cap and freed her hair. The wind was still playing in the tangles, whipping them around her face. She loved it. Her body would have to return eventually, but her spirit would remain here, untamed like the wind.

14

Mom was the only one shortening his name. Unless he was in trouble and she dug up his middle name too. And yet he'd chosen not to correct Hayley.

Jameson had taken the bait. She was cute as hell. She had that librarian thing going for her the way she glanced up at him over the rim of her glasses, almost scowling, and then pushing them back up the bridge of her nose. It was so hot.

He'd never seen eyes like hers before. They focused on him. *Really* focused on him. They were the equivalent of two diamonds, sharp and brilliant. So brilliant, in fact, that he blinked and then averted their beam of scrutiny. Two jewels that promised an even greater treasure on the inside.

Hayley radiated an incomprehensible beauty that put him under a spell. And that delicate fragrance that clung to her, whirling his senses…

It took everything out of him not to hold her down and lick his tongue over every inch of her skin. She smelled like cocoa butter. Perfectly edible.

After their excursion through the woods, she took to hanging out at the lake after breakfast, always in safe proximity to him. She sat in the shade under a tree with a book, looking up occasionally to steal a glance. He did the same, hiding his face beneath a baseball hat.

It was their secret.

And then, there were the actual secret meetings, when they talked for hours about books, music, and other things. He would hang out on her window sill, keeping his respectful distance, never taking the liberty of venturing into her personal space.

Honestly, he wasn't looking to get off with her. He was chasing the flutter of the butterflies he got in his belly every time he was with her, and he was afraid they'd stop once he crossed that line.

But he'd touched her. That one time. And he'd been shamefully grateful for the opportunity. For a split second, her guard had slipped. When he'd tossed her the berry. He was sure of it. Jameson had been tempted to sling his arm around her waist to hold her closer when he had the chance. He couldn't fault her for protecting herself from what they both knew was inevitable.

The acute defenses of her diamond eyes had warned him off, though. For some reason, they reminded him of the Sphinx Gate in that old movie Mom once made him watch. The image was burned into his memory.

Would they strike him down like lasers, or would they let him pass? Did he measure up to her scrutinizing judgment?

The last days passed with stolen glances at any chance, hidden smiles, or that stupid grin that was stuck on his face every time she was near. But the gnawing hollow in his chest grew with the approach of departure day. He wondered if she felt the same.

There had been no awkward goodbye. He wasn't going to see her off. He was going to head straight to the tree house now that he was relieved of his watch duty at the lake. He didn't want the last image of her to be of her getting on that bus. He wanted to remember her watching him on the slope.

Jameson rubbed the remaining traces of sleep from his eyes and left home without breakfast. He wasn't hungry. His stomach was in knots.

How long could it possibly last? Two weeks? Three weeks tops. It would pass. He knew it would. *Dammit.* He wasn't going to pine over her for an entire year like some lovesick dog.

Maybe it was better that she didn't come back. He was hoping she wouldn't. Wishing she would. He was so fucking angry at himself. For feeling the way he did. For walking right into it. For even laying the goddamn groundwork himself.

His jaw ached from the pressure of his molars. His mood was downright putrid. He wanted to punch something— already pictured the hammer in his hand. He'd find something to drive a nail through.

Hayley was still occupying his mind as he made his way to the tool shed, dragging his feet, and keeping his eyes on the ground. He noticed the ugly pair of shoes shifting in the gravel too late. Then there was the familiar sandy-blond hair.

Carter.

It was beginning to feel like a ritual. Stance wide, his fists were down by his side, he was braced for a fight. Clearly, he'd been lying in wait. He was alone, though, as far as Jameson could see when he stopped dead.

Neither of them moved for minutes, it seemed, staring off like two gunslingers at high noon. This wasn't going to end well.

Forty-nine weeks, he reminded himself. Forty-nine weeks of serenity lay ahead of him, give or take. Once the buses took off, he was free. He was so close. *Don't fuck it up now.*

But Jameson wanted to hit him. Wanted to let all his rage out on the boy in front of him. It was in his blood. In every cell of his body. A genetic precondition.

His fingers twitched, itching to strike. He worked them on both his hands, cracking his knuckles to let Carter know he was primed. Lengthy breaths heaved through his chest in anticipation.

You can't control his actions. Only your own.

He repeated his mantra, going through the same motions to calm himself. His thoughts went back to his dad. He'd used his skills in the name of his country, but he'd had a temper, too. Jameson had seen it firsthand, though never directed at him or Mom. He'd been a protector. A guardian. And that was what he wanted to be.

You're in control.

Jameson unclenched his fists and turned toward his aggressor.

"Take your free shot, asshole."

15

He left her cabin before she started packing. Didn't ask whether she was going to return next summer either. Of course she would. How could she not? Still, Hayley wondered if Jamie was even thinking that far ahead. There'd be plenty of pretty girls in town to keep him occupied. No doubt, he'd forget about her. Write her off as some girl he took on a hike once.

He'd made her feel special, though. He'd picked the wallflower over the rose, and she told herself it didn't matter if he'd done it merely out of pity. But lowkey, she'd hoped he would show up at the bus stop. In her stupid little fantasy, he'd kissed her goodbye, too.

Oh, what a stupid girl she was… always dreaming of things that would never happen. In her imagination, she could do whatever she wanted. She could climb mountains. She could come back here. She could kiss Jamie, and he would kiss her back. Hold her. Touch her in a way she wanted to be touched. They were her fantasies. No one could take them from her. She wrote the script. She was the director.

Her eyes scanned the parking lot again. Departure was scheduled for 7:00 a.m. sharp. Hayley checked her phone. It was 6:58. Aaron and Joey were already in their seats, but Carter was missing. She had a bad feeling about his absence. It twisted her insides into gnarly tangles. *He wouldn't confront Jamie on his own, would he?*

Carter finally stepped on the bus at four minutes past seven. Naturally, he expected the whole world to run on his schedule.

What took him so long?

The selfish prick walked down the aisle past her, his expression unreadable. She turned her head over her shoulder, watching him with rising dread in her gut.

Sliding in beside Heather, he took his spot in the back. As he hooked his arm around her neck, his eyes connected with Hayley's, and the corner of his mouth shifted into a sneer.

Oh God no…

His arrogant stare drilling into her, Carter swiped the thumb of his right hand across his lips, and that was when she noticed his bruised knuckles.

He'd punched Jamie.

And he wanted her to know.

Back in his room, Jameson took the folded blueprint for the tree house out of his pocket and flattened it against the desk. He would have to revise some of his measurements. The design in his head was constantly changing.

Leaning over the desk, he marked the problem areas on his sketch off with a pencil, then straightened to look at it again. Something was missing.

When he raised his eyes, they landed on the old book on his shelf. He put the pencil down and tugged the slim, green paperback copy free. He stared at the hatchet on the cover for a moment, contemplating giving it a second read. Mom had gotten it for him when he'd turned eleven, and he didn't remember much about it.

"Will she be back?" he asked out loud, as if he were holding a magic eight ball in his hands.

Running his thumb along the edge of the pages, he pictured a little girl plucking the petals of a flower. Did he want to see her again? Or did he NOT want to see her again?

I do… I don't… I do… I don't, he repeated in his head, flipping through the book, trying to figure out exactly what it was that he wanted.

I do. I don't. I do. I don't, he sped up his pace. He was over halfway through the short book, close to 150 out of 185.

I-do-I-don't-I-do-I-don't. Slowing the skipping paper, he recited faster, making sure to get every last page.

I—

the thick back cover slipped past his nail

—do.

And that was that.

Queuing the new Stone Sour album on his phone, Jameson stretched out on his bed with the book. He had something to look forward to now. She'd made his summer bearable. And he hoped she'd come back.

Because he really *did* want to see Hayley again.

2014

16

The black Samsonite lay open on her bed. Three weeks' worth of clothes were already packed, and her backpack on the floor was nearly full too. Hayley was giving everything a last once-over. Heather had gone to Teresa's to pick the appropriate outfit for the road, like it mattered what they wore sitting on the bus for the next four hours. They had about thirty minutes until roll call in the school's parking lot.

Hayley snapped the straps inside the suitcase into place when the door behind her opened without a knock, and Carter entered her dorm room.

"Heather isn't here." She gave him a wary glance over her shoulder. His short hair was spiked on top, God knowing how much wax tamed the curls.

"I know. I wasn't looking for her. I was looking for you… Hay-ley," he drawled her name, his greedy eyes wandering over her backside.

She recoiled inward, refocusing on her luggage. His stare raised the hairs on her skin as if he were actually touching her. And she hated the way he said her name. Hated the sound of his voice, period.

Carter had been coming on to her all year behind his girlfriend's back, via texts or stalking her in the halls, forcing her into a dark corner—

Always touching. Always taking what he wants.

Granted, the idea of sleeping with him had its advantages. She could hold it over Heather's head that he'd chosen the outcast over her. And by God, she wanted that satisfaction. Wanted to hurt that evil bitch. She'd contemplated it. Played it out in her head. But as much as Hayley would love to stick it to her hellish roommate, the dog wasn't worth it. He probably cheated on Heather with other girls. There was no shortage of interested candidates at school.

She had to admit he was a catch, though. He was good-looking. He had a classically Roman babyface that resembled his mother more than his father: her rounded cheekbones, straight nose, elegant chin, and somewhat curly blonde hair. He was also athletic, smart, and a smooth talker if he tried. A skill he needed, should the rumors of his ambition to go into politics hold. He was captain of the debate team. So he was on the right track for that.

Her spine tensed as his fingers brushed her hair forward, draping it over her chest. She could sense the heat of his body closing in. Hayley braced herself for his touch, and the weight of his hands immediately felt like a ton on her shoulders. Beneath her skin, she was screaming.

From the angle of his chin in her periphery, he was taking in the view down her low-cut camisole for a moment, then his breath lowered to her exposed neck. "I want you, Hayley. We got three weeks... and no roommates."

"But you have a girlfriend," Hayley emphasized. "Doesn't she stay with you?"

Not everyone stayed in a private cabin during summer camp. Some had rooms in the resort's main building. She knew Aaron did, but she wasn't sure about Heather.

"Don't worry about her," Carter purred in her ear as if Hayley had already agreed to hook up with him. His thumbs bit into her shoulder blades, kneading the stiff muscles. "I can take care of Heather. She has her whole itinerary planned out. I made sure to keep her otherwise occupied."

Ah, yes. He would keep her his dirty little secret so as not to ruin things with his girlfriend. Nothing official had ever been said, but everyone presumed the two of them would get married eventually. His family was loaded, and Heather was a spoiled girl. Her husband-to-be would have to be able to meet her high standards.

Carter was perfect. They'd been dating for more than two years now, and with the way she conducted herself, she appeared to be pretty sure about her future with him. Hayley was merely someone he wanted to cross off his list. Like a challenge on his bucket list before tying the knot.

But she couldn't be the only one who'd ever turned him down. What was his big fascination with her? Yeah, her boobs had come in at last. They were by no means as big as Heather's, but they fit her silhouette because, unlike her roommate, she also had the rest of the curves to match her top half. Hayley was probably more proud of her ass than her boobs. Especially in these jean shorts.

Well, he could watch her backside all he wanted while she strode off.

"Not even if you were the last person on earth," she snapped, bending slightly at her waist to slam her suitcase shut.

Then she slung the strap of her backpack over her shoulder and yanked the Samsonite off the bed. As she whirled around to shove past him, his grip trapped her left wrist. The sharp momentum of his pull ripped the weight of the suitcase backward.

Caught by surprise, her breath clipped in her throat. An amber glow flared in his irises. She'd never seen him angry before.

"Dammit, Hayley. Why are you so fucking prideful?"

"Prideful?" she repeated offensively. "Try self-assured."

"I'm not going to hurt you."

"Damn right you're not. You'll never get the chance."

His words sounded sincere, but she didn't trust the rage in his expression. She tore herself free and charged for the door.

"How's your dad?" he called after her down the hallway. "I heard he's been racking up debts faster than he can pay 'em."

His words made her stall. What was he talking about? And how would he know that?

Roy!

Of course, he was talking to his son. He would want him to follow in his footsteps one day. Probably expected the two of them to run the business together, pinching her father out.

Hayley refused to look back at Carter. It was exactly what he wanted. She picked up her feet and resumed her escape.

Dragging her suitcase behind her, she wobbled through the parking lot. It was hard to storm off in a dramatic exit when you were wearing wedge sandals.

Aaron looked up from his iPhone and shot her a quick nod when she stepped onto the bus. He was the only one on the back bench. Like Hayley, he was one year behind the foursome, so they had a few classes in common.

Closing her eyes, she leaned her head against the window, but the moment of tranquility didn't last. Heather's high-pitched laugh pierced her ears like nails on a chalkboard. Hayley slammed her temple into the glass to make the ringing stop.

It was Carter who came on first. His shoulders squared, he didn't spare her a glance as he steam-rolled down the aisle. He wasn't taking her rejection well.

Aaron picked his backpack off the floor and rose from his center spot to let them pass. Carter took the window. Heather snuggled up to him.

Trailing her were Joey and Teresa. They slid into their designated seats at the opposite window.

The only friendly face in the back row was Aaron's, wedged between the girls, his shaggy chestnut hair like a curtain over his eyes, which Hayley knew from close examination were hazel-green. She wondered if Carter was as bad a roommate to him as Heather was to her. When they played chess together, he never talked about the others. Though he hung out with them, he'd never been mean to her.

Mr. Simmons did the roll call, and the moment the bus started moving, the switch in her mind flipped. Her thoughts were no longer on school. They were on Jamie now. She would see him again. In just a few hours, she would see him. The real Jamie. Not the one from her fantasies.

A whole year was a long time, wasn't it? People changed so much in a few months—not only their looks but their likes, too. Especially at their age. Jamie was done with high school now. Would he still be interested in wasting his time with her?

So many things went through Hayley's mind as she waited for the bus driver to unlatch the doors and release her into the freedom of Bishop Park.

17

Hayley dropped her suitcase at the foot of the bed in her cabin, not bothering to unpack. Or change.

Okay, fine, she'd chosen her outfit with a little bit of thought behind it, too. The bright red top and dark blue shorts looked killer in the mirror over the door. She was going for the ultimate wow factor that would knock Jamie on his ass.

She pulled her brush from the side compartment of her backpack and gave her hair a quick fluff. Then Hayley went on her quest. She took a stroll to the homestead first, trying to act casual around Beth. Keeping her ears perked, she listened for any sounds besides the two of them in the house.

There were none. They were alone. No laughter. No hushed voices. Not even Carl, who practically belonged to the furniture.

Where was Jamie?

Beth sat down across from Hayley at the kitchen island. "Look at you. You've gotten so tall," she said, flashing her renowned bright smile.

Her dark brown hair was fastened with a butterfly clip at the top of her head, making the curls bounce around her heart-shaped face. "I bet you have to chase the boys away with a flyswatter," she laughed melodiously, her sparkling blue eyes pinched tight. "You look like you stir trouble. I always wanted a daughter, you know? Not that Jamie isn't causing me enough headaches on his own these days." A deep crease formed between her brows as she dropped her chin on the heel of her hand. "He's growing up too fast."

Right. Hayley knew a thing or two about the active libido of a seventeen-year-old male. A shudder crept over her, remembering Carter's hands on her this morning.

"How's school, sweetheart?" she asked, changing the topic.

Hayley gave her the gist. She was still at the top of all her classes; grades had never been a problem for her. She kept the pesky fly issues out of her recap.

After half an hour of their little back and forth, Hayley couldn't take the suspense anymore. The urgency to lay eyes on him was killing her. She had to put her mind at ease in regards to where they stood after a whole year.

Was he purposely avoiding her?

She had to find out for sure. But where did he hang out? She couldn't simply ask Beth. It was still their secret, wasn't it? Had he told his mom?

Nonsense. There was nothing *to* tell.

Hayley politely excused herself and went roaming the property in search of him. She checked the lake first, but open swim didn't start until tomorrow, so he wouldn't be on lifeguard duty yet.

Is he out in the woods?

He didn't have to stick around the camp all day. He could be in town, hanging out with friends. Or hooking up with a girl somewhere. The possibilities were endless, and Beth's comment about him causing her headaches echoed in her ears. She hadn't seen the black Silverado sitting in their driveway.

Hayley was about to turn back toward her cabin when the rusty metal door of the tool shed slammed shut, making her jump.

Could it be him?

She charged around the corner, and her eyes landed on the familiar figure perched on the pile of chopped wood.

Startled by the sudden movement in his periphery, his body jerked, and his boots lost their contact. He slipped off, toppling down the short rows of wood, and landed square on his ass, dropping his cigarette in the process.

So much for knocking him off his feet.

Hand to his chest, he expelled a sharp breath. "Holy shit! I thought you were my mom. She'd kill me if she knew I smoked."

Jamie pushed himself to his feet and brushed the loose dirt from the seat of his blue jeans.

Holy growth spurt, Batman!

His t-shirt stretched tight across his chest and shoulders, biceps bulging out. And, oh, his face…

Where Carter's features were aesthetically Roman, Jamie's were all Greek: the sharp angles of his cheeks, a tall, defined nose, square chin.

Nobody made her heart race like Jamie. Not Aaron. And definitely not Carter.

"She can't smell it on your clothes?" Hayley prompted after unscrambling her thoughts.

"Nah. I blame it on secondhand from Carl. Dude's a chimney." A wide grin replaced the mask of shock on his face. "It's good to see you—"

"HAYLEY!" someone called her name.

She cranked her head around and saw Aaron glaring at her from the common hall.

Damn. She'd forgotten about him. She owed him a rematch. Was it really that late already?

"Shit. I gotta go," she said, already in motion.

Fuck me!

Hayley spun around to leave him in the dust, and he was totally checking out her ass. She was an hourglass on stilts in obscenely short shorts. The front pockets were longer than the hem. And those legs… they went on forever. The tan wedges blended with her feet, making them appear even longer.

Jameson pictured her legs coiled around him. Waist. Neck. It didn't matter. He simply wanted to be in between her thighs.

Drooling from his open mouth, he watched her leave, her hips swaying side to side. He noticed the hint of uneasiness. She wasn't confident in her steps. And what do you know? That little detail told him everything he needed to know.

She was still a virgin.

Which meant he needed to stay the fuck away from her. Far, far away from her.

18

A freaking virgin! Immaculate. To be revered, not touched…

Hayley was off-limits. It was a no-brainer.

Aaaand, of course, that only made him want her more. It was a primal impulse. No matter how many times he tried to clarify the rules to his upstairs brain, his body refused to get with the program. The noose of his wild imagination involving her was drawing dangerously tight. Like cutting-off-circulation-to-extremities tight.

All the things he fantasized about doing to her…

She'd been his last thought before falling asleep and his first thought upon waking up.

And then again, in the shower, but who was counting?

Jameson skipped the shave. He didn't mind the scruff along his jawline. He dressed and found Mom in the kitchen with Carl. They both got abruptly quiet as he entered. Their shifty glances kept up some mental conversation between the two of them.

Awkward.

He ignored it. He didn't want to know the truth. Ignorance was bliss.

After his shift at the lake, he returned to his project out back of the field house that stored all the watersports equipment. One of the doors had come off its hinges, and he'd been fixing things here and there over the past few weeks. He was good at building things. Good with his hands at a lot of things.

He stared up at the dilapidated arch his grandfather had built years ago. The wood was chipped, and the white paint badly faded.

"What's this?" Hayley came up behind him. "Looks like an old wedding gazebo."

His eyes locked onto her face like a homing beacon, and his lips automatically curled into a smile. They were back. The butterflies.

"It is," he replied. "My parents got married under it."

"Thinking about fixing it up?"

He shifted his focus to the tools lying on the ground. There was a lot of work to be done. It would take months. "One day, I will."

"And get married under it yourself?" She raised her voice at the end, toying with the suggestion.

He huffed a little laugh. "Yeah, maybe."

Whether he would or not, the neglected arch deserved to be restored.

Jameson missed his dad. He had the sudden urge to tell her that his parents had been in love and that leaving hadn't been his choice. But what did it matter to her?

Hayley swapped the weight on her feet from one side to the other, hands stuffed into the back pockets of her jean shorts. She seemed uncomfortable standing around, watching him work.

"Mind giving me a hand?" he asked, holding out the drill.

He didn't need help, but he wanted her to stay a little longer. Whatever he could offer to keep her here.

He pointed the grip toward her with his fingers closed around the top. She stepped up to him and took it in her right hand, wrapping her small palm around the handle.

One brow arched, she gave the trigger a quick double squeeze. "You trust me with your power tool?"

Oh no, she didn't.

Jameson let the innuendo slide. Wasn't even sure she'd meant it. "Yeah, I trust you." He smirked. "You don't look like you got two left hands."

Bullshit. She'd probably never held a drill before in her life. Or anyone's 'power tool' for that matter. *Daddy's sheltered little princess.*

Hayley batted her full, long eyelashes up at him. "Oh, I got experience," she implied, jaw cocked, waving the DEWALT in the air.

Is she for real? She just kept going with the spunk.

Jameson was beginning to reevaluate his previous commitment. Maybe he should take her up on it. How long would she keep the taunts going? They both knew this wasn't going anywhere. They had three weeks. That was it.

If things were different, he knew he could fall for her. She was so down to earth for someone who came from money. And not afraid of manual labor, either. Hayley was everything he was looking for in a girl.

But as it were, they lived in opposite worlds—two ecosystems colliding briefly before being ripped apart again. She couldn't stay, and he wouldn't leave. They didn't belong together.

He watched her mount the new signs on the other side of the entrance to the field house. In his periphery, of course, not making it too obvious that he couldn't take his eyes off her. It wasn't that he felt shy around her. It was the fact that he knew he shouldn't go there. Not even in his mind.

Her long ponytail swayed with her motion. She moved without hurry but with efficiency, driving screw after screw into the wood and making sure they sat straight. The placement was already marked by the slightly faded paint on the siding from the old signs that had been weathered and needed replacing.

"What do you think? Up to your standard?" She stepped back, gauging her work, one hand on her hip.

Okay, he had to admit she *was* handy with the drill. "Decent," he acknowledged with a chuckle.

She was beaming with pride at the little accomplishment. The sight made his skin prickle. It was too cute.

They finished and gathered up the tools, stuffing them all back into the two boxes he'd brought out this morning. She latched the lid of the small one shut, and he expected her to take off after that, but when he rose to his feet, her hand closed around the handle.

"Lead the way," she ordered, picking it up.

Looking over the frame of her glasses, she waited for him to move. He was awestruck by the radiance of her character. Taking off hadn't even crossed her mind. How could she be so goddamn perfect? It was impossible to find a flaw in her.

On their way back to the shed, Jameson kept racking his brain for anything to turn him off this girl at his right. Cradling the object against her chest, Hayley appeared suddenly nervous. She glanced back over her shoulder as they left the footpath and went toward the secluded area where the shed stood. It was pretty isolated, but you had a view of the lake from in between the trees.

Not so brave with your words anymore, huh? Now that they were leaving the security and comfort of a public place.

A wicked little flame sparked in his chest. He liked taking her out of her comfort zone and pushing her limits. Like he'd done last year on the hike. But the two of them, out there in the middle of nowhere for hours, spelled trouble. It was a temptation he wasn't sure he could resist.

Especially if the little tease continued running her mouth. He would take her up on it. And he would find out exactly how far she wanted to go.

Jameson dropped the heavy box by his feet, using the keys from his pocket to undo the lock. He pulled the right side of the double doors open and put the 24-by-12-inch crate on top of the workbench. Hayley didn't follow. She held the significantly lighter box out to him by the handle without stepping foot inside. She probably didn't want to get caught in the tight, dark space alone with him.

He suppressed the urge to grin. What did she think he'd do?

Or maybe she didn't trust herself. What would she do, if he made a move on her? Physically. Not just a little innocent flirting while standing at a five-foot distance.

Nailing her with a level stare, he slapped his palms to the sides of the toolbox and jerked it toward him. Hayley didn't let go immediately. Glued to the object, she took a subtle stumble in the same direction, her eyes steady on his, unblinking.

Jameson felt the sparks between them. Felt them down to his marrow… an all-consuming blaze… surging…

She folded first. Releasing her grip and breaking the contact.

He set the little cube down beside its big brother and vacated the dim storage. Fully aware of her attentive stare on him, he swung the door shut, replacing the padlock, and when he pivoted to face her, she was right there, leaning into the left half of the doorway, less than a foot away.

Jameson couldn't resist. He went for it.

Mirroring her stance, his right shoulder bumping the metal surface, he reduced their proximity by an even more significant amount. Hayley looked up through her lashes, the perky tip of her nose four inches from his. There was a minuscule twitch in her lip, and he noticed the hitch in her breath.

"Am I making you nervous or something?"

She shifted her hips away from him, the apprehension evident in her motion. It was so obvious.

"You're still a virgin," he called her out.

"What makes you think that?"

"The way you walk. The way you move—"

"The way I walk?" she scuffed, appalled, her mouth hanging slack.

If that offended her, she wasn't going to like the next bold punch. "Like you haven't been fucked... but want to be," he emphasized.

That shut her up.

Her throat bobbed with a flustered swallow. It took a few seconds for her to recover her voice. "I'm sixteen."

"So? Your friend over there," —he tipped his head in the direction of the group at the pier— "The one twirling her fake blond hair while flirting with the coach. She's had sex. A lot. See how her body angles toward him, highlighting her curves."

She rolled her eyes. "So I'm not a slut like Heather. That doesn't mean I've never been with a boy."

Wanna bet?

Jameson straightened. Moving over her, he tilted his head and leaned in for a kiss.

Hayley flinched, caught off guard.

"Holy shit! You've never even been kissed."

Her blush flared bright red in her cheeks, and she couldn't deny it. She lowered her eyes, flattening her upper back against the metal door.

Jameson raked his eyes over her features, making note of all the little details he'd missed before. She didn't wear makeup. Her skin was impeccable beneath a stretch of freckles across her cute nose. She had a fair complexion that also showed faint signs of sun exposure on her cheeks. He figured she spent time outdoors instead of hauling herself up inside the walls of her school.

Tiny diamond studs pierced her earlobes, two on each side. They were the only jewelry he could see. Further proof that she didn't like to show off.

The color of her hair was a stunning chestnut with natural caramel highlights, which shimmered like pure silk in the sunlight. A lock had come loose from the tie and fell down by her cheek. His fingers itched to reach up and sweep it behind her ear, just to touch her. He wanted to pull it free and watch it tumble over her shoulders.

He imagined holding her while fanning his hand through the smooth mass and inhaling the intoxicating scent of her shampoo.

Jameson shoved his hands into his pockets to keep them in check. "What do you want from me, Hayley?"

There was something there. He knew it. They both felt it. But he got the sense that she was closing herself up. Hiding something. Her eyes reminded him of storm clouds, mysterious and full of secrets, but also stunningly beautiful with their threat of imminent doom. He'd always loved thunderstorms. There was something compelling about the forces of nature and the destruction they could leave in their wake. Would her clouds break open and spill their secrets to him?

"It's okay if you don't know. Just tell me that." He would still want to hang out with her. Even if it went no further than that. He was that much of a sucker for her at this point.

114

19

She couldn't look at him, but she damn sure felt his expectant stare on her as he waited for an answer.

"I like you," Hayley told him in all honesty. "I like you a lot. But I don't think I'm ready to go there yet."

"I'm not trying to pressure you. I enjoy spending time with you. If that's all you want, then that's okay with me."

No pressure, he'd assured her. That was all she'd ever wanted, but lately, she was feeling it from all sides. Like a trap slamming shut. Everyone always expected things from her. It was exhausting. No one had ever asked what she wanted before. Dad had made every decision.

Hayley wanted a chance to figure herself out. And that took time. Not pressure. Jamie understood. Instead of considering his pursuit of her a waste of time, he stuck around. Whether she would change her mind or not didn't seem to be a concern. When he came by, he never actually stepped foot in her cabin. One leg bent, the other one dangling outside the window, he lounged in the frame, as if he tried to keep as much of himself as possible out of her room. A knee and an elbow were practically the only parts of him crossing the threshold.

Leaning back against the headboard of her bed, she watched him over her shoulder. His hair was a bit longer this year, with unruly bangs hanging down over his eyes. The glowing morning sun behind him made his shape little more than an ominous silhouette lurking in her periphery. So forbidden. So tempting.

"Why do you perch on the sill? You can come in, you know?"

"Nah, it's alright. I don't wanna make you uncomfortable. This being your bedroom and all." He gestured loosely around the space, his face scrunched in jest.

Didn't want to invade her private space? How considerate. And surprising, coming from a boy his age.

Hayley wanted to go hiking with him so badly, but she'd be damned if she made herself look desperate. He hadn't brought it up again.

He glanced at his phone. "I also don't wanna overstay my welcome. I have to report to the lake." He shifted his weight, preparing to jump. "Catch you later."

And then he was gone, his boots landing on a *thud* in the soft grass outside her window.

It was frustrating. He did exactly what she asked of him, keeping himself at a physical distance from her and respecting her choice. And it only made her want him more. She knew once she was ready to give up her virginity, she wanted it to be with someone like Jamie.

Not Carter.

Back at the tool shed, her heart had pounded up her throat with him so close. It had been hard to draw air into her lungs. The thrill was exhilarating. And the second his eyes had dropped to her lips…

Why had she flinched?

The comparison to Heather hadn't helped. She didn't want to give him the impression that she was easy. So, to make matters worse, she'd unintentionally done a one-eighty, *after* she'd been flirting with him nonetheless. That was so messed up. She wasn't a tease.

Hayley was so confused between what her mind told her and what her body craved. She shouldn't have turned down that kiss. First base was definitely on the table, but she was too shy—and inexperienced—to initiate it herself. How could she bring the topic up now? She couldn't get the words out. She was more likely to bite off her tongue and choke.

Small steps, she decided. She would have to make a move to show him that she wasn't opposed to his proximity.

Sweat dripped down his back. It was hot. Upper nineties. Jameson kept looking up at the sun, watching its path, and counting the minutes until his shift was over.

How had he gotten so whipped in a matter of three days?

But it hadn't really been three days. This had been brewing under his skin over the course of two years. Only it was different now that Hayley was here. He couldn't get her out of his head. He'd been at her cabin for almost an hour this morning, and he was already itching to go back, even if he would only be watching her read. She was like a breathtaking landscape he didn't get tired of admiring.

"How much… was that?" Carter's words came in clipped breaths. Dude nearly hacked up a lung trying to catch his wind from the buoy.

"Minute and three seconds," *Tweedle Dum* said, checking his phone.

He gave the water a hard slap in frustration. He looked like a thrashing toddler.

Jameson watched him haul himself onto the ledge, wondering if he was going to give it another try. He'd been at it since he got here at ten. Apparently, he was trying to break his dad's old record of fifty-seven seconds.

"Are you seriously going to let a boy who looks like he can't even grow facial hair yet show you up? I mean, look at that babyface. Smooth as a Ken doll."

Carl's comparison made him snort a laugh.

"You know he's itching to challenge you."

"He can't show me up if I don't race him," Jameson argued.

"You don't have to race him. Just take off your shirt. Show him who's boss."

He shook his head at Carl. "I don't need the attention. Not gonna make it any more personal than it already is."

Carter was still on the scrawny side compared to him.

Jameson's phone chimed from inside his boot with a text. He tugged the kicker closer and pulled the message up on the screen. It was from Jill asking him to come over. She gave him the green light whenever her parents were out of town.

His thumb made the decision faster than his brain.

'Can't'

—Send.

Fuck. Had he really turned down a booty call from the head cheerleader only to breathe the air around Hayley?

Yup. It was official. He was a dumbass.

He followed up with a quick 'Raincheck?' that didn't get a response.

No surprise.

He'd lost the sure thing he had going with her. And didn't that put a damper on the next three weeks? Looked like he wouldn't be getting laid any time soon.

Whatever. It wasn't like they were dating.

He dropped the Samsung back into his boot and tossed it aside.

"You actually have your phone on you for once?" There was genuine surprise in Carl's tone.

No offense there. It *was* unusual.

"Don't get used to it." No need to keep it close now. He wasn't going to hear back from her anyway.

Worst part? He'd lowkey been hoping for the text. He needed the distraction. But once the opportunity presented itself, he had a change of heart. It didn't feel right anymore.

Jill didn't feel right anymore.

20

Someone's soft whistle caught her attention as she strolled down the main trail. The staff's golf carts went regularly back and forth on it, but it wasn't much of a road. The gravel was mostly overgrown with weeds, keeping up with the idyllic ambiance of the place. There was only one major vehicle allowed on the property. All others had to be parked in the lot out front.

She gave the area a wide sweep and didn't find anyone at first. Then her vision zoned in on Jamie's Silverado. It was facing into the driveway, passenger side toward her.

She pivoted her stance a tad to the left and spotted him sitting behind the wheel, windows down. He was wearing a dark baseball cap, his face nearly hidden in the shadow of the bill.

Their eyes met, and he nudged his head to beckon her closer.

Hayley glanced over her shoulder to check the coast. When she determined it was clear, she shifted in his direction, leaving the footpath.

He quickly finished his cigarette and dropped the butt into the can sitting in one of the double cup holders.

"You headed to lunch?" he asked, blowing the last of the smoke out the driver's side. Right elbow propped on the center console, he turned his body toward her.

"That depends on what else you have to offer," she drawled somewhat seductively while sauntering up to the window.

It brought a smile to his face, and his teeth gave his lower lip the slightest tug before he spoke.

"My mom wants me to run an errand in town. Wanna come?" He nodded at the passenger seat, his brows arched in a dare.

She'd never been in his truck before. A small, confined space? Only the two of them?

Her hands gripped the bottom of the window frame, and she took a step onto the board that ran along the side of the truck. He was wearing another Grunt Style shirt. This one had a faded and tattered American flag on it that covered nearly the entire front of his chest. The base color was black. Like his jeans. His look practically screamed the word 'rebel'.

"Errands? That doesn't sound very fun," she taunted in a flirtatious lilt.

His grin got sharper. He cocked his head to one side, and his left arm flexed at twelve o'clock on the steering wheel. "How about I take you for ice cream after? Make up for the missed lunch."

Hayley squinted, pursing her lips as if she were contemplating it, only to torture him.

"Okay. I'm game," she chimed, hopping off the ledge to rip the door open.

She slid into the seat beside him and buckled up, enjoying the attention of his eyes on her.

As Jamie started the engine, heavy metal started blaring from the speakers at full volume.

"Sorry," he cringed, reaching for the knob. "Forgot what I had on pause."

"No. Leave it." Her hands shot out but didn't touch him.

He frowned. "You sure?"

"Yeah. It's your car."

"Alright." She watched him shift his butt on the seat to tug his phone from his back pocket. "But you get to pick the next one."

He held his Galaxy up with a wickedly hot grin beneath his hat and a look that said, 'Come and take it'.

Hayley accepted his challenge. She closed her fingers around his, letting them linger before freeing the cell from his grasp. He kept his focus on the road, but the smirk dangling at the corner of his mouth told her he relished their brief touch as much as she did.

While she scrolled through the various artists in his library she wasn't familiar with, she made a mental note of the song playing. Though the verse was all screams, the chorus broke down into a catchy melody, and she found herself liking it. She was glad she hadn't skipped it. It gave her a little more detail to fill in the blanks about this charismatic boy next to her.

His taste in music was more adventurous than her own, but it didn't take her long to find common ground. Hayley added the song to the queue list and set the phone down in the cup holder next to the can of ginger ale.

Jamie shot her a sideways glance. "What d'you pick?"

"You'll see."

When Stone Sour's *Say You'll Haunt Me* came on, he tipped his head back in a laugh. "Nice choice," he noted. "That's probably my favorite album, though it's a few years old."

Hayley thought it was fitting.

Jamie reached for the volume knob again, this time to turn it up, and she leaned back in her seat, enjoying the ride-along.

The rays of the sun glimmered through the branches as he weaved and curved around bends. Bumps had her swaying in her seat, but not enough to reach for the dash.

The unpaved road through the woods wasn't as bad as the trip on the school bus. His Silverado had big off-road tires that were built for this terrain, and the loose gravel was no match for the tread. He veered around trees with the same ease he showed off while skipping over rocks.

Taking turns choosing songs, they ended up with an old album by Black Stone Cherry. Jamie picked *Like I Roll*, and she watched him sing along from the corner of her eye. She loved this side of him. So carefree and bewitching.

Windows down, music blasting, they made it into town, the metal frame vibrating from the bass notes. At the first stoplight, he took a right. Across the intersection, a tall blonde in a tiny ruffle skirt and cowboy boots craned her neck after the truck. Jamie attracted attention wherever he went, whether he noticed it or not.

He pulled the truck into an angled spot at the curb and cranked it into park, the veins and muscles in his forearm contracting as he shut off the engine. How could such a simple movement have such an erotic connotation? She hadn't been able to take her eyes off his hands on the steering wheel. Her mind kept slithering back into the gutter. It seemed to like it there.

Jamie cracked his door, and she followed as he went around to the back to unlatch the tailgate. Two medium-sized moving boxes sat in the covered truck bed. He pulled one forward, and she automatically reached for the other.

"Thanks," he said, closing things back up. "I knew I brought you along for a reason."

Hayley pressed the heavy-ish rectangle to her chest. "More like an ulterior motive, if you ask me," she fired back.

"Ha! You think *this* is my ulterior motive?" Cradling his box in one arm, he rounded her backside, his eyes making the shameless—and very obvious—dip to her ass, then returning to her face. "Girl, you're so naïve."

He swung his head around and walked up to the shop straight ahead. The large sign above read *'DONATIONS'*. Leaning his shoulder into the door, he pushed it open, and a bell chimed.

Hayley hustled after him.

He removed his hat first thing when he entered, shoving the bill into his back pocket and running one hand through his hair to give it a ruffle.

"Hey, Beau," he greeted the middle-aged man behind the counter with a polite smile.

Jamie was such a paradox. He looked like a punk kid, but he had the manners and charm of a gentleman. All evidence of his mom's exceptional parenting, Hayley figured.

Her eyes did a quick scan of the miscellaneous items, from clothing to home decor and small furniture pieces. The whole shop had a vintage flair to it that was adorable. Except for the ceramic dolls on the shelves. They were just creepy.

"C'mon back." The man, *Beau*, who was roughly Jamie's height of six feet, raised the old flip counter to let them through.

He led them down the hallway into a storage room, where more inventory filled the space from floor to ceiling. Weaving through, Hayley slid the moving box onto a shelf in the corner.

Beau waited by the door of the room and gave Jamie a clap on his shoulder. "Thank your mom for me, will ya? Carrie is gonna be thrilled with all this stuff."

Just when she thought Beth couldn't be any more perfect.

"Sure thing, man." Jamie shrugged like it wasn't a big deal.

Facing Hayley, he jerked his head the way they'd come. "See you later," he told Beau.

She returned the owner's cordial nod and brushed past him.

The shop door chimed as Jamie pulled it open, holding it wide for her. The sweet gesture made her blush. She held eye contact, shooting him a *thanks*.

"You're welcome," he said, offering her the same half-shrug he'd given Beau.

It sent another buzz across her skin. Because for her, it *was* a big deal.

Once outside, she pivoted toward the truck when his hand slid against her palm.

"This way," he said, tugging her in the opposite direction.

Her body complied on command at the sound of his voice.

He let go almost immediately after the reroute, but the sense of his touch somehow remained, like her skin wanted to hold on to the sensation and commit it to memory.

He reached for his cap and slid it back on, tugging the bill low. Again, the top half of his face was cloaked in a dark shadow. The hint of a beard enhanced his sultry, renegade look.

"So, how come you don't swim?" he asked out of the blue.

She wondered how long the question had been burning on his mind. "Eager to see me in a swimsuit?"

"Maybe," he chuckled, letting the word dangle in the air. "Okay, definitely. But that's not my reason for asking."

"I'm not a strong swimmer."

"That's why there's lifeguards."

"Ha-ha-ha. You mean there's *you*." She wagged her finger at him, hinting at his intentions. "There you go again with the ulterior motive. Still waiting for me to pass out so you can do '*CPR*'?" she prompted, using air quotes. His pick-up line from their hike last year was also burned into her memory.

"Actually, I'd much rather have you conscious when I make a move on you." He flashed his teeth in an offensively bold grin that matched the sexy swagger in his step.

"When!" —Not if. "So you *are* planning on making your move," she drew her conclusion. "And you're just… what? Biding your time until then?"

Hands in his pockets, looking down, he shook his head. "You can't blame me for trying, Hayley," he muttered quietly.

Few people crowded the sidewalk on a weekday afternoon as they continued strolling down the street of the picturesque mountain town with its little shops and mom-and-pop restaurants. Colorful flower baskets hung from every light fixture and signs on both sides of the road. Hayley saw shades of purple, orange, yellow, and red. It was every tourist's dream.

"As promised," he said, tipping his head toward the ice cream shop. "You earned it."

His hand shot out, closing around the handle. The sweet aroma blasted her senses as he ripped the door open. The inside of the store smelled like freshly baked waffle cones and caramel. Vanilla, too. It was so palpable, she could taste it.

Oh, heavens. Did they bottle this scent? 'Cause they could sell it.

She wondered what it would be like to work here. The skinny boy across from them looked about her age. He must not be tempted by the abundance of deliciousness.

Out of the twenty-some flavors, Hayley picked strawberry cheesecake, and Jamie went with the controversial mint chocolate chip—or the gum of the ice cream flavors, as she liked to call it. She teased him about it, but he laughed it off with his nonchalant attitude. And then he pointed out that only the best kinds came in white mint instead of green.

"So there's a little fun fact for ya, Miss Top-of-the-Honor-Roll," he mocked, beaming with glee.

If she'd been wearing pigtails, he probably would've given them a tug, too.

They left the ice cream shop through the rear door, where he claimed one of the blue powder-coated picnic tables on the patio. A second was empty, and a couple with two small girls sat at the third.

Jamie straddled the flat bench, his elbow on the table. She parked herself sideways, leaning back, with the sun beating straight down on them. The risk of walking away from this date with a burn was worth it. The crochet lace racerback would leave a funny tan line to remember.

The patio didn't have a fence around it, and they watched people pass by on the sidewalk.

"We can go somewhere else if you want," he said, jabbing his lime green spoon into his cup. Hers was purple, matching her top.

"What's wrong with where we're at?"

"It's kinda out in the open."

"So?"

His tone turned ambiguous. "Are you sure you want to be seen in public with me?"

She knew what he meant. At the camp, they kept themselves hidden. They didn't want to start rumors.

Only they weren't at the camp now. "People here don't know me."

"But they know *me*." He scooped another heap of white mint chocolate chip into his gorgeous mouth. She couldn't stop staring.

"And you have a reputation of sorts?" she joked. "Like the town's official heartbreaker."

"Is that the vibe I give off?" he choked out, sounding slightly offended.

Or maybe it was actual surprise at her accusation. Did he not know how irresistible he looked?

"Just something your mom said about you giving her headaches." She'd assumed it was from him running around town.

The spoon stilled in his mouth. Then he pulled it out slowly, nailing her with a narrow stare. "Since when do you talk to my mom?"

"Since my first summer here."

His stern expression changed as if an epiphany had struck. He stabbed his spoon at her chest.

"It was *YOU* who ate my cookies!" he cried, putting the pieces together.

"Sorry. They were *reeeally* good."

"I KNOW! I gave Carl an earful," he tagged on, filling his mouth again.

Hayley giggled through her nose while the sweet, creamy texture melted down her throat. She felt a little guilty.

Jamie finished his ice cream before her. Reversing the spoon, he raised it to his sinful lips, licking the inverted shape clean. She imagined his tongue working the smooth curve. Hayley had never been jealous of a spoon before. Or wished to trade places with one.

What if he'd been thinking the same thing while watching her?

His eyes flipped to her, and she was sure he could read her mind like her forehead was a billboard. Was it possible to send out some sort of psychic mating call that the opposite sex could sense? Humans didn't secrete pheromones. And yet she had the notion there was an awful lot of nonverbal communication going on between them.

Her skin flushed. Was it getting hotter out here? There was no breeze going, either.

Jamie broke the intense link between them, chucking his empty cup and spoon into the bin behind him. He wiped his palms down the front of his thighs, then put his right elbow back on the picnic table. Dropping his chin on his thumb, he watched her finish her last scoop.

It wasn't irritating at all.

His chest heaved with long breaths, and his index finger dragged across his bottom lip in slow motion. She wondered what he was mulling over.

Hayley got to her feet and went to the trash bin. Swinging his leg around, Jamie followed her movement. Propped on the ledge, knees spread, he squinted up at her into the sun. His expression gave the idea he liked what he was seeing. His eyes were practically level with her chest. They never wavered from her face, though.

This boy—

No! *This young man,* she corrected herself.

—had the kind of confidence she could only dream of having, with none of the arrogance. Jamie oozed sex appeal, lounging on the bench, hands hanging lax from his wrists.

"I guess we should probably head back," he suggested with an apathetic shrug.

"Ugh! Do we have to?"

Why does he have to be so responsible?

Her displeasure amused him, and he chuckled. "Someone might report you missing."

"No one is going to miss me," Hayley moaned, letting her shoulders sag.

"I highly doubt that."

Scooting his boots in, he slapped those powerful thighs of his she remembered sprinting down the clearing and pushed himself to a stand. He hovered over her for a long second, then hooked the front belt loop of her shorts and tugged at her. "Come on."

She couldn't argue with that. Or the sparkle of his eyes.

Despite his sense of duty to get her back to the camp, he wasn't in a hurry, and when he finally pulled the truck into the driveway of his home, neither of them made a move to get out.

"Thanks again for your help."

"I didn't do much."

"You saved me from having to take two trips. Don't underestimate how much that means to me," he exaggerated. "I hate taking two trips."

"Your mom donates a lot?"

"Anything she can find. I make the trip three times a month."

Hayley was about to commend the woman's generosity when his phone started rattling the cup holder. Instead of a name, the caller ID showed four stars.

"Speaking of the General," he muttered with an eye roll, reaching over.

Hayley frowned at him, confused.

"A running joke. It's what my dad used to call her," he explained, then answered the call.

"*Where you at?*" were the first words from the speaker.

"I'm back. I'm in the driveway," he said, unbuckling.

"*Took you long enough.*"

Hayley undid her seat belt quietly. He could deal with the wrath of his mom by himself.

Cracking the door just wide enough, she slipped out. She kept her eyes on the open windows of the house to make sure Beth wasn't looking at the Silverado to check if he was telling the truth.

The curtains shifted, and she froze. Palms at her sides, flat against the truck, she held her breath for a moment, still craning her neck. His mom's face never appeared—

"Sneaking off?"

"*JESUS CHRIST!*" she shrieked. Adrenaline flooded her veins, her heart hammering inside her ribcage. He'd managed to get the jump on her from the back of the vehicle, while her focus had been at the front. "You gave me a flippin' heart attack."

"Payback's a bitch," he grinned beneath the bill of his navy blue baseball cap. "I can teach you a thing or two about stealth." He tipped his head at an angle in suggestion.

Hayley scowled and pushed her glasses back up her nose. He had startled them right off her face.

"She's at the common hall."

"Not inside?" Hayley asked, surprised.

He shook his head slowly, his expression unreadable. "It'll be a while. Probably an hour."

So they were alone? Was he implying—

"Wanna come in?"

WHAAAAT?

Her jaw fell open. Jamie shifted toward her, his size dwarfing her in comparison. His blue eyes were alive with lightning, and fire was coming off his body, flames licking at her…

He was making his move. RIGHT NOW. Jamie was making his move on her.

Shifting over her, he pinned her against the truck, as he'd done at the tool shed. It all became clear.

MAYDAY! MAYDAY! A shrill voice rang in her head with the distress call. *WARNING! YOU'RE GOING DOWN!*

He flipped his baseball cap around and lowered his head to her right. "I'm trying to stick to your rules, Hayley, …but you're not playing fair."

His fingertips grazed her bare shoulders with the lightest touch. He let them wander lazily down the side of her arms to her elbow, out of curiosity, she guessed, to see if she'd mind.

She didn't.

Hayley reached up, tugging on his shirt at his chest. She needed to hold on to something.

"You'll get me in trouble," he said in a gravelly voice, his lips brushing the shell of her ear. "Batting your eyes at me like that."

His breath down her neck excited her. Her heartbeat was frantic. Her thighs twitched. Her body tingled all over, with every cell and every nerve on high alert. An unfamiliar sensation bloomed in between her legs.

This was it.

That was what she wanted from him.

"You make me question the definition of trouble," she admitted openly. "Touching you is a slippery slope. I don't know how fast it will go… or where it will lead. I don't know where it ends."

"And that scares you?" he speculated.

Hayley nodded. Would she be able to jump off the ride before reaching the bottom?

She feared kissing him would be her undoing.

A sob hitched in her throat. "I don't mean to play games with you." She felt awful for leading him on. Again. What the hell was wrong with her?

"You're not," he assured her, his voice tender and free of criticism. "I don't want to persuade you into having sex. If it doesn't feel right to you, then it's not. And I made no assumptions that your stance would change. I promised you not to overstep into your comfort zone, so I never expected anything out of this. You don't have to worry. We're good," he emphasized.

Tilting her chin up, he flashed a smirk, then withdrew his warm touch. Hayley watched him round the truck and skip up the steps to the front door.

21

Why was he putting himself through this torture? Every day he spent with her was making things worse, his hands twitching, fighting the urge to run up her naked legs and take a hold of her hips. Those shorts that hugged the curve of her ass made his head spin. And the hem that traced the crease where her thighs began…

That was where he wanted to put his grabby paws. Pull her down on him and squeeze her perfectly shaped glutes as she ground herself against him until she came apart. He didn't care if he finished. He simply wanted to watch her come.

Before his shift at the lake, he stopped off at her cabin. She had the habit of keeping the back window cracked for airflow since there was no A/C.

Jameson slid it open, then climbed in to leave a batch of his chocolate chip cookies for her.

Mom had thrown him a suspicious look. He'd grown up helping her in the kitchen and always enjoyed giving her a hand, but couldn't remember the last time he'd baked.

They were still warm. He wanted to surprise her while she was out for breakfast. Or maybe showering—

The visual of her under the stream, all wet and slick, formed in his depraved mind. Her head tipped back… hands in her hair, lips parted…

Fuck! He needed to get out of her room, stat.

He'd planned to leave the cookies on her desk by the window but reconsidered. He wanted her to eat them on her bed, thinking of him. And he wanted her to know that he'd been right there… where she slept…

Yup, *STAT!* As in RIGHT FUCKING NOW.

Jameson swung his leg over the window sill and bolted.

His shift at the lake was quiet. The usual suspects must've found something else to entertain themselves with. Jameson tracked the sun's path and took off thirty minutes early.

Passing by the common hall, he saw Carter leave. He tipped his diet Dr. Pepper back, then launched the empty drink in the general vicinity of the recycling bin. He didn't bother aiming. He missed the two-foot opening, and the can landed beside it on the ground.

So much for a career in sports.

Jameson bent down to pick it up, and Carter glanced over his shoulder. "Thanks for taking care of my trash, Inbred. Glad everyone knows their place." He winked, pointing a finger gun, then strutted off.

The aluminum crinkled in his grip. If only it was the arrogant prick's neck.

Jameson was tempted to *yeet* it at his head to show him what aim looked like.

He dunked it into the bin instead.

He kept focusing on making good choices. No matter how hard it was to do the right thing sometimes.

22

Hayley was leaving the common room around 4 p.m. after playing another round of chess with Aaron. She'd hoped for Jamie to show up at her cabin, but eventually gave up the wait and accepted her friend's offer. He'd beaten her twice. Her head hadn't been in the game today.

Jamie was avoiding her.

Sure, he had work to get done, and she didn't expect him to spend all his free time with her, but he wasn't suddenly too busy. He was pulling away. He hadn't even given her a chance to thank him for the cookies.

The fact that he'd climbed through her window after pointing out her bedroom should be off-limits to him was exhilarating. He was doing something forbidden.

Was he regretting it? Leaving them on her bed had seemed intimate, like that was where he wanted her to eat them—which she had done, sprawled out on her belly.

She wished they could have enjoyed them together like that, lying side by side, their legs entangled, their bodies rubbing up against each other…

Okay, she knew that probably wouldn't have been a good idea, but she wondered whether a part of him had wished the same. He could have simply handed them to her instead of leaving them on her *bed*, of all places.

Maybe that was why he'd made himself scarce the last couple of days, which were running regretfully thin. They were both incredibly aware of how little time they had left together.

Was it the secrecy and fleetingness of their little romance that made it so exhilarating? If there were a chance for them to grow into something real, something steady, would the fire keep burning or would it fizzle out within a matter of weeks?

They would never know. And the heartache cut deep. At least for her, it did.

She dreaded the uncertainty of next year. Though not having Carter and Heather around once they graduate was a big plus.

Would Jamie still be here? What were the chances of him being single?

Probably slim to none. It was incomprehensible that he was single now, and selfish to hope he would hold out for her. She wasn't worth the wait. She couldn't ask him to put his life on hold for her. Not for the three meager weeks she represented. She didn't want that kind of future for him. He had a right to be happy.

As for me…

Hayley didn't finish her thought. Carter was lurking by the exit when she turned the corner into the lobby. Brows drawn low over his eyes, his field of vision swung to and fro in a searching motion. Heather was nowhere in sight. Hayley had a distinct feeling that he wasn't looking for his girlfriend. He was looking for *her*.

She'd been on the phone with her father this morning for their weekly check-ins. He still hadn't dropped any hints regarding the truth behind Carter's allegations.

Her palms felt sweaty. She cut the distance to the doors, and he straightened from his lean.

"Hey." Annoyance flashed in his eyes, and a little of it melted into his tone.

Her feet kept up the steady stride. They made no motion to stop. He went after her, remaining in tight pursuit.

"Come on, Hayley." Two hands ripped her back and held her in place, biting into her upper arms. "The least you could do is gimme the common courtesy of a *hello,*" he grunted out, his expression showing no humor.

Then his head snapped around. A small group of students was spilling out of the common hall, moving their way. Hayley recognized some of their faces. They were seniors like him.

His grip tightened, his fingertips digging into her flesh hard enough to leave bruises. With a quick shuffle of his sneakers, Carter pulled her off the trail and shoved her against a tree.

"Ow!"

"Shut up!" He kept his voice low, watching the group pass over her shoulder. They were hidden from view behind the trunk of the large elm.

Hayley rolled a growl in the back of her throat. She didn't like being manhandled. And she didn't want to stay quiet. Hands to his chest, she pushed him off.

As he stumbled back two steps, another spark of frustration crossed his face. For some reason, her mind made a note that his height fell short of Jamie's by a few inches.

"For the love of God, why are you wasting your time with me?" she yelled, not caring who overheard. "I won't be another notch on your bedpost."

"It doesn't have to be a one-time thing."

"Oh, wow!" she gasped sarcastically. "I'm flattered that you want to keep me as your side piece."

Carter didn't buy her act. His face remained stoic. It was the first time he showed any resemblance to Roy.

A cold sensation snaked along her nape and up her skull. Maybe she shouldn't antagonize him.

Hayley got serious. "You assume I'd ever consider that?"

"You should," he suggested, his tone eerily calm. "You should think about your future real hard, Hayley."

It came across like a threat, and the lines of his features deepened in the shade the tree's dense canopy threw off. His anger made him appear bigger, menacing even.

A cold sweat was spreading through her body to her hands, and her fingers felt numb, but she didn't waver. "My future doesn't involve you," she said, forcing her voice steady, her stance firm. "I wouldn't spread my legs for you if you had a gun to my head. Find someone else to screw."

The hazel in his irises turned a hue darker as his mood worsened. "No one rejects me. Don't try me, Hayley."

"Or what? You're going to tell Daddy? We both know the only reason you get everything you want is because your father makes sure of it. He's the one everyone's afraid of. Not you."

"I don't need him. I take whatever I want."

"Oh, yeah? What are you going to do?" she heckled. "Prove to the world that you are your father's son? That you're just as much of a bully?" She leaned toward him and raised her chin higher. "I'm not intimidated by you, Carter. I'll never be your whore. And you'll never live up to your father's expectations."

She challenged him with her glare, waiting for him to respond. His lips twitched in anger, and he stepped forward.

"You're going to regret that," he hissed, baring his teeth. The sharp points of his canines gleamed from spit, primed to take a bite out of her. "You just wait. I'll make you eat your words," he finished, then sheathed his fangs and strode off.

Hayley's sigh of relief exploded out of her chest, her pulse punching up her throat. She didn't move for an entire minute. The ick factor from his touch reached so deep into her bones that she needed an emotional palate cleanse after that confrontation. And she knew exactly the right bottle of *feel-good* to sample from.

Was it fair? Probably not. But it gave her the extra push to search him out.

She hunted Jamie down behind the fieldhouse, where they'd worked together that first day. He was sitting in the shade with his back against the building, one leg stretched out in front of him, the other one up, arm resting on his knee.

As she took a few more steps toward him, she noticed he was sitting in silence. No headphones were blaring into his ears. Head straight ahead toward the woods, he appeared to be deep in thought.

A half-eaten sandwich dangled from his hand. He turned it dismissively in between his fingers like a fidget spinner. If he noticed her approach, he showed no reaction until Hayley queued up the conversation.

"Not listening to music?" Lowering herself down, she slid in close, bumping his rock-solid shoulder.

He stayed firm like a brick wall but graced her with a sideways smile. "Nah. Didn't bring my phone."

"What if your mom needs to get a hold of you?"

"Eh, they know where to find me. The property is not that big, and I'm a creature of habit."

"True. *I* found you." She bumped him a second time, only to see the faint smile again.

"Exactly. Who needs a phone? Being available 24/7 is overrated."

There was something haunting in his voice, and a small glimpse of it reflected in his demeanor. His tousled hair was damp. Little sweat beads clung to his forehead. He must have been out here for a while.

"Is that lunch or dinner?" She nodded at his sandwich, recalling that she hadn't eaten since breakfast.

"Both, I guess." He grimaced, eyeing it wearily pinched between his thumb and middle finger. "Kinda lost my appetite an hour ago."

Hayley reached across his body to snatch it from his hand like a starving animal, nearly knocking him over this time.

He didn't jerk away, and his husky laugh brushed her ear. "I see how it is. First my cookies, and now my sandwich?"

"Calm down, *Goldie Locks*—'hm ma gawd. 'S delicious," she mumbled while chewing. "Wah's your secret?"

Jamie watched her through the dark bangs of his hair as if he couldn't tear his eyes away. "Butter instead of mayo." His lips moved, but he didn't seem aware of speaking the words. His expression was blank. His stare hazy.

"Mmmm, amazing." Hayley closed her lids briefly, relishing another bite. When her vision came back, she found him pulling away.

"Have at it," he said, sitting up straight.

"Thanks. And thanks for the cookies, too," she added.

His lips drew tight. "You're welcome." Shifting his gaze, he wiped his palms on the front of his jeans. "I'm glad you liked them."

Jamie angled his body back toward the woods instead of facing her. His shoulders no longer touching the siding of the fieldhouse, he pulled his left knee up to match his right. Crossing his arms on top, he dropped his chin and stayed quiet.

Hayley didn't like the distance between them. A week ago, he'd wanted to kiss her, and now he didn't even want to touch her anymore?

Maybe she'd misjudged the connotation behind the cookies.

Her gaze drifted over the defined muscles in his torso that flexed beneath the off-white shirt. The sleeve cut into the crease between his deltoid and bicep. His back was huge. She wondered if he'd played on his high school's football team. He could easily tackle any of the senior linemen at her school.

Jamie let out a sigh that startled her. She hadn't realized how tense she'd gotten while pining over him. He raked a hand through his hair and gave the top of his head a rub before settling it at his neck.

"I read your book," he blurted without context. "Or reread, I should say."

"What book?"

"Hatchet."

"You did?" Now she found herself sitting a little straighter. "What was your favorite part?"

"The fool hens. Definitely. I could just picture them exploding left and right. Feathers everywhere." He made a bursting motion with his hand, splaying his fingers.

Of course, the birds hadn't actually exploded but had instead taken flight abruptly after being startled. It was still funny.

"I thought it would have been the moose."

"Hell no! That shit was fucked up. But exactly what I'd expect from a moose," he added with a jerk of his shoulder. "Getting a fire started would have been the easiest part, though. I got this."

He shifted to unhook something from his belt loop on the other side, then held up a black cartridge on a carabiner clip. He flicked the lid open with his thumb and pressed the button. Dual arcs ignited in purple.

"A plasma lighter. The flame can withstand a storm, and the case is waterproof. Just touch it to something flammable, and, voila, you got fire." He snapped the lid shut with a grin. "It gets 300 uses per two-hour USB charge, which you couldn't replenish in the wild, but that's more than you'd get out of a butane lighter."

And he would know.

"Alright, *Smoky*. I guess you could have lit a few fires before you ran out." Hayley matched his enthusiasm. It was pretty cool.

Before she realized what he was doing, he leaned in and clipped it to her shorts. His hands worked fast. Too fast. In a flash, his touch was gone.

"And here," he reached over to his right again, "I want you to have this, too."

He dropped the object on her lap, and she burst out laughing. "A hatchet!"

And of course, the whole thing was blacked-out, except for the bright orange paracord attached to it. The heavy-duty nylon sheath had the same white Frog & Co logo as the lighter. She tugged it off to get a better look.

"Wow! This is awesome." Brian Robeson's simple hatchet had nothing on this baby.

Turning it in her hand, she was surprised to discover more than one sharp edge. It was a multifunctional tool. The blade had four hex sockets of various sizes, as well as a hammer head, nail claw, and a pry bar on the other end. The black handle matched the plasma lighter's case and also had the logo on the side. At the bottom was a metal spike.

"A gift?" Hayley frowned. She was uncomfortable accepting it. They had never exchanged anything. And for good reason. It made what they had intimate.

"Let's call it a loan," he proposed on a lighter note. "Do something with it. Go on an adventure. A real one, I mean. Or just change a tire, for fuck's sake. As long as you use it."

Hayley chuckled as he slipped in another f-bomb. He was uncomfortable, too. Which was very unlike him. He rubbed his palms over his thighs again, then brought them back together in front of him, right hand cuffing his left wrist.

Hayley looked at the lighter dangling from her belt loop. It also had a built-in flashlight on the butt end. He made sure she was all decked out in case of emergencies.

"They're a set. They should stay together."

Her head snapped up at the sullen sound of his voice. Was this his way of saying goodbye? They never did the official 'See you next year.' Too dramatic. But she got the feeling this would be their last night together. That was why he'd been distancing himself.

23

*W*hoa!
That moment her lips closed around his sandwich…
and that moan—

Instant hard-on.

Not that he wasn't already at half-mast around her and painfully pressed up against his fly, pleading to make introductions.

He wanted to kiss her. Wanted to touch himself *while* he kissed her. Or better yet, have *her* touch him.

His fantasy from that day at her cabin flung itself into the foreground. He envisioned her sprawled out on the bed before him, squirming in anticipation, her body yearning for release.

He needed to watch her—feel her—take that plunge. The desire consumed him. He wanted to claim the blood of her innocence, have it coat him, and lick it from in between her legs.

Jameson had never been with a virgin. Not even his first time. Too much pressure. Too much responsibility. He wanted none of that shit. Every girl he picked up had at least a bit of experience.

With Hayley, for the first time, he wondered what it would be like to breach that threshold, to lead her to the edge, to be someone's first.

Yeah, he had things under control. 'Cause he wanted none of that.

He forced himself to leave before anything happened. It was getting late anyway, and he shouldn't be hanging out with her after sundown. All kinds of bad things happened in the dark.

But Jameson didn't go home. After taking his abrupt leave without many words, he headed into the woods.

God, it hurt to want her. He physically ached for it. He imagined her hand closing around his shaft, stroking him in a steady rhythm. Head to base, she covered his length, working him. And he wanted to taste her lips. *Feel* them on him.

Unfortunately, it was his own hand doing the deed, squeezing while picking up the pace.

Jameson bit down on his shirt that was hiked up his stomach, and his eyes rolled back into his head. Everything went on a spin. His body twisted sideways, arching on his thrust, her name hitching in the back of his throat as his shirt remained pinched between his teeth.

His muscles steeled, then slacked. *INTENSE.* It was so fucking intense.

If pretending to be with her had such an overwhelming effect, how much more acute could the real thing be?

Jameson sagged back onto the wooden planks. Sprawled out on the lower platform of the tree house, his breathing slowly returned to normal. He relished trees sounds of the forest at night. The chirping of the crickets. It sparked his inspiration.

Lightning had hit the structure in the spring, forcing him to start over. He'd changed his sketches up, too. The tree no longer went through the dead center of the base. He'd shifted the placement to the side, where a short, three-rung ladder led up to the *second floor*. It was the larger of the two platforms, suspended between the first tree and another. He was merely getting started on that part. It would be huge one day if he kept at it.

Still no stairs, though.

Jumping off the side, he caught the edge with his fingers and dropped the remaining four feet to the ground. He reached for his pack of smokes as he started walking toward the trail before he remembered he had no lighter.

Disappointed, he stuffed it back into his pocket. He really wanted to light one up right now. He wouldn't get another chance tonight.

His steps landed on the gravel in noisy crunches, the dense rubber tread of his kickers scraping against the gravel and grinding it into smaller rocks. It was the only sound emitted in the park. And it was dark by now. No light was coming from any of the cabins; everyone was asleep.

He wasn't sure what time it was. He'd lost track. The dim yellow orbs flanking the trail were the only things showing him the way home, floating in the air like little beacons.

He was still some distance from the docks when he heard thrashing coming from the lake below. Panic kicked in. He broke into a sprint, hurdling the underbrush until he reached the tree line. And then he spotted him out in the water—not by the buoy—but near the island.

Jameson charged down the slope without thinking and dove head-first into the blackness at the bottom. He didn't hear the splash. The lake swallowed him up, as if welcoming him.

Pushing to the surface, he picked up speed, kicking his legs and gaining quickly on Carter. He tried to keep his eyes on him, but the guy's head kept disappearing, arms splashing uncoordinated as his strength was fading.

Jameson was nearly there. Only a few more yards—

He blinked to clear his vision, and Carter was gone. Vanished, right in front of him.

FUCK!!!

He filled his lungs with a great gulp and went under, his hands fumbling in the dark. He didn't care to whom Carter thought he had to prove himself. It wasn't worth his life.

He brushed against something and blindly reached for it. The bare skin slipped his grip. He tried again, both hands pulling with all his might.

They exploded out of the surface together, panting for air. Carter more so than he, forcing the stale out, wheezing on the inhale.

At least he was conscious.

Jameson leveled him off and hooked his arm across his chest to tow him back to the shore. He didn't focus on how tired his muscles felt from the ordeal. Or the weight of his boots dragging him down. He only focused on each sidestroke that reduced their distance.

Within minutes, they reached the slanted edge by the dock. Jameson heaved the prick up and flopped onto his back beside him, drawing more breath into his lungs.

His muscles were screaming now that they were no longer under tension. In his periphery, Carter crouched on all fours, hacking up a lung with spurts of water.

"My record is forty-seven seconds, asshole," Jameson sneered, kicking to a stand. "You owe me."

24

Jameson picked up the bag of white icing and gave it a twist. Adjusting his grip to get the pressure right, he touched the metal tip to the intended target while his left hand rotated the base. His wrist moved steadily and with consistency, though the delicate work wasn't his forte. He was surprised at how therapeutic it felt.

The thing was, he didn't care what needed to get done. He'd just do it. No questions asked. He was like Carl that way. He helped out wherever he could and didn't have to log his hours. In return, Mom paid him a fixed monthly salary.

He'd saved up most of his paychecks for the new all-black Anthem wheels, and they looked sweet as hell on the Silverado. Once summer camp was over, he was going to apply for a job at the off-road truck shop in town. They didn't only sell parts and accessories, they had a full garage, too. He was self-taught when it came to fixing his truck, but he'd be happy doing either. And he could still easily manage the work around here. All positions were currently filled, and his odd jobs were hardly more than busy work. He needed something on the side. He didn't want to be a freeloader.

Mom's light steps filled the kitchen, closing in on him from behind.

"Where's Carl?" he wondered as she came to stand beside him. He was so much taller than her now—six-one to her five-eight.

"I don't know. He's not here 24/7."

He couldn't place the tone in her voice. Was she annoyed by his insinuation? They were the ones keeping secrets. Didn't he have a point? "Isn't he, though?"

"What's that supposed to mean?"

Jameson lowered the squishy bag and met her eyes. "He is here an awful lot."

"So?"

God, he hated the lying. He wished they would just spit it out instead of sneaking around. He could take the truth. He could be mature.

"Bullshit!" he cursed under his breath.

"Excuse me?"

Fuck. "Sorry."

He hung his head apologetically for swearing in front of her, but it *was* bullshit. There had been plenty of opportunities for her to come clean, yet she kept up the stupid charade that wasn't fooling anyone. They were treating him like a child.

"What's going on with you?"

"Nothing." *EVERYTHING.* Beginning with a girl he couldn't have and ending with his mom and his best friend hooking up. But he wasn't going to divulge his secrets either.

Her fingers went for the cross hanging from her neck. She wasn't religious. He knew the necklace was an old family heirloom. Her mother had passed it on to her the day she got married to Dad. Though she'd quit wearing her wedding band, the simple chain never left her throat.

Jameson stared at her more closely than he had in a while. When he was younger, he'd wished for a sibling. A friend. Someone to play with.

His parents had sat him down and explained about the complications during his birth and that Mom could no longer have children. Something about an emergency hysterectomy, but he hadn't known what that meant. Then his father had died and, a few years later, his grandparents, leaving only the two of them.

He remembered Hayley's words. Why was he giving his mom headaches? Was she worried about how he would take the news? He wanted her to be happy. She had nothing to feel guilty about.

"Mom—" he clipped out.

He'd been about to put her mind at ease, then changed his own at the last second. He figured she'd tell him on her terms when she was ready. He wasn't going to push the subject.

She looked up at him expectantly, waiting for him to speak.

Letting it go, he pivoted back to the cake for the Mitchells' big day. The wedding was tomorrow. There was barely enough time to turn the place upside down once the summer campers left.

"Don't you think you're taking on a little too much?" he asked to divert.

He brought the silver tip back up to the edge of the tier and gave the piping bag another firm squeeze.

"Eileen's the wedding coordinator. She's got it all under control. I hardly have to lift a finger."

Eileen was family. There had never been a question about the venue for her oldest daughter's wedding. The park was the obvious choice.

Mom gasped as her sight fell on the half-dozen white roses he'd prepared, sitting off to the side. "Have you been practicing on those? They look better than mine. And your piping is so thin and even. You should be a surgeon."

Jameson chuckled at the suggestion, nudging his free elbow into her side. *A surgeon? As if.*

The roses had come out nicely, though. She could choose the placement herself.

"I'm dead serious. You deserve better, Jamie. You shouldn't be stuck here with me."

"I'm fine, Mom," he said, putting the icing bag down. He knew where she was going with this. "I like it here. This is our home." It was the most beautiful place he'd ever known, and he wouldn't trade it for a life in the city. Not even if someone offered him a mansion.

Her expression was somber when her hands reached up and clasped his cheeks. "You are my light, Jamie."

The gesture. Her words. He towered over her, and yet she could still make him feel like he was six years old.

Her mask of seriousness melted into a smile, and she gave him a shove. "Get out of here. Do something fun. But stay out of trouble," she tacked on her motherly advice.

With a "Yes, ma'am," he bent down to give her a hug and a quick kiss on her temple. "Love you."

Grabbing the second half of his sandwich in one hand and his ginger ale in the other, he darted for the door when she called after him in disapproval. "Is that all you're having for dinner?"

He winked, clamping the ham on rye between his teeth, and reached for the door.

"Keep your nose clean."

Keep my nose clean? He could do that. And the rest of his body as well.

After the shit Carter had pulled the other night, he thought it best to keep watch at the lake. Just to be sure. He hated the guy, but he didn't want him dead. Kids drowning made a bad headline.

Hayley let the lid of her suitcase drop shut. Except for her toiletries, everything was packed, and her alarm set for 6:30 a.m. Physically, she was ready to go. Emotionally? Not so much.

Summer was over.

At least the best part was. All she had to look forward to was a week with Dad at his estate. And that wasn't half as much fun as it sounded. She'd be alone with him. A driver would pick her up at school in Jackson two days from tomorrow and take her on the five-hour trip south to Salt Lake City, where she would meet her dad before the two of them got on a private airplane together.

None of that sounded fun.

She sank down on the corner of her bed, flipping the lid of the plasma lighter open and shut. She hadn't seen Jamie in two whole days. Though it felt longer. She'd played the conversation at the fieldhouse over and over in her head, analyzing the little indicators in his demeanor. The bigger picture had clicked into place before his rapid escape:

He still wanted her.

It was like that nonverbal transmission at the ice cream shop. A carnal pulse hummed through her, this time emitted by him.

Then there was his gift—which wasn't a gift—and that last comment about the lighter and the hatchet staying together. She couldn't be sure he'd meant it that way, but it had come across like a metaphor for them.

She thought about those hands of his at the waistband of her shorts. If he'd gone for the button, would she have stopped him?

No. Because she wanted to feel his touch. Wanted to feel even more of him.

Damn his moral code. He was good at keeping his promise not to tempt her. But Hayley wasn't a nun. Something had started to build inside of her. An ache. A longing. A fire spreading. A need she couldn't describe…

And it was answering his call.

What if she would never feel this way again? If she let this one chance at something amazing slip away? If she let *him* slip away?

She would never forgive herself. Come what may, she couldn't leave without seeing him one last time.

It was pretty dark when she shuffled her way down the slope to the lake. She recognized Jamie's characteristic shape at the end of the dock from a distance. His silhouette was so familiar. Legs crossed, leaning on his thighs, he turned a green can of ginger ale in his hands. Smoke drifted up from the cigarette wedged between the index and middle finger of his right hand.

"Shouldn't you be packing?" he asked without turning.

He was still about ten feet away, straight ahead. She had no clue how he knew it was her. A sixth sense?

His question sounded gruff.

"Do you want me to leave?"

He shook his head solemnly in response. Not a rejection, but not exactly encouraging either.

Maybe this was a mistake.

Hayley stuffed her hands into her back pockets and ambled across the rest of the boards. Some creaked beneath the soft *shlop shlop shlop* of her flip-flops.

When he glanced in her direction, she motioned with her chin toward his cigarette. "So, I assume you have another lighter."

"Like I'd give you my only one," he mused as she sat down on his right.

"How did you know it was me?"

His cocksure smirk was back after the momentary lapse at the fieldhouse. "A hunch."

"You knew I'd come?" Why did it feel like he was pulling the strings even though she'd made the decision on her own mere minutes ago?

"No. But I hoped."

His sharp blue eyes remained fixed on her, studying her reaction. They were the same brilliant color at night as they were during the day. They had a supernatural glow to them.

She forced herself away, looking at anything but him.

"Why did you?" he probed, his finger tapping the aluminum can expectantly. Some ash fell from the cigarette. "We both know it wasn't for a swim. You were looking for *me*."

Hayley hugged her knees closer to her chest and sighed. "I was."

"Why?" He paused. "Nothing has changed. We're right back where we were three weeks ago. You're nervous. Glancing around like you're searching for something, only you don't know what."

Her spine tensed at his callous remark.

"Or is there something you're itching to lose?" he asked with a suggestive edge. "What's burning on your mind, Virgin?"

When he waited for a response, she turned to look at him. Jamie quirked a questioning eyebrow, raising his hand to his mouth. "Spit it out."

His cheeks hollowed as he took a slow drag on his cigarette, the tip flaring orange. She held his scrutinizing stare, teeth chewing up her bottom lip.

He broke eye contact to blow the smoke out to the side, away from her, and flicked some more of the ash. "You afraid your virginity's going to evaporate in my presence?"

She was thinking more along the lines of *combust.*

"Relax. It's safe from me. I have no interest in claiming it."

"You don't?" Hayley finally found her voice. "And here I thought you were trying to get into my pants."

Jamie didn't laugh. "I'm not gonna lie. I'd like to," he admitted openly. "But the only thing I can give you is regret. I don't want to be your baggage. It's not worth it."

He brought the soda up to his perfectly kissable mouth and added, "No, you should hold on to your virtue. It's admirable. God knows I couldn't do it."

She watched him take a swig. His Adam's apple jerked as he swallowed.

Why did the seemingly ordinary movement excite her?

"How old were you… when… you know…" she asked, breaking from the spell.

"Just turned sixteen." He lowered the can and took another long drag on the cigarette. The lit end burned quickly down toward the filter.

"And that was your birthday present?"

"Sort of," he replied with a grin, expelling the cloud. "She was twenty."

"Wow! Twenty, huh? That's statutory rape, you know?"

"Fuck off," he choked out, coughing up little white puffs of smoke from his last inhale. "Summer didn't rape me. She's eighty pounds wet. And I was very willing."

"Yeah, I bet," Hayley shot back, joining in his laughter.

"I fooled around plenty before that with girls in school."

Girls in school? "I thought you were homeschooled."

His features became stern, as though the comment had struck a chord. "Only until high school." He stubbed the gleaming butt out on the wood planks, then stuffed it into his soda can. "Don't believe everything you hear. Carter doesn't know what he's talking about. My dad didn't ditch us. He was in the military. I was ten when he got killed overseas."

"I'm sorry," Hayley murmured. Not only for his loss, but also for her ignorance.

"He was my idol. I worshiped him," Jamie went on in a pensive state. Left palm to his chin, he rubbed his fingers along the stubble on the opposite side of his jaw. "Taught me how to handle a rifle when I was eight. I shot the tail off a rabbit from a hundred yards away."

She watched his head tip back a little as his hand slid down the length of his throat.

Hot damn, even his neck was sexy.

Hayley dropped her inappropriate gaze. Looking down at the planks beneath them, she noticed the gap between the water and the dock. There appeared to be a foot and a half of space above the surface.

Jamie remained glum.

"So, what do you do out here alone?" she prompted to coax his spirit back.

"You really want to know?" He shot her a narrow-eyed look as if he were contemplating. A wicked determination crossed his face. "Fuck it."

With that, he grabbed the bottom of his shirt and chucked it over his head. Then went for the zipper on the inside of his boots. The gleam of something metal tucked between his laces caught her eye.

"What are you doing?"

"Going for a swim."

Hayley regarded him with apprehension.

Tugging his socks free, he jumped to his feet and dropped his jeans next. "Never been skinny-dipping either, Virgin?" he mocked, his cocky signature grin dangling at the corner of his mouth.

To her relief, he stopped after the denim layer. In nothing but his black boxers, he did a backflip off the dock. Water splashed up and out in all directions, catching her in the spray. Her hands flew up as she squealed.

He re-emerged a second later with a whip of his head, splattering more drops around him. "What's it gonna be? You getting in or chickening out on me?"

She glanced back up the hill over her shoulder. The lake sat so low that they were invisible from the trail. There were no lights around either, which was probably because the lake was off-limits after sundown.

Hayley felt a burst of encouragement ignite in her chest. Setting her glasses down on the dock, she slipped her flip-flops off and slowly rose to her feet. She crossed her arms in front of her body, lifting the hem of her peasant blouse over her head in an awkward strip tease. The foolishness of it made her giggle.

When she went to work on her jean shorts, Jamie's eyes remained glued to her with intensity. She could tell, though her vision was slightly out of focus now. She wished she was wearing prettier underwear than the simple blue and violet cotton. Something with a lace trim, maybe. Or at least a matching set.

Hayley straightened her arms and dove in head first, keeping the splash on her entry to a minimum. Eyes closed, she aimed upward, paddling her feet.

When she broke the surface, there were only inches between them. She swept her hair back from her face and blinked away the water. Jamie beamed in satisfaction. With her collarbone above water, her toes were barely touching the

160

ground. Which meant his six feet were standing firm, giving him all the advantage.

"Look at you, all up in the water and shit," he heckled.

"Yeah, well, I'm with a lifeguard, so I'm not too worried about drowning."

He gave her a measuring look, lips twisted at an angle. "I have to admit I'm surprised."

"What can I say? You're a master manipulator. And you're not even trying."

"You think I'm not trying?" Eyes hooded, he made a sharp tsk sound, and then she found herself chest to chest with him. "Still so naïve. Have you learned nothing?"

His low timbre was brimming with erotic greed. Hayley's heart dropped several notches. It settled in the cradle between her legs with a heavy thud, and her thighs twitched as if to catch it. She'd played right into his hands. He was in full control of the situation. "You planned this?"

He baited her with his silence, then broke into the most sincere laugh. "I'm kidding, Hayley. I swear I wasn't lying to get you to let your guard down and lure you into the lake."

Ah! The ulterior motive.

She drew up a pout. "You're an asshole." Then she leaned backward and expressed her opinion with a slap at the water, splashing him.

"That look on your face was worth it. I love coaxing you out of your shell. I want you to trust me. I didn't *make* you get in. That was *your* choice. So, I'm guessing you trust me a little bit, or you wouldn't have left your comfort zone for me."

Hayley wasn't mad. He had a point. She'd followed the spider into its web, not knowing if it wanted to eat her alive or merely play. It was shocking how easily Jamie could switch his conduct from one to the other.

And on cue, his humor sobered.

Below the surface, his hands found hers, lacing their fingers. He gave a soft pull, and her body drifted toward him as if of its own accord, drawn to him like a magnet.

Noses nearly touching, his eyes lowered to her lips. "Will you let me kiss you?"

Hayley's heart fluttered in her chest. Her mouth went dry. Despite all the water surrounding them, she had a cotton ball stuck in her throat.

She cracked the seal on her lips, but no sound came out, so she nodded.

Tilting his head, Jamie closed the distance between them in slow motion, his heated gaze on hers until the very last second.

The vision of him fell away when her lids became heavy, but she didn't need her eyesight for this. A primal instinct guided her. Hayley was barely aware of her chin tipping up, reaching toward him in nervous anticipation. She had no control over her body or the way it responded to him.

The feathering warmth of his breath magnified against her lips as his chest nudged her breasts. A prickling sensation raced through her veins, chasing his movements like striking a match, and with a spark, they were joined.

A flame burst to life behind her ribcage, so hot she thought she'd caught fire. Jamie's fingers twitched in his hold on her. With a groan, he deepened his kiss, pressing his chin against hers and parting her lips further.

The tip of his tongue sought her out. Slanting his mouth over hers, he tipped her head back with his height. Eyes closed, she felt everything: his fingers sliding against hers, the heat of his body, the longing in his kiss…

It was so much more than a physical connection. He was in her head and under her skin. He was in every part of her. Jamie was awakening something in her that had been screaming to be set free.

The warmth of his kiss spread lower, quenching an ache in the depths of her core. Hayley knew she was crossing the threshold for something unfamiliar. And there was no going back to the girl she had been.

Her nipples tingled from the touch of his chest, and she arched on reflex, wanting to feel more of him pressing against her.

Jamie's slick tongue traced the shape of her mouth, caressing every contour with sensual attention. She was the spoon. Or maybe she was the ice cream, melting against the heat of his explorations. She was becoming one with him.

His mouth on her soft, the stubbles rough, were the perfect, exhilarating combination. Hayley's mind was swimming. She didn't realize he was walking her backward until she bumped into the inclining edge of the lake. The dock was now blocking them entirely from view, even if someone happened to walk by.

The water wasn't as deep here. Jamie released her hands, running his palms along her sides and toward her back, then reversing the path. His thumbs traced the crease below her breasts, never venturing higher.

Roaming her curves, he kept his touch above her waistline, gentle and without demand, taking only as much as she offered.

Hayley reached for his strong shoulders, arching her back. Her chest strained to feel his body against hers, seeking the warmth radiating from him. No one had ever made her feel so wanted.

Her hands went upward, fingers spearing into his hair, clasping the back of his head. Raw desire passed through his kiss. It evoked the same lust in her, and the throbbing between her legs became unbearable.

A plea formed in her head. Her mouth refusing to break from their motion, she gasped for air. "I want you closer."

He exhaled with restraint, and his voice came back hoarse. "I'm already pretty damn close, Hayley."

She hesitated to vocalize her request for what seemed like an eternity, and he must have guessed her mind. "Where do you want me?"

His tone carried the confidence of someone who knew the answer to his question. Already on her tiptoes, she replied by opening her thighs wide enough for him to nudge in between while scooting her rear onto the cusp of the grassy edge.

He groaned as if fighting some kind of internal battle. "You want to feel me between your legs?"

Her voice was nearing a whimper, and she choked on her *yes*.

With the moan of someone who knew there was more to come, his hands rounded her ass, smoothing down the back of her thighs. He lifted her higher up on the edge of the shore, bringing her hips flush with his. Then he was *THERE*. Ardent with intent. Right where she wanted him.

Breaking from her lips, he dipped lower, his chin scraping along her throat like sandpaper. It was so hot. So arousing. Her body felt liquid as he molded her to his contours. He wasn't a boy. He was *all* man. And he wanted *her*.

Jamie led a fiery trail with his tongue down her throat and kept going, kissing inch by inch along her front to her breast. His breath scorched the sparse cotton fabric covering her.

Mouth sealed to her, his deep moan hummed through her sternum and reverberated in every cell of her being.

And that was when her mind spiraled. She forgot about everything else around her, utterly lost in the movements of their bodies.

Hayley locked her arms around his neck. She was afraid she might splinter apart in his arms. She forgot that they were surrounded by water. She felt as though she were floating on air, somewhere high above the clouds.

The soft splashing of the water from their motion lulled her into a stupor, the sound dragging her under. And yet somehow, she was climbing. Toward what she didn't know. But her arms tightened around his neck, desperate to find out.

"Oh God. Please don't stop."

"Chase it, Hayley. You're almost there."

Almost there, his words echoed in her head. Her muscles trembled. She couldn't make it stop. Couldn't keep herself together. She was going to shatter into a million pieces.

Almost there.

"Oh God, Jamie, don't let go."

"I got you."

His tone was calm, and she believed him. He was right there with her, his arms securing her to him as she squirmed in need.

Almost there.

Sparks ignited everywhere. Hayley chased the fuse with bated breath.

Almost—

The force ripped through her from the inside out, detonating like a bomb. It sent her body into a jolt. Her nails dug into his skin. She became a livewire, twitching, as wave after wave rushed her from head to toe.

A sob broke free, and tears formed in her eyes. She couldn't hold them back any more than she could've fought the climax. The feeling of euphoria flooding her was overwhelming.

His face pressed against her cheek, and she felt his lips curve into a smile. "You wanna feel that again?"

"God yes!"

She didn't want it to end.

25

Reclaiming her mouth, he adjusted his position, hiking her leg higher to change the angle. Hayley circled her hips, grinding herself against him, her body hungry and desperate for another release.

He thought he heard someone call his name, but he ignored it. Nothing could deter him from his quest. He wanted to draw that sound from her again. That cross between agony and euphoria. He didn't care about himself. He wanted her to come undone.

Her nails bit into his skin again. She knew what she was looking for now, and she worked herself against him with more urgency, no longer timid.

His temperature rose from all the friction without penetrating her. She was an inferno, catching him in her blaze. Her grind was slick and needy, matching his slow rhythm. He could feel how wet she was, and not from the water. But he wanted more. Wanted her drenched and dripping, her fluids mixing with his own.

He fantasized about pulling her panties down and delving in between her legs. About being her first. About how tight she'd feel, gripping him and milking him with every pulse. The suction. The heat. *His Virgin—*

God, the mind was a powerful thing. He was about to come.

"Imagine me inside of you, Hayley," he groaned, the raspy sound of his voice so rough and foreign. "Imagine how I'd feel."

He rocked into her. Harder. Offering more of himself as her body began to quake underneath him. Hayley matched his motion. The two of them chased the high together as though it were the most natural thing. Their kisses turned sloppy. Their breaths jagged.

He met her hips, again and again, until she gave a violent spasm. Her muscles convulsing in his arms, she surrendered that second orgasm to him, and he came too. The instant her soft cry reverberated in his skull, the force behind his own release cut through him like a knife.

Her name formed on his lips in that moment of bliss. Just like it had that night in his tree house.

Jameson dove into the curve of her neck. Face buried, he stifled a final moan. His pulse continued to race. Warmth pooled where their bodies were joined, coating them with their combined ecstasy.

Coiled around his hips, her legs stilled.

He lifted his head to find her face. "You okay?"

Hayley nodded. Under the pale purple cotton of her bra, her nipples perked from the wet chill. The distinct, dark circles around them were visible, and he couldn't tear his eyes away. She was so fucking perfect.

He'd left a small hickey right below her nipple. In her bliss, she hadn't noticed him shifting the material, but she'd notice it later. She'd see it in the mirror and think of him. He could picture the smile it would bring to her lips, and that was priceless.

Panting for air, he kissed her again, holding on tight as he dragged them both off the ledge and back into the water. Only their heads remained above the surface.

Left arm hooked around her waist, he brushed his palm across her lower belly to wash all traces of him away. There would be no physical evidence of what they'd shared, and yet she would remember him as the one who'd set her free. He might not have claimed her virginity, but he had claimed something far more valuable.

Her soul.

With gentle guidance, he took her hand in his. He led it between her thighs, stroking her with her own touch.

Her legs gave one last quiver at the contact with her still-sensitive nub. Jameson reveled in the satisfaction.

Curving her palm over her clit, he weaved his fingers in between hers and let them hover at her opening. "Promise me you'll think of me," he whispered. "Just once."

Her eyes were alive in the dark, two silver stars gleaming up at him. "I promise."

"You're beautiful, Hayley. Don't let anyone take that away from you."

Bringing their entwined hands up, he kissed her knuckles before releasing his hold on her.

Jameson hopped up the ledge first, then held a hand out to her. He watched her, amused, as she scrambled out of the water. Her long hair was plastered to her shoulders and boobs, all dripping wet. The shorter ends curled around her head, framing her radiant face.

He enjoyed the view very much. Her cheeks blushed. She was glowing.

He didn't realize he was sucking his bottom lip until it drew her attention. Running a hand through his hair, he shook some more water from it, then stood up.

Jameson went back to the edge of the dock, where they'd left their clothes. Hayley was right behind him, a little skip in her step. It was the best ego boost any guy could imagine. She was giddy and so fucking cute. He'd kill for another go at her.

Discouraged, he shoved his legs into his pants and locked that idea up tight behind his fly. While he dropped to his ass to put on his boots, Hayley remained standing. She shimmied her shorts up those long, perfect legs and did that little bounce at the top for the last inch.

Goddamn, he wanted back between her thighs right now. Didn't even need the usual ten minutes to get hard again. It had been what? Four minutes? Five tops.

She went for her blouse and pulled it over her soaked underwear with a cringe. He had to chuckle. There was no hiding it. The second her bra touched her top, the material clung to her full mounds.

"It's not funny. Everyone's going to know what we did." She tugged on the fabric to adjust the fit, but it didn't make a difference. She looked like a pinup for a car wash calendar.

"The only thing they're gonna know is that you went for a swim after hours."

"Oh my God." Her eyes went wide behind their black frames. "Am I getting in trouble for that?"

"Nah. You were with a lifeguard, remember?" He winked, yanking the zipper on his boot the rest of the way up.

Hayley grimaced. "That's what I'm afraid of. I'm sure anyone can put two and two together real quick. I hope I don't run into anyone on my way back."

She gave the fringed hem of her shorts another pull, too. The light blue denim covering her ass was also showing a darkened triangle from her wet panties. His jeans were black, so no worries there.

"Speaking of which," she picked up the conversation again. "Aren't you bothered by your own damp situation?" She motioned at his crotch, then shivered. "It feels weird."

"Eh, I'm used to it," he said, popping his head through the top of his t-shirt.

Hayley slipped her feet into her flip-flops and started to move across the planks. He pushed up too, but didn't move from his spot. Tipping his head to one side, he watched her gain some distance.

She must've felt his gaze because she swung back over her shoulder to catch him staring. Hands teasing through her hair, she continued moving backward, swaying her hips intentionally. She relished the attention. He couldn't help but note the subtle change in her demeanor.

Technically not fucked, but she got a first taste.

She gave him a clueless look. "What?"

"I like the way you walk," he hinted at his remark from three weeks ago.

She rolled her eyes at him and whipped around. Her hair followed the motion with a *smack* against her upper back.

He wouldn't mind giving her *rear* a smack.

Jameson took a step in her direction, then jumped back, remembering his empty can. He knew better than to litter. Mom had drilled her values and virtues into him at a young age. Leaving trash around was disrespectful to the park's heritage.

He swiped the can off the ground and broke into a jog to catch up with her at the end of the dock. He rushed past the bin before falling into step to her left.

She acknowledged him with a smile she was trying to suppress by pinching her lips between her teeth. She hadn't stopped grinning since they'd left the water.

Her hands gathered her wet hair at her nape and twisted it into a rope, which she draped over her shoulder. The side of her neck showed faint signs of abrasion, where his facial hair had scraped against her skin. It didn't compare to her plump, succulent lips, swollen from his thorough attention. He wanted to kiss her again. But he didn't. He needed to rip that band-aid off and forget about the sting.

So, when they walked back up the hill together, he didn't hold her hand like a simp. Burying them in his pockets, he looked down at his boots, dragging one in front of the other through the grass. He glanced to his right at her feet too, matching her pace in their steady ascent. At the end of the slope, they would go separate ways: she to her cabin, and he…

Home, he guessed.

344 days lay before them. Would she come back in December if he asked her to? 147 days was a little more bearable. But how desperate would that sound?

Jameson didn't ask. They reached the top of the hill in silence.

"What the—"

Hayley spoke first, but he was thinking the same.

Ambulance lights cut through the dark of the night. No sirens. That was never a good sign. It usually meant there was no need to hurry because whoever needed the ride was already past saving.

As they drew closer, Jameson could see the crowd gathered around his home. People were muttering to each other, their faces in shock.

The weight of an anvil plunged into his stomach. Only one word left his lips.

"Mom."

26

Things seemed to happen in slow motion: Jamie breaking away from her side, kicking into a dead run toward his home, pushing people out of his way, elbowing through the gawking mass. Voices erupted behind him. He ignored them, barreling further.

All the lights in the house were on, and the front door stood wide. Hayley recognized Carl at the head of the crowd. Calling his name, the large man lunged at Jamie before he could brush past and reach the porch. Strong arms locked around his chest from behind, pulling him back. He howled at his friend to release him, thrashing in his hold. He threw the big man off balance with his kicking and screaming. But he didn't let go.

"You can't... you can't go in. I'm sorry," he hollered, wrangling Jamie.

They had to keep him out to give the EMTs room to work. Carl was the only one big enough to hold him. It looked like someone had chained a feral wolf to a tree. The mass of onlookers parted for them, giving them space. No one wanted to catch a flying fist or boot to the face.

Jamie was frantic. His cries of denial went on, tears streaming down his cheeks as his mind tried to refute what he was seeing, telling himself it wasn't real... couldn't be true... couldn't be his mom.

But it was. Everyone knew. The faces surrounding them bore masks of equal shock and disbelief, but they all knew.

Hayley felt his pain. Every ounce of it permeated the air around them. More people were crying. Staff and guests. Her own tears ran unchecked.

A paramedic's dark uniform appeared in the doorway, then Beth's body was carried out on a stretcher, her face covered by a white sheet. She was moved into the ambulance in the driveway. There were no sirens. No one rushed to work on her. A second paramedic climbed in afterward, then the doors slammed shut.

That was when Jamie fell to his knees, a scream so gut-wrenching ripping out of him, it tore her open.

Hayley watched it all and her heart broke for him. She'd stayed at the back of the crowd because, after two years, nobody knew how close they had become.

Hands clasped over her chest, she stood on the sidelines. She wanted to go up to him. Push a way through. Console him somehow. But what could she do? Put a hand on his shoulder? Carl was already doing that.

The gentle giant crouched beside him, speaking into his ear. Jamie didn't acknowledge him. Hunched over, he remained on his knees. His body became a statue, his mind somewhere lost in between this new reality and the old. Not even Carl could reach him there.

What was it that people had told her when her mother passed? She couldn't remember. She'd been too little. The only thing she recalled was that their condolences had made no difference in her grief. No amount of words could make this hurt any less. She knew that from her own experience.

But how had Beth died? Had she been sick like her mom?

Hayley was trying to come up with a possible cause when the sheriff arrived.

"Who called it in?" he barked at the female police officer in charge. She was a tall woman of Native American descent. Her dark hair was weaved into a strict braid at the back of her head, not one strand out of place.

"Carl did, sir. He found her on the kitchen floor a little before 10 p.m. Apparently, she had a brain tumor. Got the terminal diagnosis a few months ago."

"Oh, man," the sheriff muttered, hanging his cowboy hat. Beneath the rim, he didn't look much older than the female officer. Not even in his forties, Hayley guessed. He had a strong jaw and a classic Dallas mustache that nailed his cowboy look.

Hands on his belt, he let his shoulders sag, then looked back at the uniformed woman beside him, who was displaying the same official pose. "What about her boy? Where is he?"

"Carl's with him now." She jerked her chin in the direction of the guys. "Poor kid. He had no idea."

Despite her professionalism, her tone was full of compassion. Her almond-shaped eyes with their somewhat upswept corners gave a hint of tears being held at bay.

Had she personally known Beth? Hayley was beginning to think everyone in town did.

The sheriff gave a groan, eyes searching the sky for help as he paced a few steps. "Fuck. This is bad. Really bad. It's going to break him. His eighteenth birthday is the day after tomorrow. He's going to inherit everything." The man rambled off more to himself than to his subordinate.

The female's head bobbed along in agreement, her lips drawn into a thin line. Hayley searched her features for any sign of surprise, but the details of Jamie's circumstances weren't news to her. Her pronounced cheekbones and long, straight nose remained stoic.

After the ambulance took off, the crowd started to disperse. Everyone was either returning to their quarters or leaving to go home, she assumed.

Hayley went back to her cabin to change into dry clothes but found herself too restless to stay put. The walls felt suddenly confining. Jamie had pushed off the lawn and vanished into the woods. She couldn't shake the thought that he was out there somewhere. Alone.

Hayley strolled along the trail, mindlessly putting one foot in front of the other. It was nearly two in the morning. The entire staff was gone. The resort felt like a cemetery. It was too quiet. Even the wind in the trees had died down to pay its respects.

She could still hear him screaming in her head.

God, that blood-curdling scream…

She didn't think she could ever forget it.

His mom had always been so kind to her. The only woman she'd ever looked up to as a mother figure. Her dad's acquaintances hardly measured up. Now Beth was gone. Just like that.

"Did you find him?" a hushed voice asked from the dark front porch of the homestead. It sounded like the female manager she'd met a few times.

Hayley poked her head around the corner, keeping her feet light on the gravel.

Yep, the young woman from the reception desk was sitting on the steps, talking to Carl, who was shaking his head in response. "He's not answering his goddamn phone. No one has seen him in hours."

"I'm so worried. Where could he have gone? You know him best, where does he go when he wants to be alone."

"Dunno. I checked the lake twice. And the tool shed. He's not there either," Carl said, in low spirits. "I don't think we'll see him for a while. He can get lost in the woods for days. Trust me, he won't be found until he wants to be."

Hayley retraced her steps to give them privacy and took a different trail back to her cabin. When she unlocked the door, she noticed right away that something was off. The window that she always kept propped open a few inches was still the same, but a sixth sense raised the hairs on the back of her neck. It was somehow colder in here.

Hayley shut the door without making a sound and stood in silence for a moment. To her left was a closet. To her right was the tiny bathroom with no more than a toilet and a pedestal sink.

She rounded the corner of the short hallway, and that was when she noticed the puddles leading from the window sill across the room to her bed.

Someone had climbed into her cabin.

Only the foot of the bed was visible from her angle, but it appeared to only go in one direction. *He's still here.*

The cause of her dread was suddenly crystal clear, though it brought her little relief.

Hayley kept going until the entire length of her bed revealed itself. The back of Jamie's head protruded at the top end, beside the nightstand. She knew what to expect, but the sight of him hit so much deeper. Arms crossed on his knees, he huddled on the floor. His dark shirt stuck to his body, soaking wet. He was freezing and shivering.

He was also barefoot.

Where are his—

Hayley looked around the room and saw that he'd chucked them by the window where he'd entered.

She lowered herself to his level, kneeling in between his legs. Water pooled around him as though his heart was bleeding out onto the floor of her cabin. His eyes were slightly downcast toward the floor and didn't shift to her as she moved into his field of vision. They looked black in the dark. No vibrant blue was left.

"You hid in the lake, didn't you?" She remembered the air pocket below the deck.

Jamie didn't speak. He stared straight ahead.

"You need to take your clothes off. You'll get hypothermia."

He didn't move. Didn't hear her.

"Jamie!" She shook him by the shoulders. "Jamie, look at me."

His eyes went up but remained glazed over. He wasn't looking at her. He was looking *through* her.

Screw this. She would do it herself.

Hayley took a hold of his shirt and pulled it over his head. He didn't oppose.

So far, so good, she thought.

Then she reached for his belt and realized she'd cheered too soon. Jamie snapped out of the trance. His hands cuffed her wrists, keeping her from proceeding. She could feel his muscles trembling beneath his firm grasp.

"Jamie, please."

"No!"

The single word came out so harshly. He'd screamed his voice hoarse. But Hayley understood. He was raw. He didn't want to make himself any more vulnerable.

She watched his chest heave in the seconds of utter silence, his grip never relenting. "It'll be alright," she said to assure him.

His features contorted. His lips quivered, and his eyes filled with tears again. "It hurts... I can't breathe."

"I know." She crushed a sob in her throat. "I'm sorry."

Without further resistance, Jamie's hands fell from her wrists. This time when she tried, he let her remove his jeans, bridging his hips off the floor.

She worked them down his legs, then tossed them to the side.

As she scooted up next to him, she noted how exhausted he looked. His body slumped against the bed behind them. His head swayed, as if too heavy to hold up.

Hayley pulled him toward her chest, her right hand at his nape, left clasping his cheek.

In their embrace, she felt his dam break. With his arms wrapped around her waist, he curled into her and let himself go. His armor crumbled. The confidence of the young man from mere hours ago was gone. He was simply a boy who lost his mom.

She watched over him while he wept, her t-shirt collecting each drop of his grief and sealing it away.

Entangled with him, she twirled her fingers through the wet ends of his hair. "It *will* be alright, I promise you. But not for a while." She decided to speak from her heart and tell him the truth. Something she wished people had done for her.

"I remember how much it hurt. And I can tell you that it will get a lot worse before it gets"—*not better*—"tolerable," she punctuated. "A few days or weeks from now, when everyone stops coming by to distract you and they get back to their routine, that's when you'll feel more alone than ever, your mind trapped in a small, dark space it can't get out of. It will never hurt any less, Jamie. But one day it will be alright."

Hayley continued grazing her fingers through his soft hair. He found a sliver of peace at last. His breathing became shallow and even with sleep. She reached her left arm above her head and tugged the blanket off the bed to keep him warm.

Something landed on the floor beside her with a startling *smack*. It was her notebook.

His temple resting against her shoulder, Jamie's eyes stayed closed. Keeping her right arm around him, she pulled the pen from the spiral binding with her non-dominant hand. She flipped the top cover open and wrote the note in an awkward left-handed scribble on the first page. Then she ripped the corner off and stuffed it into the pocket of his jeans.

27

The alarm woke her at 6 a.m. sharp. Hayley jerked off the pillow and found herself in bed, the covers tucked around her. Jamie was gone, the wood floor dry as if he'd never been here.

Had he put her to bed before leaving?

She threw the blanket aside and gathered the rest of her things before marching off to the parking lot. As she passed the clusters of students, she overheard the same topic in every conversation. Last night's tragedy was front-page news.

Hayley didn't engage. She kept her head down and kept walking to the front of the bus, trolling her suitcase behind.

The petite, blonde manager was standing beside the open door. Her eyes were red and had bags under them. She looked like she hadn't slept at all.

Hayley wondered if Jamie was still MIA; officially anyways. It meant a great deal to her that he'd chosen her cabin as his refuge.

She wanted to say something but wasn't sure what would be appropriate. She settled for the classic, "I'm sorry for your loss," then followed up with, "She was very kind. I'm going to miss her."

The woman blinked, perplexed. "You knew Beth?"

"Not really. She offered me cookies once." Hayley figured it would be best to keep the details to a minimum.

"She will be greatly missed." The young woman sniffed. "Have a safe trip home."

A line of students was beginning to form behind her. Hayley stepped on the bus but turned back over her shoulder. "Thank you," —her gaze drifted to the tag on the woman's white button-down blouse, searching for a name— "*Summer*," she gulped in surprise.

"You're welcome, honey."

Her large peridot eyes gave off a subtle sparkle. She was very pretty. Hayley figured she was… what? Twenty-two. Approximately.

'She's gone, Jameson,' Carl's voice droned on in his head. *Gone?*

His words made no sense at first. How could she be gone? *'So sorry.'*

Then it started sinking in: *The headaches.* He'd urged her to get them checked out. When she stopped mentioning them, he assumed they were gone. He should've pressed for answers. Should have pressed for the truth.

Goddamn secrets.

Jameson dug his fingers into his temples, drawing little circles. Now he was the one with the headaches. The space between them was pounding harder than his heart. Lack of food, water, and sleep could do that to you. It didn't take a brain tumor.

He didn't know how long he'd been sitting at the dock, legs dangling off the edge. The entire day was a blur. He remembered scaling a tree after leaving Hayley's cabin. He'd perched on the highest branches that could hold his weight and watched the buses take off.

How had he ended up at the lake?

Jameson dropped his hands into his lap. His cell phone lay on the planks beside him. Like his climb down, he also didn't recall swinging by the house to grab it. And yet here it was. Mocking him.

32 missed calls.

At least twenty of them had come in between ten and ten-thirty. While he'd been otherwise occupied.

He stared down into the black abyss below. He could hold his breath for almost six minutes—had counted the seconds out himself last night. But it felt like he was holding it still. His lungs burned as if he were drowning. And he wanted to be. Wanted to drift off in peace. No more pain. No more nothing.

It had been quiet underwater. No screaming in his head. Nothing but silence. He wanted to feel that numbness again. The darkness. The cold.

He thought of the heart carving he'd discovered in one of the supports. It was well hidden on the inside of the post closest to the shore. Somebody had etched it into the wood years ago. Time had aged the grooves of the initials. He didn't know whose they were. Another summer romance that never stood a chance. There was probably an infinite amount of love stories the lake had borne witness to, whispers and promises shared, swallowed up by the depths of the waters. So many secrets no one would ever uncover.

Jameson pulled the small piece of paper from his pocket and unfolded it. The blue ink had bled from getting wet in his damp jeans, but it was still readable: *'Call me if you ever need to talk.'*

He held Hayley's note in one hand, his phone in the other. 32 missed calls. And not one of them would've made a difference.

Talk!? he laughed. What good would that do?

No. Talking couldn't save anyone.

He flicked the paper into the water first, watching it dissolve the rest of the ink, erasing the digits as though they'd never existed. Then he flung his phone across the lake.

28

Jameson flicked the lighter open and shut, listening for the clank of metal on metal. It wasn't a plasma like the one he'd given Hayley. It was his dad's old zippo with a butane torch insert that worked better on smokes.

The case had the skull of the Marine Corps FORECON battalion etched into the side, but it was mostly covered now by the black piece of bicycle inner tube he'd slid down. When closed, the simple rubber over the two halves of the case made the lighter practically waterproof.

"For fuck's sake, open a freakin' window once in a while, will ya?" Carl's voice came from the direction of the hallway to his left. "It reeks in here."

Jameson was too high to care. Besides, it was his house. "No one's asking you to stay, old man. You know where the door is," he remarked, snapping the zippo in his right hand shut again.

Carl didn't take the hint. Instead, the rustle of his motion approached the bed, and then his weight settled on the edge beside him.

Jameson opened his eyes, but it made little difference. His room was dark, the blackout curtains shut tight. He had no idea if it was day or night outside.

Unfolding his left arm from behind his head, he scooted back against the board to sit up. He didn't repress his contempt for the intrusion.

"What do you want?" he asked the large black silhouette in front of him. The quicker they got this uncomfortable conversation over with, the quicker he could light up another joint. Every interaction was awkward now. There was always the morose subtext, the elephant in the room no one wanted to bring up. But they all thought of it whenever they saw him. The sad undertone that traced their voices. He was so fucking tired of hearing it.

Carl dropped a flat rectangle wrapped in brown packing paper into Jameson's lap. "Happy birthday," he said with a weary grin. "I know it's late, but you're hard to get a hold of these days."

True. That was because the day after the wake, he'd kicked everybody out and shut the place down. Eileen's daughter's wedding had gone off without a hitch. Thanks to the staff. His absence hadn't been noticed. *'Everyone understood,'* they assured him. Like he gave a shit. He'd spent the night high at Jill's. And the next somewhere else after she'd kicked him out. Didn't even remember where. None of it fucking mattered. None of it could fill the void in his chest.

Carl let his massive shoulders hang with a sigh, and Jameson braced himself for the lecture that was to come. "I know you're hurting right now, but isolating yourself is not going to make the pain go away. Sooner or later, you have to find a way to move on. You want space... you want time... I get it, Jameson, I really do. But you can't shut this place down for good. Your mother wouldn't have wanted that."

"And you would know what she wanted, wouldn't you?" he interjected.

"I know she wanted you to be happy. That's all she ever talked about."

Talked about. The words stung.

"My mother died while I was off with some girl I'll never see again. I should have been there. I should have been with her." Jameson raised his voice out of guilt. She'd died alone, and he was the only one to blame for that. He would never forgive himself.

"There's nothing you could have done. She was dead before her head hit the ground."

"Were you fucking my mom?"

"Whoa, what?" Through his narrowed view, Carl looked genuinely taken aback by the accusation.

"You heard me. Were you?"

"Why would you think that?"

"I saw you with her in the hallway… whispering. Always whispering around me."

Carl stared back, his expression blank. "I don't think that's the question burning on your mind." He paused. "What do you really want to ask me?"

"DID YOU KNOW?" he finally shouted. "Did you know she was dying?"

Through the blur of tears, Carl lowered his eyes before he answered, "I did. She needed someone to talk to."

"Why would she tell *you* but not *me*?" It hurt to find out that she'd chosen to confide in someone other than him. There had never been any secrets between them. Sure, on his part, there was the smoking and Summer, but nothing life-altering. Nothing big like this.

"She wanted to. It was so hard for her to keep it from you, but she didn't want to ruin the little time she had left. She didn't want to see you like this."

"So, you lied to my face. Every day."

"I thought it was for the best. I'm sorry, Jamie—"

"Don't call me that! You don't get to call me that!" Jameson yelled, shoving the present off his lap.

He jumped off the bed, glaring at his former best friend on the other side. "Get out. Get out of my room, and get out of my house. I don't ever want to see you again."

Carl remained composed. There was no resentment in his voice when he spoke, only pity. "We'll leave you be if that's what you want. Just know that whenever you're ready… we'll be there." He tapped the corner of his gift, then pushed off the bed and walked out.

Jameson bit his lower lip until the copper tang of blood flared on his tongue. His high was gone, and he wanted to be numb again. Wanted to burn this whole motherfucking place down.

He picked up the flat shape he'd so callously rejected, holding it by the short sides. The paper made a soft crinkling sound, and he could feel the beveled edge of a picture frame as his thumbs traced the contours inward. He had a vague idea of which photo it held. He didn't want to see it.

Crouching by the side of his bed, he pushed the gift underneath and out of his mind.

It wasn't long after that when the familiar fog settled back over him. He didn't feel the lighter in his hand anymore. He merely stood there, watching the hungry flames rise above his head and turn everything they touched into ash.

29

He woke to the foreign sound of metal on metal. Keys jingling. Jameson sat up in the corner of the cell, leaning his head against the wall. A jackhammer had taken up residence, pounding away without breaks.

His eyes stung, and he really wanted to keep them closed. His tailbone was sore from slouching on the brick of a bench.

How many times had he been arrested in the past three months? Four?

"Fifth time's a charm." Paul's voice brought his memory up to speed.

He jerked his head up too fast and immediately regretted it. The buzzing and throbbing from last night were still in full swing.

"Underage drinking. Vandalism. Aggravated assault. The list escalates as it goes on. They are no longer misdemeanors, Jameson. You're an adult. You'll be charged *as an adult*." the sheriff enunciated, his voice growing angrier with volume. "Shit. You would've beaten that man's face to a pulp if they hadn't pulled you off of him."

"He should've kept his trap shut," Jameson snickered, flaunting a proud grin. It had taken three guys to peel him away.

"He said you hit on his girlfriend right in front of him."

Oh, he'd done more than that. He'd banged her in one of the bathroom stalls.

"She liked me better than him." She'd given him looks all night before the fight broke out. Her dumbass boyfriend had been oblivious to that.

"You think this is funny? This shit would've gone on your permanent record. You could've gone to prison for this. You're lucky I talked him out of pressing charges. Cut you some slack."

"I didn't ask you to do that—"

"*You* didn't. But your dad did. I owe him. He wanted me to keep an eye out for you. And a fine job I'm doing at it," he tagged on quietly, sounding disappointed.

Face toward the wall, eyes closed, Jameson ignored the remark. Paul's guilt trip wasn't going to work. Something in him had snapped. Without a moral compass, his violent tendencies had taken full reign. Like a boiler gauge with its indicator needle stuck in the red zone, he'd reached a critical state. He couldn't shake the anger bubbling under his skin. So he instigated fights to get it out of his system. The sheriff didn't even know half of it. His knuckles had already been cut and bruised. Had been for months. The guys he usually picked off preferred to keep a low profile with the cops. No way would they come forward.

"I can't continue cleaning up your mess, Jameson. It's been six months. I know it's not nearly enough time to cope with what's happened, but you need to stop. This self-destructive route you're on is going to ruin your future. Your mom wouldn't have wanted that for you."

His mom was dead. So was his dad. They couldn't care anymore. Whom did he have left to impress?

No one.

"We all loved Beth. Everyone here feels for you. Why do you think we've looked the other way for so long? But how much longer until you kill someone?"

He didn't wait for a response to either question. "You're a good kid. I want to help you get back on your feet. I think the best thing for you is to leave here. Leave this whole damn town behind."

Leave? Fat chance.

Jameson kicked his boots off the uncomfortable bench and crossed the holding cell. Deputy Harris was sitting behind her desk, pretending like she wasn't listening in. Stepping up to the bars, he curled his fingers around the iron, glowering through the gap. "You can't make me leave."

Nobody could make him do anything anymore. The only way he was abandoning his home—the only place he'd ever known—would be in a body bag. They'd have to drag him out of here.

"No, I can't," Paul agreed with a heavy sigh of defeat. "I can only appeal to your common sense and hope that you'll see reason. For your own sake."

Jameson straightened, letting his hands slip off the bars and dropping them by his side. He stared at the man across. His dad's friend was no taller than him. Slightly bigger in mass, but still in great shape for a Marine vet. He used to respect the hell out of him. His cropped hair showed gray streaks along the sides that even his hat couldn't hide, and his short handlebar mustache was a nice touch. He pulled that Texas Ranger vibe off well. His dad had told him stories of them serving together. Funny how they'd both ended up here.

"Promise me you'll keep your nose clean," Paul said, putting his key in the lock.

The irony made his chest pull tight. They were the last words his mom had spoken to him, though the sheriff couldn't possibly know that.

Jameson didn't commit. He wasn't sure he could keep his word. He had the feeling things were going to get worse before they got… tolerable.

2023

30

Hayley's hands sprang up on instinct. "Oh my God, please don't shoot." Heart thumping wildly behind her sternum, she squeezed her eyes shut.

There had been no sound of an approach. Whoever it was had to be an exceptional hunter.

"You're trespassing on private property," he said in a low timbre devoid of any empathy.

Jamie?

The air stalled in her throat. *Could it really be? Is it really him?*

"I-I'm sorry. I didn't know—"

"Liar!"

She didn't hear him take a step, but the hard muzzle suddenly pressed into the back of her head. "You move like you know the area."

His crude tone made her wonder what kind of man he'd become. Was he really going to shoot her from behind?

Hayley panicked and blurted out the first thing that came to her mind. "I know you shot the tail off a rabbit from a hundred yards away when you were eight."

Okay, probably not her brightest choice, but the silly comment didn't fall on deaf ears because the pressure of the rifle disappeared.

"Turn around." A hint of curiosity mixed with the commanding authority in his voice.

With a little flutter in her belly, Hayley complied, lowering the hood from her head as she rotated in slow motion.

"Holy shit." The rifle dropped at his side, and his look of confusion melted into utter surprise. "Virgin?"

She scoffed at the outdated label, folding her arms over her chest. "I'm twenty-five, you know?"

Jaw slack at an angle, he blinked as though considering the likelihood that he might be hallucinating.

Then the corner of his mouth twitched and his expression lit up, flashing her that same cheeky smile she remembered, blue eyes sparkling in recognition.

"Hi." She lifted her hand in an awkward little wave.

"I'll be damned."

They both stood there, rooted to the ground, transfixed by each other. She wished she knew what kind of conversation was playing out in his mind. Her own thoughts were racing. His loose plaid shirt hung open, sleeves pushed up his forearms. The excited butterflies in her belly multiplied. In front of her towered the man-version of the boy she once knew. And, holy moly, he was as big as an oak, staring down at her from his high vantage point. Her thighs twitched in response, urging her to start climbing and begging to be wrapped around him.

His brows drew together, forming a deep crease. "You're hurt."

Huh? Oh, right. Her hand. The wave.

"Uh, yeah." She thumbed over her shoulder, trying to deflect her embarrassment. "I slipped in the creek back there.

You wouldn't happen to have a first aid kit on you, would you?"

Other than the black hunting rifle in his grip, he appeared empty-handed.

"Not *on* me, no," he replied apologetically, affirming her.

"So much for 'Be Prepared'. The Boy Scouts would be disappointed."

Her remark made him laugh. "There's little demand for medical care. I shoot to kill. Not wound."

And judging by the scope mounted on the gun, he had no problem accomplishing that.

"Let me see." He pulled her close and brought up her palm to inspect the deep cut before she could decline.

Hayley held her breath unintentionally. His touch was gentle. The brush of his thumb across her tender palm was much softer than the callous notes in his tone.

"Doesn't look like you need stitches," he said, releasing her hand. "Come on. I'll bandage you up at home."

Whoa, wait. HOME?

Hayley swallowed hard. He was taking her back to *his house*?

Slinging his rifle over his shoulder, Jamie led the way. It took her a moment to fall into step beside him. Panic settled over her again. She would *actually* step foot into his house.

Him. And her. At his house. Alone.

What the hell was she thinking? He was probably married. There had to be a wife waiting for him. Maybe kids. Why had she never encountered him on her visits before? Why didn't anyone else in town know he was here?

Hayley got a grip on herself and noticed his eyes dipping to her shoes. "Nice footwear. How'd you manage to slip in those?"

"Mad skill, I guess," she answered sarcastically.

Yeah, she had a real knack for getting into sticky situations.

"And I assume the fall's why you're wet, too."

Ah, so he did *notice.*

She nodded her head in shame, but she'd rather stew in her damp gear than ask his wife for a spare set of clothes.

As they kept walking, Hayley didn't want to let on how familiar she still was with the property. She usually avoided Beth's homestead and the entire north side, where her former cabins stood, turning back once she reached the south end of the lake. Jamie took that same route, bringing them straight up to the common hall.

Hayley's hands were sweating. She curled her fingers, and the salt leaked into her wound, making it sting. She knew his house sat right around the corner.

The driveway came into view first, and she almost burst into a laugh. Lo and behold, his black Silverado loomed out front like a rabid guard dog, blocking almost the entire house with its size. It was bigger than she remembered.

And then it revealed itself. Bit by bit, in all its pristine beauty, his home appeared behind the truck.

The last of the gravel crunched under their soles and then quieted to dull *thuds* on the steps. She flanked him up to the covered porch that ran along the whole front side. In between the foot-wide posts, her eyes were immediately drawn to the imposing set of doors. The pair was made of solid, dark-colored wood with a slim window panel on either side. They were massive. Hayley figured about eight feet in height, even more in width, counting the panels.

Using the front door felt strange. She'd always entered through the back, never seeing more than the kitchen of the rustic ranch that was his home. And she didn't want to think about the only time she'd seen the large double doors open.

Jamie extended his hand toward the black iron grip. It wasn't locked. Depressing the top switch with his thumb, he gave it a push and stepped inside.

Hayley followed and braced herself for God knew what: kids running toward their dad…a dog barking…

She crossed the threshold with her eyes closed, one hand gripping the inactive side of the entryway for emotional support rather than to keep her from stumbling.

The house was quiet. No voices. No laughing children. Not even the sound of a TV playing.

He lives alone.

At least for the moment.

She watched him lean his rifle against the wall and unzip his boots one by one. They weren't the tall ones he used to wear, but they were taller than her mid-height Merrells.

He dropped them by the door beside only one other pair—his size, same tactical style, tan instead of black.

Is there really no one else?

Hayley did the same with her own shoes, and had to acknowledge that they looked pretty good lined up with his.

"I'll get the kit. Make yourself at home," he told her, already turning away.

Her hands went up to remove her hat and pull her hair free on reflex. The jacket stayed on. She only wore a black sports bra underneath.

As Jamie disappeared in the back, Hayley canvassed the space. It *was* eerie to see it from this side. It was still the same house. And also not. The archway that had divided the kitchen from the living room was gone. She could see the stool at the island where she used to sit. He'd knocked down the wall to make it an open concept and give it a modern makeover. A barn door now split the two halves of the home, providing privacy for the bedrooms while creating a sizable area to entertain guests. The high wooden ceiling made the space appear larger than it was. It was a modest ranch. Two, maybe three bedrooms.

Her heart felt heavy. The interior was warm and inviting, every bit like Beth. Lots of sunlight flooded through the large windows facing south, eliminating the need for artificial lighting. The modern seating furniture had navy blue upholstery. Made of cotton twill, not sticky, rigid leather.

Hayley ran a hand along the velvety texture of the chair's backrest. She could picture Jamie stretching his long legs across the sofa on the opposite side. His mom curled up in this one, reading a book. And Carl…?

Probably in the kitchen stealing cookies.

"Sit!"

Hayley whipped around at the command. Jamie nodded at the sofa chair, a gray canvas case in his hand. "Please," he tagged on.

She sank onto the seat and held out her hand when he crouched in front of her. "I probably should have washed it instead of ogling your place."

"Looks clean," he said, laughing. "And I have nothing to hide. What you see is what you get."

Hayley wished she could say the same. If only things were so simple.

She slumped deeper into the soft cushions. Fluffy throw pillows engulfed her on all three sides, as if swallowing her up.

Jamie focused his attention on dressing her wound, applying a thin layer of Neosporin, and gently pressing a gauze square to the center of her palm. Hayley held it in place while he got the cotton bandage out of the first-aid kit.

His hands worked with the kind of shocking ease that came from experience. He started with a locking turn around her wrist, then carried the bandage along the back to the base of her little finger. He completed the turn across the middle, rounding her thumb, and brought the bandage back up to her pinky. From there, he drew it across her knuckles, diagonally down her palm, and finished with a circular turn around her wrist.

It looked like he'd done this a million times. His motion was a program playing without much awareness behind it.

"Not your first time playing nurse, is it?"

"No," he replied wryly, securing the bandage with a small strip of adhesive tape.

Hayley tried to get a read on him. He had the same half-cocked grin, stunning blue eyes, and dark hair that was almost black. There was a lot of his mom there. She recognized the woman's spark that lived on in him.

But that was where the familiarity ended. He didn't dress like a punk kid anymore. His plain t-shirt was red; he'd taken the black and white top layer off. His hair was shorter and a lot more tame these days. The sides were neatly tapered to blend with the two-inch length on top. The ends of it fell forward as he looked down. He'd caught the small cut above her ankle.

His hand dropped to the inside of her right leg, rotating it to get a better look. He nudged her leggings up to inspect the cut, and his fingers brushed her bare skin.

"I can slap a Band-Aid on that if you like, but it's really just a scrape," he suggested, his palm giving her calf a light squeeze.

The pitter-patter of her pulse became louder in her ears. She swallowed a few times to wet her throat. "I think I'll be fine. Thanks."

He'd also grown a beard. It was short and didn't hide his chiseled jawline, but it was longer than the bit of scruff he'd sported nine years ago.

Who is this intriguing man?

Jamie held on to her lower leg a split second too long, and she thought she caught the hint of something flashing across his eyes. Then he pushed to a stand, and it was gone before he pivoted. "Can I get you a drink?"

She watched him wander off into the kitchen behind her and contorted her body to track the enticing view. Propping her chin up with her elbow on the armrest, she drawled, "Got any wine?"

"Fuck no! What do I look like?" He scowled over his shoulder, taking offense at her bold presumption. "I got beer."

"I'll take that," Hayley chuckled. "Mind if I use your bathroom."

His back turned, he pointed down the hallway. "Second door on the left."

She took his direction, facing the hall. The first door turned out to be the laundry room. She could see the matching set of washer and dryer through the gap. It was the only one that wasn't shut. Past the bathroom on the left was a third door, and two more were on the opposite side of the hallway. The folding-type one at the far end, she assumed, was a linen closet, judging by the classic layout of the ranch.

When she returned to the kitchen, he'd finished unloading the dishwasher. He dropped the empty silverware basket into the bottom rack and closed it up before going to the fridge right beside it.

"I can't believe you're still driving that old beat-up Silverado," Hayley teased. She could see it through the window above the large dark, concrete farmer's sink.

"Hey now, it was brand new at some point." He pulled two bottles of Pabst Blue Ribbon out, holding them by the neck with his left hand.

"When? In two-thousand?"

"Oh-five." He swung the fridge shut with a somber look on his face. "It was my dad's," he elaborated, twisting the caps off and tossing them onto the counter behind him.

Yikes! She put her foot in her mouth on that one.

Holding his own in his right hand, he extended the second *PBR* out to her.

Hayley cringed, accepting it. "Sorry. I never considered its sentimental value."

She focused on the void on his left ring finger. There was no wedding band, and the interior of the house lacked a certain feminine touch—other than what was left of Beth's original décor.

No wife. No live-in girlfriend.

"That's alright. It still runs smoothly. And I had it lifted by six and a half inches."

That's why it appeared bigger.

Stuffing his free hand in his pocket, he leaned back against the sink across from her. In his red shirt and blue jeans, he looked like Superman.

If Superman had a beard.

What was he like with a woman? His hands were gentle, but they could get rough, too.

He tipped his beer toward her in question, "And what do you drive these days? A Lamborghini?"

"Audi. The Lambo is no good in the woods," she joked. She hated flashy cars.

Holding the cold bottle in her lap, Hayley mirrored his pose. The sharp edge of the island pressed against her rear.

His eyes narrowed on her. "Why are you here, Hayley?"

And there it was, the question she'd been dreading this whole time. But, oh man, did she love the sound of her name on his lips.

"I sneak back here every summer." *Besides skipping the first year*, she kept that to herself.

"Why?"

Another warranted question.

"Nostalgia," she grimaced, embarrassed. "I thought the place was abandoned."

"It is. Or was... I don't know." He gave his head a subtle shake as if he was still figuring that part out for himself.

"What happened to you after?" She didn't want to say it out loud, but the tragedy of that night was the elephant in the room. She'd replayed it in her mind so many times. How long had it taken him to come back from that?

"Got in trouble for a while. Drank too much… got high too much," he dragged out. "But then I quit and went to college."

"College?" That got her attention. Her eyes shot to his. "For what?"

He took a long sip and swallowed before answering. "Architecture."

Hayley wasn't sure she bought it. There was no sign of that in his home. No drawing table. No sketches. No models.

Was he making it up to impress her? She couldn't picture him in a white-collar profession.

Hayley pushed off and rounded the white granite slab to sit on the corner stool. There were three on each side.

"What about you?"

"International business." She set her beer down, keeping her hand wrapped around it. "But I didn't finish. I dropped out after the first year." Her brief time in college was a mess. She didn't know if she was ever going to pick it up again.

"That doesn't sound like you. The quitting things, I mean."

"Priorities change," she told him before her voice choked. A lump formed at the back of her throat. She bit her tongue to fight the emotions bubbling up. She wasn't going to break down in front of him.

Jamie straightened and kicked another one of the backless chairs out from under the island. Elbow propped, holding up his drink, he slouched down in the spot opposite her, three feet of pristine white between them.

"You wearing contacts now?"

"No. I had my vision corrected. Less of a hassle." That was the simplified answer, but it was the truth.

"Hm. Too bad. I liked the glasses," he revealed into the mouth of the bottle.

It was news to her. She'd never hated them herself.

"Your turn," he prompted. "Quid pro quo. Two for two."

He clasped the longneck loosely with three fingers and dangled it back and forth, giving her his most honest 'ask me anything' expression. Did he really not have any secrets?

Sweat from the bottle soaked into her bandage as she rubbed at the condensation on the glass with her thumb. She didn't want to play this Hannibal Lecter game—wasn't ready to bare her skeletons to him. She felt more like reminiscing on the good times.

Luckily, Jamie agreed.

Without effort, they were able to share laughs the way they used to. The chemistry between them was still there. They jumped from one random topic to the next, cracking jokes, never running out of fuel.

At some point, he started a second beer while she nursed her first. Hours must have passed like minutes; neither of them bothered checking. They talked and talked in a steady flow. The conversation never ebbed. Until—

Crap!

Hayley jumped off her chair with such force that it skipped over the hardwood floor. "I gotta go."

She'd lost track of time as she was being sucked down memory lane. In the window behind him, the sun was setting. It was getting dark. Low light made the forty-minute hike back dangerous.

Beer in hand, he got up too, and went for his key on the counter by the back door. "Where are you staying? I'll take you."

"NO!" she blurted out, rushing toward him with her hands up. She couldn't accept his offer. No matter how chivalrous it was.

The overblown rejection raised his suspicion, and he frowned.

"I-I appreciate it," she added quickly. "But you don't have to. I'll find my way."

She backed off as he gave her reaction another critical once-over. Whatever his bloodhound senses picked up wasn't in her favor, because he shook his head and said, "Not up for debate. Either you let me drive you or you'll have to spend the night."

Hayley raced through her options in her head. A: split right now, beat the darkness rolling in, and never return here. B: let him take her back to her cabin and run the risk of someone seeing them together. Or C—

"Stay," he answered for her.

He took a step closer. She didn't pull away. "You want me to spend the night?"

"I want to finish what we started, Hayley. We're not done catching up. You still got half your drink left. And don't tell me you weren't enjoying this as much as I was."

He paused, waiting for her to deny it. His level stare challenged her to capitulate. "What's it gonna be... *Virgin*?" he stressed. "You in or out?"

He brought the mouth of the bottle up, and Hayley couldn't look away. She wanted to feel his lips crushing down on her, chilled from the drink. She wanted the taste of the cold liquid on his tongue, enhanced by his kiss. She wanted everything he was offering...

And she wasn't walking out of here without it.

"Look at you, smooth-talking your way into my pants again."

His head tipped back on a laugh. "I'm pretty damn sure you left here with your virginity intact," he argued, taking a stab at her chest.

"Physically maybe. But not emotionally," she clarified. "You were my first in everything *but* that. My first crush. My first kiss. The first boy who made me feel beautiful."

"I vividly remember."

Her eyelashes fluttered, perplexed. *"Vividly?"*

"Every little detail of that night… locked away in here." He tapped the side of his head with his left index finger.

"So, you thought of me?" Her hands tangled in the ends of her hair. She didn't judge him if he had. She had her own highlight reel.

"I did," he replied, scooting his *PBR* onto the counter beside her. The fierce beam of his spotlight remained focused on her.

Moving in, he snaked his arms around her waist and eliminated the gap. An instantaneous blaze radiated from his body, burning through the thin fibers of her clothes, which still posed too much of a barrier between them.

He leaned down, hovering over her. The warmth of his breath made her want to curl up inside of him. "Did you ever think of me?"

Hayley nodded. "All the time."

His eyes, dark and hooded, drifted over her face as the corner of his mouth gave a satisfied twitch. Lust bloomed between her thighs in an acutely familiar way.

Dipping his gaze, he feathered his lips across hers in the lightest kiss, then skimmed along her cheek.

Her lids fell shut to focus her awareness on the heat that filtered through her palms resting on his pecs, even the bandaged one. It rose up her arms, with his muscles shifting under her touch.

Jamie tilted his head at an angle, nudging her temple. Her heartbeat hammered against the steel cage of his chest. She knew what he was going to ask.

"Did you ever think of me when you touched yourself?"

His distinctive timber hummed through her eardrum, vibrating her bones to the marrow. The question mixed with the desire in his embrace. His hands grazed higher up her torso, thumbs going under her jacket to find bare skin.

"Yes." Hayley grinned. "I did." She remembered the promise she'd given him. And she'd made good on that a hundred times over.

His hold on her tensed. Scraping his coarse facial hair along her jaw, he dragged his mouth back to hers. "Show me," he urged in a grating voice. "Show me how you imagined me touching you, Hayley."

He came down on her before she could take another breath. Fingers digging into her sides, he parted her lips with his tongue, flicking past her teeth. He felt so good. The taste of him crashed through her, making her hot all over.

He rolled his hips into her, his hands sweeping under her top to dip inside her leggings as he backed her up against the low-mounted sink. Sliding under the sides of her thong, he pushed the layers down, kneading her flesh along the way.

Hayley hadn't realized how deprived she'd felt. The hard bulge behind his jeans pressed into her hip with insistence, and the thought of him inside her made her ache with need. She clutched his shirt in her fists. His kiss was laced with an indisputable demand that lit her up like a flare.

Jamie didn't restrain his own aspirations. His calm composure was gone, and she loved how roughly he handled her. With his mouth slanted over hers, their tongues tangled. His fingertips rounded her curves, settling in the crease below her ass while he ground himself into her. He ravaged her body, claiming all of her at once without apology.

One palm firmly grasping her cheek, he took her left hand from his chest and led it to the throbbing part of her that begged for his attention.

She gasped.

He moaned.

She wasn't sure who was more surprised by the slippery impact—he or she? She'd never been so wet in her life.

"You must want me pretty damn bad if your body's making it that easy for me," he speculated with an amused lilt. "But I still don't think it's good enough. I need you dripping before I give you even an inch, Hayley. If you want me to fuck you properly, you need to come first. So, show me," he repeated, giving her hand a squeeze. "I won't ask again."

His left arm hooked around the small of her back as she cupped herself, drawing soft little circles. Her clit pulsed. Her needy flesh swelled under the caress.

Jamie remained patient, studying the rhythm and pattern of her motion, listening to the cues her body was giving off. Hovering over her, foreheads touching, he let her fingers do the walking, sliding along her seam and in between her folds.

She knew how to draw the pleasure out, keeping a slow pace, but with him right there, every sensation was heightened. Foreplay with him was on a whole other level. She wanted it to last longer.

Her libido was not on board with that. It was edging dangerously close to the finish line. He caught on to her desperate squirming, and when her panting grew in urgency, his dominant hold took over, picking up the pace.

"No! Not yet." She wasn't ready.

"Enough teasing," he growled. "My turn."

Trapping her palm in a hard grind, he weaved their hands to slide one of her fingers inside next to his own. She gasped again, and he deepened his kiss, sinking into her.

His lips were like velvet, his tongue bold and assertive as he entered her body over and over. Each sharp in-and-out thrust stroked the tender bud at the cusp of her sex, sending bursts of lightning through her core. She couldn't fight the trembling.

"Please…" she whimpered.

What was she begging him for? To stop? To keep going?

Jamie didn't miss a beat. He pulled out, and then Hayley felt the increase in pressure as he added another one of his long fingers beside hers, slow and gentle, while his body trapped her against the concrete slab.

"Goddamn, you're tight. Just like I always imagined you'd be."

His lips cruised the shape of hers, nudging her further back over the edge of the sink, relentless in his pursuit of her climax.

He buried his knuckles inside of her again in the same steady glide, riding her body higher and commanding it with intimate proficiency. Warm slickness pooled where they were joined, and he groaned into her throat, savoring their combined erotic greed.

"You feel that?" he asked, nipping at her bottom lip. "That's how fucking wet I want you."

Oh, God! Her hips rolled involuntarily to meet his deep thrusts, flashback after flashback replaying in her mind. She was caught in a whirlpool. She couldn't think. Couldn't speak. The slick suction was too much. There was only the blissful chase of friction.

Hayley cried out as he triggered her release. The jolts spread to her toes and fingertips, sending her muscles spasming.

"And that's how you finish," he whispered. "Hard and deep."

He followed up his statement with another prolonged thrust. Eyes closed, she let her head fall back. His teeth moved over her chin to the front of her throat, biting and kissing the vulnerable tissue while his motion between her thighs slowed to a lazy grind.

As her breath returned to normal, Jamie straightened and steadied her against him, his arms coiled around her waist. She skated her hands along his biceps, grasping the solid muscle. The sleeves of his shirt were drawn tight over the crest of the well-defined mass. He was magnificent. And she couldn't wait to feel more of him.

"Are you going to hold up your end now?" she asked when he pinned her back against the sink. "Quit stalling. I'm not a virgin anymore."

"You sure?" His left hand came up and wrapped around the side of her neck, his thumb moving across her jugular. "Whatever inadequate dick you've been riding can hardly count. I have to assess your condition myself. And until you fit all of me," he rasped, "you stay my virgin." He captured her mouth in another fervent kiss, his tongue flicking past her lips, playing with her own.

Jamie exuded masculinity. And yet his dominance didn't threaten her. She wasn't scared of him. Hand heavy at her throat… and yet nothing. No fear. She knew he wouldn't hurt her.

Her hands ventured underneath his shirt to his lower back. His jeans hung low on his hips, and the waistband of his boxers stuck out on top. He wasn't wearing a belt.

"You could've had me, you know?" she prompted, running an acrylic nail up and down his spine, feeling his muscles jerk beneath his skin. "At the lake. I wouldn't have turned you down."

"I know. Stupidest damn decision I ever made. But then you wouldn't be here right now. You're the one who got away." His voice was all sultry. His eyelids heavy with need.

From the back, her fingers traced the edge of his pants at his waist, brushing along his skin as she brought her hands together at the front, teasing, "I couldn't have been the only one."

"The only one that mattered," he answered in a pant against her mouth when she undid the button and released his fly. "I'm not that foolish anymore, Hayley. This time, I'm taking what I want. And if I get you in my bed… I'm keeping you there."

"Then I guess I have to stay clear of your bed."

She reached into his boxers, closing her hand around his massive erection. Jamie groaned, rocking into her stroking motion.

Hot blood pumped beneath skin that was like silk. She imagined the feel of him on her tongue, his stiff shaft sliding to the back of her throat, stretching and filling her.

"Anything else fair game?" She quirked a brow toward the couch.

He let out a broken laugh before sending her on a spin and pushing her leggings further down her thighs.

"We're not going anywhere," he said in a husky tone.

Jutting her rear out at him, she watched over her shoulder as he pulled a condom from his back pocket. He ripped the foil square open and rolled the rubber down.

His lips curled. With eyes on her, he gave himself another stroke and then came in, grasping her neck.

His mouth captured the underside of her jaw, biting and kissing. He traced the curve from her earlobe to the base, where it disappeared into the collar of her jacket. Hayley's skin buzzed, and she arched more to give him free rein.

Her bra chafed against her overly sensitive nipples. She wanted it off. Wanted to be fully naked to feel him, skin on skin. His hands weren't enough.

His ragged breath lingered in the crook as his palm smoothed over the swell of her ass, spreading her to give him access. She pressed her curves into his groin and felt the ridge of his arousal. Her legs quaked from anticipation.

He slid the hard length of him across her slick entrance, making her shiver. The waist of her leggings stretched tight across her mid-thigh, restraining her movement like a rope.

She leaned forward a little more, adjusting her hands on both sides of the sink. They shook. The ripples crawled up her arms, and she broke out in chills at the thought of him.

Sliding her thumbs down over the edge, she gripped the countertop.

With a languid drive of his hips, the tip breached, forcing her slit open. He smothered a moan against her skin and followed up with another inch, delving deeper only to retreat immediately.

He was toying with her.

 "How much of me do you want to feel this time, Virgin?"

"Stop calling me—"

She didn't get the retort out. His hand at her nape grabbed a fistful of hair, yanking her head back, and his sharp breath fell across her cheek.

"I asked: How. Much?"

Fuck. She didn't think it was possible to get any wetter, but a discrete little trail ran down the inside of her thigh at the twitch of her muscles.

"All of it," Hayley mewled. She hated how desperate her voice sounded, but she was ready to beg him for every last inch he was holding out.

He grinned wickedly, mirth in his eyes, and then his fist tightened in her hair, twisting her head to the side. He crushed her mouth beneath his to devour her breath while he readied himself at her entrance again.

The head prodded her seam, and she angled her ass higher, craning her neck and arching on her tiptoes—*So. Fucking. Needy*—But she didn't care anymore.

Hayley pushed off her hands to come down on him, taking him off guard.

Jamie sucked in a breath. He drew his hips back a little, his hot kiss not straying far. "Naughty girl," he hissed. "*I* wanted to do that."

Mouths open, hovering over each other, she flicked his lip with her tongue. He chuckled darkly and then released his hold on her hair, shifting to the dip of her thigh. The tip of him now crowning her, he hauled her hips toward him and plunged the length of his shaft deep inside of her, splitting her in half with one punishing drive.

She yelped, trembling badly.

"You want it?" He retreated, then railed into her again, sliding even deeper. "Then fucking take it, Hayley. All of it."

He didn't give her a chance to utter another plea. He came at her again and again.

She couldn't form clear thoughts as her brain turned to mush. They were on the steep ascent of the rollercoaster now, with nowhere to go but down.

And what a drop it would be. The anxious excitement tingled in her gut and built in intensity each time he slid home.

His breath came in jagged tides, his hands roving her body up her sides and to the front. He reached around, one hand cupping her breast on top of her clothes, the other wedged in between her legs, rubbing her clit. Fire spread through her thighs and coiled in her womb.

Caught in their moment of passion, Hayley lost her grip on the sink. Her palms found the flat surface of the counter to brace herself right before their bodies met again.

Two strong arms encircling her, he pulled her upright and caged her against his chest with a possessiveness that made her knees weak.

She held on. To him *and* to the violent force that thrashed beneath her skin.

Hayley reached up, clasping his cheek, to bring him closer still. Her lips brushed his jawline, and a deep rumble built in his chest. She loved the sound of him. It was rough. It was raw. She couldn't get enough.

"All *this*, pent-up for you." He panted hard, grunting in her ear.

The barrel of his chest rose and fell rapidly against her back, and sweat skated down her spine in the hollow between them. His fingers bit into her flesh. The orgasm began to peak in her womb a second time.

He tugged on her bottom lip, then let go, growling in her ear, chasing the release with her. She curled her toes and swallowed a sob. She was almost there—

"Ah… fuck, Hayley…" He cried out her name, rearing back, and they both climaxed together, her walls gripping him tighter as every muscle in her body tensed.

Her sight caught on his profile. His flushed face was beautiful. Breathing hard, he jerked into her a few more times, releasing every last drop.

Disappointment rushed her. She wanted him to jet into her. Wanted to feel the drip of him between her thighs.

Jamie straightened. Without lingering, his arms fell from her, and he pulled out, ripping the warmth of his proximity away.

"Did you get what you came for?"

31

There was a drop in her stomach. His tone was brusque and laced with resentment as he zipped himself up. He stepped to the side, and then the metal garbage can lid slammed shut.

"Is that your way of asking me to leave?" She shimmied the tight spandex back up her thighs. She suddenly felt way too exposed in front of him. More than just physically.

Jamie didn't meet her eyes. He swiped the beer off the counter beside her and brought it up to his mouth, turning away. He left her in the kitchen with the same affection he'd given the trash.

She yanked her leggings the rest of the way up, glaring at him as he gained distance.

"So, all *that* was only a farce?" She waved her hands, despite him not being able to see her. "You didn't really give a shit if I got lost?"

"Nope." He kept walking into the living room, not looking back.

Anger bubbled under her skin, and the cut on her hand stung from putting too much pressure on it now that the high from the exhilaration was gone. Her fingers curled into fists. "You know I could accuse you of the same thing, right?"

"If the shoe fits," he mumbled.

Asshole! "A quick fuck was not what I was looking for." She slammed the heel of her foot down on the wood floor, giving the chair next to her a rattle.

This time, he halted. He pivoted around halfway and tilted his head to one side, keeping his expression cold. "Then what exactly *were* you looking for?"

"I was looking for a friend." Which sounded ridiculous considering they'd just had sex. That wasn't something you usually did with friends.

Shaking his head, he scoffed in amusement. "You have a funny way to connect with friends." Then he dropped into the corner of the three-seater sofa facing the kitchen. "Well... I'm afraid you're not going to find him. That fool left."

He blithely kicked one ankle over the other. If there had been a coffee table, he probably would've propped his feet on it. He looked so smug, sipping his *PBR*, and slouching low.

The shift in his demeanor was an unfortunate turn of events, yes, but she had dealt with worse. She had no intention of walking away from this. She could change his low opinion of her.

She marched toward him, stopping beside the sofa chair she'd sat in earlier. "Alright. Fine. You got me. I wasn't really looking for a friend. But I wasn't expecting *this* either." She gestured back and forth between them in her defense. "I didn't use you."

"Yeah," he drew out. "Ye did."

218

"You believe sex is the reason I come back here every year?"

He didn't want to vocalize his reply to that. He hoped the hard lines on his face and the tight jaw spoke for themselves.

She came back every summer. If not for him, then why?

The moment she stepped foot inside, he knew she wasn't going to leave unfucked. Life was short, and he'd never expected to get a second chance with her. He wasn't going to pass it up. Fate wouldn't grant him a third.

He simply had to figure out the logistics. He'd lured her into the kitchen because it was the most neutral ground. Unassuming. But he'd had it all planned out. Make her feel comfortable… get her to drop her guard. Then his snare snapped shut. And she thought she'd initiated it. Laughable. She was as naïve as ever.

Okay, he *was* presumptuous. Asking her to stay hadn't been a shot in the dark, though. He'd picked up on the little signals she'd sent his way: chewing her lip, twirling a lock of her hair. Maybe she'd done it without realizing it, but her body had responded to him nonetheless. It didn't take a sniper to nail the target. She'd wanted to stay. Merely needed to hear him say it.

Then they both had gotten what they were after. Finally crossed each other off their bucket lists. So why did he feel bitter?

It felt wrong. Rushed.

After years of hyping her up to be this unicorn beyond his reach, he'd captured her at last. It was over. No more wondering. No more chasing butterflies.

Jameson was angry with himself. He would never see her again. She had no reason to return now. He'd given her exactly what she wanted. The one thing all her money couldn't buy. So, he wanted to hurt her to make himself feel better.

"I swear I didn't mean for this to happen, Jamie."

He chuckled into the mouth of his bottle.

"What?"

"You and my mom were the only ones who called me that."

She blinked, dumbfounded. "What did everyone else call you?"

"Jameson," he told her. "Or *JD* back in school. Last name is Davis, in case you were wondering." He jerked his shoulder derisively, bringing the beer back up.

"Not Bishop?" She knitted her brows, and then comprehension struck. "Of course, that was your mom's maiden name."

Folding her arms in front of her chest, she leaned her hip into the side of the chair's backrest, the wheels in her head visibly turning, and her voice was quiet when she dropped her eyes as if talking to herself. "This whole time, I never knew your full name."

"We weren't that close. How much did you really know about me?"

They both knew he had a point. They had never exchanged personal information. Two perfect strangers. No last names. No phone numbers.

Well, she'd given him hers that last night, but—

"You never called." Her words came out in another whisper, though this time they were directed at him.

"Did you honestly think I would?" He leveled his stare with her as she raised it to him. "I tossed it in the lake that very same night. I thought it was fitting. It was where the two of us should have ended."

He watched disappointment wash over her face. Jameson had many regrets from that night, but the worst one was searching her out afterward. He didn't want her to remember him like that. So weak. So pathetic.

She swiped her thumbs behind her ears to gather her long hair at the back, then twirled it into a rope and draped it over her shoulder. The hem of her nylon zip-up rode up her waist again with the motion, grazing her belly button. It was short, but below the midriff, and hovered right at the line of her leggings, so no skin was directly showing.

Unless she shifted.

Then the outfit would grant him the tiniest glimpse. Like it was now. The smooth skin was practically begging for his touch. He had felt the goosebumps pucker beneath his hands. Her waist was so small that he could wrap his arm around her twice. She was too thin, and something about that didn't sit right with him. He had the urge to feed her—*not* fuck her—but whatever. Priorities and shit.

And ditching her glasses? He hated to think that some prick made her believe she needed to change any part of herself.

Her fingers weaved through the ends of her locks in a meditative gesture, and her gaze hovered somewhere ahead, not focused on the physical space around her.

"I guess I should probably go, then." She pushed off the chair and started moving toward the door.

Don't let her walk out, asshole, the voice in his head screamed.

Jameson ignored it. It wasn't his fault if she slipped and fell to her death in the dark out there. She was obviously clumsy.

But she didn't leave. Instead of picking them up, she stared down at her shoes for a long second when something changed her mind and she whipped around.

"Fuck it!" Her hands shot up. "I'm not leaving. You want to know what I was really looking for?"

He gave an apathetic shrug that was hardly encouraging, but she went on anyway.

"Hope!" she answered her own question. "I was looking for something I was cheated out of. The freedom of choosing my own life."

Her voice had taken on a quiver, and she swallowed. Then something shifted in her demeanor. Raising her chin, she straightened…

…aaaand began to strip in front of him. Exactly like she'd done that night at the lake. Her nimble fingers tugged the zipper down her front, slowly exposing her belly.

His stomach flipped, and his pulse sped up. She was wearing nothing but the black sports bra he'd already gotten his hands on. His palm buzzed with the memory of her. It had no padding. He'd felt her hard nipple through the material.

Hands behind her back, she pulled the cuffs over her wrist. Her chest jutted out as she shrugged out of the sleeves and let the thing drop to the floor by her feet. Crossing her arms, she reached for the tight band around her ribs.

His erection gave a hard kick behind his fly, watching her raise it over her head.

This isn't a dream, right? She's really doing this? Right in front of me?

Her tits bobbed in affirmation as she chucked the bra aside, too. Then her pink nipples stood out at him from six feet away.

His mouth watered. Slipping her hands into her leggings, she bent over and scooted them down her smooth legs. The gray pants matched the top, but her thong was white—*virgin-white*, go figure.

Her hands went over her heels, brushing her socks off in the same motion, and then she stood in front of him in all her naked glory… and his brain stroked out.

THAT he hadn't seen coming.

His cock swelled with need again. She was so damn perfect, he couldn't stop his eyes from roaming her curves.

But talk about being clumsy. There were other faded scrapes and bruises on her arms. On her thighs, too. He could see them in the meager light of the living room. It was pitch black outside now, and the glow from the street lights through the kitchen window didn't reach this far into the house. The ones on the back porch behind him were off.

Eyes hooded, she swayed up to him in the darkness of the room and straddled his lap. He clenched his teeth as the blaze between her thighs scorched through to his own. His groin throbbed, melting against her.

"You asked me to show you how I imagined you," she said in a seductive voice.

His pulse punched up his throat. She leaned closer, hands pressed to his chest.

"Now it's your turn," she went on, whispering against his lips. "Show me how you wanted me."

She kissed him, and he didn't move. Not because he didn't understand her request, but because his brain was still on the fritz. He was simply stunned. His Adam's apple did an involuntary jerk at her challenge.

She feathered her lips across his in another fleeting kiss, then moved down, her teeth scraping his chin through his beard and along his throat. His heartbeat hammered in his ears.

Keeping his eyes closed, Jameson leaned his head back. He squeezed her hip, feeling her grind on him. She was so goddamn wet between her legs. She smelled fucking irresistible, too. Her skin. Her hair. Like green apples or something.

The beer disappeared from his clasp, and then her hands found the hem of his shirt. She dragged it over his torso without the least bit of resistance from him.

Her hands shifted to his thighs as she leaned backward, still rocking her hips. His bleary vision focused on her full breast, swaying with her movements. He felt parched. He couldn't swallow. All moisture had evaporated in the heat between them.

His hand drifted up as if compelled. It engulfed her breast, fondling the soft mound. He teased her left nipple and let his thumb linger on the spot where he'd left his mark. He circled the area with the pad of his thumb, and another moan escaped her. She remembered too.

On an impulse, he jerked up, capturing a mouthful of her flesh. She gasped, her fingers spearing into his hair, then moaned and arched more as he suckled her, flicking the perked tip with his tongue.

His arms snared her waist and lifted her off him only long enough to lay her out beside him on the cushions. Stretching her out on the couch, he lowered himself back down on her. He dragged his nose along her immaculate skin, inhaling deeply, drawing ounce after ounce of her down into his lungs until she filled every cell of his body.

Legs entwined, his thigh rubbed against the wet heat of her seam. She quivered beneath him, fingers teasing through his hair, and he knew the anticipation was killing her.

Shifting around, he shoved his jeans down one-handedly and hooked her leg behind the knee, aligning himself at her opening.

The feel of her had his eyes rolling into the back of his head. He'd only grabbed one rubber from the nightstand and never screwed any randoms without one—had no intention of knocking some girl up—but he would make an exception for her. He wanted to feel her skin on skin, and he didn't hear her object, either.

"I'll pull out before I finish," he muttered. He wasn't sure the words had come out right. He was barely coherent.

"You don't have to. I'm on birth control."

Ah fuck! He drew his hips forward and almost came right there when she said that. The thought of actually finishing inside of her was enough to push him over the edge.

Her wince snapped his attention to her nails digging into his scalp. He hadn't meant to go all the way yet, but her body welcomed him back in one slick glide.

Cradling his head in her hands, she brought his mouth up and kissed him tenderly. Her legs closed him in, immersing him completely in her warmth. With the simple act of intimacy, she turned the clock back.

Jameson retreated, pulling out to the tip and then easing himself home again, letting her feel every inch of him on his unhurried thrusts. It was everything he wanted that first time but had been too afraid to seize. He knew she would ruin him if he let her. He wanted her to be no more than some girl he finally got out of his system.

But she wasn't just *some* girl.

It was *her*. Hayley.

32

J ameson stared out the window, catching a last glimpse of the sunrise. He tried, unsuccessfully, not to think about what they'd done in this very spot last night. She was the perfect height. Kinda tall for a chick—five-nine, five-ten maybe.

His mouth threatened to break into another grin at the image of their reflection in the glass that was now burned into his memory. In his mind, he'd had her so many times in so many different ways. And yes, the fantasies were vivid, but they'd never been close to the real thing.

He reached for the coffee pot on his right and poured himself another cup. It was still hot, but no longer steaming.

Hayley's lithe body stirred soundlessly under the blanket on the couch behind him. He caught her movement in the window, and it made him downright giddy.

A naked girl on my couch…

He pivoted around to take in the unfiltered view of her. He'd slept in his own bed after she'd fallen asleep in his arms. The intimacy with her came so effortlessly it scared him. He didn't want to admit how good it had felt. Too good to be true, in fact.

She swung the blanket off, kicking her legs over the side, when her eyes locked on him in the kitchen. "Morning," she greeted him with a weary half-smile.

"Morning yourself."

He hid his grin behind the mug. Leaning back against the counter space between the sink and the fridge, he watched her get dressed, a flush burning on her cheeks.

She grabbed her underwear first, then her bra and socks, the leggings last. The fingers of his empty hand wrapped around the edge of the countertop beside him. She took her time sliding the fabric over her long legs. She went inch by inch, wriggling them up like they were a pair of sheer nylons. And what-do-you-know? He was enjoying the show in reverse, too. The pants were practically a second skin, clinging to the sinful curves of her backside.

Goddamn, that ass…

Jameson swallowed the sip of coffee that he'd forgotten was sitting in his mouth and shifted his attention. "How's the hand?"

"Better. Thanks," she gave a clipped reply, doing a little wave to prove her motor skills before bending over one more time for her hoodie.

She stuffed her arms through the sleeves and skipped down the hall for a quick escape from the awkwardness.

He sighed through his nose. He wished he knew what she was thinking. Rubbing a hand through his hair, he pushed off the counter. He put his mug down on the island and turned to the stove, firing up the pan on the burner. He needed something else to focus on, and he was hungry anyway.

He pulled the few things he'd gotten yesterday out of the fridge. As always, he'd skipped the local store and stopped at the market off the highway on his way into town instead. He had zero interest in running into anyone he knew—even managed to avoid Carl on his sporadic trips to the park.

God knew why he still felt responsible for taking care of the property.

Hayley came out of the bathroom, glowing. And not only from the rays of the morning sun on her face. She seemed genuinely happy. No sign of unease or regret.

She pulled her hair up in a high ponytail and twisted the tie from her wrist around it. "You cook?" she remarked, sounding almost shocked.

"What, like it's a difficult skill?" She was a lot easier to impress than he'd anticipated.

"I remember you baking. I didn't know you could cook, too."

Setting her butt down on the short side of the island, she picked up his mug and raised it to her mouth. He drank it black, and from the look of her indifference, she was used to the taste.

Her tongue swept across her lips, and he found himself briefly mesmerized by the glossy sheen. He wanted to kiss her again.

"My mom taught me a few things," he told her, turning his sight back on the pan. "She used to say, 'the way to a girl's heart is through her stomach.'"

"You're interested in my heart, then? I thought you were out for my soul."

Jameson reared back with laughter. He couldn't wrap his head around how unforced things felt with her. She was too damn cute. It was addicting.

"Tell you what." He shut off the heat. "I'll take any part of you that you're willing to give." And her ass was already on the table, so he considered it on the menu as well.

Scraping the scrambled eggs onto the plate next to the stove, he shot her a sidelong glance. "I didn't want to assume you were staying for breakfast, but I'm eating either way, and it would be really nice if you joined me."

She broke into a smile that reached her eyes. "I'm starving, actually."

YAHTZEE! Maybe he should stop at the gas station for some scratch-off tickets later. His lucky streak just kept going. It was hard not to gloat.

He pulled two forks from the drawer below and set the plate down in between the same seats they'd sat in last night. Hayley's ponytail whipped around as she dropped onto the stool, which he now considered her spot.

He slid her one of the forks.

Braced on her elbows across from him, she squished her boobs together and dug in. Talk about a lean-and-squeeze. They nearly popped out of her black sports bra. How was a man supposed to focus on food?

Jameson's mouth watered, though he'd lost his appetite for the scramble. Tugging on the plate with his index finger, he dragged it closer to his side to make her work for it a bit more.

The elusive green amid the gray in her eyes flashed a little brighter when she caught on, but she played along. Kneeling on the stool, ass up, she leaned over the middle of the island. And, oh man, did he like that view—from all angles.

He let her finish his coffee and polish off most of the food, too. He didn't mind. On the contrary, his chest swelled, seeing her so comfortable and content. He couldn't help but wonder what they might've had together if things had gone differently that night.

If I had asked her to come back…

If mom hadn't died…

Nine years wasted; there was so much they'd missed out on.

Jameson jostled his head to clear it from the past. He didn't want to die with regrets. You never knew when your time was up.

He rose from his seat and took the dishes to the sink, letting the water run to get it hot.

Hayley came up on his left. She leaned into his side and hung her hands from his shoulder.

His insides steeled. He stared down the drain, afraid to look at her. She was about to launch into her 'goodbye/been nice knowing ya' speech and he had a hard time keeping his food down at the thought of it.

"Thank you," she said, her cheek pressed to his arm.

"For?"

She laughed. "Not shooting me on sight, for starters."

His grip on the concrete edge tightened, waiting for the other shoe to drop.

"But also for being here after all these years," she went on, the soft tone of her voice stirring something he didn't dare to dwell on. "I had no expectations of ever seeing you again."

Their encounter had been nothing short of dumb luck. He wasn't supposed to be here—didn't actually live here anymore.

"You really thought I'd shoot you for trespassing?" He angled his chin toward her, but she wasn't looking at him either.

"I didn't know what became of you. No one knew. You simply disappeared. I thought you were dead."

There had been a lot of times when he'd wished he were.

"Every day I hoped you'd call… just to hear your voice… to know that you're okay. But you never did."

Fuck! He wanted to tell her that he'd missed her. How could he do that without sounding desperate?

Coward. No regrets, huh? he reminded himself.

Well, then here goes nothing.

The next thing he knew, his fingers were splayed in her hair at the back of her head, and he was kissing her. Her lips were soft and sweet. She felt amazing.

Her hand clasping his bicep, she was kissing him back. Her mouth opened to him, her tongue seeking his.

The moment didn't last long, but it was enough to leave them both hungry for more. No matter how many times he had her, he would never get his fill. He was a bottomless pit, ravenous for her.

Hayley pulled back an inch, peering up through her lashes. "Was it worth it?" she prompted. "The wait?"

No question about it. "Hell yes!"

She flashed a dim smile that could've meant anything. Those stormy eyes of hers were full of secrets he couldn't begin to grasp.

She blinked, then curled into his chest.

Jameson dismissed the nagging feeling and dropped his arms to her waist. Holding her tight, he kissed the top of her head.

"You showered," she pointed out, burrowing into his neck.

His skin heated under her touch. She nuzzled the soft spot below his ear, and his insatiable appetite roared to life. His greedy hands sloped over her ass, pressing her into his raging hard-on.

"I have to go," she groaned, slipping from his embrace.

Right. Because this was only a weekend trip for her. A vacation. She had a life somewhere else. He didn't know where she lived, but he knew it wasn't close. She didn't belong here.

"I slept on the couch, not your bed. Does that mean I'm free to go?"

"I suppose so," he muttered.

He recalled her strong position toward accepting a ride, so he didn't offer again. If she didn't want him to know where she was staying, then he would respect that. But he wasn't ready to have her walk out of his life just yet. It was only Saturday.

"I'll have you know I make mean fajitas, too. If you can take the heat, that is," he challenged, not letting go of her hand.

"Oh, I can take the heat." Hayley swung back into his chest. Clasping his face in her palms, she feathered her lips over his in a teasing motion.

"Good." His fingers dug into her hips, his teeth nipping at her. "Come back for dinner."

"What's for dessert?"

"You."

33

Hayley took a step back and reached for the button in the top right corner. As the trunk hatch slowly lowered in front of her, she watched her suitcase disappear.

It was hard to believe she'd only been here for a little over a day—hadn't even worn half the clothes she'd brought. A shower and a quick shopping spree later, she felt like a new person.

She'd packed up what few belongings she had to avoid an unnecessary trip back to the cabin tomorrow. She wanted to stay with Jamie for as long as possible before she was forced to return to her cage, and she would bleed the weekend to the very last minute. Missing out on her usual hikes was a small price to pay.

But she was well aware of the dangerous game she was kicking into motion. Though she paid cash wherever she went to prevent a credit card trail, the Airbnb was the one thing she couldn't hide. It wasn't hard to find if someone bothered to look into her PayPal account.

She had to assume eyes were on her here, too. Being seen in town didn't raise much suspicion, but she couldn't afford to be linked to the park directly. How would she talk her way out of that one?

To eliminate her chances of being noticed in the area, she dropped her car off at a remote access road near Bishop Park. Knowing it was deep in the woods and wouldn't be visible to anyone making the drive up was a little extra comfort. The lack of a trail didn't bother her either. With the shortcut through the brushwood, she was only a couple hundred feet from Jamie's home. She knew the way by heart.

She came up on the park's main strip from the direction of her old cabin, the side of the property she usually avoided on her trips. She was struck by how little the place had worn down over the years. The lawns were cut and the hedges trimmed. It was remarkable. Everything looked exactly the same as the day she'd left. Like the park had never closed.

Hayley sidestepped the gravel road and let her toes brush through the soft grass, savoring every memory that rushed back to her. How many times had she walked this stretch to meet Jamie at the lake or to visit his mom at home?

Time threw her for another loop when she came up to the house. The kitchen window was open as always, and the door propped. A sob hitched in her throat. It was a bittersweet feeling to be standing here again, and she half expected to see Beth leaning into the jambs.

The soundtrack to the familiar clip in front of her was new, though. Whiskey Myers' *Die Rocking* was blasting from the kitchen. She bit back a snicker. It was so Jamie—easygoing and carefree.

She recalled him singing along to Black Stone Cherry back in the day. She wanted to hear that wholehearted laughter of his again.

Hayley halted for a moment outside, giving her appearance another check before poking her head in the door. She knew

236

she was making too much fuss about this, but she wanted it to be perfect.

She swallowed and brushed a strand of hair behind her left ear. It hung loose, tickling her bare shoulders and making her neck break out in a sweat.

Why was she so hot all of a sudden? The breeze had felt nice a minute ago.

More sweat was dripping down her back, and her hands were sweating too. *Dammit.*

She wiped them on her hips, but that only made her more aware of her dress rubbing against her skin.

She was overthinking this. Jamie wouldn't be this nervous. He was the epitome of confidence.

Fuck it. Just go already, she told herself, hurdling the first step up to the door, trying not to trip over her own feet and make an utter fool of herself.

Eh, who was she kidding? That was exactly her shtick.

Hayley leaned in and saw Jamie, head down, staring at the phone in his hand, his shoulder braced against the fridge.

And *DAYUM!* was he swoon-worthy. His plaid shirt was two different shades of denim blue with a white base that looked simply stunning in contrast with his dark hair and black jeans. And he was barefoot.

How does he do it? How does he make this rustic attire so dashing?

His eyes snapped up beneath a rogue curl of hair as her presence triggered his awareness. They made a brief dip down her naked legs before coming back up.

"Hi," she breathed out, her pulse racing.

Instead of returning a hello, a smile stretched across his face, and his chest doubled in size. He looked at her as though she were a dream come true.

Her cheeks heated under his speechless approval. The expression was worth every penny she'd spent on her own outfit. She'd bought everything new for him, from the dress to the strappy heels to the white lace lingerie.

He chucked his phone onto the counter and swooped in, picking up right where they'd left off. He still smelled as good as he had this morning: orange and cedar.

She could have sworn his soap had pheromones mixed into it because the lace between her legs began to melt when she inhaled the intoxicating fragrance. She was practically drooling. And she couldn't get over how tall he was. Most men were intimidated by her in heels.

A contented purr rolled in his throat as he slanted her backward, his arms secured at her waist. Hayley remembered the taste of cigarettes in his kiss. There was no trace of it now. But there was something else. Something she was very familiar with.

"You've been holding out on me," she mumbled in a daze. "You got whiskey, too. Mind sharing."

He pursed his lips at an angle, and his brows pinched together. "That depends. Are you a fun drunk?"

"I'm a horny drunk… aaaand then a sleepy drunk. It's a thin line." She grimaced, tacking on that last bit.

Jamie cracked into a laugh. "Then I better measure your liquor carefully."

He straightened them out, then tipped his head, frowning with concern at the tan, four-inch Steve Maddens caging her feet. "You didn't hike here in these, did you?"

Counting her luck, she probably would've broken an ankle. "No," she admitted, rounding her eyes. "I carried them in my hand."

Jamie snorted and shook his head at the silly effort she was making to impress him. Then the wicked spark reemerged in his vibrant blue irises, his teeth jabbing into his lower lip.

She caught his face in her palms as he dove toward her mouth. His own hands went south… under her dress.

238

Without breaking away from the kiss, he gripped the back of her thighs and lifted her off the ground to move them over to the kitchen island. "I've been hard all day thinking about you," he said, his voice thick with arousal.

She chuckled into his mouth. "You want to fuck me again?"

"*Hell* yes!" He pressed the aforementioned erection against her throbbing clit to prove it. "But I'm going to fuck you with my tongue first."

He sat her down. The modest hemline of her dress bunched around her waist, and Hayley flinched when the cold granite touched her skin.

"I'm going to eat you out right here. On my table. So I can think about this every time I have breakfast… and lunch… and dinner." His teeth nipped at her with each addition, drawing a whimper from her.

"I thought you said I was dessert." Through the narrow slit of her eyelids, she caught a glimpse of the used chopping board next to the sink. What were they having again?

He smiled against her lips. "Did I forget to mention you'd also be the appetizer?"

Her sex pulsed at the promise of him making a meal out of her, and she could already feel the friction between them dampening.

Tipping her head back, she let her eyes fall shut. Jamie urged her further, dragging hot kisses down her throat and chest. The cotton of her dress heated under his breath, then stuck to her skin, where he licked the material covering her.

Laid out on the granite slab before him like a willing sacrifice, she arched up, cradling his head and smothering his moans between her breasts.

His tongue explored her as much as his hands did, thumbs stroking the crease of her hips, and his large, warm palms caressing the outside of her thighs. He slid the lace down her legs, and flames licked in the wake of his touch.

Her fingers in his hair ceased their grazing. "Um… Jamie?"

"Yeah," he drawled as if only half-listening. His mouth kept going lower down her front, his greedy paws equally undeterred.

"What kind of peppers did you chop for the fajitas?"

"Anchos. They're not that hot."

"Oh, but they *are*!" she argued, pushing against his shoulders since he wasn't catching on.

He straightened with reluctance. "You said you liked spicy."

"I'm not talking about the food. It's your hands. They burn."

"Oooh…" His brows winged up as her words clicked. "Well, shit! I swear I washed them three times." Shamefaced, he lifted his palms, offering her an apologetic shrug. Hayley scowled. It wasn't funny.

"Fine," he growled in surrender. "I'll keep my hands to myself. But I can't say the same about my tongue."

Fingertips biting through the cotton layer, he grabbed hold of her hips and pulled her ass over the edge. "This is for making me wait."

And then he went down on his knees, draping her thighs over his shoulders. Hayley yelped when his tongue darted out, but his arms snared her waist to keep her from moving.

His kisses were ruthless. He took without remorse…

And nothing had ever felt better. She locked her ankles behind him, bucking against his face. *This* was what he'd picture every time he had another meal at the table.

Not touching her was too damn hard. His arms wound around her hips, trapping them against his mouth as she squirmed. One palm flat on her belly, the thin cotton layer of her dress was enough of a barrier between his hands and her bare skin.

The taste of her was divine. His tongue lashed at her, unable to get enough.

She came then, her cry of pleasure a sweet melody to his ears, and he sucked her harder, faster, until he nearly came himself. He was so goddamn ready.

"Fuck, Hayley," he growled while straightening between her knees. "For nine years, I have pined over you… Imagined you on your back before me. You're so fucking beautiful."

Her legs draped over the edge of the island as he let go of her to fumble with the fly of his pants. He shoved them down his hips, and—

Shit! He was about to grip his cock to align himself when he reconsidered. No hands on that either. *Damn capsaicin residue.* He really *had* washed his hands three times.

Gripping her sides on top of the cotton instead, he angled his hips and eased into her. Slippery from her arousal, her body gave no resistance. It swallowed him greedily, taking his full length in a single glide until the last inch disappeared inside her folds.

A groan ruptured from his throat. His head fell back, and his mind went blank, safe for the sensation of her wrapped around his shaft.

His hips must've picked up their pumping without conscious thought because Hayley arched to meet him, rocking her body in an undulating motion to match his thrusts.

"Jamie…" Her voice cracked into a whimper.

When he directed his eyes back to her face, he found her stare on him, her eyelids hooded. Beneath her lashes, the pupils were two large black voids.

She was chasing another release.

"God yes, Hayley. Just like that. Let me feel you come."

Her culminating tremors leaked into him. Jameson pulled back. He retreated, almost to the tip, and slammed into her again, urgency tugging at his self-control.

Lips parted, her fingers curled around the hem of his shirt— the only part of him she could reach to pull him closer. Her breaths came in little gasps, shooting out of her in short, quick bursts. Her tits bounced each time their bodies met, nipples taut beneath the thin fabric of her dress.

He watched, eyes glued to her. She looked glorious. Her sounds turned desperate, her movements needy. It was the most beautiful thing he'd ever seen.

A cry broke free as her orgasm peaked. Despite his body screaming for its own release, he didn't rush things. He wanted to savor every clenching pulse she granted him.

But she felt too good. Too hot. Too slick.

Jameson couldn't fight it. A switch flipped. He sped up, pumping faster in and out of her. Hayley's moans and whimpers turned into a chorus of pure euphoria, her body giving into the spasms of her climax, her walls squeezing him.

Bone-breaking tension wound through his muscles. His balls tightened, and he knew this was it. Rearing back, he plunged into her slick passage with a deep thrust that had him seeing stars. A guttural roar ripped from his throat as he let himself go.

Hands fisting her dress, Jameson's body collapsed on top of her, the beat behind his sternum pummeling her chest.

"My sweet virgin," he murmured, his forehead pressed to hers.

Damn. It was over too quickly.

Hayley's arms slid over his shoulders to link at the base of his head. Her fingers grazed through the short hair. "You're never gonna let that go, are you?"

Jameson shook his head, and she sighed in defeat.

They stayed like this, reveling in the afterglow, her legs wrapped around him still, until their breaths deepened.

Slipping from her, he wound his arms around her waist and pulled her up to a sit. "I hope you worked up an appetite."

"I'm starving," she replied in the next beat.

But her tone held a teasing note. The tip of her nose nudged him, and he met her gaze briefly before her lips sealed to his, sweet, gentle, but full of lingering heat nonetheless.

Her palms came down, sliding over his pecs and giving them a squeeze. If she kept at it like this, her touch roving his body, she would have him going back from six to midnight in two minutes flat. The blood would stay down in his cock and never return to his head. She had him begging for a slow death at her hands.

Hell yes! was he going to think of this every time he sat down at the island for a meal.

And it didn't matter that it was over faster than he had liked. The quickie on the island was only the appetizer. He still had the main course to look forward to.

And not to mention dessert.

34

Braced on his elbow beside her, Jamie pressed a kiss to her shoulder. His beard tickled, and Hayley tucked her arm closer to her chest.

"How much time you got left?" he asked, his gaze following the gentle path his fingers were tracing down the curve of her spine.

He couldn't seem to take his eyes off her, as though she were some kind of priceless artifact in a museum to be admired. But apparently, neither could she, as she craned her neck around like an owl. She loved his attention on her. Loved the reaction on his face.

After cooking dinner together, they'd had sex again. On the floor this time. And he'd found the delicate, hidden zipper in the side of her dress without a map—tugged it down so slowly, it had sent chills up her arms from anticipation.

Then they'd fallen asleep on the rug in the living room, tangled, and surrounded by half a dozen throw pillows from the sofa.

His question caught her off guard—snapped her right out of her beautiful daydream. How long had they been lying here?

The sun was shining through all the glass on the south side of the house. In between the windows, a set of French doors she hadn't noticed the first time opened to a porch. It was bright. Hours past sunrise. She had to make it home before it set at six.

Hayley rolled onto her back, avoiding his question. She didn't want to leave. Her eyes traveled up the tall stone fireplace. It had a heavy beam for a mantle that matched the ones that ran across the vaulted ceiling. It was such a beautiful home.

Sliding his knee in between her legs, Jamie moved over her in an attempt to block her view. When she didn't look at him, he pulled her chin toward him. "I don't want to wait another nine years to see you again."

Oh God, what am I doing?

This was wrong. She shouldn't be here. How could she be so selfish?

"Come back next weekend," he pressed.

"I don't know if I can get time away." A scratchy dryness clung to the back of her throat. She dropped her gaze to his bare chest. She couldn't look him in the eyes. They were so open and sincere. *She* was the fraud.

"I'll make it worth your while," he hinted suggestively.

"Oh, I have no doubt that you would." She chuffed a little laugh. He'd probably do that thing with his tongue again.

His finger tilted her chin higher, and his thumb brushed the edge of her bottom lip. "Please."

Her chest tightened. "I'll try," she told him. Because that was all she could promise him in honesty. "And next time, *I* cook," she offered.

"You cook?" He cocked his head to the side. "Don't you have staff at your dad's mansion who do that for you?"

His offhand remark hit a sore spot. "You think I'm that spoiled?"

246

"No. Forget it." Leaning down, he captured her mouth to silence her worry.

His hand dropped to her breast, and her body came alive as he caressed her contours. They felt tender and swollen in his grasp. He drew circles around her taut nipple with his thumb, while his palm fondled the full mound.

Hayley snaked her arm around his waist to his ass. With her nails biting into his skin, she gave his firm muscles a squeeze, too.

A groan ruptured his kiss, and his hips jerked forward.

"You're hard again," she noted.

"No shit! All this talk has me starving. I want to ravage you." He pressed his face against her cheek, breathing heavily. "You going to tell me what's on the menu other than yourself?"

"You strike me as a meat-and-potatoes kinda guy."

"True," he snickered. "I love me some steak. But I like greens too."

Tight glutes, ripped abs, pecs the size of her head… *Yeah, you wouldn't get a formidable physique like that without well-balanced nutrition.*

He tapped her temple with his forehead. "It's a deal, then."

Hayley got behind the wheel and unwrapped the bandage from her right hand. The perfect dream was over, and all she had left was the white strip of cotton. There would be no scar. No mark to prove it had really happened.

She leaned over the center console and unlatched the glove box. Her cell phone was still in there, powered down so it wouldn't send a signal of her location. She'd only brought it along for an emergency. Which was ironic. She'd rather die than make a call for help.

She stuffed the used bandage in between the vehicle's manual and the other crap she hoarded in there like it was her treasure chest. No one but her ever drove this car, and even those times were rare. It served her well as a way to keep secrets.

Blowing out a sigh, she buckled up and pushed the start button for the engine without giving herself another round of guilt. It was time to lock this away like all the other memories she couldn't afford to dwell on.

She'd changed out of the heels and into sneakers for the drive. She knew she had to floor the pedal for the next five hours to make it home before sunset. The staff never inquired about her whereabouts, nor did they mention her absences; it wasn't their place to pry. But she couldn't trust Mateo. If he beat her back, he would make it his business to find out where she'd been, and he definitely wouldn't keep his mouth shut about the fact she'd left the nest all weekend without his supervision. He wasn't on *her* payroll. He only answered to the 'higher power' of the household.

The wild beauty of the Red Rock Lakes National Wildlife Refuge was long gone from her rearview mirror when she pulled up to the estate's gate at a quarter to six. The two black halves winged open slowly, revealing the Tudor castle that was her prison. The exterior was all gray stone, and it lacked the charm of the exposed beams. Overgrown ivy vines made up for that.

Hayley felt suffocated by the mere sight. The huge property was surrounded by eight-foot-tall, solid brick walls on all sides, as well as a top-of-the-line security system. It was anything but homey. Luckily, she was left alone most of the time due to booming business all over the U.S. She preferred to have the place to herself.

She put the wheels of the car back in motion. The driveway was long. It split at the front steps, circling a large oval flower bed to the left and bending around the house to the right.

She maneuvered the Audi around the greenery to the stand-alone garage and all other reserved parking.

The gravel made little popping sounds beneath the tires as she turned into one of the angled spots of the carport. The tense sensation in her shoulders eased when she saw Mateo's spot on her left, still unoccupied. He hadn't come home unexpectedly. Her secret was safe another day.

She shut the engine off and clicked the belt buckle when something else abruptly triggered her sixth sense, drawing her focus out of the passenger side window.

The garage door was open.

She dragged the seat belt slowly back across her body. Cold fingers snaked up her nape. The Levante, of course, wasn't in, but her eyes halted briefly on the car that was. The black beast of a Bentley was slumbering in its den.

The hairs on her arms stood on edge, and she swallowed a dry gulp as her throat constricted.

Her fingers wandered to the center console, popping the latch, her eyes glued to the other vehicle with rising dread.

She found the ring without looking down—the collar that chained her to this place. She slid it back on her left hand, immediately feeling the vise tighten further around her throat.

Before swinging the driver's door wide, Hayley snatched her phone from the glove box, then hopped out to retrieve her suitcase from the trunk.

Dragging it behind her through the gravel, she made her way to the front door. No one greeted her at the entrance. The staff had already retired to their quarters for the night, which suited her just fine. Hayley went up the steps, her Merrells unusually quiet compared to the clicking of heels on the stone.

She unlocked the door with her own set of keys and stepped into the empty foyer. Smokey immediately let out a bark. He came hustling around the corner, his little paws sliding along the tile, bringing a smile to her face.

Hayley crouched to pet him, but he pressed his cold nose into her palm before letting her touch him.

"What are you sniffing, buddy?" she wondered, watching his tail wag from side to side.

The four-year-old Pit Bull dragged his muzzle along her arm and into her chest, picking up on the foreign scent clinging to her.

"You can smell him on me, can't you?" She brushed her hand over the dark gray fur between his perked ears and down the side of his head, nudging his nose with her own. "He'll be our little secret," she whispered.

She needed a shower.

Hayley ruffled his fur some more. He did that kind of happy dance like he was stepping on hot coals, bouncing all over the place with excitement.

"Yeah, I missed you too—"

Smokey's head jerked the same moment she caught the agitated voices upstairs. Both of them were unmistakably familiar to her. One of them was her father. The other...

Her heart plunged into her stomach. Why was Dad here? She hadn't seen him in years.

That was what she'd sensed outside. If he'd come all this way to talk in person, there had to be a reason. What were they plotting? What did they know?

The acidic taste at the back of her throat rose so quickly she barely had time to shoot for the small bathroom in the foyer. She was glad she was wearing sneakers, or she would've broken that ankle after all.

As she hunched over the porcelain bowl, the little pitter-patter behind her drew closer. Smokey had followed her through the cracked door. He shoved his little face into her side, whimpering with concern.

"It's alright, buddy. You know I'll be fine."

It was meant to assure *him,* but she needed to hear the words out loud just as much.

"I won't let him break me," she added quietly under her breath.

Smokey snuggled up in her lap to comfort her as she leaned back into the wall. The old Tudor had never felt like a home to her, but he made it bearable.

Once the front door slammed shut, Hayley snuck upstairs into her bedroom. Her little shadow trotted along silently.

She went into her closet, brushing past the drawers with all her priceless jewelry—rings, bracelets, necklaces... enough diamonds to financially support a small country.

She set her Merrells down on the floor and slipped back into the black Louboutins with the five-inch heels. The sad thing was, her feet didn't even hurt anymore when wearing them. She really *had* grown into the role.

LADY OF THE HOUSE—Blegh! She'd rather live in a cabin in the woods, get her hands dirty digging in the yard, or break a nail climbing a tree.

There was irony in *that*, too. With Jamie, she'd felt like she could finally be herself, and yet around him was when she hid behind a mask. She couldn't tell him the truth. She was forced to slip back into the position fate had dished her. Be the good girl who did as she was told until...

Until when? The day she died? Did her sentence have an expiration date? Was there any hope for her to get out eventually?

If there was an end to it, she couldn't see it. Not until she stopped breathing. Then she'd be free.

35

"Are you cheating on me?"

His gruff voice jolted her focus, and Hayley's guard slipped. "WHAT?"

He tipped his head to the side, and his dark eyes narrowed further into slits. "You sparring with anyone else?" Trevor hinted at her upper arm with a concerned expression when she just stared at him, dumbfounded.

"Bad circulation. I bruise easily." She shrugged, then swung another right hook at him, which he promptly blocked with the padded glove.

In the two months he'd been her personal trainer, he'd never once commented on the dark blotches. She should have worn long sleeves, but it was too damn hot in here. Even he wore a muscle shirt.

"Maybe if you gained some weight, you wouldn't have that problem. You don't have an eating disorder, do you?"

"God, no!" She loved to eat. But she wasn't always able to keep her food down around certain people.

Trevor was a bit taller than her and kept the pads high, blocking his face from view. All she saw of it were his stern brows slanting down and a deep crease in the middle. She wasn't sure he bought the excuse.

Hayley continued her assault. Her fist battered the targets, picturing a particular face. Her knuckles burned, and honestly, it felt good. Every day, she fought the urge to punch a hole in the wall, but she knew it wouldn't get her out of her cage. He would only draw the steel bars closer. Working out was her escape. Here, he couldn't control her.

Outside of the house, she didn't interact with anyone; she didn't have any friends. That was why Thursdays were the most fun. There was no stress about getting sweaty with Trevor in public because everyone knew he was gay, and since the mugging four weeks ago, she'd started to put more effort into it. You never knew when you were going to need it. Things had happened so fast that morning. One second she was drawing money from the ATM, and the next she had a knife to her throat.

What were the odds she was attacked on the one day a week Mateo had off?

The guy hadn't been interested in her wallet, though. He'd jostled her into the alley around the corner to get a piece of *her* instead.

Good thing it had been a knife and not a gun. Thanks to her self-defense training from Trevor, she'd been able to get away mostly unharmed.

The cops had never followed up. Which was no surprise. They had no leads since she hadn't been much help in describing the perp with a ski mask—average height, average build, average everything.

After the workout, she took a shower, then Mateo escorted her back to the house, presumably to lock her up and throw away the key.

He wasn't the chatty type, so they usually rode in silence, but the stoic lines on his face appeared harder than they'd been this morning. Hayley assumed he was in his early forties. It was difficult to tell. His features were carved from stone, without laugh lines or wrinkles around the eyes to give him character. She'd never even seen him flinch in the seven years she'd known him.

She fussed with the zipper on the gym bag in her lap, thinking about tomorrow and the promise she'd made. A heavy feeling settled in her gut. What would Jamie think if she didn't show? She didn't want to be a liar, but what had she really done to try and make it?

Mateo pulled the Lincoln up to the front steps, then came around to open the coach-type door on her side. Sunlight flooded in the second he cracked the seal, blinding her. The tinted windows had bathed the backseat in darkness, and her vision needed a second to adjust.

When she climbed out, he didn't meet her eyes. Her braid, which was still damp, lay heavy across her shoulder, and a chill rolled down her spine. Something was off.

Hayley took the steps up, and someone opened the door from the inside. She wasn't sure who, because her attention was immediately drawn to the slender figure rushing down the stairs, a suitcase in each hand, and his ass on fire.

Not literally, but he sure was in a hurry—

Hayley froze mid-thought, her heartbeat quickening. They were *her* suitcases.

What the fuck?

Her hands clutched the rough straps of her gym bag tighter. Right behind the diligent butler was Tia, beaming like a child despite her fifty-three years of age. She was carrying her own suitcase and paused next to Hayley in the middle of the foyer.

"He will meet you at the airport," Randall huffed, brushing past her on his way out the door.

He will WHAT? She never went on business trips with him.

Her head followed his direction, and she watched in horror as his skinny arms hefted the luggage into the trunk of the car. She could feel Tia beaming behind her, and the pain was like a knife in her back. The woman was her personal maid and the only confidant she had besides Smokey. What fresh hell awaited them.

"Where are we going?" Hayley spoke over her shoulder, her muscles so stiff she couldn't turn her head.

She'd had more nannies than she could count, but Tia was her one constant maid since her mother's passing. The plastic wheels of her suitcase squeaked on the pristine mahogany floor as she put it into motion and cheered, "Home!"

Marcus' throaty laugh coughed through the speaker like he was choking. "How's that hand, by the way? Would suck to lose function of a tight grip. You'd have to start jerking off with your left."

"Blow me," he grunted, putting the phone down beside him so he could keep typing.

"Pass. But I can find you someone who will. You just need to get your ass out here."

"Not gonna happen."

It was that *helpful* attitude that had kicked the shitshow off last time when the surprise birthday party his college buddies had thrown him went from bash to *bashing-in*.

Yeah, he might have stopped starting fights, but he was still always the one to finish them. Usually with his right hook. That was why he didn't like parties. Or surprises. Or secrets. His blood still ran hot too easily.

He should've known not to go to the second bar. Nothing good ever came from that. Much like decisions made after 2 a.m. You either stay at the first location or go home. And he should've gone home.

"Come on, man. They want you to take a look at the project on site."

Jameson's fingers stopped sweeping over the keyboard, and he took the phone back in his hand, adjusting it to his ear. "They're paying me to fly to California?" *Shit.* Was that good or bad?

"They want to hear the opinion of the guy who came up with the insane design."

He ran a hand through his hair and leaned back against the headboard. That had never happened before. "And they can't do that over the phone?" He held his breath for the reply.

"Apparently not."

Damn. The air shot from his lungs with a sigh. He really didn't want to go. He'd have to drive all the way home to get the plans he hadn't brought down to the park with him. He didn't even have a desk here; that was why he currently worked from his bed. But the view out from the back porch was a bonus.

Of course, he had another reason for not wanting to leave on a Thursday. He probably wouldn't return until Saturday.

Though, to be honest, he had a bad feeling about Hayley coming back. Something in her eyes had told him not to get his hopes up. They'd had an amazing weekend together. End of story. He couldn't put shit on hold for her. He'd worked too hard for this.

"So, does your silence mean you're coming?" Marcus poked. "I didn't think I'd have to use her to twist your arm, but it was actually Tatum's request. She's been asking for you."

Jameson chuckled and relaxed into the pillow. Maybe the problem wasn't as bad as he'd feared. "Does she want to chew me out again?"

"I don't know what she has in mind, but you're the only one who can give her exactly what she wants. You have a way with her."

He had a way with her? Of all the people close to her. Who'd have thought? But Marcus knew Jameson couldn't say *no* to her.

"Fine," he relented. "Whatever the boss wants. I'll take the next flight out."

If she requested to see him, then it ought to be important. And who was he to keep a lady waiting?

36

Hayley kept her nose buried in her Kindle, still pretending to read. Well, on the flight, she'd actually *been* reading—while sipping champagne—so now she was too buzzed to focus on the letters in front of her. They all blurred. Never mind, though. She could still pretend. And hey, maybe if she threw up, she could blame it on some bug she'd caught, giving her a reason to fly back early.

The nausea was worth avoiding conversation. They'd never shared any common interests. Better to save her breath—

Her body lurched left, then forward, the seat belt cutting into her skin at her chest as the car veered. Their driver slammed on the brakes and cursed at the "fucking redneck with a cowboy hat" who'd cut them off in his bright red F350.

The engine of the beast roared and quickly left them in the dust, but their driver continued his verbal assault, shaking his fist and cursing at no one.

Under different circumstances, Hayley would've laughed. In her current situation… not so much.

The AC made the temperature inside bearable, but the few seconds out in the heat had been enough to get a sweat going.

Her face itched under all the makeup, and so did her scalp. It was torture not to dig her fingers into her hair and scrub the whole mess.

The leather seat stuck to the back of her arms and legs. She'd changed into more 'presentable attire' on the private jet, but the dress was uncomfortably short; not something she'd pick on her own.

Her eyes dropped below the tablet in her hands to her crotch, and she could almost see her underwear. No matter how many times she tugged the hem down, it crept back up. How was she expected to walk around in that?

Hayley clenched her teeth so hard they ached from the pressure. She hated this. Hated being a puppet. Hated all of it. She wanted to scream.

It was the alcohol that kept her rage at bay. But it was there. Bubbling right beneath the surface.

Traveling light had its advantages. The fact that he only had a backpack and no bag to check had definitely saved his ass. He'd nearly missed his flight because of his little detour home. Thank God, he hadn't run into any Amber. It had been a quick in and out.

The drive north from the airport was under an hour, according to GPS, but traffic always sucked. It could take him longer, and he hated wasting time on the road. Between the car and the plane, he'd spend more time traveling than actually getting stuff done.

Jameson kept his fingers crossed that Marcus could handle the rest on his own, as long as he got things sorted out. Hopefully, he could fly back tomorrow.

260

He didn't like the West Coast heat. It stoked his temper.

He came up to the gate and rolled his window down to press the button on the intercom. Instead of a request for his name, the gruff voice from the speaker greeted him with a flat "Welcome, Mr. Davis" and the iron hinges went into motion.

Mr. Davis, he chuckled. He could picture the dusty old butler in his stiff tailcoat suit standing behind the front door. That guy was a hoot. Jameson would never get used to that shit. Such formality for him? Made him feel all tingly on the inside, he might blush. He wasn't merely expected, after all. His presence had been *requested.*

On the drive up to the main house, he tried not to gawk too long. The place looked like old money. Smelled like it too. It wasn't his world, and he had no interest in getting sucked into it.

A familiar face waved him down at the front, in the casual attire of blue jeans and a plain button-down that were right up his own alley and equally ill-suited for a place like this.

Jameson hopped out of the rental and marched toward Marcus, who was awaiting him on the lawn.

"How you liking them wheels?" His friend nodded back at the truck he'd reserved for him at the airport.

"They'll do," he barked. "But I prefer a Chevy."

It had handled the damn limo blocking the lane pretty nicely, though.

"How's Emily?" Jameson asked to the side, where his friend paced him to the back of the house, hands in his pockets.

"Eh, you know, about ready to pop and cranky as fuck."

"Wasn't she due two days ago?"

Lips drawn tight, he gave a frustrated *mm-hmm* sound for a reply, keeping his eyes to the ground. His black hair was matted down by sweat, and his deep-set brown eyes had dark rings around them. His worry made him appear way older than Jameson instead of a year younger.

He and Emily had been married for less than a year. To think of him as a dad seemed crazy. He'd be the first one out of their circle. Though he wasn't the only one married. Only two remained single.

"Terry's getting hitched next month."

Scratch that.

Jameson stopped walking. He turned toward Marcus, throwing his hands up. "He's known her for three weeks! How can they even *think* about getting married?"

"I don't know, man." His friend gave an easy shrug. "The heart wants what the heart wants."

"Oh, spare me that bullshit, like you believe in love at first sight." He swung back around and kept walking. "It's a load of crap. Only girls believe in that shit." Yeah, he knew he sounded like a cynical old grump.

Marcus' heavy sigh came across as a personal attack.

"Shut up," Jameson snapped before the wiseass could open his mouth. And here he thought he'd dodged all talk of his own marital status today.

"Look, I'm not saying you should rush into something like this. But you shouldn't be too picky, either. You might miss out on the perfect thing that's right in front of you. Amber is—"

Nope. He didn't want to talk about her. Jameson whipped around, pinning him into the Greek balustrade of the deck that ran around the house. Fist twisted in the man's shirt at his shoulder, and forearm pressed into his clavicles, he hissed low. "Drop it! I'm not in the mood."

"It's cool, man. None of my business." Marcus didn't take offense. He'd known Jameson's temper long enough. He raised his palms in surrender, no shock or fear in his eyes. They were the same calm brown, staring back at him.

262

He exhaled a sharp breath through his nose. What the fuck was he doing attacking his friend? All he did was offer some advice.

His empty stomach twisted. The guilt reminded him of the lunch he'd skipped in his rush. "I'm sorry," he muttered as he backed off, looking down.

He stabbed his forefinger and thumb into his eyelids to rub out the frustration nagging at him. Low blood sugar and the heat were a bad combo.

"Don't worry about it. We're good," he said, burying his knuckles in Jameson's shoulder.

The return punch came like a reflex, knocking Marcus back a step.

Lightweight.

They both broke into a laugh right when a text came in on the other's phone. Marcus whipped it out and stared at the screen, eyeballs popping out of their sockets in full-blown panic mode.

"Shit! I forgot. She wanted me to pick up more ice cream."

Jameson reared back, a hand pressed to his chest. "Dude, you should see the look on your face. She's got you pissing your pants." He shook his head. "Seriously, your little woman is not that scary."

His friend shot him a quick glance as he typed a reply. "Oh, you have no idea. I gotta split. She's gonna be so pissed," he added in a low mumble to himself.

"Sounds like someone's sleeping in the dog house tonight. Good luck with that."

"Yeah, you just wish you had my life."

Bold claim.

Jameson drilled a finger into his friend's chest. "You're whipped. Ain't nobody wanting that. You used to be a tough son of a bitch, Rodrigues. You've gone soft." He gave him another shove to the chest, with both hands this time.

"Stop. I get enough of that from my wife."

"Your wife calls you soft, too?" he heckled. "Wow! Not sure my male pride could take that hit."

Marcus rounded his eyes and stuffed the phone back into his pocket, but Jameson didn't let up. He kept poking. "Look at you all, smitten and shit. Always smiling. What happened to that grouchy motherfucker I used to know, huh?"

The accused tipped his head, then said, "He fell in love, asshole. You should give it a try instead of running from it."

Yeah, maybe he was jealous. So, he held his tongue and cut the man some slack.

His eyes flicked over Marcus's shoulder to the shifting curtain in the window.

Okay, *awkward*. Now the butler was glaring out the window, watching them act like idiots instead of grown-ass adults.

"Go." Jameson jerked his chin. "Tell her I said *hi*."

Marcus started walking off, then turned back. "Hey, you staying at the same shady motel again?"

Jameson scoffed. "Yeah. It suits me."

"You should stop by for dinner."

"And play buffer between you and Em?"

"Oh, she won't hold back in front of you." He grinned. "You're family."

"Alright. I'll be there."

Marcus nodded, then started moving toward his truck.

"Don't tell the guys I'm in town," Jameson called after him over his shoulder. "I don't need them throwing me another party."

First bloody fight in a long time. He shook his head again as he trudged up to the object in question, wondering why the fuck he was back here at all.

37

Jameson regarded the structure, tilting his head to the left. Sometimes ideas came to him while he stood back and simply stared at it from a different angle. He was the one devising the construct, but Marcus was in charge of putting it into reality.

They were a good team. Together with his crew, they created immersive play environments beyond the average tree house. All with a rustic flair. The wood looked weathered and worn, giving each project a unique, not to mention slightly haunted, appearance. Kids loved it.

This was their largest undertaking yet. Two stranded halves of a pirate ship emerged from the ground, painted in faded black and red. Tattered sails that fluttered in the wind were hoisted on the masts, with the skull and crossbones flag flying on the very top. There were rope ladders dropped from the eagle's nest and cross beams, as well as functioning water cannons that shot off the sides. The balloon launcher sat at the bow of the ship, ready to take out the enemy from a distance.

A warm feeling of accomplishment settled in his chest, along with pride. The details were perfect, exactly as he'd imagined. It was nearly finished. He couldn't, for the life of him, figure out what the problem could be.

The rich couple who'd commissioned him were a bunch of stiffs who hardly gave him the time of day. Everything had been arranged through their personal assistant, and Jameson had been prepared to hate the job from the start.

Luckily, it hadn't been all bad. The build was for their kids, and funny enough, he liked the rugrats better than he liked their parents. They weren't the spoiled brats he'd expected. Probably because they'd been raised predominantly by nannies with better manners than the adults around them.

So what do you know? He actually liked kids. Little ones anyway. Fuck teenagers and their low work ethic. He'd fired enough of them already.

He'd scrapped his original design for the tree house after meeting the two for the first time. It was the girl's personality that inspired the change. He wanted to create something special that was unique to them both, engaging for the older girl but also accessible for the short legs and small hands of her three-year-old brother, Elliot.

In the end, the outspoken young lady had given him all the ideas herself. He liked to think of her as his boss. If she didn't approve, it was back to the drawing board for him.

What could've gone wrong?

Jameson glanced over his shoulder at the sound of a door falling shut. Tatum came skipping down the yard, beaming when she saw him. There was a big gap where her left front incisor should've been.

"Hey," he pointed out, "You lost another tooth."

"Yep. Fell out dis morning. Toof Fairy gave me ten dollars for it." Her grin stretched wider, and she poked at the empty space with her tongue.

"Ten, huh?" He popped a squat to her eye level. "I only used to get one."

Tatum pointed her big, green eyes—the size of headlights—at him. A spark of expectation twinkled in them. "Do you like it?"

"I do."

How could he not? She was proud of the pirate reference. That one had been *her* big contribution.

Tatum wasn't a girly girl who wanted to dress like a princess. She liked the villains. She currently stood in front of him, barefoot, in tan cargo shorts with a saber dangling from a wide leather belt. It was wrapped loosely around her hips instead of going through the loops. Her top was multi-layered despite the heat; white cap sleeves protruded from under her dark brown tank top. She'd also tied her long blonde hair back with a red bandana to show off the golden hoops bouncing below her ears every time she moved her bobblehead.

So there's a little girl under there after all.

"Will you build one like it for your kids, too?"

He shook his head. "I don't have any," he said, as if apologizing for a deficiency.

"Why not?"

"I'm not married."

"You don't have to be married to have kids."

Damn. Talking to her was like a tennis match, and she was on the serve. "True. But I prefer it in that order," Jameson admitted.

He wanted the kind of love he'd seen in his parents every single day. Dad had been four years older than Mom. He'd worked at the camp part-time as a teenager to get away from his foster parents and still off and on after joining the Marines. Dad had told him that he'd always had a crush on Mom and that she was the reason he'd stuck around.

"You should get married soon. You're old," Tatum pointed out, her little voice laced with a reprimand.

Gee thanks. And another point for her.

"Not really on my to-do list at the moment," he informed her sheepishly. Her curiosity knew no boundaries. She was kind of intimidating.

"So, what's the big problem, little lady? Why'd you call me all the way out here? Your parents can't be too thrilled about paying unnecessary expenses."

"You know how there's more parts to a galleon, right?" she remarked in an authoritative tone.

Of course. Silly me!

Counting on her fingers, she rattled off, "There is the captain's cabin, a dinghy, and just lots more wood to use."

He chuckled, catching on. "Okay, so you want a third piece?"

"Yes! A tall one. Like a tree house." Her eyes sparkled even brighter now as she reached her hand up above her head and went onto her toes to emphasize how tall she wanted it. "With a rope going all the way to the top."

Jameson stared off at the vacant space between the two ship halves that would put all three in a triangle formation and let his imagination run free.

He could see the pointed bow of the dinghy as a door frame leading into a tree house made of the cabin's parts... a five-foot climbing wall... a second level with a corkscrew slide attached to it, and another straight out on the opposite side...

The longer he stared at it, the more details came together. Tatum was his muse.

"You know," Jameson said, smiling back at her, "I think I can work with that."

He winked, then pushed off to stand. "Is Andrew inside?" Her father's PA had to approve of the addition. "You know I have to run this by him first, right?"

"Oh, my parents are on board. 'No expenses spared,' Daddy said."

Jameson blinked. "You already ran this by your parents? And they're okay dropping more cash on your little adventure land?" She really was on top of her priorities.

"Of course." She flashed him another toothy grin. "No one can say *no* to me."

Yeah, Jameson fucking loved his job.

38

She was running out of time. But she couldn't let on how desperate she was to return to Salt Lake City. Or why. She needed to cause a fight. Anything to give her reason to fly back home early.

Hayley tipped the narrow glass back, avoiding the view of him in front of the mirror, fidgeting with the cufflinks. He knew better than to ask her for help. He stood there, judging her from across the room with his condescending stare in his fucking Armani suit—all black, even the shirt, but no tie.

She wanted to hurl the crystal flute at his back.

"I see you started your drinking early this morning." His reflection darted her another narrow-eyed glance over his shoulder as he tugged on the cuff, his wrist up.

One mimosa hardly counts as 'drinking'.

"I ordered you breakfast." He went on talking over her because she wasn't going to argue the obvious. "Have some food with that, will you? I don't need you to make a fool of yourself this afternoon." He turned, and this time his actual eyes bored into her. "And maybe try to be less of a disappointment for a daughter while we're here."

"And you would know what it means to live up to your own father's expectations, wouldn't you?"

The large vein in his forehead throbbed, and his eyes darkened. Yes, it was always a sore subject for him—*the dutiful son.*

She wondered whether her grandfather would approve of the theatrics or roll over in his grave? Hayley had never met him. The old man had died before she was born, leaving his business empire to her father. But the full weight of its survival rested on her shoulders alone.

His eyes shot to Tia and then back to her. He didn't want to make a scene, not even in front of staff, but behind closed doors, it was a different matter. The remark would have earned her a slap across the face. Hayley was very aware of that. She played the game, too. And Tia knew her place. She'd keep her mouth shut.

His freshly shaven jaw ticked, his voice forced low with practiced restraint. "Nice try. But you won't get a rise out of me today, *darling*," he stressed through his clenched teeth and strode over to the desk. Even his gait was eerily calm.

He took his suit jacket off the back of the chair and slipped one arm inside, then the other. "I'll be back before lunch to pick you up."

He straightened the lapels without a double-check in the mirror and swung toward the door of the room, shutting it quietly behind himself.

Right. Because they had to make regular public appearances together. Didn't want people talking behind their backs.

Hayley dragged her tongue along her teeth, gripping the feeble stem of the champagne flute.

Fuck lunch!

She slammed the glass down on the side table. "Pack your bag, Tia. We're flying back to Utah."

272

39

Jameson shut the fridge and popped the cap on the last *PBR*. He was back in his own kitchen by Friday night. The trip had been smooth, and all worries were ungrounded. Marcus would take care of the rest.

Stalking through the dark living room, he started the playlist on his phone over. It was almost 10 p.m. and pitch black beyond the trees now.

He dropped his phone on the small glass table and ran a hand through his still-wet hair. There was a subtle breeze going. It felt nice on his skin, as he was wearing only sweatpants. No shirt.

Sinking into the wicker chair, he kicked his feet up on the stone ledge of the unlit fire pit and leaned his head back. He couldn't wait for fall. He'd sit out here every night.

Marcus was right. The motel had been shady. It had also been noisy. Jameson loved the quiet out here, besides the music. No cars, sirens, yelling, or other city noise. Only peace.

He wondered how much longer it would take him to finish. The wall separating the kitchen from the living room had been the first thing to go. Then he'd refinished the cabinets, switched the handles for more modern hardware, and installed the barn doors in Mom's old—now *his*—bedroom for access to the bathroom and closet.

Ah, yes, the closet. His next project. It had always been too small. He'd never understood why Mom had refused to rip out the wall between that and the storage closet from the hallway. It would make the whole thing so much bigger. There wasn't much stored in the other room anyway. Just a few boxes.

He raised the bottle to his mouth, hardly taking his eyes off the twinkling stars above.

"Got any more?"

Jameson jerked forward, spilling from the top of the bottle and coughing up what had already made its way down his esophagus.

What the fuck?

He hunched over, neck craned to his right. Hayley grinned from the edge of the deck as she leaned her shoulder against the house. She looked like a fever dream in that flowy dress, the color of seafoam. The hem brushed along her ankles in the breeze.

He wondered if she could see his heart trying to leap out of his chest. It was pounding so hard, it hurt.

"Do you?" Her eyebrows winged up, waiting for an answer.

Did she ask a question? Jameson blinked rapidly, then cleared his throat. "Sorry. Fresh out," he replied once he recovered his speech.

She kicked off the siding and strolled his way. "Share?"

"Sure."

He ran a hand down his crotch to wipe the spilled beer, discreetly adjusting the tent in his sweats while he was at it.

Hayley dragged the second wicker chair close and dropped down beside him. He held the bottle out to her.

"You look surprised to see me," she said, taking the *PBR* from him. "Did I catch you in your PJs?"

A smirk danced on her lips before they parted and touched the glass rim, the tip of her tongue making a quick appearance.

It was so hot. His throat suddenly felt as dry as bone. He needed that drink back, stat. Either that, or suck what he needed to survive from her directly.

"Just the top half." He put his hand on his chest in a suggestive manner. "I usually sleep naked."

He leaned over, snatching the beer from her grasp, but he didn't lift it to his mouth yet. "And *YES*, to answer your question," he extended his pointer toward her, the rest of his fingers clutching the bottle. "I *am* surprised to see you."

"Why?" Training her attention on him, she propped her left elbow on the armrest, tucking in her legs and curling more into the basket.

"I wasn't convinced you wanted to."

"I promised I would."

Jameson shook his head. "No. You promised to *try*. Don't think I didn't catch the loophole." He leaned back again, repositioning his legs on the fire pit.

Hayley crossed her arms over the tall side of the chair and lowered her chin. She was so drop-dead gorgeous in the golden glow of the porch lights, her eyes like two silver stars looking up at him from underneath her lashes. He couldn't stop staring.

"But I *did* want to. I came as soon as I could." Her gaze dropped apologetically. "I'm sorry about dinner."

Shit. He'd been home for hardly thirty minutes—only enough to take a shower. If he'd taken the later flight into West Yellowstone, he wouldn't even be back for another two hours.

Talk about close calls.

Jameson really hadn't expected her to show. But that didn't mean he'd been prepared for the disappointment to kick him in the jewels when he came home and didn't find her waiting out front.

"Eh, don't sweat it." He wouldn't complain. She was here now. That was all that mattered.

But he did wonder what kind of obstacles she had to hurtle that prompted her to use the term 'try' to come see him.

Jameson brought the bottle up and took another drink, then handed it back to her. He noticed that her dress had a modest neckline, something Mom would have worn when she was younger.

The thin straps draped loosely over her slender shoulders, like they were barely hanging on. Combined with the pale hue of the cotton, there was something pure about her appearance. She still looked like his virgin.

He dropped his legs and rose from the chair. Standing tall in front of her, he brushed a lock of her hair from her face, tracing the curve of her cheek with his thumb.

Warmth flooded every inch of him, and his cock twitched as he hovered over her for a moment, regarding her from his high vantage point.

Yeah, he fucking loved the view of her like that. Her face was all innocence, but behind those eyes, she was thinking the same thing.

He let his hand drop and tugged the almost empty longneck from her fingers. He set it down at the edge of the fire pit, then took her soft hands in his, pulling her to her feet.

Hayley's coy grin melted into something seductive right out of a playbook. Palms to his pecs, her body was warm and soft against his hard contours.

As he wrapped one arm around her waist, the fabric of her dress slid across her smooth skin. With a gentle nudge, he angled her chin toward him and pressed a kiss to her lips. Subtle at first, then becoming more bold.

Hayley reciprocated his fervor with a moan, sinking into him.

Jameson jerked away abruptly, cutting the connection.

"What are you doing?" she cried when he dipped down and swung her over his shoulder.

Hinged at the waist, her nails clawed at his ass, and all his blood rushed from his head to his groin. He felt himself swell, growing thick with an erotic greed he couldn't wait to satisfy. He'd keep her up all night.

Left arm around the back of her legs, he pinned her thighs to his chest. "You owe me dinner." He gave her rear a slap and spun toward the living room.

An hour later, Hayley slipped from his grasp. She reached for his hat on the side table, putting it on her head and shooting him a skeptical look. "Cowboy hat, huh? Did that punk finally grow up?"

"Nah." Jameson snickered, rubbing his hand across his jaw, the bristles of his beard rough on the pads of his fingertips. "He still lurks around. Especially at night. He prefers the dark."

She moved her body to the music still coming from the Bluetooth speaker hooked up to his phone. She was wearing the shirt he'd left on the sofa chair—the blue Harleyville, his favorite.

The fabric was insanely soft, and he could imagine how it felt on her bare skin. Her hardened nipples stood out even with the distracting plaid pattern. It looked great against her tan complexion. And that cowboy hat... *fuck*. The only thing missing were the boots.

The shirt was held together only by a single button in the middle of her perfect tits, straining and begging him for its release. She teased the lucky little fucker with her fingernails, rolling her shoulders back seductively.

Whiskey Myers *Frogman* was playing, and she made the rhythm work for her. The way she swayed her ass made him see stars. She put her hands on her knees, spreading them apart as she lowered herself down and then rose back up.

How she still had the strength to stand after their heavy oral foreplay earlier was beyond his comprehension.

He'd have to fix that. And he didn't care that it was three thirty in the morning.

Placing her palms on the armrests on either side of him, she bent forward. His eyes dropped on a reflex as gravity got a hold of the shirt, giving him a clear shot in between her tits down to her lace panties.

He'd taken off her dress but left them on as he'd eaten her sweet pussy from behind while bending her over the back of the chair he was now sitting in. Twice, she'd climaxed. Three fingers deep, her honey had poured like water down his wrist, primed to receive the full size of his shaft.

But he'd only given her a little taste. After making her come again, and the pulsing of her walls had subsided, he'd pulled out and spun her around.

She'd scooted down on the seat between his knees and taken him into her mouth without a moment's hesitation. He'd slid along her tongue and the roof of her mouth to the back of her throat in one thrust, so deep he'd choked back a whimper.

Her eagerness to taste herself on him had made him snap. One fist in her hair, the other one gripping the backrest of the chair, he'd retreated and driven in again to the hilt, the glide so smooth she'd felt like heaven. He couldn't get enough of her. And when he'd finished, and her throat bobbed from swallowing all of him down, he'd pulled out to claim her mouth with his.

Jameson's chest fell and rose faster as he watched her dance. He'd *never* get enough of her.

He was only partially aware of his teeth tugging on his lower lip. In front of him, Hayley straightened and spun around, showing off the lacy butterfly-back panties that only covered half of her ample cheeks—and would undoubtedly be the death of him. He wanted to sink his teeth into the plump flesh again.

Her smooth brown locks spilled out beneath the hat and bounced with the swing of her hips. Not able to hold himself back any longer, he kicked to his feet and came up behind her.

The heat between their bodies increased to a blaze. She threw a kinky smirk over her shoulder before turning to face him.

He snatched the hat from her head and put it on himself, lowering his lips to hers. He curled his tongue into her mouth, feeling her shiver against him.

At last, he reached up to pop the button. Using only his index fingers, he split the two halves of the shirt further, dragging it over the pebbled tips and exposing the full view of her magnificent breasts.

He picked her up, one arm around her waist, the other hooked around the back of her knee. He wanted to carry her to his bed, but then remembered the deal they'd made and reminded himself that he needed to let her go again.

So he dropped to his knees instead, taking them both to the floor.

Hayley could hardly keep up. Four times he'd already made her come—had climaxed twice himself. The man's sexual appetite was insatiable.

And now they were in the shower, his hunger as voracious as the moment his mouth had first claimed her. Blue gaze low and heady, Jamie caged her against the wall with his enormous body.

Hayley baffled about the conflicting sides of him. There was tenderness in his touch… in his kiss… in the way he looked at her. But there was also raw passion he couldn't hide. His hands became rough. His fingers dimpled her thighs as the harshness of his mouth bruised her lips, depriving them both of oxygen.

Yes, he was fierce as he took her. He squeezed, pinched, and bit, but not to cause harm. Only to draw more pleasure from her. With the steady drive of his hips, deep and unrelenting, his hard chest crushed her breasts against him. And yet there was nothing brutal about his movements. He sank into her again and again, caught up in the combined ecstasy of their bodies.

Hayley dragged her nails over his back. Water rained down on them, washing away the sweat they'd worked up.

Jamie's kisses dipped lower. Hot, labored breaths rolled down her sternum, and his eyes were so dark and hazy there was no blue left.

The sight was startling. He was an image of pure male lust, drunk on his desire for her.

Holding her gaze, he captured one of her breasts in his mouth, while at the same time filling her to the brim again. Hayley gasped on her inhale. A matching groan caught somewhere between Jamie's throat and the seal of his lips on her full mound. His heavy lashes fluttered.

Trapped in the heat of his mouth, his tongue drew little wet circles around her nipple. Whimper after whimper, his sensual attention coaxed from her.

Hayley watched. The vision of him pushed her closer to the edge, and the pressure built in her womb. Her thighs trembled around his waist. Her breath juddered.

"Jamie, please… I need to come."

He fucking smiled then. She caught that glint in his eyes as he sucked her harder, teeth dipping into the tender flesh while his fingers teased the other side.

The pain was sharp. As was the climax that lanced through her at his command. Her breasts surged against him. Her spine arched.

Hayley cried out his name, and he increased his tempo. The rapid pace behind his hips as he pumped into her made her head spin. She forgot how to breathe. There were no conscious thoughts. Only the force of his thrusts, reaching the very last parts of her each time he retreated and slammed home again.

His large muscles contracted under the strain of his exertion. His voice was no longer human; a predator's deep growl filled her ears. And Haley embraced it. She gripped him tighter. She wanted it all. Both sides of him. The tender with the rough. The sweet with the depraved.

Because that was passion. More than simply lust. More than an obsession. And far beyond any obligation.

It felt like freedom.

But it felt like something else too. Something she was afraid to name.

Hayley buried her face in Jamie's neck, hoping that he wouldn't notice the tears… that the shower would hide her shame.

She was fully aware that each moment they shared could be their last. She would have to return to *him*.

40

Hayley had left him a phone message, telling him to shove his lunch up his ass. What was he going to do? He couldn't come after her immediately. He had business to handle in Cali until late Sunday morning. She would deal with the fallout of her petty tantrum then.

She'd left Jamie's early to give herself plenty of time to return. As she curled up in the tufted green velvet, awaiting her punishment, the front door opened, followed by a gruff "Is she here?" and Randall's "Yes, sir. In the library." response.

The butler's words were muffled through the door, but she was familiar with the routine reply.

Her spine steeled, and her thumbs pressed into the pages of the open book in her lap. She expected him to barge in any second now to rip into her.

But he didn't. His footsteps thudded up the carpeted staircase, then died in his bedroom shortly thereafter.

Her eyes rolled toward the high ceiling apprehensively, tracking his movement. He was right above her, his room adjacent to her own. She still had to face him tonight. This wasn't over.

Hayley blew out the breath she'd been holding. Her gaze landed back on the book. The ink had smudged where her thumbs sat. She didn't want to apologize for ditching and embarrassing him in public. No doubt, he'd come up with an easy excuse for her absence, but there was only so much his suave charisma could sell on its own. He needed her by his side for appearance reasons.

He'd be furious with her, and this time he wouldn't have the same inhibitions holding him back. It was just the two of them in the house. Tia didn't live with them. She only came around to help her get ready for special events—hair, makeup, dress, the whole spiel. Oh, yeah, and to pack her bags for short-notice trips Hayley herself wasn't informed about, naturally.

The gardener came by once a week; the cleaning staff twice. Randall was in charge of the daytime housekeeper and kept things in order, though both of them were little more than ghosts to her. They hardly crossed paths. Hayley lived in the library—mostly—and, yes, she did also make her own food. Except for dinner. That was usually prepared by a personal chef with all the pomp and circumstance that was necessary to fake a family meal together. Including a small wait staff.

She couldn't imagine he'd want to share a meal with her tonight. He needed to cool off first.

Is he afraid he'd overstep and take his anger too far?

She wasn't scared of him. She would survive him.

Half an hour later, Hayley closed her book and pushed off the French chaise. Holding her chin high, she went upstairs.

She was marching down the second-floor landing when his voice stopped her at the open door to the office.

"Feeling better?" he prompted from inside.

She pivoted around to spare him a little attention. He'd changed into a t-shirt that had a relaxed fit on his frame. It was dark green. Hands splayed, he braced his weight on the desk.

"I do. Thanks for asking. Must've been some 24-hour bug. Maybe something I ate." She shrugged blithely, ready to move along.

"Aren't you interested in what we discussed?"

"No, not really."

She was more interested in the weather report. The news had warned of this year's monsoon season catching a second wind. More severe storms were expected over the next few weeks that could cause highway and interstate closures going north due to the lake flooding.

The area around Willard's Bay was most affected. And with the storms getting so bad, his flights would get canceled too. Then they'd both be stuck here.

But maybe it wouldn't come to that, and he would soon hop on another plane to Las Vegas, Phoenix, Denver, Dallas, or wherever else he needed to build connections.

His shoulders flexed under tension. She waited for him to say something else as he held his stare in a level challenge and his jaw twitched. But he didn't.

"Anyway, enjoy your night." Hayley flashed a curt smile and kicked off toward her room at the end of the hall.

Smokey's collar jingled after her with a clear declaration.

Hayley touched her shaking hands to her temples. Her skull was pounding from inside. She'd skipped dinner on Sunday only to avoid going by his room again, then barely made it through last night, relying heavily on wine.

Nursing the hangover now, she wondered for a moment if her rebellion was worth it. But she didn't want to roll over and die. Her pride wouldn't let her. Giving up would mean letting them win. And that was unacceptable.

"You thinking white or tan for the shoes?" Tia asked, pulling the zipper up on Hayley's dress.

"Hmmm." *The dress is white, so…* "How about red?"

Her maid's eye twitched like she was about to have an aneurism. They both knew the prick in the adjoining room wouldn't approve of her drawing that kind of attention, especially with him being tonight's guest of honor. And he was already in a foul mood. Holed up in his office, he'd been making agitated phone calls all day. It sounded like he'd dropped the ball on some major shipment, but other than "snooping around" and "buyers getting nervous", the only words she'd caught were of the swearing variety. He'd kept his voice down on the significant details.

Hayley straightened her body in front of the mirror. Hands on her hips, she rotated from side to side to get the full view. The new dress wasn't simply white. It was white glitter. The bottom came down to her knees, but it had a slit that ran up her right thigh. The half-sleeves hugged her arms like a second skin.

Yes, the rebel in her cheered with glee. The scarlet-red ankle boots would be perfect. "And the red clutch, too," she said, pointing toward her closet.

Rolling her eyes, Tia disappeared. She reemerged ten seconds later with a shoebox and the mini purse in her hands.

She opened the box and slid it onto the bed. "I don't want to be responsible for this."

"Yeah-yeah-yeah," Hayley waved her hands in the air, "I'll take full responsibility."

She plopped down on the edge of the mattress and took the right boot from the box. Slipping her foot in, she zipped it up, then did the same with the left.

She walked back over to the floor-length mirror to assess the outfit while Tia scowled over her shoulder, muttering something in disapproval.

She couldn't think of a better way to make a statement.

"Need anything else before I go?"

Let's see: hair—check, make-up—check, dress—PERFECT.

"Nope." Hayley popped the *p* between her lips. "I'm all set."

"Alright then. I'll see you Friday."

"Friday?" Her fingers stopped combing through her hair.

"Yeah. Dinner with the Gibsons.

Right. *Crap!* She'd forgotten all about that. She had obligations. Commitments to keep. It could be weeks before she'd get another chance to see Jamie.

41

They snuggled up on the three-seater, her body stretched out in front of him, her head lay back on his shoulder. The ceiling fan above them was on, and from time to time, a single long billowing hair of hers would tickle his face until he swept it back behind her ear. He loved running his fingers through the silky strands. Loved touching her, even if all they did was talk.

The early evening breeze from outside shifted the curtains of the French doors to the back porch. Her flats, which she'd kicked off on their way in, lay strewn about haphazardly, one upside down.

She'd dropped in on him late this morning—on a Tuesday—which meant she would leave again tomorrow at dawn. The last time she'd come by on a weekday, it had been the same. She was stealing time for them wherever she could, but she always left too soon. She swept in like the breeze, then split just as quickly at first light, leaving no trace of having been there at all.

And he never knew when he was going to see her again. Or *if*. It had been two weeks since the last time. Three before that.

Jameson frowned unintentionally, his thumb stroking the skin beneath her t-shirt. One arm around her waist, he dropped his chin into the crook of her neck.

"Actually, my first time wasn't that great. To be honest, he didn't measure up to you." She reached for his cheek, affectionately combing her fingers through his beard. "It should have been you."

His right hand, which was brushing up and down the outside of her leg, halted its doting motion. "What happened?"

Something in her tone triggered the wrong nerve. How had they ended up in this conversation? They'd been talking for hours; he couldn't remember.

"Nothing worth dwelling on," she answered, waving him off.

Scooting a little higher up his lap, she went back to grinding the swell of her ass against his front. It had the desired effect and distracted him.

He let his hand drift across the top of her thigh, his fingers dancing up the inside. Her shorts definitely lived up to their name. The frayed hem was cut off right at the junction of her legs. He could slide his hand straight into the candy jar.

As the tip of his forefinger grazed the edge of the denim, her stomach gave a hungry growl. He could feel the rumble against his arm around her naked belly.

Squeezing her legs together, she curled up in his lap and giggled, embarrassed.

"Maybe I should feed you first." He wrapped his arms tighter, tickling her sides.

He liked feeding her. She was too skinny. Which was strange considering what she could put away. It seemed their coupling encouraged her appetite.

"No." She wriggled in his hold. "We can eat after."

Jameson relaxed his arms only enough to let her get turned around, then he rolled them onto their sides, pinning her into the back cushions, his ass hanging over the edge of the sofa. If he slipped off, he'd take her with him.

He nudged his leg in between her thighs, searching out the heat that seared through his clothes. The ache in his groin locked on to her needy flesh.

Coiling her hair around his fingers, he pulled, forcing her head back to give himself access to her throat. He pressed his teeth into the dip beneath her jaw, feeling his own groan resonate in her chest.

He had her whimpering, right where he wanted her, when there was a rap on the front door.

Motherfuck.

Jameson growled as he drew back and slipped out of her embrace.

Fucking cockblocker. Who the hell…

Marching across the room, he peered through the narrow glass panel next to the door. "Is that a Maserati in my driveway?"

A *Levante*. Not the kind of ride you saw a lot of up here, but he could make out the distinct Trident emblem in the grill as he reached for the left side of the door and swung it wide—

"I apologize for the interruption. I'm looking for my wife?"

Jameson froze, the blast from the past hitting him like lightning straight to the chest. On the other side stood a man with sandy-blonde hair, dark beady eyes, and a baby-smooth jawline he'd recognize anywhere.

Even after all these years.

"She's known to hike in this area. You haven't seen her, have you?"

Carter spoke in a much deeper voice that still carried the same condescending note, and Jameson wasn't at all surprised that the asshole didn't recognize him. The entitled never really looked at someone they considered below their standard. *He* certainly didn't make the cut. The man hardly even looked up as he scrolled through his phone.

"She drives a white Audi Q7. Here's a picture…"

He kept talking, but Jameson stopped listening at that point, bile churning in his gut. He glanced back over his shoulder at the empty sofa and the curtain blowing in from the back porch.

Suddenly, it all made sense. He could see the whole picture unfold in front of him.

"…this is her, right here."

Jameson focused back on Carter, who was holding up his phone, showing a picture of him with Hayley leaning into his side, her clasped hands draped over his shoulder, the asshole's arm around her waist…

Something inside of him cracked.

"Never seen her before," he gritted through his teeth, then shut the door in Carter's face without looking him in the eyes.

It was the truth. Though her body was angled toward her *husband* in an affectionate manner, her face appeared sad. There was no smile on her lips.

He didn't know *that* woman at all.

Jameson let his head fall back against the solid oak wood. How could he have been so naïve?

42

*T*he gun clicked right by her temple as he cocked the hammer back. "That's what you wanted, wasn't it? Me holding a gun to your head?"

Hayley screwed her eyes shut. Her arms were stretched out above her. Aaron had pulled the cuffs tight around her wrists. There was no slipping out, and the slats of the headboard didn't budge either.

Her legs trembled, trying to shift on the bed where Carter now kneeled, having taken his former roommate's place. His left hand squeezed her throat. She couldn't stop him. She was too scared to even scream. Her muscles were stiff, and fear froze the blood in her veins.

He leaned down to her ear, pressing the cold steel against her skin on the opposite side. "Bet right now you want to recant that dare?" he mocked, his words sharp and painful like a knife in her back.

The floorboards creaked as Aaron shifted toward the door.

"Stay!" Carter ordered him, his voice pulling away as he straightened on top of her. "I want you to watch this."

His hand slipped from her throat, but the muzzle of the gun stayed right at her temple. "You too, baby girl. I want your eyes on me."

She wished he'd pulled the trigger. Her nightmare had only begun.

Hayley's lungs were burning as she raced through the woods, hurdling the brush at full speed, barefoot, while clutching her shoes in her hands. Twigs poked at her soles, but she didn't have time to put them on until she got to her car. She didn't look over her shoulder. The blood drummed in her ears, and she just kept running.

She slammed into the driver's side door, scrambling to get her fingers around the handle and rip it open. It unlocked automatically with the key fob in the front pocket of her shorts.

She climbed into the seat and yanked the door shut before slipping her shoes on. Then it was only a matter of buckling up and punching the gas.

Her pulse matched her speed the entire drive home. Her heartbeat never recovered its natural rhythm. Every muscle in her body was so tense, her back ached.

"C'mon, c'mon, c'mon. Open already."

The gate creaked as it widened in slow motion. She gunned through as soon as it was enough to fit the mirrors. She didn't know how much of a head start she had on him.

Hayley made it through the door and took the stairs two at a time.. She showered, then raced back downstairs, swinging around the newel post on the bottom and sliding toward the library.

She flung herself onto the chaise and opened the book in her lap to a random page the moment his key slipped into the lock of the front door.

And right when she thought the tattered pump in her chest couldn't take anymore, her adrenaline peaked a second time as his footsteps approached the library. He was ambling, the sound almost taunting—a cat playing with a mouse.

Dread twisted her gut, the *boom boom boom* of her heart bouncing off the walls like thunder.

He knew.

He fucking knew.

But how? She'd left the house this morning, not ten minutes after him. He was supposed to fly out at 6:30 and not get back until tomorrow night. What the hell happened?

"My flight was canceled." He stopped in the doorway, crossing one ankle over the other as he tipped toward the frame.

Fuck! He'd come back and found her gone.

Her hands gripped the hardcover tighter, and she kept her eyes down, catching only the outline of his body at the top edge of her vision.

"Where were you?" He studied her with his hands in his pockets. She could picture his expression, eyes dark and unreadable.

"Out." She held her tone light and indifferent to his suspicion. "Am I not allowed to leave?"

"Of course you are." He kicked off and came strolling her way, hands still in his pockets. "Why didn't you call Mateo?"

"He's running an errand for your father." At least she hoped so since his car wasn't here. "And I wanted to drive myself," she tacked on matter-of-factly.

How had he known where to look for her? If he'd had a hunch on where she was, why had he taken his car instead of flying? He could've beaten her home by two hours. Was he fucking with her? How much did he know?

She wondered if he'd noticed the significant climb on her car's odometer. She'd been up to Montana four times in the past six weeks. That was over 600 miles per trip. And then there were the security camera feeds that showed her coming and going from the property.

She hadn't thought this through at all.

He stopped his lazy stroll right in front of her. She could feel his stare narrowing, but she refused to meet his eyes. She flipped a page, feigning ignorance of his concerns.

His fingers fiddled with the keys in his pocket. She hated the sound of that. It was the sound of his irritation whenever something didn't go his way, and he was trying not to lose his temper.

Trying because the distraction didn't always work.

The first time she'd noticed it, she hadn't known what it meant. Hadn't been prepared for his one-eighty mood swing. She'd humiliated him in front of his friends. Taunted him for not being able to satisfy her and suggested Heather had faked it too.

He'd retaliated by cracking her cheekbone with his fist. That had been the last day she'd worn glasses.

Over the next year, he'd sprained her wrist by twisting it behind her back, ripped her shoulder from the socket, and bruised her ribs on several occasions simply because he could.

She stayed quiet to survive. When there were bruises on her neck, she'd wear her hair down. When the marks were on her wrists, she'd layer bracelets. When he chose to whip her back with his belt, her dress would have to be less revealing. And when things got too bad, she'd come up with an excuse not to make a social appearance.

There was always a way to hide their secret. They played their roles in public well. According to everyone else, they were happily married.

But after six years of studying his tells more closely, she knew how to read him.

And how to defuse him.

296

With a sigh, Hayley slammed the book shut, then tossed it onto the seat beside her.

"Is there something you wish to say?" she asked, finally lifting her eyes to his.

He was still wearing the same black suit and burgundy shirt he'd left in this morning. The top two buttons were undone, as if he needed more room to breathe.

She watched his chest expand. Was he going to accuse her right here? Right now?

The seconds ticked by, but Carter didn't say anything. Head tipped to the side, jaw cocked, he merely glared at her from his high angle.

She knew he relished the rare opportunity. In average pumps, they were equal. In her plateaus, she was two inches taller. He hated that.

He stopped his fidgeting and yanked his hands from his pockets. He shifted his weight toward her and reached for her hair, twisting a wet lock in his fingers.

Hayley didn't flinch. She allowed his touch.

"I called your phone," he said, scrutinizing her reaction.

Yes, he had. Twelve times, to be exact. It was still plugged in on her nightstand.

"I was worried. Why didn't you answer?"

She recognized the tone of his voice. He was fishing. And that was when she knew he had a suspicion but no proof.

"Is that where you were?" she prompted. "Out looking for me?"

"I feared you were lying dead in a ditch somewhere."

"Feared? Or *wished*?"

His fake affection dropped abruptly as he removed his hand. He didn't need to pretend in front of her.

Carter's expression was hard, but his features had never quite caught up with maturity. The subtle softness remained, and he still resembled his mother more than Roy. Maybe that was why people fell so easily for his charades.

He pinched his lips between his teeth, and his breath arrived with sharp force before he spoke. "Do I need to remind you that you were attacked just a few weeks ago?"

No, he did not. But she wasn't buying his phony concern. The only thing he worried about was protecting his assets and his business affairs.

"Well, I'm safe and sound, so you can rest easy now." She assumed his meeting had been rescheduled for tomorrow.

"Yes, I can." He gave her a wink and pivoted around to leave.

Thank God, she wasn't expected to share a bed with him. She needed sleep.

Hayley glanced at the clock on the table beside her. It was past midnight, and she felt exhausted. She couldn't make the drive up to Montana again right away, but she needed to get back to Jamie. Needed to tell him the whole truth. She never meant to drag him into her mess. She had to apologize to him.

Carter was nearly out the door when she remembered to ask, "Why was your flight canceled?"

"Storm down in Phoenix. It's pulling north, so it looks like I won't be leaving anytime soon." He threw a malicious grin over his shoulder. "Hope you don't mind me hanging around."

43

*K*aren nudged her with her elbow again. She could never remember the woman's actual name. "You're so lucky you're married to one of the most influential and powerful men in the entire state."

Hayley stifled a snort. Carter was none of that. His father was. Roy was the man behind the curtain, pulling the strings. As governor, he was God to these people. It was no secret that Carter wanted to run for Senate—with Wilkins Pharmaceutical at his back financially. Too bad he was still a few years shy of the requirement.

"Not to mention good-looking."

Yes, yes, her husband was very attractive. Hayley rolled her eyes. She was aware of all his physical attributes. Unfortunately, it was the character underneath that was shit.

Leaning back in her chair, she tapped her half-full champagne flute with a freshly manicured nail.

"And his father… mmm-mmm-mmm. That man ages like fine wine. If Carter looks anything like him in his mid-forties…" the harpy's voice trailed off in a daydream.

Gross!

"I bet he'll be president one day. I can just picture you as First Lady."

Calm down, *Karen*. This was Utah, not New York State. Or California. And Hayley would know; she was originally from there. Carter, on the other hand, was born and raised in Salt Lake City. She was expected to be a good little wife to him, sit at home, and care for the children like all their friends with their brood of five or more kids.

But she wasn't made for that. So, yeah, Carter's friends and acquaintances never considered him part of their inner circle. They saw him as less of a man for his lack of offspring. Hayley didn't care if they thought he was impotent. It was the only power she had over him. He would never consult a physician about the issue, either. He was too afraid of the prognosis that the problem was him. Ignorance was bliss, she figured.

The large diamond cuffs that wrapped around her wrists like shackles shifted when Hayley lifted the rim of the glass to her lips, nursing the first of undoubtedly many drinks to get her through the evening. The storm had passed, and the weekend was starting to look up.

The ostentatious woman sitting at the table with her was one of many leeches that flocked to her only to raise their own social status. There were no friends among these backstabbing brownnosers. Everyone was out for themselves. This woman in particular, Hayley knew, was recently widowed—not divorced, because that would have instantly ejected her from the circle. Men held the power. Women were merely the pretty things they wore on their arms. Like a fancy watch.

So, *Karen* here was currently on the hunt for a new husband; hence, the flashy attire. Her boobs were on full display with the plunging neckline of her dress. Hayley's keyhole was much more modest in comparison.

The woman's cleavage distracted from her face, though, which was haggard despite being in her early thirties. Her translucent skin and dark circles under her eyes made her appear much older. Hayley pitied her, and yet she couldn't shake the feeling that, in less than ten years, that could be her.

The only upside? Being a widow.

Martini in her left hand, *Karen* brushed her fingertips along her blonde chignon, which was as solid as plastic. Her eyes swept the surroundings for possible suitors when her face suddenly lit up at someone approaching from behind Hayley. "Governor Nolan, you made it. So pleased to see you again."

The words crashed like ice water down Hayley's back. She could feel the legs of her chair sinking into the soft ground as the vulture circled slowly around her to reveal himself. He loved dramatic entrances. Fed on them like air. The same air that was now being sucked from her lungs.

His clean-shaven jaw gave a minuscule tick, but he didn't return the woman's smile. He took her extended hand, keeping his sole focus on Hayley.

His eyes were much darker than Carter's—almost as black as his hair and most definitely as dark as his soul. His head showed no gray even at forty-six. Roy wasn't like his son. He was a different kind of animal. He was a shark. A Great White. A natural predator with vicious teeth who hunted for fun. He smelled blood, and he followed it.

She shrank deeper into the grass beneath her as his scrutiny left her strangely breathless. If the ground could get a move on and swallow her up already, that would be great.

"A governor *and* a senator in your family, Hayley. Can you imagine?" *Karen's* voice droned on.

Together, Roy's connections and Carter's charm threatened the financial and social ruin of anyone who opposed them. Possibly even bodily harm. With all the politicians and government officials on their payroll, who was there to challenge them?

The lump in her throat swelled. She wanted to throw up. She clenched the crystal in her hand.

"I couldn't do any of it alone." Carter raised his glass, strolling toward them. Amusement tugged on his lips, but not enough to show any teeth. "I owe it all to the beautiful woman by my side," he said, coming to stand on her right.

That was her cue.

Hayley rose and faked her response to the bogus flattery as he leaned in, pressing his lips to hers. It was brief because it was a formal event, but sometimes he took the theatrics further. And still, she was expected to play along. They were a team.

A team of liars.

She took a drink to swallow the sickening acid rising in her throat. *Karen* shrieked out of the blue.

"Oh, you two should dance!" she exclaimed as though it were the brightest idea she'd ever had.

Hayley choked on her champagne, spitting it back into the flute while bubbles tickled her nose. *No wa—*

"Yes! We should."

Her eyes snapped toward Carter, who was beaming at the suggestion. He extended his hand in an overzealous gesture, waiting for her to take it.

What was he doing? They never danced. Up until now, she hadn't even noticed the soft music playing in the background. And there actually was a small dance floor, too. What kind of sadist had put that in the middle of the lawn?

Hayley slipped her hand into Carter's, not sure what else to do. Why did he suddenly feel the need to crank this into a higher gear?

Karen took the champagne flute from her, and the next thing she knew, he steered them past the tables toward the square shape at the far end.

She slid her left hand up his shoulder as he switched his grip on her right. He clasped it gently, pulling her toward him, all in line with his affectionate appearance, but it was his arm around her waist that reminded her of her place next to him. It was like a boa slowly drawing tighter with each breath.

They didn't speak during their dance, but she felt the irritation roll off him, his fingers doing the same twitching motion they did with the keys in his pocket.

"I ordered you the salmon," Carter said, pushing in her chair when she returned from the lady's room.

Karen could barely contain her approval of him. Her pale green eyes sparkled with glee as she leaned in and whispered, "Isn't he the sweetest? And so attentive."

Sweet? Please. Ordering her food was only another way for him to control her. She could kill for some Omaha beef right now.

Dammit, the salmon here was amazing, though. Even more so paired with two glasses of a full-bodied, white Pinot Noir.

Hayley was starting to feel buzzed. She lost track of the conversations as the voices around her dulled. She was vaguely aware of her own among them.

Sharp pain rushed her out of nowhere, and she flinched. Carter's fingers bit into her thigh under the table, stopping her from saying what she was about to say.

"Watch it," he hissed through his teeth so no one could overhear.

She plastered on a smile and nodded as though she wasn't screaming internally. She was losing her damn mind sitting here. She needed out. Needed to move to clear her mind.

Carter let her go, but instead of heading to the lady's room to splash water on her face, she somehow ended up on the first-floor balcony on the opposite side of the manor. It was dark by now and quiet, so far away from the festivities.

Hayley put her fingers up to her neck, massaging away the tension, and taking her first deep breaths of the night. As she tipped her head back and looked up at the stars, she wondered what Jamie was doing. She couldn't stop thinking about the horrible way she'd left him with no explanation.

The awareness of someone watching her stretched up her spine with an icy chill. Goosebumps rose on her arms from the heavy presence. If she believed in demons, she'd have guessed he'd found her.

She turned her head gradually, eyes leading the way. Her stomach dropped before her sight landed on the huge shape emerging from the shadows of the mansion. He was one of the tallest men she'd ever met—not counting Mateo, that man wasn't human.

Governor Nolan.

The title left a sickening taste in her mouth. Politicians, as well as law enforcement agents, were in his pocket. That was how he'd found her so fast in her escape six years ago. She knew his threats were real. She hated the *old man* more than she hated his progeny. No good could come from his bloodline, and she'd never be the breeding mare for Carter's offspring.

Hayley followed his broad shoulders down to his arms. His hands were hidden deep in the pockets of his pants, his suit jacket still buttoned. His son had that same condescending strut down pat. *Like fucking genetics.*

"He really does have a soft spot for you, doesn't he?"

Carter? Hardly. Hayley opened her mouth, but no words came out. Tongue-tied, she slowly dropped her arms by her sides, watching every move of his toward her.

Had he followed her here? Her anxiety grew with every silent step he took, her stomach rising and falling in the frantic rhythm of her pulse. The tension knotted its way back through her shoulders.

Roy slipped his right hand from his pocket and drew it to his chin, thumb scratching the chiseled edge of his jaw as he clasped it loosely. "I mean, why else would he allow you so much freedom?"

His lips twisted at a curious angle as he recounted, "The backtalk, the coming and going as you please…"—*he knows too?*—"I would never tolerate this kind of behavior. I would've locked you in the basement by now."

Was he implying she was lucky she didn't have *him* for a husband?

She took a step backward. He came to stand on her left, facing the front lawn. His large palms clasped the balustrade in front of them, and an image of them wrapped around her neck popped into her head. She shuddered. The thought alone was enough to constrict her windpipe so much that she couldn't swallow.

"My son is useless. Got too much of his mother in him," he said, looking out into the distance.

Her hands curled into fists. How could he talk so coldly about his late wife? Carter's poor mother had committed suicide via prescription pills three years ago. No wonder she'd gotten addicted in the first place… with a husband like that. The egomaniacal bastard kept women all over the place.

"He's weak," Roy stressed. "Maybe I'd have better luck with a grandson."

Hayley scoffed and then sucked in a panicked breath when his hand shot out. He jerked her around to face him, his grip crushing her elbow. "Why is it that in six years, he can't seem to put a baby in you?"

She made sure he wouldn't. *That's how!*

His eyes narrowed with malice. "Maybe I should take matters into my own hands."

Fuck that. She'd rather have her tubes tied.

"Hayley!"

They flinched simultaneously as Carter's voice erupted from inside. He stepped out onto the balcony, looking both perplexed and suspicious at finding them together. "Dad?"

He didn't like his father around her any more than she did, but he never voiced his disapproval. He *was* weak.

"I found your wife," Roy's grip on her elbow tightened, "Wandering around by herself out here. You should keep her on a shorter leash," he suggested, then released her, practically shoving her into his son before storming off.

Carter caught her as she tripped over her shoes and landed in his arms face-first. He looked after Roy until he was gone, then lowered his voice to a whisper-shout, both hands clutching her. "What have I told you about talking to him?"

"Careful. You're going to leave a mark," she snapped back, glaring at him. She was done being manhandled tonight. "People will talk. And nobody wants to elect a wife-beater."

Without breaking eye contact, he removed his grip around her upper arms and straightened.

"Besides," Hayley tacked on, "He's your father. What do you expect me to do?"

"What did he say to you?"

"Nothing," Hayley lied. "You showed up just in time."

She assumed he'd seen Roy approach the table earlier this evening, too. That was why he'd interrupted them.

"I thought you said he wouldn't be here," she remembered.

"I didn't know. He was supposed to be in Atlanta until Monday."

There was resentment in his tone from being left out of the loop by his father. They didn't trust one another, and she was caught in the middle. She'd give anything to get out of this.

Carter reached into his back pocket, retrieving his iPhone. She herself was more of an Android fan.

"I'll have Mateo take you home," he said, already marching off through the Gibsons' library back to the front door.

Hayley followed suit, for once not arguing with his authoritarian nature.

Mateo pulled up in the Continental not two minutes after he hung up the phone. Carter opened the rear door on the passenger side himself and jerked his head impatiently for her to get in. He couldn't get her out of here fast enough. He was pissed that he had to come up with yet another excuse for her early departure.

She scrambled into the backseat, wondering how much longer he'd stay behind. Mateo had to return to fetch him later.

"Wait up for me," he blurted, then slammed the door shut.

WHAT! Why?

The words choked in her throat. Mateo put the car in motion before she could process Carter's request.

Why did he want her to wait for him to get home?

Hayley downed another glass of wine, pacing the stretch between the window and her bed. Mateo had dropped her off and watched her disappear inside before driving off again. That had been forty minutes ago.

She'd kicked off her shoes but not changed out of the dark red dress. The fabric felt tight around her chest, despite the keyhole between her breasts. The clasp at her neck was also irritating. It wound around her throat like a dog's collar.

She put the empty glass down on the little round table by the window. Her bracelets made soft rasping sounds, and for some reason, it made her look at the diamond on her ring finger. Was it really morally wrong to cheat on her husband if she'd been forced to marry a man she hated? She was neither

Christian nor Mormon. The vows meant nothing to her. It was all a lie—

The gravel crunched in the driveway as a car rolled up. A blanket of dread settled over the bare skin on her back and arms. She hugged them closer to herself, stepping up to the window.

She exhaled in relief when it was the white Lincoln Continental and not Roy's Bentley. He had a penthouse apartment downtown and the formal Governor's Mansion too, but the family's Tudor remained his private residence. And that threat he'd made earlier…

Carter waltzed into her room through the adjoining door from his own. His fingers swept over the knot of his tie, unwinding it as he came toward her. He tossed it onto her bed to his right, then his hands went back up to the collar of his shirt, unbuttoning the top.

Hayley felt nauseous. The loss of her Jimmy Choo's made her legs no steadier.

"Don't you dare." She shook her head and took a wonky step back.

His dominant right hand taking aim at her throat, he caught her before she got too far. "Or what?" he baited.

He crushed his mouth to hers in an unrequited kiss before she could respond, then threatened in a coarse whisper, "I touch you anytime I want."

Hayley swung out to slap him, but he jerked back and seized her by the wrist with his free hand. His nostrils flared.

"Not the face," he snarled, reminding her of his grasp around her fragile neck.

She could scratch him anywhere else, though. The long, red streaks down his chest or back were always covered by his shirt. He'd button it to the very top, too.

He dropped her hand, still glaring. "You're drunk," he noted with disapproval.

"Of course I am! How else could I tolerate you?"

"So you're tolerating me now? And here I thought you were trying your hardest to reject me." He scoffed over his shoulder, then said, "Or maybe that's just when you're sober. 'Cause we both know, *darling*, when you're drunk enough, you'll forget about that damn pride of yours. You'll be on your knees begging me like your life depended on it."

His hold shifted higher, so his thumb captured her bottom lip. He pulled it down gently to nudge his way inside. "I'd love to have that view again…" His voice trailed off as his stare fixed on her mouth, the tip of his tongue licking across his own lips.

His left hand slid to her ass, and then he pressed her against his body, nudging her awareness toward the ridge of his hard-on.

Where does he think he's going to put that?

His breath feathered across her cheek. "We've had some good times," he whispered. "Surely you remember."

Yeah, she knew he liked the dress—dark red was his favorite color—but wearing it tonight hadn't been an invitation, dammit. Why had she picked it? And the Romy pumps, so she wouldn't be taller than him? Because she wanted to appease him after his suspicions, keep him content, *not* give him a hint that she was open for business.

"It's all a sham, Carter. There's never been anything real between us."

All motion came to a stop. His hand at the small of her back, the one on her chin… the whole scene froze with her validation. The temperature in the room dropped, and neither of them even breathed.

"You want something real?" he gnashed, baring his teeth.

She caught the tearing of fabric at her backside, where his hand had been when Carter flung her toward the bed. The tops of her thighs hit the edge of the mattress, and her face smashed into the comforter.

Disoriented and dizzy from the booze, her hearing caught the clanking of his belt as he undid it and then yanked it through the loops.

Before she could comprehend what he was doing, his hands gripped her wrists, pulling them back. Her spine bent from his use of force. The hard leather cut into her skin, and he wound it tighter still, around and around and in between her hands to fasten the buckle.

Taking a hold of her left elbow, he flipped her onto her back. Her chest arched up from the position of her arms, and sharp pain traveled along the pinched nerves. Hayley gave air to a small cry.

"Does it feel real yet?"

Her fuzzy vision refocused on him. He stood over her, almost straddling her hips.

Gloating, he bent down, bracing one hand on the bed next to her head as the other one clamped tight around her jugular again.

"Or how about now?" he taunted.

"You're an asshole," she croaked through his unrelenting grip. "You've always been an asshole."

"And you've always been a cold bitch. But you're still my wife, and you still live under my roof."

"*Your* roof? Don't you mean your *father's*?"

There weren't a lot of things going through her mind right now with the oxygen running thin in her lungs, but if she got him angry, the night could end right here.

The vein on Carter's forehead flared again. No keys or nervous ticks could diffuse his rage. His fingers delved deeper into the soft tissue of her throat, his palm squeezing the front.

This was it.

His left hand reached past her head for his tie. He balled it up in his fist and shoved it down her throat with two fingers, making her gag.

"Say good night, baby girl," he rasped, placing his hand over her mouth and nose.

Hayley didn't fight him as her vision narrowed into a tunnel. The ire burning in his eyes was the last thing she saw before everything turned black.

OF APPLES AND TREES

44

Was this a fucking game they played? People like them used others for their amusement all the time, didn't they? He hoped she'd at least gotten a good laugh at his expense.

Jameson kept thinking about that picture of them together: Carter in a perfectly fitted suit, and Hayley in that short dress that highlighted every curve of her body. They might not have looked happy in the photo, but they looked like they belonged together. Like they were made for each other.

That had just pissed him off more.

Pissed him off so much, he'd slipped up and gone home. All because he didn't want to be alone. Needed a distraction. And then one thing led to another...

But it hadn't felt right. He'd known it wouldn't. He was playing a fucked up game of his own by giving Amber hope they were back on when they weren't.

He couldn't blame that on Hayley. That one was all him.

Fuck! What the hell was he going to do? He needed to get her out of his head. It had been four days, and here he was, the anger roiling through him like the moment the truth had come crashing down.

He glanced at his phone—*2:13 a.m.* Why the hell was he sitting out here? He should be asleep in his bed instead of slouching in this damn wicker—

The knock on the door was so soft, he almost missed it.

Then the air in his lungs froze. He knew the small hand that made the sound. *Nuh-uh.* No way was he going to open that. *'2 a.m. rule' and shit.* He knew better. It bit him in the ass last time.

He launched from the chair and shut the French doors behind him… which, of course, she heard. She knocked again, barely harder, now that she knew he was awake.

Nope. Not fucking happening. He stood, rooted to the ground, in the middle of his living room. He didn't move a muscle as he glared at the front door like he had x-ray vision, daring her to turn around and—

"I'm not leaving," she countered through the barrier.

But her voice didn't sound half as resolute as the solid oak keeping her at bay. He could wait her out. He had a bed. She didn't.

Jameson closed his eyes and sighed. Then he was the one turning away.

He crashed down on his stomach, pulling the pillow over his head, and for a moment, everything was quiet. He was hoping she'd catch his drift. He didn't want to talk to her. Didn't want to see her. He was still too angry and afraid of what he might do. He'd never hit a woman, but God-help-him his blood was boiling.

How could she lie to him like that?

Tap… tap… tap…

The little ticking noise of her fingernails against the glass forced his eyes open. It was in the steady rhythm of a clock, annoying the shit out of him.

Tap…

—a rumble worked its way through his chest—

…tap…

—he clenched the sheets, trying to ignore it—

…tap… tap…

Jameson whipped around with a start, the sheets rustling with his motion. The sound wasn't coming from the porch. She was standing on the other side of his bedroom door.

How the fuck did she get in?

"You forgot to lock the French doors in the living room when you ran, coward," she chanted without hiding her glee.

Son of a bitch!

A deep growl ruptured in his throat, and he flung his pillow across the room. "Go away, Hayley!" he barked as it thudded to the floor.

Jameson could tell his reaction took the wind out of her. He felt the shift in the air as the clicking of her heels trailed further down the hall. He expected to hear the door open next, but it didn't.

She stayed.

The woman had bigger balls than him. He was acting like a damn child, hiding out in his room.

Alright, fine. He'd indulge her.

Jameson got up and threw the door wide, giving her a fair warning by nearly ripping it off its hinges. He waited a long second for the dust to settle before he stalked down the pitch-black hallway. That was how far he got when his feet balked.

Hayley was seated on the stool at the corner of the kitchen island. In *her* spot. Not a single light was on, safe for the dim glow at her back through the kitchen window.

He flicked the switch to his right for the under-cabinet lighting, but she didn't acknowledge him. She was staring down at her clasped hands, pinched between her thighs. She didn't look like she wanted to be here. So why was she?

"What do you want?"

His tone was harsh. As it ought to have been, matching his killer mood. He had no intention of changing it anytime soon.

Hayley set one foot down on the floor and then the other as she lifted her eyes to him. Jameson looked at her—really looked at her this time. She had makeup on, neck-breaking heels, big diamond bracelets. And that dress…

The fake highlights in her hair irked him too. Nothing about her was genuine.

Or maybe it *was*. Wherever she'd come from, she hadn't bothered changing. This was the *real* her. The one everyone but him knew.

How had he ever considered that he could make a woman like her happy?

She held her chin high and started off with an encouraging shrug. "Go ahead. Have at it. Whatever you want to say to me, get it out."

"Why? You get a kick outta that too?" Nah, he was done jumping through hoops. "Haven't I humored you enough yet?"

"I didn't mean to hurt you—"

"You *lied* to me." He shot her a hateful glare, then pivoted his weight from one foot to the other. He couldn't stand still any longer.

Pacing the living room, he lowered his voice. "How could I be so stupid? This… this was a fantasy that was never supposed to become reality."

"Please, let me explain."

"I have a better idea," he snapped as he spun in the other direction. "Why don't we both just pretend that you told me and I didn't give a fuck?"

"I thought you quit."

Quit what?

Her head jerked toward the opened pack of smokes on the side table. He barely slowed his strides to look at her. "I'm a bit on edge. Don't judge me."

He hadn't actually lit up. Merely rolling one between his fingers had been enough to remind him why he'd quit in the first place. It was a bad habit. He'd found a different way to relax.

Hayley folded her arms over her chest. His eyes fell to her hand. She'd taken her wedding ring off again. Did she ever wear that thing? There wasn't even a fucking tan line. Talk about bad habits.

"I drove all night. Aren't you even going to hear me out?"

"From where?" Fuck him, but some part of him wanted to know everything now. Every personal detail she'd swept under the rug.

"Salt Lake City."

Shit. That was over 300 miles, if he remembered correctly. Had taken her what? Five and a half hours or so?

"Will you please sit down?"

"No."

But he stilled his pacing. His body angled away from her, he shoved a hand in his hair and rubbed the top of his head. His brain had never felt so useless.

"What was this to you?" His voice cracked from the anger he was holding in. "A little escape from your boring housewife life? Unfinished business or something?"

"You know, I could ask you the same thing."

"At least you weren't lied to! I've been sleeping with another man's wife."

Her palms shot up again. "What does it matter? It's not like you like the guy."

"*What does it matter*?" he enunciated, raising his voice. "That's not who I am, Hayley."

Fuck, his chest was heaving. Was he hyperventilating? He felt like throwing up. "How could you marry him?"

"What makes you think I had any choice in the matter? Our fathers have been best friends since middle school. My future was sealed the day I was born."

"What fucking world do you live in where women get married off to the highest bidder?"

"A world of power, Jamie."

"Then divorce him."

"It's not that simple."

"Bullshit! Don't tell me you're one of those women who gets off being in a toxic relationship. Or is it the posh lifestyle you don't want to leave—"

Her open hand slashed through his vision so fast her diamonds blurred.

The crisp sting of her slap across his face had caught him by surprise. Grinding his molars, he allotted her the free shot. It had been a shit thing to say, and he was man enough to admit his emotions were getting the better of him. He deserved it.

"Don't you dare." Her voice shook from holding back tears. "You have no idea what I've been through. You don't think I tried to run away? I made it two states over before I was dragged back. I had a huge black eye at my wedding, with so much makeup covering it that my tear ducts were glued shut. I couldn't even cry. He threatened to break my legs if I ever tried to run again."

She dropped her face into her palms.

"Carter beat you?" His fists balled on their own as fresh rage coiled through his veins.

Hayley shook her head. Jameson was confused. "Your father, then?"

She lifted her eyes and focused on him. "Carter's."

Her father-in-law put a hand on her?

318

A single thought occupied Jameson's mind: MURDER. He wanted to kill the old man. And his progeny too. For hurting her. For touching her. For…

No! His heart plummeted when his fragile mental state flipped suddenly from outrage to trepidation. *Please no!* The comment about losing her virginity that hadn't sat right with him.

Jameson connected the dots. "Tell me it wasn't *him*. Tell me Carter wasn't your *First*."

Hayley shook her head slowly, shoulders sagging with regret and shame. "I was dating Aaron at the time."

Is that Tweedle Dee or Tweedle Dum?

"I had always wondered why he hung out with Carter and Joey. He wasn't like them." Eyes downcast, she rubbed a hand down her arm. "Carter had instigated the whole thing. Even recorded it so he could use it to humiliate me."

"Fucking bastard," Jameson muttered to himself.

"There's more."

His spine steeled as she gathered her courage to confide in him. He wasn't sure he wanted to know the extent of the asshole's cruel game. The icy dread creeping down his back told him he didn't.

"Carter recorded it. He was there… that night in my dorm room. I didn't realize anything was wrong until Aaron handcuffed me to the bed. Then Carter took his turn—"

Jameson's needle was creeping back into the red as her voice broke off. Bile rose in his throat, and the acidic taste was right at the back of his tongue.

He forced it down, drawing a deep breath in through his nose.

Hayley sniffed. When she wiped a few tears from her cheeks, he noticed that her hands were shaking. "Carter knew I would never let him get close. He figured if he couldn't be first, he'd make sure he was second."

Her bottom lip quivered. "Aaron used a condom, but he didn't. He finished. He was trying to get me pregnant. I had no idea why," she rambled off quickly.

Jameson felt the sharp pain in the center of his palms where his nails had drawn blood. He wanted to kill the guy with his bare hands. Strangle his skinny neck and drain the life out of him.

"I thought it was over after that," she went on. "Then Roy approached me the day after my graduation. Told me that I was going to marry his son. I was a transaction… a part of a deal he'd made with my father. My plan for college and all my future dreams went up in smoke. My dad sold me like cattle."

Her light hand brushed the last tear from the inner corner of her eye. "That's when I ran." She wiped it down her little black dress. "I couldn't trust anyone."

"He still found you," Jameson concluded.

Hayley's head bobbed in confirmation.

His lungs ceased thinking about what she'd gone through. Her pain. Her fear. Entirely at their mercy…

But he had to protect his own heart. He couldn't let himself fall for a married woman. Hayley had given no indication that she was going to leave Carter. If he hadn't found out, she probably wouldn't even have told him.

How long would she have strung him along?

Jameson took a defensive stance, crossing his arms in front of him. Somehow, he'd ended up back by the hallway.

He didn't know how to respond without driving a stake through her heart. So, he stayed silent until she forced his hand.

"Please say something." Her eyes flicked nervously back and forth. The dramatic dark eye shadow made the green in her irises pop. No doubt she had lash extensions on too. He knew the type. He hated everything she stood for.

Jameson steadied his voice. "What exactly do you want from me, Hayley?"

Apprehension pinched her brows as though she didn't like where he was headed.

"Is it pity?" He shook his head. If she wanted to live in their world, that was the price she had to pay. "I don't feel it. I feel *pissed*. You're only using me to make yourself feel better."

He straightened and took a challenging step toward her. She was damn near eye-level with him. "Go back to him," he bit out. "Go live in your *'world of power'*."

He should've left with that and gone back to his room, slamming the door on his way, but he didn't. He stayed right where he was, daring her to bite back. To take a stab at him in return.

"I'll go," she answered, her face twisted with bitterness from his provocation. "I'll let him touch me. And every time we fuck, I'll think of you, because that's the only way I can get off."

Damn right, she would. Because he knew she hadn't faked it with him. That shit had been real.

Her hair whipped through the air as she spun away from him. His hand shot out, closing around her arm and ripping her back into his chest.

"You're not leaving until I'm done with you," he growled, his mouth hovering over hers. "I'll ruin you for him before I give you back."

"You already have."

Her hands captured his face as their lips met in a fiery kiss. Teeth clashing, they annihilated the air between them. His lungs burned from lack of oxygen, and still, he didn't stop. He devoured her.

The thought of Carter touching her drove him mad. Her clothes, her jewelry… everything bought with his money had to go. Jameson wanted the unsoiled version of her, bare to the bone and free of the man's contamination.

He stripped her naked, piece by piece, the shoes, the dress, even her black lace panties. Nothing would cross the threshold into his bedroom.

Shifting the diamond bangles on her wrists, he noticed the red marks underneath.

"Ignore them," she said, dropping the rings to the floor, where they clattered against the dark walnut.

And then she was pure, immaculate in his white sheets… and yet his anger remained, simmering beneath the surface. He couldn't shake it. He drove into her with deep, punishing thrusts again and again, chasing the release. Beads of sweat clung to his forehead. The drenched tips of his hair brushed along her skin as he dragged his nose up her chest.

Breathless, he buried his head in the curve of her neck. "Whose name are you going to cry out when he makes you come?"

"Yours," she answered in the same beat. Her hips rolled in sync, hands just as restless, roving through his hair.

"Let me hear it, Hayley. Come for me."

Squeezing her leg that was hiked at his shoulder, he picked up the pace, railing her harder, retreating, and diving back in.

"Jamie…"

Thrust.

"Jamie…"

Thrust.

"Oh God, Jamie—"

Her body arched violently, hips bucking, tits jutting out at him.

He reared back on a final grunt, but his own climax didn't bring relief. His persistent erection called for more.

He flipped her around beside him. Left arm slung around her neck, he gripped her jaw to angle her face toward him.

Using his knee to spread her legs from behind, he let his fingers wander the entire stretch from her clit to her ass, back and forth, marking his territory with more of her slick arousal until she was wet and slippery all over.

His touch lingered at the back, drawing maddening little circles around her puckered opening. He applied pressure, nudging only the tip of his finger inside.

Her chin jerked in his grasp, and she whimpered.

"That's mine too, Virgin. You're *ALL* mine," he rasped into her ear.

Right hand squeezing her thigh, his lips never straying far from hers, he buried himself deeper.

And then he took what he wanted, intending to toss her aside after he was done using her.

But he couldn't. When he finished and pulled out to roll her over, his arms wrapped around her of their own accord. He pressed her to his chest so tight he couldn't breathe.

All the hate drained from him. He felt deflated. Exhausted. He'd given her everything he had left, and now he was just empty. Again.

He couldn't hate her. He saw the bruises for what they really were. Carter's fingerprints: one dot opposite a crescent-shaped cluster of four.

The ones on her wrist and neck were different, but he'd seen similar marks before too. The abrasions were like rope burn, only not quite. Fabric or leather bindings, he assumed.

Fuck.

45

Hayley slipped out from under the tangled heap of their limbs and gathered her clothes scattered in the hallway. She wondered what time it was. Jamie had dozed off, but she'd been too restless to keep her eyes closed. She didn't want to wake him. It wasn't even light outside yet.

She slipped back into the ridiculous black dress Ashley had sent her for the event.

Oh, there was a theme, alright. That being *Gothic Chic with a Touch of Dominatrix!* A layered ruffle skirt with a dovetail gave it a playful edge, but the top was a nightmare. The mostly sheer, floral lace bodice was sleeve- and backless from the high neck collar down, and the front didn't have much more coverage. A thin chiffon ribbon fell in between her breasts like a tie, drawing attention to the deep plunge there.

It also came with a wide leather belt that cinched her waist. The only thing missing was a whip.

Hayley wondered if it was one of Ashley's own designs. She'd been tempted to ignore it, but in the end, didn't want to hurt her friend's feelings. Because maybe they really *were* friends. Or could be. She'd even taken a page out of her book and worn her hair down for once.

Shunning the mirror in the guest bathroom like the plague, she scrubbed at what was left of her smokey-eye makeup and weaved her fingers through her hair to detangle the mess. She wished she had a tie to pull it into a ponytail.

After Carter had departed for the airport, she'd gone to the fashion show only to make sure people saw her in public. Mingling with the crowd provided her with an alibi in case he got suspicious again; the more people, the better; especially when she hadn't enlisted Mateo to take her. Then she'd sneaked out through the back door and come straight here. Hopefully, Roy had slept at his condo and not noticed that she'd been gone all night.

But the clock was ticking. She had to get back.

Down the hallway, her eyes fell on the closed door opposite the master bedroom. She tried the handle, and it opened.

The scent emanating immediately pulled her back into the past. It smelled like Jamie, woodsy with a hint of smoke.

She pushed in further. It was dark; heavy black-out curtains shut out the light. She hit the switch on the wall to her left, flooding the room with instant brightness. She squinted through the discomfort until her weary eyes adjusted. His bedroom was big. Almost as big as the master.

Curiosity gripped her. Without much thought, Hayley's feet started moving into his private space, absorbing it all.

He had a dresser against the wall to her left, dark wood matching the various floating bookshelves. The top was completely bare. No pictures or loose items. The entire room was very neat. Not what she expected from a teenager at all. The only thing out of order was a black and gold football jersey tossed haphazardly into the corner, crumbled, and forgotten.

So he *had* played in high school. She wondered what position. Defensive Lineman, maybe? She could picture him barreling into people, mowing them over with ease. He was built for that.

She'd seen pictures in the living room of his mom and dad, a tall military man with broad shoulders and a heroic presence. There had been one with him carrying Jamie on his shoulders at maybe five or six years old. His personality had already shown through in his quirky grin. The same one she'd come to look forward to every summer.

Hayley ambled past the dresser and read the two award plaques hung up on the wall above:

Benjamin F. Davis

United States Marine Corps Special Operations

Force Reconnaissance

She recalled a picture of his dad in uniform, cradling a newborn Jamie, a proud grin on his face. He'd been very handsome: dark blonde hair and pale blue eyes, according to the old, faded photo on the mantle. Jamie had been proud of him, too. A large US flag was mounted in between the two plaques, brandishing their patriotic spirit, for which his father had made the ultimate sacrifice. He'd been there for the most impressionable years of his childhood, and then his mom had finished shaping him into a truly remarkable young man.

Hayley skipped over the slightly ajar door to his closet. His desk sat in between two windows covered by dark curtains. She dragged her pointer across the surface in a long, diagonal line and noticed the thin layer of dust coating it. There was more of the same on the bookshelf above. He really did have a lot of books. All four shelves were stacked full.

She smiled to herself when she found the familiar green spine of *Hatchet* amongst the masses in front of her. He still had *their* book.

Hayley resisted the urge to pull it out and feel its pages again. She couldn't remember the last time she'd read it. She didn't have her copy anymore. She'd been forced to leave it behind, along with most of her other personal things. There was no room for dreams in her new life. She had to erase that foolishly hopeful girl from existence.

Rubbing the dust between her forefinger and thumb, she turned over her right shoulder. Her eyes scanned around, keeping the clockwise motion going.

They stalled on the rustic, brown shiplap wall beside his bed. It was the only one with wood panels. They were stained in two different shades, but what caught her attention was the distinct discoloration that stretched from the floor all the way to the ceiling. An eerie melancholy emanated from it.

"How many girls have you brought back here?"

"None." Jamie entered her periphery with the silence of a bear. "I haven't been in here in eight years."

"Why not?"

She watched as he lowered himself onto the edge of the desk. It gave a soft creak, adjusting to his weight. "Because the boy who used to sleep here died that day too."

She turned back toward the wall, brushing her fingertips over the charred surface of the wood. "What happened here?"

He hadn't given her any details on the nine-year gap—on what he'd gone through. At least he hadn't been alone. He had Carl. He had friends who cared. Didn't he?

"There was a fire."

"Only at this wall?"

She glanced at him over her shoulder when he didn't reply. His eyes were down, his mind deep in thought. She could see the hard lines of his clenched jaw through the scruff of his beard.

And then she knew.

If they had stayed in contact, could they have saved each other from the pain? Or was that something they had to go through on their own to become stronger and make it out alive on the other side? To prove their will to live?

Suicide was the coward's way out. Every time she resisted the impulse to slit her wrists, she felt superior to the pain. Conquered the demon whispering in her ear. It *did* make her stronger.

Hayley strolled over to him on her bare feet. Sliding in between his powerful thighs, she clasped the sides of his head in her hands. She pressed her lips to his forehead and inhaled the fresh scent of him, a mix of mint, orange, and cedar.

The ache in her muscles lingered after everything he'd put her through so recently. But she didn't mind it one bit. There were no regrets. Her body willingly surrendered to the possessiveness in his touch the way it never would to Carter.

She combed her fingers lazily through the wet, black waves of his hair. It felt so soft, she wanted to sink deeper into it.

How long had she been in here if he'd already showered?

"What time is it?"

"Almost eight," he replied, hands engulfing her waist, his face buried in her chest.

Shit. It was later than she thought. The long black-out curtains were doing a hell of a job. Or maybe it was overcast.

"I have to go back."

"Fuck that!" His head snapped up, and his crystal blue eyes cut into her. "I'm not letting you go back to a man who beats you. I'm not making that mistake twice."

Hayley dipped her thumbs under his chin. "I'm not your responsibility, Jamie. I wasn't then, and I'm not now. It's not your job to protect me." No, that job had been her father's. "I can handle Carter. Whatever he does to me is nothing compared to what Roy will do. I've been gone for too long.

It's only making things worse." She dropped her hands and took a step backward, sliding from his embrace.

"What story can you possibly come up with that won't?"

"I'll think of something."

She had a quick mind and quick reflexes in life-or-death situations, as the mugging in the alley had proven. "I know how to defend myself. I'm still alive, aren't I?" She shot him a wink, pivoting toward the door.

Jamie slid his hand into hers and swung her back as he rose to full height. He lowered his forehead to hers.

"Leave him," his voice pleaded.

"I can't."

With a heavy heart, she freed her hands, pulling away from him.

"Then don't come back."

Hayley faltered in her steps. She felt the downward drag all the way to her toes. "So it's over?" she asked, too afraid to look at him.

"Don't ask me to keep this up. Don't ask me to share you with him."

His voice was thick with emotion. She turned slowly to face him, but he wasn't looking at her. His eyes were down to his right, brow pinched in pain. "If I can't have all of you, then I want none of it."

"Do you love me?"

His Adam's apple jerked in the expected silence that followed her question. She'd surprised herself by asking.

He pinched his lips between his teeth, choosing his answer carefully. "It's too soon for that," he said with a steady breath.

He was suddenly calm. Too calm. She hated it. And why was he still not looking at her?

"I like you, Hayley. A lot. Every second I'm not with you, you're on my mind, and I can't wait to see you. I like spending time with you... even when it's not for sex. When you're just here and we talk. I love *that*. And I know I don't want it to end. That's the only truth I can give you. Anything else would be a lie. I'm sorry if that's not enough to make you stay."

He finished his little speech, but he didn't move. Hands in the front pockets of his jeans, shoulders drawn forward, he avoided looking her in the eyes, as though he didn't want them to reveal what he was thinking. Was there more to what he let on? What was he waiting for?

"Thank you for your honesty. It's refreshing to hear the truth in a world where everyone lies to get ahead."

"You should know." His voice hardened. "You're the one who chooses to run back to them."

"Jamie—" Hayley opened her mouth, but she didn't know what else to say.

He shook his head. "Don't leave him for me. Leave him for yourself."

He had no idea how ironic that was. Protecting herself was the reason she had to go back. If she didn't, they would come for her.

Dragging his gaze along the ground, Jamie pushed past her toward the door. She stared after him. The thought of not returning here was tearing her apart. Didn't he know how badly she wished she could stay?

Turn for me, she begged, remembering the boy in the book watching the plane turn away to abandon him—his only means of escape.

He'd waved his torch in desperation, knowing he'd die in the wilderness without help. Her survival depended on this one moment right here, and Hayley clung to the same hope with all she had left.

Please. Turn.

She held her breath as he paused with his right hand on the jamb, chin tipped toward his shoulder.

His tone froze the cold blood in her veins to ice. "Don't come back," he repeated.

Jamie left without looking at her. She heard the front door open and shut. The rumble of his truck. And then nothing.

She was on her own.

Abandoned.

46

Jameson didn't go far. He just needed to get away. He couldn't watch her leave. *He* had to be the one doing the walking. Or driving, in this case.

The way she kept staring at him…

He'd felt her eyes, the heat of the awareness spreading across his face like the full blast of the sun. But he'd refused to look at her, too afraid of what his own eyes might give away— thoughts teetering on the edge of his mind, words he wasn't ready to voice.

He kept asking himself if *that* had been the moment. That moment people say you looked back to on your deathbed with regret. Would that be his last thought before he passed on? The moment not seized?

The truck's seat belt chime cut through the thumping inside of his skull. He hadn't even bothered buckling up. The alert kept nagging him to make up his mind. Eyes closed, he growled back, while flipping through the past five and a half hours of his memories in a photo montage. Every time his heart gave a beat, the picture in his mind changed.

His grip on the steering wheel tightened, making the leather creak. It wasn't over. A blaze ignited under his skin in the center of his chest. He wanted her. Feel her. Taste her. Smell her. He wanted more of what they'd had last night. And she'd known exactly what to say to trigger him.

Jameson ripped the idling truck into reverse and floored the pedal as he jerked the wheel around. The tires spun, kicking up dirt from the coarse turf underneath, rocks clanking against the undercarriage until it pointed back in the direction he'd come.

He veered the Silverado onto the park's gravel road toward his home. His heartbeat quickened, doubling its pace.

Did she leave yet?

He couldn't tell as he drove up. Hayley's car hadn't been out front when he'd made his dramatic exit. There was no way of knowing until he got inside.

He pulled up and paused in the driveway, the engine still rumbling. He stared out the windshield, his left forearm flexed with his grip at 12 o'clock.

What was he going to do if she was gone?

What if she wasn't?

He had no plan. All he knew was that he wanted her to be there.

Jameson twisted the key in the ignition before yanking it free, then hopped out onto the gravel. In long strides, he stormed the front steps to the door he'd left unlocked…

…to find the house silent…

…and empty.

Hayley cranked the steering wheel to the left more and more, while her toes screamed from being squashed inside her

334

high-heeled shoes. The plateaued bottom helped to put force against the brake pedal, but it was also unsteady. She shouldn't be driving in these.

The scene in front of her windshield blurred, and everything was spinning… spinning so fast, she was pressed back into the seat. She couldn't see the oncoming traffic anymore.

Was there any?

The tires skidded along the road before all movement stopped. Her car came to an abrupt halt in the middle of the intersection, facing the opposite direction she needed to go.

That damn blacked-out Yukon!

It had been hauling ass through the red light and nearly crashed into her passenger side. She'd ripped the wheel to the left in a panic, avoiding the collision with sheer luck.

What if there had been another car in the lane beside her?

She didn't dare think about it. The Audi could've ended up in the trench or wrapped around one of the massive oak trees flanking the highway, with the driver of the SUV completely oblivious to the more serious damage he could've caused—

Or had *her* light been the one on red? She was so distraught, she couldn't remember.

'Don't come back.'

Jamie's words cut so deep they severed her soul from her physical form. Her whole body felt numb. He hadn't torn her dress or left his marks on her, other than searing his name into her very being. But he had the ability to make her feel more vulnerable than anyone ever had.

Damn. The averted accident had been a close call. She needed to get a grip on herself and focus. Her head ached and her vision swam as she finally peeled her fingers from the steering wheel. She'd gripped it so tight that her hands were ice cold. She couldn't feel her toes, either. The urge to vomit rose with the acidic taste at the back of her throat.

A voice cut through the drumming of blood in her ears. It was muffled. She couldn't make out the words. She blinked, still staring out the windshield into the empty intersection.

Someone was standing beside her window, banging against the glass with his fist to get her attention. His lips were moving in the corner of her eye, but all she could hear was, *'Don't come back!'*

Absentmindedly, her hand went to the window switch to lower it, and the old man's round face came into focus.

He lifted the bill of his trucker hat a few inches and tipped his head at an angle toward her. "Are you okay?" he asked, raising his bushy eyebrows in high arches.

He must've seen the whole thing from his vehicle and gotten out to check on her. A driverless blue Suburban was pulled over onto the shoulder of the road.

Hayley assured the considerate man with a blank nod. She wasn't physically hurt, as far as she could tell, though she couldn't get a word past her sealed lips.

Some of the wrinkles in his worried expression eased, and he stepped back from her car. His body pivoted toward his truck, but his wary eyes remained on her for a few more seconds.

Hayley raised the window back up, then turned her car around to keep going. Her nerves began to settle. She was only half an hour from home.

The garage was still down, and Mateo's car was gone, the same way she'd left things last night. She was looking forward to the empty house. It was early in the afternoon, and she still had hours before Carter's flight from Phoenix landed.

She'd need every minute to put herself back together. There was no more escape for her. She needed time to cope with that. Time alone. She'd left his house in a hurry to keep from falling apart right there in his bedroom, but the breakdown was coming. She could feel it. The second she was safely hidden away, her emotions would crash down on her and drag her to the bottom. She just had to climb her way back out before Carter returned home.

In the foyer, Smokey darted up to her with his tail wagging. She bent down, setting the shoes in her hand silently on the wood floor, and petted him. He promptly shoved his big muzzle into her, sniffing all over at the scent that was no longer foreign to him.

Paws restless, he let out a stifled bark and got agitated. His acute sense knew something was wrong. Nudging her chest, he huffed through his nose as if asking her to spill.

He must've noticed the tears she was holding back because, in the next moment, his tongue shot toward her. She had barely enough time to turn her face before he slapped it across her cheek and then along her neck, showering her with his sloppy kisses.

"Thanks," she said, hugging him around his muscled neck.

Her belly twinged with an angry growl she could've mistaken for the sound of a hungry animal. Then she remembered that she hadn't eaten in almost 24 hours.

Hayley pushed off her knees, and the two of them strolled toward the kitchen on the left when suddenly her feet aborted their mission. She became very aware of the cold sensation against her bare soles as the low voice from upstairs drilled its way into her vertebrae.

Roy's here? The two of us alone in the house?

No. There was a second voice. Another man, blabbering incoherently. His speech was rapid and in a pitch that exuded fear.

What the hell is going—

Hayley jumped, but the man's scream was cut off as quickly as it had arrived. A heavy *thump* followed the silence.

Was that—

She froze. The grip around her spine paralyzed her to the core, and the air left her lungs.

—a body dropping?

Her scalp tingled as all blood drained from her face. And just like that, she lost her appetite again. Bile climbed up the narrow passage of her throat instead. No matter how much she swallowed, it didn't go away.

One Mississippi…

Two Mississippi…

She took deep breaths to keep from hurling onto the polished mahogany floor. Randall would have a fit.

Three Mississippi…

The entire foyer was in impeccable shape. Not a speck of dust.

Four Mississippi…

It would be a shame to—

Nope.

She veered right, back through the foyer, and past the bottom of the stairs to the little bathroom around the corner. *Boom… boom… boom,* her heart thundered with the cold surge of adrenaline.

She gripped the lid with both hands as her stomach initiated the evac, but the result was mostly dry heaving. It wasn't until the spasms stopped that her survival instincts kicked back in. Roy was still upstairs.

Wiping her forearm across her mouth, Hayley straightened and scooted backward to hide against the wall. In the same instant, the office door swung open, and his footsteps approached the top of the stairs.

Had he heard her? Did he know she was back? Had he monitored the security feed from the front gate?

The door to the bathroom was still wide open, but she was too scared to try to close it now. She held her breath and listened for his steps, staring at Smokey by her feet, compelling him not to make a sound.

After a minute, there was some rough shuffling as he retreated into his office to make a phone call. From what she gathered, he was commissioning someone to get rid of the body.

At last, Hayley shifted to nudge the door closed, leaving only an inch for her to peer through.

The man who arrived a little while later entered with his own key. He was wearing a casual dark gray suit and black tie that flopped around with his motion. He moved fast… he knew where to go… he was familiar with the place.

What the fuck? How many times had he walked in and out of the house as if he owned it?

She watched him disappear up the stairs, and voices broke out—Roy's and his. They were composed, not ruffled by shock or reproach. The whole thing seemed almost routine.

Her mind zoned out. She imagined how many times he'd done this before. She was living with a cold-blooded murderer. He'd touched her… wanted to do even more to her…

Hayley felt sick again. His blood was rotten to the core. His and his son's. But at least Carter backed off when she was unconscious. Something told her Roy wasn't so inclined. In case he chose to move forward with his agenda, she was thankful for the nifty little gadget nestled in her uterus. Even *he* couldn't get past that.

If her husband only knew…

Very heavy footfalls thundered down the stairs as the man made his way back to the bottom. She could only see him from behind as he moved toward the door and ripped it open with his free hand. The extra weight hardly restricted his movements. The other man was only half his size and rather scrawny.

Is he really dead? There was no blood.

"Jonas!" Roy called from upstairs.

His accomplice swung around, and that was when Hayley saw the incapacitated man's bludgeoned eye. Yep, he was definitely dead. It looked as though something sharp had been forced through the socket.

Hayley gulped and shrank lower in her stance. The gnarly wound wasn't the only thing she was now able to identify. When the large man's jacket shifted, she noticed a glimmer at his belt—the shield of a cop.

Her eyes shot back up to his face, and this time she recognized him. It was the same detective she'd reported her mugging to.

"Carter will take care of the next shipment himself," Roy said in a gruff tone. "I need you to take a little vacation."

"Where to?"

"Montana. There's an issue I need confirmation on before it causes bigger problems."

Hayley's hands sprang up to cover her mouth.

He knows about Jamie.

47

Smokey perked his ears and lifted his head from her lap. He hadn't left her side since she'd gotten home.

"She's in the library, sir," Randall proclaimed in his usual submissive tone, though she hadn't heard Carter asking.

"She is?"

He sounded surprised. Had he expected her to be somewhere else while he was out of town?

Hayley sank deeper into the cushions and flipped a page when Carter strolled through the open door. Apparently, he needed his own visual confirmation.

Smokey took an alert position whenever her husband approached, always on the defensive.

"Good little guard dog." Holding the book with her right, her free left hand patted his head in praise.

She had bought him when he was only a puppy. His fur had been lighter then, but his chest was still as white as snow. So we're his paws. It looked as though he was wearing socks. Carter disapproved. He didn't consider a pit bull a refined choice. But like she gave a shit about his opinion.

Oozing confidence, she stretched out on the French sofa, crossing her ankles. She wasn't going to cower in front of him.

Carter kept somewhat of a distance, thanks to the little sentinel in her lap. He sank onto the rounded lip of the desk by the foot end of the chaise, hands in his pockets. "How was the show?"

"Inspiring. I took a few pictures."

As proof. Not that her dress wouldn't leave a lasting impression on everyone's mind. She couldn't forget to thank Ashley.

"Mayor Townse asked about you. I told him how sorry you were that you couldn't make it due to the unfortunate rescheduling. Good thing at least one of us showed. He'll remember our support for his daughter." That should earn her a few points of gratitude in his book. The mayor had influence too, and he would therefore return his support to Carter when the time came.

"I stayed the night at the casino," she mentioned offhandedly, flipping another page. She observed him only in her periphery.

"You did?" He tipped his head sideways, sounding more skeptical than surprised this time.

Well, she'd rented a room as a cover. Not that she'd actually slept in it. She'd entered before leaving the venue and left the keycard on the bureau, so she could check out electronically the next morning.

"It was late, and I decided to have a few drinks." She gave an easy shrug with the book in her hand, assuring him that she had nothing to hide. "Figured it would be safer than driving."

He couldn't have her causing a scene of drunken, disorderly conduct now, could he? So naturally, he had to agree with her reasoning.

"So you've been home all day?"

"All afternoon," she chirped. "Your father was here." He could confirm with Roy later if he wished. It was the only reason she'd brought him up. He'd become an unsuspecting part of her alibi.

Hayley noticed Carter's posture stiffen with the unexpected piece of information. "You were alone with him?"

"Yes. Briefly. He was already on his way out the door when I ran into him in the hallway."

She'd stayed in the foyer's bathroom for another half hour or so before sneaking upstairs to take a shower. Roy must've heard the water running. He'd surprised her by lurking in her bedroom when she came out, wearing nothing but a towel wrapped around her body.

Needless to say, the situation had taken an awkward turn with his carnal gaze roaming her. He'd come to find out if she'd seen anything, probing her in the same sly way Carter had adopted, but he'd stayed for the view of her dripping wet and practically naked in front of him.

He'd hovered over her, way too close for comfort if there ever was any with the man, his sharp, dark eyes trained on every muscle twitch of her face that could've given her away. Hayley had felt rooted to the ground under his scrutiny. He was terrifying. Even more so now that she'd seen him kill a man without the least bit of scruples.

Roy had lifted her chin to meet his greedy stare, her throat too dry to swallow with all six-foot-two of him coming down, shoulders twice the width of hers. He'd appeared to buy her pretense not to know that he was home. She was off the hook for eavesdropping on his extracurricular activities, but she wasn't free from his net.

Carter chewed his thoughts over. "Did he talk to you?"

As he'd dropped his hand to leave, his fingertips had brushed across the bare skin on her thigh—not meant in affection but as a threat.

"No," she lied bluntly to his face. Roy wouldn't divulge that part to his son either.

She wondered if Carter was indirectly involved in the murder. His father had mentioned his name in reference to a shipment. But a shipment of what? Drugs? Was that what his business in Arizona was about?

It was a bold move to use Roy as an alibi without letting either of them know what she'd witnessed. It would only make her another loose end. Like the dead man. But she needed to kick off her own investigation into their affairs.

"Is he coming back tonight, or will he be staying downtown?"

Carter's gaze drifted over her legs. It was the same possessive look his father had rendered in her bedroom. It suddenly made her feel just as naked in front of him, and it wasn't like she was giving him unintentional signals again by showing off skin. After her shower, she'd put on a pair of navy leggings.

The corner of his mouth twitched. He straightened, pulling his hands from his pockets.

"The other night was fun. We should do that again," he suggested as he kicked off the desk.

Fun for whom? She'd rather have the tie shoved down her throat again. Did he need a reminder of how she'd rejected him? "You ripped the zipper on my dress."

"So buy a new one. I don't give a shit."

The thought of Roy alone in the house with her spurred something in him. The urge to assert his predominance, maybe? It made no difference if it was the man's eyes or hands all over her.

Or did he know about his father's controversial agenda for keeping his lineage going?

Hayley's spine went rigid. Smokey picked up on the abrupt change in the air too. He emitted a low growl before her husband took another step toward her.

He stopped, glaring down at her dog. Smokey didn't yield. She could see his dark lips curling to reveal the tip of a white canine ready to strike. It was a wild standoff.

Carter's fingers shimmied by his side, but he caved, knowing he was likely to lose at least one of them if he made a wrong move and tried to pry the obstacle in her lap away. So, he turned on his heel instead, tail tucked between his legs.

"Who's the big dog in the house?" she asked, ruffling the fur on Smokey's neck. "That's right. You are."

Hayley pressed his muscled body into her chest, and he swept his rough tongue across her face in reassurance. Yup, the 60-pound pup would sleep in her bed tonight.

Hayley arrived at the gym with every intention of pulling through, but once the smell of rubber mats and sweat assaulted her sinuses, the exhaustion in her muscles became overwhelming. Her heart simply wasn't in it today. She'd been restless all night, and her breakfast smoothie hadn't energized her either. The mixture churned slowly in her stomach. It felt like cement.

She was still in her pristine gear when Mateo took her back home; she'd spent more time in the Lincoln than at the gym. She hated bailing on Trevor. His workouts were the only thing keeping her from losing her damn mind at the house, but since she was back early and Carter would still be at his office in town, maybe she could find something on his desk here.

Hayley dragged her feet up the stairs as female laughter erupted on the second floor. Her hand halted on the polished rail. Carter's voice came next in a sensually low rasp that raised the hairs on her neck.

What the hell?

Her feet resumed their ascent at a more apprehensive pace until she reached the top. She let go of the banister's support and crept down the length of the second-floor landing. The plush carpeting made no sound under her sneakers, but the erratic drumming of her pulse made up for that.

She stalled in front of the office right as the door swung open—

Hayley jumped back. "Heather!"

"Oh! Hi, Hayley," she said, flipping her blonde hair over her shoulder.

Neither of them bothered disguising their fake smile. They'd been at this for too long. The infamous foursome had remained a tightly knit circle after graduating. Teresa probably would have married Joey had he not died of a heroin overdose in college.

After graduating a year after them, Hayley had been forced to attend the same one to stay under her husband's watchful eye. Heather had never forgiven her for ruining her plans to become *Mrs. Carter Nolan.*

He, on the other hand, had very much enjoyed the turnout. Deep down in her gut, Hayley knew why he never wanted to marry Heather. She was a clingy gold-digger. Carter didn't like suck-ups either, but he permitted them where they served a purpose. Apparently, he'd found a new one for his ex.

Hayley gave the short black dress she was wearing a quick once-over, then marched past her into the office.

Carter narrowed his eyes at her. "Wife."

"Husband," she returned his cold greeting.

An iced Mocha Frappuccino sat on the corner of his desk. She wished she could say it was Heather's—only girls drank that shit—but no. It was his. Hayley had created her own habits only to spite him.

"'You fucking her?" she burst out.

Okay, now she sounded like a jealous wife, which she wasn't. But why did it have to be Heather? And how long had this been going on behind her back? Was he trying to get a kid out of *her* instead?

"What if I am?" he challenged her reaction. "Don't act like you care. When was the last time you let me touch you?"

Months.

But willingly? Never!

"Frankly, I've grown tired of trying."

Ha! He made it sound like he'd actually been a faithful husband to her until now, which she knew he wasn't, and that was fine. She'd never expected that from him. He had no romantic feelings for her, only the possessive kind. No woman could tolerate that for long. Better that he fell asleep on top of someone other than her.

But he'd never cheated on her so openly. Why did he no longer feel the need to hide it?

Hayley's mind jumped back to Jamie's condition. She was too afraid of Roy to file for divorce. The company would only remain in his name, with Hayley by his son's side. Otherwise, it would revert to her father. That was why Carter couldn't divorce her either.

"Let me be clear. I don't care who you're screwing. Just make sure you use protection. You don't want to catch anything contagious"—she nudged her head back toward the door his slut had taken—"and who knows where that's been."

Then Hayley left him standing there, with his hands in his pockets and that smug grin on his face. Maybe he really did think she was jealous.

Arrogant prick.

She retreated to her bedroom, waiting for him to leave the house, so she could return to his office and conduct her search. She'd never spent much time in it before. It gave her the creeps. It had always been Roy's office and was, therefore, adjacent to *his* bedroom, not Carter's.

She hated the idea of going back there. It was where they made their deals, and probably where they had made the arrangement with her father to *acquire* her, as well. Hayley's skin crawled at the thought, and her stomach gave another pang.

Was she getting sick?

Or was this her new permanent state around them as her body adjusted to the idea of being trapped in the house with the two of them?

Hayley stepped out onto the large second-story balcony to take a breath. The length of it stretched from her room all the way around the corner to Roy's, though she never dared to venture far past Carter's doors. It felt as though the second leg of the balcony was some forbidden corridor she had to avoid.

Not this time. She lurked by the bend, out of sight, but ears perked.

Her hair billowed in the soft breeze, and the scent of freshly mowed grass filled her nostrils. Yes, they had a gorgeous mountain view here, too, but it wasn't the same. It was suburban life. With manicured lawns. Domesticated. Not the wilderness she so longed for.

And she wasn't the first woman to have suffered under this roof. Her eyes didn't go up to the third floor of the mansion, where the old master suite was. It had been occupied solely by Roy's late wife. She'd haunted the upper floors for years prior to her passing… *an absent mother, leaving her son to the vices and whims of his father.*

But that wouldn't be her. That would never be her.

Hayley heard the ring of Carter's cell go off through the French doors of the office. He answered it in a curt tone, and his voice became more agitated as the back and forth went on. His replies were short.

Who's he talking to? Roy?

There was the sound of movement, like he was rifling through stuff in a hurry, and then the unmistakable slam of the office door inside the house.

Ten seconds later, he hustled down the front steps. She watched him pull the Levante out of the garage and burn rubber through the iron gates.

Hayley pushed off the banister. If he'd left in a hurry, maybe he'd left something behind. What was he plotting? Was Heather really content being his side piece?

She entered the office through the French doors of the balcony. It wasn't unusual for them to be unlocked during the day, and besides, she didn't want to take the chance of running into Randall on the floor's landing.

She kept her ears perked for any sounds past the door as her feet fell silent on the dark carpeting. The scent of his expensive cologne lingered in the air.

Straightening behind the desk, she took in the interior from a foreign angle. The armchairs were all in the classic Chesterfield style, tufted dark brown leather with a low back and rolled armrests, except for his throne behind the desk, which was a high Wingback. The room had the vibe of a classic cigar lounge and was about as suffocating.

Hayley swallowed and scanned over his desk for anything that looked out of the ordinary. Nothing appeared disheveled; not even after what he'd supposedly done here with the whore. All papers were still neatly stacked—

The commemorative letter opener that normally sat in the right corner was gone. Was that what Roy had used to stab the man's brain through his eyeball?

How many people has he killed under this very roof we share?

There was no doubt in her mind that Roy had a hand in her father's ruin. He'd been itching to get his hands on the majority share for years. He'd swooped in like a savior in disguise and seized everything. Including Hayley. Her father had rolled over to save face, throwing her under the bus in the process. The man meant nothing to her now.

She recalled the last time she'd faced him. She'd stormed into his office, demanding an explanation, but he'd only confirmed the nightmare.

'You have no idea what I've sacrificed. The things I've given up… I had a legacy to uphold. As do you.'

'Fuck your legacy!'

She'd never spoken to her father that way before. Called him a spineless bastard for caving to Roy, and the strike to her face had only served to make things clearer. He would never come to her aid. That had been the last time she'd seen her father.

Are they using his Pharma business to move illegal drugs?

Hayley wished she hadn't heard a thing. She'd rather be oblivious to their dealings.

She dropped into the chair and leaned back. Lacing her fingers over her stomach, she twiddled her thumbs while canvassing the rest of the room.

Where's his safe?

She swiveled the desk chair around to her right, staring up at the oil painting of a landscape. The problem wasn't finding the damn thing, it was cracking it open.

She pushed out of the black leather and reached for the corner of the frame. The magnet unlatched. She swung the painting to the side, finding herself face-to-face with the standard solid steel box of a wall safe. No way could she guess the combo.

Disappointed, Hayley moved the cover back into place. She pivoted toward the balcony and was about to leave the office when she glanced down at the large bottom drawer of the desk. It had a lock on it, but that wasn't what made her stall. She noticed the little white corner sticking out of the top. A piece of paper.

She lowered herself onto her knees and gave it a gentle pull until she managed to slip all of it free. It was a long sheet with very fine print. It looked like a legal form. Thomas Wilkins' and Roy Nolan's signatures were at the bottom.

Her eyes darted across the paper, catching words here and there. Something caught her attention, and she repeated the line she'd just rushed over.

Her heart leaped into her throat. She couldn't believe what she was seeing. Her father had signed ownership and his shares in the company over to her, making *her* the major shareholder, not Roy or Carter.

The bastard had been acting head of the company on her behalf this whole time, running things without her knowledge?

Hayley forced herself to blink and read the following passage again. In the event of a divorce or her death without children, Roy and Carter stood to lose her shares of the business.

Had her father done this to protect her?

Hayley froze reading the clause at the bottom of the document, above their signatures:

After turning twenty-five, ownership would automatically transfer to her *husband* instead of reverting back to her father.

48

She'd found her way out. They didn't need her anymore. Carter and Roy could keep the business and run it into the ground for all she cared. She wanted nothing to do with it.

Hayley stepped up to the imposing set of doors and knocked. She had already contacted a lawyer, but she needed to tell Jamie before she dropped the bomb on Carter. They could be together now, and Roy had no reason to send his watchdog after him. He would be safe. *They* would be safe.

She waited. There was no reply, and no sounds of shuffling came from inside the house. Everything was dead quiet.

She frowned over her shoulder at the backed-up Silverado in the driveway, then knocked again, rapping on the heavy door with more force.

Nothing.

She stepped off the porch and went around but didn't find him lounging out on the deck either. She peeked into the bedroom. His bed was empty; all doors were locked.

Where the hell is he?

Hayley marched back to his truck, feeling more anxious now. Had Roy's man gotten to him already? He'd only been dispatched two days ago.

His cell phone number wasn't listed, and she had resorted to calling the park's old landline as her only means to reach him, but it had never been reactivated since the closure. She had no way of warning Jamie of the threat.

Hayley tried the handle on the driver's side, and the door unlatched. She climbed into the seat, looking for God-knew-what. Anything that could tell her where he'd gone off to.

A piece of mail was shoved between the seat cushion and the center console. Hayley pulled it out. The name on it was Jameson Davis, but the address didn't match Bishop Park's. The envelope was made out to a place further east of Lima, an apartment unit in West Yellowstone.

Does Jamie not live here?

Her focus was still on the envelope when there was movement in her periphery. A hand shot to the back of her head and ripped her out of the truck by her ponytail so fast.

Hayley crashed into the gravel, the coarse rocks cutting into her arm. White-hot pain flared in her left shoulder and elbow from the unimpeded fall. It knocked the air out of her lungs.

She sucked in a sharp breath when her eyes landed on the familiar set of brushed leather Armani lace-ups. Before she could utter a scream, the lug sole of Carter's shoe drew back. In a jolt of panic, she tried to push off the ground to get away, but it was of no use, her limbs didn't respond quickly enough. He nailed her hard in the ribs, and she thought she'd throw up from the pain.

"You forgot your phone, *darling*," he sneered, his fury rippling off every word. "But no worries. I was still tracking your car."

Another blow hit her side as she winced.

"Every year you drive up here to meet with him behind my back."

"No," she coughed out.

"You thought I didn't know? I always knew about your little trips. But I let them slide. Gave you just enough freedom to come crawling back. You knew better than to run."

Dirt clogged her throat. She blinked through the cloud of dust surrounding her—

Please no!

Her arms twitched on reflex, then wound around her stomach as he took aim again. More pain exploded behind her ribcage. She rolled onto her back, coiling inward from the agony.

Carter crouched beside her, leering down, his voice full of malice. "By the way, your doctor called… to schedule an immediate appointment. As a concerned husband, I asked her what it was about. Imagine my surprise."

Right. Because after contacting a lawyer, she'd drawn another pivotal conclusion. And the home pregnancy test had come back positive, confirming her suspicion.

That's why he's doing this.

He rose back to his feet. Through her narrowed view, she caught the flapping motion of his jacket as he swung back a fourth time. He struck her again with a blow to her jaw, and her arms went lax, then slipped to her sides.

Her eyelids fluttered, too heavy to open, and her skull was ringing as the blackness pulled her under.

Jameson put the paintbrush down and wiped his hands on the rag before picking up his phone. The pressure on his eardrums ceased as he disconnected the Bluetooth.

Pulling the headphones free, he slipped the little buds into the front pocket of his jeans. A few white stains now mingled with the red and black spatter that had already been there.

He'd picked up on the renovations to distract himself. He would be alright. Just had to keep moving forward.

Sitting back on his heels, he squinted up at the old arch. The paint was still wet, but all in all, he'd given it as much TLC as he could currently muster. He felt content with the result.

He gave the cell's screen a quick glance, then returned it to his back pocket and pushed himself to his feet. He'd been out here for over four hours, skipping lunch even. It was five-thirty.

He gathered his supplies in the back of the RZR. The little off-road vehicle had saved him from all the walking back and forth. It was a lot easier to maneuver around the property than his truck. More fun, too. He liked drifting it on the dirt roads after a long night's rain, when the scent of water still hung in the air, fresh and musty where it seeped into the earth.

Jameson parked it by the tool shed to unload, then trotted the rest of the way up to the house. He didn't go in. He rounded the front of the Silverado. Eyes on the ground, he reached for the driver's side door when he noticed the piece of junk mail by his feet that he must've dropped earlier. He'd stopped by this morning to check on things.

He bent down to pick it up, then hopped behind the wheel.

'The hell?

There was a folded note trapped under the wiper. He leaned around to pull it loose, then sank back into the seat as he straightened the corners out.

THE TRASH IS ALL YOURS. ENJOY.

What's that supposed to mean? Did Carl leave this? Jameson hadn't seen him in months.

Whatever. He crumbled the piece of paper up and dropped it into the door before he twisted the key. Stomping his foot on the gas, he pulled out of the driveway.

He turned the radio up, barely listening to what was playing. It didn't really matter as long as it was loud. He wanted to drown out that nagging feeling that was slithering up his spine. An awareness as though he'd forgotten something… or should be doing something other than grabbing food…

At the red light, he reached for the bill of his hat and tossed it into the passenger seat. He rubbed his palms over his face, then raked his fingers through his matted hair, giving it a ruffle. His scalp was itching. So was his skin. Like something was crawling underneath it. Some kind of sixth sense.

Fuck! His hand slammed down on the steering wheel, giving his irritation an outlet. He needed a shower. *That's it*, he told himself. *Nothing else to it.*

Jameson kept his twitching boot heavy on the gas. He rolled into the sub-shop half an hour out of town. Nobody knew him here. Which was the point.

He slouched into a booth inside, choking down his sandwich. He kept staring at the back of his truck, that same uneasy feeling clinging to him. The words of that handwritten note bounced around his head like the annoying jingle of an ad you couldn't shake.

The word 'trash' specifically, rubbed him the wrong way. It was supposed to be a reference; he was sure of it. What connection was he missing?

Frustrated as shit, he flushed the last bite with water because ginger ale wasn't commonly stocked in small shops, then slid out of the seat.

The moment he turned the engine over and the initial rumble evened out, the damn tune was back:

Trash… trash… trash is all yours.

No! *'The trash is all yours.' THE trash…*

MY trash…

Then it clicked. *'THANKS FOR TAKING CARE OF MY TRASH, INBRED!'* the words echoed in his ears. *CARTER—*

"HAYLEY!" Jameson slammed on the brakes, and that was when the dull *thud* came from the Silverado's truck bed, the sound of a large weight sliding around.

He ripped the wheel to the right, pulling onto the soft shoulder, then jumped out. He lowered the tailgate, but she was so far back. He couldn't reach her.

Jameson's chest got tight at the sight of her in the small, dark space. She was unconscious, from the looks of it, and lying on her side, facing him, her head tipped at a bad angle.

He folded the top cover back, then climbed up. The box wasn't airtight, but oxygen had surely grown thin, not to mention the heat. The truck had sat in the sun for hours. How long had she been locked in here?

He brushed her hair from her face and noticed that her wrists were bound behind her back with what looked like the asshole's necktie—

Oh thank God. Her lashes fluttered, then her chest expanded with a deeper breath.

"Jesus Christ, Hayley. You scared me to death."

The side of her face was bruised in a deep shade of purple. Her arm, too. He reached over to untie her hands, and she whimpered when he pulled her into his lap. Her shirt was riding up her waist. He was afraid to find more of the same marks on her ribs.

"Why the hell would he do that?" he wondered as he wiped the tears and dirt off her face.

But Jameson already knew the answer to that. The cat was out of the bag if Carter had ambushed her at the house. Why had she come back at all? Why take the risk?

"I'm going to leave him," she said in a voice that grated like sandpaper. "I'll go through with the divorce. I'm not afraid anymore."

No, she wasn't, if she was willing to risk a beating like this. She was tough as shit. How many hits had she endured?

"I'm taking you to the emergency room." They didn't have a big hospital, but the intensive care unit wasn't far.

"No!" she interjected before he even shifted a muscle. "No doctors. I don't want anyone to see me like this. Please, Jamie."

He didn't like this. She wasn't bleeding as far as he could see, but what if she had internal injuries? "Hayley…"

"They're just bruises. I'll be fine," she mumbled. "No doctors."

But she didn't look fine. Her head slipped listlessly off his shoulder, and he got the feeling she was about to pass out on him again.

"Stubborn woman." He brushed his knuckles down her cheek and didn't want to let go of her, but they couldn't stay here. "Come on. Let's get you in the front."

Jameson scooted his ass along the bed, dragging her to the edge of the tailgate with him. He hopped down, then scooped her into his arms and carried her around to the passenger seat. Once he got her buckled in, he went over to his side.

He turned the key in the ignition, and let the truck idle for a moment, unsure where to go. He couldn't take her back to the park. That place was compromised now that Carter knew about her affair. What if he returned?

But he couldn't take her home either. It wasn't exactly neutral ground.

"I'm taking you to a friend," he said, shooting her a glance. "Someone I trust."

Damn. He hated to do this, but there was only one person who could help. He scrolled through the contacts on his phone, then pressed *Send* to connect the call.

The line picked up. "Summer, I need you to do me a favor."

"Jameson! It's so good to hear your voice. It's been too long. What do you need?"

"Meet me out back in twenty."

Summer awaited them by the south doors in the rear parking lot of the *Twin Pine*, arms crossed over her chest as she leaned back. She pushed off the wall as Jameson pulled up to the curb, an expression of worry on her face. They hadn't spoken in almost a year. Man, this was not the proper opportunity to make amends for being a dick, and she was a saint for not sending his ass away.

She stepped up to his side. Not meeting her eyes, he cranked the truck into park, then shut off the engine. He got out and went around to Hayley's door.

Summer scoffed behind him. "What, no '*hey, how-are-ya, what's-new, you-look-great*'?"

She was wearing a bright red wrap dress, her long blonde hair twisted up at the back of her head. A woman like her didn't need to fish for compliments.

"You do look amazing." And under any other circumstances, he'd be thrilled to see her like this. He was so happy for her.

"Aw, thanks." He couldn't see her ditzy smile, but he could hear it in her voice. "So what's this about that you couldn't tell me on the phone?"

He gently gathered Hayley in his arms and nudged the door shut with his elbow.

"Oh my God, Jameson, who is this?" Summer's eyes popped, mouth hanging open, when he came around the hood.

He stopped in front of her and sighed. "A friend."

"A friend?" She arched a skeptical brow, not buying it.

He was about to tell her to shove it but remembered that she was doing him a solid here. "Don't ask. It's better if you don't know."

"Alright. Fine." She threw up her hands, then concern took over, creasing her forehead. "Who did this to her?"

"Her husband," he answered after a moment's hesitation. He wasn't sure if he should tell her at all.

"You're involved with a married woman?"

"I'm not," he barked. He'd called things off.

Summer's frown only deepened. "I don't like this, Jameson."

"I know. I'm sorry to drag you into this, but I have nowhere else to take her. Can you put her up in a room for the night?"

"Yes, of course. Bring her this way."

The woman really was a saint. She pulled the steel door open wide and led the way down the long hallway to the first room on the right. "I figured you might need a place to stay when you called, though I never expected this."

She swiped the lock with her master keycard from her lanyard, and the light flashed green with the sound of the deadbolt disengaging. She pushed down on the handle and again opened things wide for him.

"You're not getting in trouble for this, are you?" he wondered. She was the manager, but still.

"No, don't worry. I'm glad I can help."

Hayley curled in on herself as he laid her down on the bed. In her semi-conscious state, her hand held on to his as if asking him to stay. He wanted to.

He gave her another look-over before pulling away.

He *had* to.

Jameson turned to Summer, still standing in the doorjamb. "I think she might have a concussion. Can you stay with her after your shift? Just in case?"

"Sure," she answered without hesitation. "But wait! Where are *you* going?"

Pushing out of the room, he pivoted his chin over his shoulder. "Home." He was already here. No point in driving the hour back to the park. "I'll be back in the morning."

"Does Amber know?" Summer's voice called after him down the corridor.

"No," he uttered to himself, both palms giving the bar on the exit door a hard shove.

49

It wasn't so much the pain in her head as it was the unimaginable sorrow lulling her into numbness. Hayley didn't want to wake up. The loss of what Carter had taken from her was too great. Even if Jamie didn't love her, at least she could've had that… something for herself.

But *he* had ripped that away.

Going in and out of consciousness on the ride, she'd gathered enough to know Jamie had taken her to a hotel in West Yellowstone. And there had been someone else. She'd heard him talking. A woman. Hayley had vaguely recognized the voice too, but it was her pretty face that had put the pieces together. It was Summer, Bishop Park's former manager.

And Jamie's *First*.

They were still close after all these years? She remembered how worried Carl and the young woman had been the night Jamie ran away.

Hayley pushed off the bed. Pain instantly shot to every corner of her body. Everything hurt. Every muscle felt battered and bruised before she even took a step. Her insides felt hollow somehow.

Summer had stepped out of the room a little while ago, but left a change of clothes on the dresser for her: a pair of dark blue jeans and a black t-shirt. Gratefully, Hayley swiped them up, then ducked into the spacious bathroom around the corner.

She avoided a glance in the mirror as she stripped off her dirty clothes and slipped under the hot spray of the shower to rinse the tragedy away.

Her hands trembled. She had to fight the tears spearing into her eyes. The pink water pooled around the drain by her feet before it disappeared with everything else. *Weeks… erased… no more… like it never existed.*

But how had it at all? The desperate little life had forced its way through. A miracle, never fully coming to be.

One thing she'd managed on her run six years ago was finding someone to put the birth control in place. It had been her only option. She now remembered something along the lines of getting it replaced in six years.

Had the IUD shifted? When? To imagine that under different circumstances, it could have been Carter's…

What if he really couldn't father any children? Heather hadn't looked pregnant in her spandex dress, either.

As Hayley slipped into the clean clothes, she heard the door to the room open. The woman was sitting on the far edge of the bed when she turned the corner of the bathroom. Her eyes fell to her round tummy. Summer was pregnant. And not only by a little bit. She looked ready to pop.

Hayley's eyes widened. "That's not Jamie's, is it?"

"What! *Psh.* No way." She waved her hand and laughed as if it were the most ridiculous thing she'd heard.

Thank God. At this point, Hayley wouldn't be surprised if he really did have a wife stashed away somewhere.

Summer's smile dropped, then her demeanor tensed visibly. Her palms smoothed over her swollen tummy in a protective manner. "I noticed you're bleeding. Um, I thought… you might want to shower and change into some clean clothes," she said, still rubbing her belly.

She knows. Knew that her husband had beaten her for being pregnant with another man's child. Hayley wanted to sink into the ground.

"Thank you," she whispered, dropping her eyes to the psychedelic pattern of the dark carpeting.

"You can keep them. It'll be a hot minute before I can fit in them again." She let out a little laugh to distract from her uneasiness, then noted, "You look familiar. Have we met before?"

Hayley took a slow stroll toward her. "Summer camp."

"You're Hayley, aren't you?"

"He mentioned me?" She lowered herself onto the foot of the king-size bed across from Summer.

"No," she replied apologetically. "Never. But I saw the way he looked at you back then when he thought no one was watching."

"I know about you and him," Hayley mentioned, clearing the air.

"He told you, huh? Yeah, I'm not proud of that, but you know Jameson. He wasn't exactly an ordinary teenager: he was sixteen going on nineteen… and already a better kisser than some of the guys I've dated," she laughed, embarrassed.

"I couldn't believe I was his first. I thought for sure he'd lied to get to me. Though, that wasn't really like him. But let me tell ya," she stabbed the air with her pointer, "he knew what he was doing. One moment I was on top of him, and the next he had me on my back, taking control. He said he'd made out with girls before, just didn't want to pressure them. I guess I was different. He was so sweet and not shy at all in pursuing me—"

Clipping her words, Summer dropped her face into her palm, shaking her head. "Oh, God. I was so ashamed by the whole thing. We kept it a secret. My husband doesn't even know. I'm surprised he told you."

"I think it slipped out," Hayley said, letting her take a little comfort in that.

She recalled how they had laughed at the lake at her suggestion that he'd been seduced by a twenty-year-old. Clearly, it had been the other way around.

Her eyes shifted around the suite, landing on the still-drawn curtains. "Where did he bring me?"

"Twin Pine Hotel," she replied, but Hayley had already gathered as much from the stationery by the bed and the soap in the bathroom. She was a little familiar with the town.

Summer held out her phone. "Is there someone you'd like to call? Jameson said he'd be back, but if you'd like to call someone else…" she let the words hang in the air expectantly.

Hayley would've liked to call a cab, but her wallet was in her car back at Jamie's. She kept thinking about the address in West Yellowstone. She had a bad feeling about it. He was hiding something. Why else would he have kept it from her?

"I just need to look up an address nearby, if you don't mind."

Summer handed her the phone, and Hayley pulled up the Google Maps route on the screen. It was about a mile from the hotel.

"Thanks," she said, handing it back.

"Alright. Imma head back to the front desk." Summer pushed off the bed and turned for the door. "Gimme a call if you need anything, okay? I'm sure Jameson will be back shortly."

Hayley returned a polite smile and nodded, then watched the door close behind the woman. If she waited here for him to pick her up, she'd never find out why he was so secretive about the apartment. She needed to go. Needed to see it with her own eyes, so he couldn't talk his way out of it.

366

Hayley tugged the keys for the Audi out of the front pocket, then dumped her ruined clothes into the bin by the door before pulling it shut.

Her body protested at each step she took, but she pressed on regardless. She was glad Jamie hadn't taken her to the clinic. She didn't want to explain herself to the doctors.

And what if they told him about the miscarriage?

No, she didn't want to see the look on his face. He'd think that she lied to him about being on birth control, too.

She followed the directions the way she remembered them from Summer's phone, taking a few rights and one left. After the last turn, the dead-end road led her to a gated community in a very homey neighborhood. Luckily, the sidewalk didn't have restricted access, and Hayley could pass right through. She kept her eyes peeled for the correct street name and address; *Unit 5A* was burned into the back of her lids.

She passed the first row of condominiums when she realized the tall, four-story buildings gave way to smaller family homes. That bad feeling from earlier returned. This couldn't be right, could it?

She checked the street name on the sign above her head again: *Jefferson Ct.* That was it.

And then she spotted the house number, too—

It was a *duplex!* Surrounded by *more duplexes*, 1 through 6, A and B, a freaking family home in the middle of a family neighborhood, complete with a playground at the small park straight ahead.

For a moment, Hayley thought of turning tail, but she had come so far. She couldn't chicken out now. She had to know.

She approached Unit 5A, the left side of the conjoined building, via its individual cobblestone footpath. The garage was down. No car in the driveway. Was Jamie inside now? Was anyone?

Would she feel more comfortable if she wasn't wearing another woman's panties?

Hayley raised her hand to knock, thinking about how unfortunate it was she didn't have a key to walk in and investigate the premises on her own. A moment later, the lock clicked, and then a hole in her chest opened up, swallowing every vital organ in one gulp.

The door pulled back to reveal a gorgeous blonde woman, almost as tall as him, and exactly what she expected to be his type.

"Um, hi. I'm looking for Jam— Jameson," she stammered, remembering that nobody but her called him Jamie.

Her cornflower-blue eyes gleamed as she smiled. "Oh, he's not home right now. I'm Amber, his—"

Please don't say wife… please don't say wife…

"—fiancée."

Yup, she sure was. There was the engagement ring on her left hand, sparkling in the sunlight as she swiped her hair behind her ear. *Very subtle.*

"How do you know Jay?"

"I'm a friend of Summer's." Hayley blurted the first thing that jumped to mind. "She told me he lives here. I don't have his phone number… I thought maybe I could catch him." Her hands fidgeted nervously, grasping at her shirt. She felt like such a fool.

"Well, he left early this morning, and I'm not sure when he'll be back, but I bet if I give him a call, he'll rush right home… in case you care to stay and wait." She stepped to the side and opened the door wide for Hayley to enter.

Fuck. She seemed so nice. What the hell was he doing?

"Um, sure. Thanks," Hayley replied, walking into the living room. She might as well wait for him here; she had no means of getting back to her car. "I'm Hayley, by the way."

"Have a seat, Hayley." She hinted at the couch across the room. "I'll just be a minute."

Yup, this was definitely his place—no, *their* place. There were pictures of them together everywhere. This is where he kept his drawing table and his sketchbooks, his desk, his work…

This was where he lived.

A heavy lump formed in her throat. Her mouth went dry.

"Can I get you a drink?" the woman called from the kitchen while she swiped her cell phone off the counter.

"Uh, water. Thanks."

"Just a sec," she shot back with a smile and disappeared around the corner. The dreamy *'Hey, baby'* was the next thing from her lips as she kicked off the call to Jamie, then the door behind her clicked shut.

Hayley dropped her face into her palms, elbows on her knees. It didn't make any sense; he'd been raving mad about her using him as an escape. Made it clear that he wasn't a cheater and wouldn't keep things up with her. He wasn't that two-faced. Wasn't like Carter.

"So, you work with Summer at the *Twin Pine*?" Amber quizzed as soon as she returned from what Hayley assumed was their bedroom down the hallway. "Is that how you know each other?" She sank into the sofa chair diagonally from Hayley, setting a glass of water in front of each of them.

It probably would've been easier to tell her that she *did* work at the hotel, but she didn't want to lie. "No, actually. We go further back than that… Bishop Park." She hoped it didn't sound suspicious.

"You worked at the park?" Amber looked taken aback by the response.

"I knew Jameson's mom."

Her surprise turned sullen. "I wish he'd tell me more about that time. He never talks about her." Her eyes went to the ceiling as she gave her head a little shake. It appeared to be a troubling subject for her. "You haven't been in touch at all since?" she probed, refocusing on Hayley.

"The park closed, so my school never went back to summer camp." Maybe Amber would assume that she'd been a lot younger than Jamie then.

"Why are you looking for him now, after all these years?"

"I always wondered what happened to him. He was in really bad shape when I saw him last. I lost my mother when I was young..." she let her words drift, playing the sympathy card. "I'm glad he made it out on the other side alive."

"Well, he has that whole violent streak in his past."

Violent streak?

"He had that in common with my ex. But after college, things turned up." Amber grinned as though she were the reason for his turning the corner. And what if she was?

"And now you're engaged," Hayley chirped to change the topic. "That's exciting."

"Oh. My. God." Amber over-enunciated dramatically.

Her face lit up like a Christmas tree as she droned on about all the planning she'd been doing for almost a year... the venue... her dress... the extensive guest list... blah, blah, blah... Hayley wasn't listening.

"...So we decided to push the date for the ceremony back a few weeks. He wanted everything to be perfect for our big day—"

The Silverado pulling into the driveway made them both snap to attention.

"Ah, told ya he'd rush right back for you," Amber said with a smirk.

370

Was that a hint of malice in her tone? That hadn't been there earlier. Was she suspecting something? But, hey, a strange woman shows up at your doorstep, looking for your man… Who could blame her, right?

Both of their heads turned in anticipation. Neither of them moved. Everything turned deadly silent for two seconds; one could've heard a pin drop. Hayley was pretty sure she'd stopped breathing, too.

Then Jamie turned the key and all but pounced into the living room. His shoulders heaved.

50

He'd sent Amber's call straight to voicemail. He didn't have a head to deal with her right now. But when he returned to the hotel, and Summer told him that Hayley had left on foot, the little voice in his head told him to listen to that message. They were within walking distance of the apartment, after all, and what were the odds of it being a total coincidence that Amber's call had come at that very moment?

Slim to fucking none.

But at least he'd been prepared for what he walked into.

Amber rose slowly from the chair, folding her arms over her chest. Her brow was arched, her hip cocked in contempt. She had no fucking right to play the victim here. He didn't have to explain himself to her, and if she thought she could hold him accountable for cheating, then she was fucking delusional.

"Hayley." He kept his glare on Amber while addressing her. "Truck. Now."

He needed to get her out of here, stat, before Amber made things worse. Hayley would probably drill him with more questions on the drive, and he wanted to tell her the truth. But he needed her to hear it from him.

Jameson pivoted in his stance to clear her way. From the fringe of his vision, he thought she looked frightened of him as she slipped past.

Amber shifted her weight, hands curled into fists down by her sides. "You're an asshole, Jay," she shouted with a tremble in her voice.

"I know," Jameson sighed in agreement, then turned to follow Hayley's lead.

She was already buckled up in the passenger seat when he pulled the front door shut and came up to the truck. She didn't seem scared anymore. Or pissed, for that matter. She appeared reserved.

"Are you hungry?" he asked to break the ice.

Staring down at her hands in her lap, Hayley shook her head.

It would be a long ride back in silence. What had Amber told her?

Thirty-five minutes ticked by on the truck's radio when he couldn't stand it any longer. "How did you know?"

"The address on the envelope."

The one he'd dropped in the driveway?

No. He clearly remembered wedging it in between the seat and console. She must've been in the Silverado when Carter found her.

"It wasn't a secret, Hayley."

"Then why didn't you tell me?"

"Because it was irrelevant."

"Irrelevant?" She raised her voice in derision. "You're engaged! This whole time, you give me shit for cheating on my husband when you have a fiancée waiting for you in your joint home—"

"Ex-fiancée," he corrected calmly.

"She said the wedding is on hold. Not off."

"There won't be a wedding. I'm not marrying her," he stressed, his eyes shifting briefly from the windshield to Hayley's pout.

"According to her, that's why you came back. To fix up the camp, so you can have the wedding here."

"I came here to think. I started fixing it up because I want to reopen."

Something had pulled him back. A longing? He couldn't really explain what it was. "I swear it was over before I ran into you."

The breakup had happened on his birthday, and maybe it was part of the reason he'd been in such a foul mood, though he was the one who'd called it quits. In the phone calls that followed, she'd tried to reconcile, and apparently, she'd gotten the impression he might come around.

He wouldn't.

'You were the one who proposed.'

'I was drunk.'

Liquid courage because, deep down, he knew it was all wrong. He didn't want to. Regretted the words the second they slipped out. But it had been too late, and the more time went by, the more anxious he got. The noose was drawing tighter around his neck. He had to get out.

So, he'd taken off. He'd hoped restoring the old arch his parents had gotten married under would loosen that knot in his chest, but it had only made things worse. He didn't know what he wanted anymore. He'd thought he loved Amber. Heck, they'd been living together for five years. Was all that complacency merely him settling for something that was convenient?

Fuck! He didn't want that. He wanted something that would send his heart racing.

Then he saw Hayley. With one look, she'd kicked that stagnant pump beneath his ribs into motion, and he knew he couldn't go back.

"Then why is she still wearing the ring?"

He gave an apathetic shrug. "I told her to keep it."

It wasn't anything special. The thought of giving her Mom's had never even occurred to him until now. And why did that suddenly feel significant?

He had the urge to reach for the thin silver chain weaved in between the laces of his left boot. It was paired with dad's dog tags in the other, always reminding him to stay on the right track. He wanted to believe his old man was still guiding his steps.

Jameson prepared for the sharp right-hand turn uphill that would take them to the main gate of Bishop Park when Hayley told him to take a left through the woods instead. He knew where the wide trail led—the far north side of the property...

And her Q7. *So that's where she hid it.*

She wasn't staying. She wanted him to take her to her car. The realization was tough to swallow, and he ground his teeth to keep his mouth shut. He didn't want her to know how much her rejection hurt.

He pulled up to the rear bumper of the small SUV and let the engine run.

"You were right," she said, unbuckling her seat belt. "I'm leaving him no matter what, but I have to do this for myself. Not for us."

Without giving sound to the turmoil inside of him, he watched her climb out of the Silverado and slide into the driver's seat of her own vehicle.

Her stormy-gray eyes found his in the rear-view mirror as she turned the key, then she took off, leaving him behind.

51

Hayley couldn't stay… couldn't breathe. Her emotions were running wild. She needed air—

No, not air; there was plenty of that here. She needed space. Yes, space. Distance to put everything back into perspective. Her first step was the divorce. Once she was free, she could focus on everything else.

Heavy storm clouds turned the sky into a threatening mass above her. They hung so low, they cut the mountains in half.

The Levante was backed into the garage, and she knew just where to find the bastard. The Lincoln Continental was also in the carport, so this was going to happen with witnesses.

Randall leaped out of her way as she pushed through the front door and marched for the stairs. She blew into his office with all the fury of the impending storm.

She found Carter across from her, looking over documents. His eyes snapped to hers, fists braced on his desk.

"Miss me?" Hayley drawled.

His jaw twitched, and there was definite displeasure mixed in with his surprise. Mateo, who was hunched over the side of the desk from his much taller height, straightened, his body poised.

Carter shot him a look, jerking his head toward the door, and his sidekick promptly got moving. He squeezed past Hayley out of the door, then shut it quietly behind himself.

She strolled closer, folding her arms over her chest, and gloated over the fact that he had failed at taking her pride down. "As you can see, I'm still standing."

Carter rounded his eyes in exasperation. "I gave you a chance to disappear quietly. Why couldn't you just take it?"

"You honestly thought I would go quietly? I would've thought you knew me better by now."

She lowered herself sideways onto the edge of the desk, trying not to throw up at the thought of Heather sitting in this very spot, batting her lashes at him.

She rested her weight on her hand as she slanted toward him and tipped her head. "I have a different proposal for you. I want a divorce. A clean break."

She paused, watching him straighten, but his expression remained unmoved, as though he thought she was bluffing.

"I know about the age clause. Let me walk away from this sham of a marriage, and you can keep the company. All I want is my share in cash, a fair split, 50/50, then we never have to see each other again."

Hayley was scared. She knew she had no leverage. Her lawyer didn't really want to defend her against Carter and Roy. Which lawyer would?

But she could go to the media. A public scandal was her only threat…

…and her only shot.

The problem was, would people believe her? For six years, they had fooled everyone with their false affection for one another. Still, sometimes all it took was reasonable doubt to sway the verdict, and it was in the aspiring congressman's best interest to go down quietly.

Carter stayed silent. His jaw clicked as he ground her proposition between his molars. Nostrils flaring, he drew in a breath, then exhaled sharply while turning away.

He paced to the small bar set up against the wall of Roy's room on Hayley's left. His back turned to her, he reached for the bourbon, pouring himself a drink.

Her phone buzzed as he kicked it back. She scanned the screen. It was another urgent weather alert: LAST GREAT STORM OF THE SEASON…HIGHWAYS AND INTERSTATES GOING NORTH CLOSED OFF DUE TO FLOODING…AREA AROUND WILLARD BAY MOST AFFECTED.

She heard more of the soft splashing as Carter poured a second, drawing out the suspense of making his decision.

Is he going to go for it?

When he finally set the decanter down on the tray and spun around, there was a glass in each of his hands. His shoulders sagged with a heavy sigh. She recognized the resolve in his demeanor—he was going to agree to her terms.

He strolled toward her, holding one drink out, and she took it. "Here's to the end of us," he said, raising his glass in a toast.

Hayley copied him. The burn felt good. The palate was smooth with its soft, rich notes of burnt sugar, cloves, and caramel. Her muscles relaxed with each sip. She won! She was free.

Over the rim of the glass, she watched the twitch of his lips into a smile and the flash of something in his eyes.

She never made it to the Blanton's strong and lasting finish. No taste of nutmeg or corn registered when the glass slipped from her fingers.

It didn't shatter. *Did he take it?*

She still saw his face, that spiteful grin. Then Carter was gone too… the office… everything was gone…

…everything but his hazy voice in her ear, "Good night, baby girl."

Working with his hands cleared his head. He had to keep busy. Not knowing when Hayley was coming back was driving him mad. But he remained convinced that it was a question of *when*, not *if.* He could be patient. She would come back.

Jameson had already cleared the side of the master closet that he was going to tear down and emptied out the storage room in the hallway entirely. All the boxes with old junk were gone. He'd moved some of it to his old bedroom and trashed the rest before taking on the wall. If he started from the hall's side, which was uncarpeted, he could leave the master's drywall mostly intact. That way, it was easier to dispose of it through the French doors to the back porch.

He stepped onto the short ladder and ran the blade of the carpet knife across the top edge of the drywall, separating it from the ceiling. Then it was time for the fun part. After he punched a hole with the claw side of the hammer, he started ripping away the drywall using both hands. It felt so good to finally let all his frustrations out. With every chunk he tore free, a little more weight lifted off his shoulders.

The interior wall had no insulation. He'd started in the center, pulling down the top first, working his way left, then right. But the lower half of the wall, he did in one run.

When he reached the bottom right corner and ripped the last two-square-foot piece of drywall free, he drew back in surprise. In between the stud spacing was a box, approximately 3 by 12 inches, just big enough to fit in the gap.

Jameson took it out, wondering who'd put it there. He didn't remember Mom ever redoing the wall.

Reaching for the knife again, he sat his ass down on the hard concrete and cut through the layers of tape that held the flat shoebox together. Curiosity compelled him. This had been his family's home for generations; whatever secrets were hidden inside, were somehow connected to him, no matter how much time had passed.

The lid loosened, and he lifted it, staring down at the unexpected contents: old photos of Mom…

…and a boy who wasn't Dad.

Jameson took a second to wrap his mind around it. Bewildered, he shuffled through them. There were four photos in total, one taken every year, so it seemed. It showed them sitting under one of the trees by the lake; he recognized the background. The two of them were roughly between sixteen and nineteen. In the latest one, mom didn't look much older than she was in her wedding pictures.

Putting the photos down, he reached for the other item in the time capsule—Mom's diary.

He hesitated. It felt wrong. She'd gone to great lengths to hide this…

But she hadn't tossed it out. Why? Had she wanted someone to find this eventually? Was there something of significance inside? No one but family would care—

Or was this meant for him? What did she want him to know now that she couldn't have told him to his face?

He stared down at the front cover:

Lizzy Bishop

The weight of an anvil pressed down on his chest. His fingers brushed her handwriting, the smooth stroke of the blue ink.

He fidgeted nervously with the corner, then bent it back and started reading at the top. The date was June 1992. She wrote about school, summer break, friends, her parents insisting she help out more with the students at camp this year… organizing clubs… chores.

July 3rd—she mentioned a boy… seeing him on the first day, and then more and more around the park… He approached her at the lake after his friend had taken off… They got to talking…

1993—more school drama, then came July: 'He is back!!!' *Three exclamation points.* 'T. and I…'

"T? Who the hell is T?"

'…started hanging out… Everything was exactly like last year… the same feelings were still there…'

Jameson stumbled over the words, repeating the line, but the meaning was obvious. "Mom had had a summer fling!" *What do you know? The apple really never falls far from the—*

The dates started skipping, only focusing on her time with the boy now; no more talk of her parents' nagging or girls at school. She mentioned their first timid kiss, making out at the lake at night, their first—

Whoa! Hello. Mom and that boy had definitely covered the bases. *Graphic much?* That was more than he needed to know about his own mother. He felt the urge to stop reading right there, before they reached home plate.

Something cold crept up his neck, a little voice whispering in his ear, but he couldn't grasp the words.

Digging! Keep digging.

1994—Jameson blew over the irrelevant stuff. The tone in her narration shifted, appearing anxious. Things between them sounded pretty serious. 'T. sneaking around to meet me, but no one knows.'

July 1995—'He's afraid to tell his dad.'

December 1995—'Mr. Wilkins nearly caught us this time.'

382

Mr. Wilkins. The name rang a bell. Jameson kept reading faster.

'Tommy is gone. He won't be coming back…

'I believed that he wanted to say goodbye. Meet for one last time at the lake…

'Ben found me after. I told him. I told him everything…

'He is so kind. He listens every time I pour my heart out to him. He's been there for me. He's the one person I can count on.'

April 1996—'Ben knows it's not his baby, and still he wants to marry me. He doesn't care. I know he will love him unconditionally and raise him as his own. He will hide my secret with me.'

Eyes wide, Jameson paused and straightened. This was three months before he was born. Mom was talking about *him. He* was the baby. Ben wasn't his dad!

Drawing long breaths, he searched his feelings on the supposedly earth-shattering knowledge… and concluded that it wasn't. Wasn't mind-numbing or heart-stopping.

Yes, his jaw had dropped for a hot moment, but it *wasn't* earth-shattering information. It was irrelevant to him that Benjamin Davis was not his biological father. That Tommy Wilkins was instead. None of that mattered. And maybe Mom had known that it wouldn't change anything. Ben was the one who stayed, the one who raised him, and the only one who'd ever been a dad. The other man meant nothing to him.

The final entry in the diary was August 1st, three days after his birthday. Mom wrote, 'I firmly believe that something good can come from something bad. Life is all about balance—the dark *and* the bright. For me, that's Jamie. Jamie is my light.'

Jameson smiled at the last line, her words of affection echoing with clarity in his ears even after all these years.

He picked up the most recent photo of the two again. Something about them at the lake rippled in the back of his mind. He turned it over, and his eyes concentrated on the drawing of the cheesy heart around the words 'Tommy & Lizzy 4-ever'. It was like the carving at the dock. The initials T. W. + L. B.

Wilkins. Didn't he read about him in the news during his time at college?

Jameson pulled out his phone and searched for the old article from spring 2017. There it was, in bold letters:

Thomas Wilkins saves family business with help of long-term partner, Utah Governor Roy Nolan.

Below the headline was a picture of the man and his daughter—

No… God no!

Jameson dropped his phone… dropped everything as his hands clutched his head. The room started spinning around him, and this time his world truly shattered into pieces.

52

Hayley sucked a huge gasp of air into her lungs, and her eyes sprang open. She was freezing. A wet coldness clung to her in the dark of her Audi. Water was rising quickly. It was already up to her chest.

Her hands shot up, fumbling around the murky liquid. She found the seat belt latch and freed herself, the river water still rising around her. The car was more than halfway submerged by now.

How long had she been out here?

She pulled on the latch of the door, but it didn't open. The pressure against it was too great. She had to break the window.

Break the window… but with what?

Her hands skimmed more of the soup that filled the Q7's interior. She took a breath and dove across the passenger side. Her finger found the lip of the glove compartment. She rifled through the contents, ripping everything out. It floated to the surface…

Yes! She'd found it.

It was still sharp; the blade cut her skin. She shifted her grip, feeling blindly for the handle. She was running out of breath.

Her hands wrapped around the long, waved shape, and she pulled, but the cord at the end had gotten caught on something. The handle slipped from her grasp, disappearing into nothingness.

No… please…

Hayley panicked. She had to come up for oxygen, and that was when she saw how high the water was getting. The bottom half of the driver-side window was gone.

Don't give up, she told herself. She could find it. It had been right there.

She took another deep breath and went back under, hunching over the center console. She couldn't see through the blackness in front of her hands—

There! It was still dangling from the glove box.

She grabbed the handle and yanked on it again, but nothing happened. She wrapped her left hand around it too, pulling as hard as she could, and finally, the hatchet ripped free.

Shoving her hand through the corded loop, Hayley aimed the handle's metal tip at the top edge of the windshield, which wasn't yet submerged. She watched the first spider webs from the impact spread. They reached out further when she hit the same spot a second time.

The glass shattered out in front of her, and she spun the hatchet in her hand, using the hook-shape of the blade to rip more away, widening the hole enough for her to fit through.

She drew in one last breath and then kicked off the seat toward freedom. Glass shards sliced her arm and stomach as she pushed through the opening, but she didn't care. She wouldn't die down here, and that was all that mattered.

Hayley reached the surface, still clutching the little black hatchet. She swam to the edge of the trench, rain pelting her head. Heavy, unrelenting drops assaulted her from all sides, preventing her from getting enough air into her lungs, but she kept fighting nonetheless. Her brain refused defeat. Her limbs moved on autopilot.

Her knees crashed into the slanted side of the trench, and then her fingers sank into the mud, too. She'd made it.

She looked over her shoulder at the rushing water swallowing her car. Only the white roof was visible in the brown swamp. In another minute, there would be nothing left.

Hayley pushed off her aching muscles and started walking. She had no idea where she was. None of the sights looked familiar, but she eventually made it to the road. No cars passed her, and she didn't know how long she'd been walking when she finally saw lights up ahead. A motel.

With her last bit of strength, she dragged herself to the office. The middle-aged woman behind the front desk gaped at the sight of her—dripping wet, coated in mud, and wielding a hatchet.

The woman made the sign of a cross over her chest, uttering the words '*Dios mio*,' and Hayley cringed. She wouldn't want to meet herself at a shady motel off a dark highway at the moment, either.

"May I use your phone?" she asked as politely as she could so as not to frighten her further.

The clerk nodded and slid the phone on the counter over to her, then took a step back. Hayley didn't blame her. What she wouldn't give for a hot shower, clean clothes, and a bed.

Lifting the top of the ancient phone to her ear, she started pressing the numbered buttons and waited. In the silence that followed, her mind put all the little pieces of Carter's plan together. He had never intended to divorce her; the mugging, the run-in with the Yukon, the death trap of her Audi…

They were trying to get her out of their way. That was why he'd kicked up his public display of affection. So he could reap sympathy points for playing the grieving husband. And of course, he'd been out of town during the first two incidents—not that anyone would expect him to do the dirty work himself—but he still had airtight alibis. She had a feeling he was sitting on a plane right now, going who-knew-where, gloating about his scheme.

He would have it all upon her *untimely demise*—or mysterious disappearance. Which, of course, no one would question. Roy's connections would make sure of that. He controlled the state. There was nowhere for her to run.

At last, the line picked up, and her words shot out, "Daddy, I need your help."

53

J ameson raised his cuffed hands and rubbed his eye sockets with the heels until they burned. He'd spent the last three days on a bender but couldn't get the images out of his head. Each time he closed his eyes, there she was, every line, every freckle of her face etched into his memory.

My freaking sister! Of all the boys who came and went through the camp for decades, it had to be Hayley's father who knocked up his mom and then ditched her like she meant nothing?

He wished she'd never come back. He hadn't exactly been happy, but he'd been better than this. In only two months, she'd managed to wreck his entire existence. How was he supposed to bounce back from that?

He couldn't. And he didn't want to tell her, either. No point in both of them living with that knowledge. He didn't wish this on her.

Jameson gave up trying to ease the jackhammering inside his skull. His wrists dropped into his lap, and he let his shoulders sag. He kept his eyes closed, reciting the chain of numbers that comforted him. Whenever he found himself nearing his breaking point, the simple ten digits reminded him why he was still hanging on.

"Here we are again." Paul's boots dragged across the floor, approaching the cell bars. "I thought we had a deal that I would never find you in this cell again. You know I don't want to have to book you."

Jameson straightened and leaned back against the cold brick. "You do what you must. It's all the same to me."

"What could possibly be so bad that you can't come back from it? I've done some fucked-up shit when I was your age."

Oh, yeah? Jameson was a second away from asking if the good sheriff had ever banged his own sister. He was sure to win the bet… but possibly end up with a black eye, so he decided to keep his trap shut.

Paul sighed, then the lock clanked as he turned it over. "I did make one call for you," he said, sliding the cell door open.

Jameson's hazy vision landed on the large, dark-skinned man strolling up to the bars, hands buried in his pockets.

He shifted his boots on the ground and slouched lower. "I should've known she'd send you."

He made no move to leave the bench, but not because he wasn't grateful. First Summer and now Carl…

He'd put them through too much crap to have them come to his aid.

"You know my wife. Once she gets something in her head…" he trailed off. "She wouldn't stop yapping until I came down here and bailed your ass out. Couldn't have her going into labor over this." He coughed up a laugh. The man's imposing presence was still the same: casual black t-shirt, blue jeans, buzzed skull, and a wall of muscle.

They hadn't spoken in years. Not since Jameson started freezing everyone out. He felt so fucking guilty for all of it. He *had* been ungrateful. And selfish.

"Beth was a good woman," Carl said, knowing exactly what he was thinking. "We all loved her, and we all wanted to be there for you... wanted to help. But you pushed everyone away, Jameson."

He remembered the look on their faces. Couldn't be sure who else had known the truth about Mom's condition besides Carl. It had driven him mad with rage.

All that anger was gone now. He just felt hopeless.

Jameson cleared the frog in his throat, then found the words he'd been searching for. They were simple, but not always easy.

"I'm sorry," he said, the unintentional tremble in his voice underscoring his sincerity. Pressure from holding in tears built behind his nose and eyes.

Why are apologies so goddamn hard?

Carl leaned his shoulder into the side of the cell door. "You don't have to apologize. I told you, when you're ready, we'll be there for you. No judgment."

He turned over his shoulder, looking for a directive on how to proceed. "So, you're free to go or what?"

Jameson didn't move. Didn't really want to go back to the park. He rubbed his thumb across his aching knuckles. He'd still been picking splinters and shards of glass out of the cuts when *Under-Sheriff* Harris—good on her for that promotion— had pulled up. She'd looked smug, grinning down at him planted on the curb.

After all this time of trying to stay under the radar...

"He didn't actually get booked, thanks to his model behavior," Harris uttered from her desk in the back of the small station, head down in paperwork. "So there's no bail to settle. Take him home and make sure he sleeps off whatever *that* was." She motioned with her forefinger in his direction, not bothering to look up.

She hadn't considered it more than a temper tantrum. Good on him, he guessed. And why run? He'd done the deed, he'd face the consequences. He simply needed to blow off some steam. The fact that he was drunk off his ass did not help his equilibrium. Hence the parking of his rear on the concrete. He'd waited for the cops to show, then casually propped his elbows on his knees and held out his wrists. Like a good little criminal.

Cigarette dangling from his lips, he'd patiently waited for her to slap on the cuffs and take him into the station for vandalism. He'd been about done with this whole night anyway. He was exhausted and just wanted to sleep. But he couldn't do that at his place. Not with everything reminding him of her. He would gouge his fucking eyes out if it helped.

If she showed up at his house, would he be able to accept the truth? Or would he hate himself for wanting her still? He had to turn her away. Quit her cold turkey. It was for the best that he never saw her again.

Jameson dropped his feet to the ground, then rose and walked over to Carl. His friend gave him a nod, smiling as he squeezed his shoulder with a firm grip. His hand didn't feel as massive as it used to, but it was still as encouraging.

"All this because some girl broke your heart, huh?" he hinted at the reason for the drunken tantrum.

Some girl—The same words Jameson had used back then. *'…while I was off with some girl I'll never see again…'* Yep, the same girl he'd bailed on his mother for.

Jameson rounded his eyes in response. "I knew I should've told Summer to keep that to herself."

"We don't have secrets," Carl scoffed.

Right. But if that were true, he'd still be rotting in his cell. Or six feet under by now.

Harris unlocked the cuffs and nudged her head toward the door, a little smile dancing on her lips.

"Don't come back!" Paul's gruff voice bellowed from his office.

Jameson stifled a grin. A warmth spread through his chest, knowing that these people had never stopped caring for him.

"Who beats up an abandoned building? You suddenly afraid of taking on live opponents… getting your pretty face messed up?" Carl heckled on their way out. "I like the beard, by the way." He rubbed a hand across his own smooth chin. "Looks good on you. Summer would shave me in my sleep."

He let the old man drone on. For the first time in days, Jameson felt… not *good*, but *okay*. Things would be okay.

54

She'd rented a room at the motel while waiting for her father to arrive. He'd paid the mortified lady behind the desk off, so she wouldn't tell anyone that she'd seen Hayley stroll into the door in the middle of the night, hatchet swinging and all.

Her car had been pulled out of the ditch the next morning; no body was found. She'd followed the news on his plane back to Sacramento. The anchorwoman had repeated the report several times— *'Windshield broken…body could have washed out… searching the lake… female owner, Hayley Nolan, still presumed dead.'*

What if Jamie saw this on the news by chance? She couldn't reach out to him, it was too dangerous. She hadn't contacted the police. Chances were good they wouldn't believe her or cover the whole thing up. So she was going to stay dead. For a while, at least.

Keeping tabs on the news feed, she'd been hiding out at her father's Georgian colonial-style estate for the past four days. It wasn't any more comforting than Roy's mansion. And felt as much of a prison to her. She couldn't stand being trapped there any longer, either.

Dad understood. At her request, he arranged a flight for her on his private plane to and from West Yellowstone to visit a 'friend'.

Hayley rolled up to the house in the rental her father had organized for her at the airport. She parked it behind the Silverado in the driveway. When she got out, she immediately tensed. The smell of smoke hung in the air.

She shut the door quietly and listened for the crackling of fire coming from the back porch. The pit, she presumed. Though it wasn't cold and hardly dark outside to need it yet. Something about that made her nervous.

As she rounded the corner and climbed the two steps, she found Jamie seated in the wicker chair in front of the fire, the soles of his boots braced against the stone ledge around it. There was an empty box between his feet, barely far enough away from the licking flames. It sat askew inside its lid, as if tossed haphazardly.

He didn't acknowledge her. He kept his eyes on the pit, ripping out the pages of what appeared to be a journal in his hands. He was tossing one at a time into the fire in front of him.

"Turn around and go back," he said in a gruff manner that didn't match the warm tone he'd implored her with the last time they spoke.

Had she heard him right? Hayley wavered. "What?"

Rrrrip! He balled the next sheet in his fist and chucked it into the flames.

"Whatever you're looking for, you won't find it here. Turn around… get back in your car… and leave."

His breathing was slow and steady, his calmness a paradox to the turmoil his words stirred in her. The heat from the fire lashed at her insides.

"Why are you doing this?" she yelled, the panic in her rising higher. Why was he pushing her away now? "Are you angry that I left? I… I needed to think… I wanted this to be right."

She didn't want to dive into this, not knowing how to handle her situation with Carter. A whole lot of good *that* had done her, she was technically deceased at the moment.

But no way would Jamie know that she'd narrowly escaped death mere days ago. So what the hell was he so worked up about? Why wouldn't he just tell her? They could work through it, couldn't they?

"Jamie—"

"Please leave, Hayley," he repeated in an even tone, feeding the flames another page.

"That's it? That's all you have to say to me? You woke up this morning and changed your mind… decided that you were done?"

He ignored her, continuing his farce.

"Don't do this to me," she begged, almost screaming. "Don't do this to *us*. Not now." Her mind was racing with a million thoughts, but she couldn't hear them over the deafening pulse in her ears.

"If you want me to leave, then at least tell me to my face." Maybe his eyes would give her something to go on.

He crushed the paper in his palm but didn't throw it yet.

Why was he so cold toward her all of a sudden? What had caused this shift in him? Was it Roy? Had he threatened him?

He sent the paper ball in his fist flying to its demise like all its predecessors.

"What the fuck are you burning that's so important you can't even look at me?" She lunged for the fire, trying to snatch up one of the pages.

Jamie jumped out of his seat, and his hand cuffed her wrist so quickly it sent her spinning. Her hair whipped through the air.

"DON'T!" he snapped, the red flames of the pit thrashing in his eyes. "That's none of your business."

Hayley swallowed in shock, utterly frozen by the aggressive reaction she'd drawn out of him. Her eyes shifted to his knuckles. They were scuffed and bloodied.

He dropped her wrist in a sharp motion, his blue eyes turning glacial. "Go home, Hayley. There's nothing here for you. There is no *us*. You shouldn't have come back."

The way he spoke her name was like ice down her back. His tone was so detached, so foreign.

He pivoted on his heels, and her hands jolted up, fists clenching his shirt at his chest to pull him back. "I love you," she blurted as a last resort to grasp his attention.

Tears started spearing into her eyes. "I've loved you for a very long time. The only reason I've made it this far is because, in my head, you were always with me. Every time I needed you… you were there, holding my hand. Even if it wasn't real… you helped me through."

He tore her hands away, as if he couldn't stand her touching him. "That wasn't me, Hayley." Her gaze flicked to his other hand, the knuckles of that one gashed too. "That was your imagination." He gave her a shove, causing her to stumble backwards.

'*Violent past*,' she heard Amber's voice in her ear.

His face had no marks, which meant his opponent hadn't landed any hits. Never gotten the chance, she presumed. Was the poor bastard still breathing?

"You're not in love with me," he went on, fists clenched. "You're in love with an *idea* of me. *You* got yourself through all that. *You* did that. Not me. You put me on a pedestal I can't live up to."

He tossed the rest of the journal into the flames too, then strode away, abandoning her outside without an explanation. The crackling fire was all that was left of him.

Hayley glanced down at the burning label:

Lizzy Bishop

Why was he burning his mom's diary… erasing her memories? Did they mean so little to him?

She wished he hadn't dropped it dead-center into the pit. Something in her wanted to preserve it.

Her eyes landed on the floor on the opposite side of where he'd sat. It was a photograph. Or what was left of it. It must've fallen off the edge without him noticing.

Hayley's eyes followed the direction he'd gone. The lights were off inside, and he'd drawn the curtain to the bedroom after locking the doors behind himself. He'd learned from the last time. *Go figure.*

Keeping a lookout, she slowly bent down to pick it up. She caught a spurt of joy when she noticed it was only partially burned. Two faces in the shot were still visible: Beth and…

… her own father?

Why did Beth have a picture of them together as teenagers? Confused, Hayley turned it over—

A lump formed in her throat as she stared down at the top half of a heart encircling the words Tommy & Lizzy 4-ever.

Carl and he had talked a lot, on the drive and afterwards. His babysitter had stayed the night after dropping him off, since he was technically on house arrest, then taken him to get his truck in town in the morning; once Jameson recalled the general vicinity of where he'd ditched it. And, hey, what-do-you-know, it had been parked in a proper parking zone, inside the lines, AND parallel to the road. How had he managed that? He *was* a model criminal.

So maybe there was hope for reformation at the end of this. He needed to go through all the steps first. He'd started with one apology already, he wouldn't stop there.

Jameson had gone to see Amber next. The conversation had been something like:

'I asked you to find a new place a month ago.'

'I'm not going anywhere. Not until we talk. You owe me that much.'

And he truly did. He'd never meant to deceive her. Her family lived in Bozeman, but the two of them had met in college, halfway across the country. Maybe it was the crazy odds that had driven his reasoning. They had moved in together after graduating. As friends. And yes, there had been the occasional benefits, but they hadn't been exclusive until he'd popped that stupid question.

"It's because of her, isn't it? That girl who came by. Hayley."

"No. It's not about her. It's about us, Amber. I'm not in love with you."

"But you said—"

"I know what I said. And it wasn't a lie. I thought I was. I wanted it to be true… I was wrong. I'm sorry. I'm sorry for being a coward… and for misleading you."

His second apology in 24 hours hadn't been any easier than the first, but it had brought them both the needed closure.

He'd returned to Bishop Park after that, and for ten miles, he'd had the sense that someone was tailing him. Then the suspicious station wagon had followed I-20 south deeper into Idaho while he'd taken the highway to cross back into Montana.

His skin prickled with the same awareness again later that night. He felt Hayley arrive before she rounded the corner to the back porch while he was in the middle of destroying the evidence. Luckily, he'd gotten rid of the photos first. As long as he held onto the diary, she wouldn't get a glimpse. And, oh boy, did he hold on.

Each page he tore free ripped a little bit of the truth away. It was liberating in a sense. The fear of her discovering what he knew was being purged by the flames.

Jameson didn't look at the ink on the paper anymore. Didn't look at her either. There was only fire.

He didn't waver. No matter how much she begged or how much it hurt to see her cry when he finally did meet her eyes. She thought this was the worst? She had no idea. She didn't understand his gift of ignorance. The flames were for her sake, purifying her with every word they consumed.

So Jameson kept his lips sealed. Would take the secret to his grave for her. That was his solace. He had a snowball's chance in hell at happiness, but she could still find it. She would forget about him, have babies, and grow old with someone else.

Yes. It was done. He had burned every last piece. She would never know.

OF APPLES AND TREES

55

Taking the steps up, Hayley stared down at the movement of her feet as she passed in between the set of pillars. The female housekeeper opened the door, and she felt horrible for not remembering the kind woman's name. She seemed to be Tia's age.

She wore a simple gray dress underneath a white apron, and her dark hair was up in a chignon. Narrow streaks of gray ran along the sides. She greeted Hayley with a warm smile that instantly made her miss her friend. She hadn't seen Tia since the day of the Gibsons' garden party.

Hayley returned her smile and stepped inside, squinting through the assault on her retinas caused by the marble flooring and snow-white paneling on the walls. It was too bright. Everything was immaculately detailed with tradition at its core: dark wood-capped banisters, tall ceilings, and high archways. The pillars throughout the home were all Roman Doric, with little frill but a base at the bottom of the smooth shaft. It screamed elegance while shoving the Roman architecture down your throat from all sides the second you entered the foyer.

More of the classic architecture was highlighted in the liberal use of niches and alcoves. Though the word '*use*' was a misleading term. They served no purpose other than being decorative. Completely unnecessary. There wasn't even anything displayed in them—no vases, no statues, no paintings… nothing. It was all empty. Like this house. She hated this house. Always had. It was cold and detached, like her father.

But she *was* grateful. He'd welcomed her with open arms, despite the way they'd left things six years ago.

Hayley marched upstairs to his office and knocked. He was usually reading through paperwork at this hour; it was only a little past nine in the morning. She'd stayed the night at a hotel near the airport, turning the photograph of him and Beth over and over in her hand. She hadn't been able to put it down since she'd lifted it off the floor. Was this the reason for Jamie to cut ties with her? What else was in the diary? Was his suspicion right? Was there proof?

Hayley could only get her answers from the original source himself: *Tommy*.

On the other side of the solid oak door, her father's surly voice prompted her to enter, and she drew a quick breath of encouragement into her lungs before following through. The interior was exactly what you expect from the outside of the house, but dark and bitter instead of the lightness the bright paint offered. The only thing that wasn't depressing here was the white marble fireplace.

Her eyes shifted nervously from his shape behind the desk to the door at her backside as she closed it.

"What is it, sweetheart?" he coaxed in a little softer tone.

Hayley felt tongue-tied while dragging her feet up to him.

"I didn't expect you back so soon. Everything alright with your friend?"

She nodded, then swallowed and opened her mouth. "There is something I need to ask you… and I don't want any evasive answers, or excuses, or lies. I want the flat-out truth," she demanded, her tone gaining in confidence as she steeled her spine.

Her father's brows winged up, then a deep crease formed in between the two halves, the wheels in his mind visibly turning to gauge the agenda behind her stern request.

Will he deliver?

Hayley set the photo down on the desk in front of him. His dark green eyes dropped from her to the exhibit in question, and a sudden mask of shock replaced his wariness. His gaze flitted back and forth between the picture and her two more times before it settled on the former.

Hayley braced her fingertips on the edge of the desk. Leaning in, she put the spotlight on him and waited.

He picked it up… His lips parted, then closed on a sigh… His Adam's apple bobbed…

Finally, he cleared his throat and recovered his speech. "You know I attended the summer camp when I was your age. We all did."

Yes, Carter's, Joey's, and Aaron's dad, too. She'd heard the stories.

"I made lots of friends there—"

"She is not one of the students," Hayley interrupted, losing patience. "I know who she is— was," she corrected, forcing her voice steady.

Her father hesitated to respond, his features twitching apprehensively. He was wondering how much she knew.

Hayley rolled her eyes. "You were more than friends," she clarified for him, helping things along. She specifically told him not to beat around the bush.

She watched him ease back into his chair. The stiff leather crinkled under the movement.

His mouth drew into a thin line, then his tongue swept across his lips. "You said your friend gave you this?"

"Her son," Hayley elaborated. "I met him back at summer camp, and we became friends."

"Her boy? I can't believe she kept this all these years… It was so… so long ago. I knew she'd gotten married at some point. I heard about her passing, too."

"It's true, then? You and her?"

"Yes," he admitted with another uncomfortable sigh. "We were in love. Wrote letters back and forth through the years until we saw each other again every summer. It went on for a few years."

Hayley recalled his words from their last conversation about her having no clue what he'd sacrificed to appease his own father for the sake of the family's legacy. "*She* was what you had to give up," she concluded.

"I told your grandfather that I wanted to marry her. He didn't take kindly to the idea, calling it a foolish notion. Told me I had no say in whom I was going to marry. He had already chosen your mother for me."

He paused and lowered his gaze at the painful subject out of respect for her, not with regard to his own feelings. He'd never cared. Had never loved her mother. That was why there were no pictures of her in the house.

Hayley watched her father blink, suddenly heavy with emotion he'd never expressed before, and for a moment she got a glimpse behind the stoic man. "I was heartbroken when I heard about Liz," he said with sincerity.

"Yeah, I can only imagine because I've never seen you shed a single tear for my mother." Fresh rage buzzed under her skin at his admission.

"Hayley—"

"Spare me any more lectures about your legacy. It's true, then? All of it?" He really *had* been in love with Beth but had to break it off because of his own father's disapproval. "How could you, Dad? How could you knock her up and leave her like that if you loved her?"

"What are you talking about, sweetheart?"

"You didn't know she was pregnant? She had a *son*. Jameson. *He* found the picture." She recited the evidence in case he had already forgotten.

"Pregnant? Wait, you think he's your half-brother?" *Bullseye!* "That's impossible. We never… I never… I was careful."

Careful? Was he implying that he'd pulled out? That wasn't a foolproof method.

"No. You're mistaken. I'm not the boy's—"

Sudden comprehension struck him, but Hayley couldn't follow his train of thought. His eyes darted rapidly in a flustered expression. "Oh, no. No-no… It couldn't be," her father mumbled to himself, then refocused his anxious stare on her. "What does he look like?"

"Not like *you*, actually."

The structure of her father's face was much rounder compared to Jamie's sharp cheekbones, defined nose, and the square chin he hid under his beard. Even if he had facial hair, she couldn't draw any resemblance to the man in front of her.

"He mostly looks like his mom: same smile, blue eyes, dark, almost black hair. He… uhm, he kinda looks like…"

Hayley raked her mind over the details when she finally recognized the similarities—

"OH… MY… GOD!"

56

Marcus' ID lit up the screen, and he answered it, already knowing the reason behind the call. It wasn't work-related. Amber had probably reached out to Em, venting to her about him giving her the boot. And, of course, she'd mentioned Hayley too, so his friend was now calling to confirm the allegations.

He didn't pussyfoot around the subject either. Marcus dove right into the interrogation as if he'd made a list of questions he wanted checked off. It was the basic stuff: *'Who the hell is she?'*, *'Where'd you meet her?'*, and *'Why the fuck didn't you tell me?'*

He evaded.

"Did you cook for her?"

Jameson chewed his lower lip in more silence, and that was enough of an answer for his friend.

"You did, you slick son of a bitch," he deduced. "Did you make the fajitas?"

"Yeah." This time, Jameson laughed in affirmation, rubbing a palm down his thigh.

Marcus popped something into his mouth, mumbling, "You're welcome," then chomping loudly into the speaker.

He was the one who'd given him pointers on the recipe. The dish was the reason Emily gave him a shot, and supposedly it had a spicy reputation that had nothing to do with the flavor—something about the men in his family cooking for their girlfriends before they became their wives—*all coincidence.*

Jameson could hear Em's elated chuckle in the background as Marcus made further insinuations and called Hayley a unicorn. He ended the call before being forced to elaborate on his nonexistent intentions toward the elusive girl they'd never meet.

He didn't blame his friends for being curious about who she was and where she'd come from. He couldn't even answer the simple questions.

'So, she just dropped out of the sky and into your lap?'

No. But she'd always been there, like a shadow attached to his body, an imprint of her spirit connected to his soul.

And now she was gone. He didn't feel whole. His chest hurt. He hadn't been able to expand his lungs fully since breaking Hayley's heart. As if he'd lost his privilege to oxygen. Didn't deserve to be breathing the air around him after sucking it out of her.

Jameson sank down on his old bed, feeling almost as wretched as he had the last time he'd sat on it. He reached over the side and retrieved the flat, rectangular shape he'd almost forgotten about from underneath. It was still wrapped in the same brown paper.

Looking down, he gave the sides of the frame a brief squeeze, then ripped the flaps on the back open. With each tear, he revealed more of the old photograph from Mom's last birthday. He remembered the day they had taken it.

That was only two months prior…

He hardly recognized himself. He was standing behind her, his arms draped over her shoulders in a tight hug. She had her head tipped toward his at an angle, hands up, clasping his forearms.

Eileen and Carl had thrown her a huge surprise party. She'd been so happy.

"I fucked up, Mom. I fucked up so bad… I don't know what to do." He felt like he owed her an apology as well.

Jameson recalled sitting in the tree, letting the wind carry her ashes away. He'd climbed as high as he could reach, early in the morning, dew drops still clinging to the leaves. He'd sat there by himself for over an hour before being able to let go of the physical part of her.

He'd done the same with Dad's, per her request, only climbing higher now than she'd let him at ten years old while she'd watched him from the ground.

This time he'd been alone, though, with no one there to hold him on the bottom after he'd made his descent… only more of the same loneliness greeting him.

That feeling had never left. Only become more bearable.

"I'm sorry for letting you down."

The sound of a car door made him tense as it slammed shut right outside his window at the end of the driveway, where it curved around the house.

Would she really come back?

Something didn't feel right. He set the picture frame down on the mattress and went over to the window. A black Escalade was parked behind his Silverado.

"Who the hell—"

Damn. The back door to the kitchen was unlocked.

Jameson rushed to the kitchen, remembering his rifle still lying on the island. He rounded the corner of the hallway and stopped short, a gasp shooting past his parted lips.

"Nice piece. I like your taste," the stranger said in a gravelly voice as he hovered over the weapon. He was wearing a dark two-piece suit with a white shirt and black tie, his jacket open at the front. He leaned into his hands, which were braced on either side of the black Savage 110 Magpul Hunter.

Adrenaline raced through Jameson's system at high speed. Staring at the man in front of him, things started falling into place rapidly, and pieces of an entirely new puzzle came together.

He knew he looked like his mom. People had been telling him that for as long as he could remember. And he'd always been able to put on muscle easily, like his father— well, Ben. But this man, the man standing in his kitchen, was his biological father; same height, same build...

And it was not Thomas Wilkins.

Motherfucker! He'd sent her away for no reason. Everything he'd been through... all the agony...

"My name is Roy. Roy Nolan." He straightened, introducing himself before Jameson could get his lips unglued to ask. "I'm looking for my daughter-in-law. You don't happen to know where I can find her, do you?"

Jameson shook his head warily as his chest tightened up with the increase in his body temperature.

His black eyes narrowed into a skeptical glare from across the island. "Are you sure? Her car was pulled out of the floodwaters after the storm four days ago, but her body hasn't been recovered. Something tells me she didn't drown. She's a slippery little thing... with good survival instincts."

Floodwater? Drown? 'The fuck was he talking about? Hayley was just here last night. Was he the last one to have seen her?

"I have no idea what you're talking about," Jameson bluffed, folding his arms over his chest, his voice level.

The corner of the man's mouth twitched with amusement. "You're a bad liar, Mr. Davis."

Because he didn't make it a habit. This guy was a politician. Governor, right? So he had plenty of practice in the department, surrounded by some of the worst liars one could only imagine. No doubt, he could sniff them out like a bloodhound.

"I can see the thoughts racing through your mind... so many questions."

Yeah, he had a few. But for now, he was glad Hayley had given them the slip. Where was Carter? Why had he sent his father?

Beads of sweat gathered along the back of his neck under the bastard's scrutiny. Jameson raised his chin and stood tall. He wasn't intimidated.

Hands in the pockets of his black slacks, Roy looked him up and down, then huffed, either because he was impressed or still amused by the unexpected defiance. He was probably used to people kissing his ass.

"You have her spunk," he acknowledged with approval in his tone.

Jameson lowered his hands, grinding his teeth in a sneer. He couldn't stay quiet anymore. "You!" he gritted out. "I know who you are."

Roy gave a weak laugh, catching on to what he was implying. He raised his forefinger toward Jameson. "So you figured it out. I knew Lizzy had a kid the right age... always had my suspicions about you."

He watched Roy push off the island and come around toward him, moving with the dominance of a predator. Jameson could see why Hayley was afraid of him. His jaw was as inflexible as granite, his dark eyes void of any emotion. The threat level behind them was clear.

If Mom was in love with Tommy, why *him*? How? What had he missed in the diary?

'*...Ben found me after.*'

After what? What happened the night Tommy left? Mom mentioned his friend but no name. It was *him*. Roy was Tommy's friend. Like Carter and the other boy... they had fooled Hayley. Had Mom become a victim of the same dirty trick?

Heat rose behind his eyelids as he drew faster, shorter breaths. His shoulders rose and fell with the climb in agitation, the familiar rage brewing in his blood. The short fuse, the violent impulse... it was all because of *him*. Jameson had gotten his temper from him—*his father*—and the more he focused on it, the hotter his blood ran.

Roy halted no more than a foot in front of him and quirked his brow. "You want to know how I did it?" Then he leaned in, lowering his voice to a whisper. "I lured your mom to their secret meeting place down by the lake with a note. I knew all about their secret. Who do you think helped him hide it from his father? So maybe I wanted a little gratitude, a piece of the action. They fucking owed me."

Slanting his body away from the man, Jameson's head shook in disbelief. His brain scrambled to find another logic behind the insinuation.

"I made it look like the note was from Tom, telling her how he wanted to take back what he'd said. And Liz fell for it. But instead of him, she found me. Imagine the look of surprise on her face."

Roy's features twisted with spite. Jameson had seen the expression before—so many times, he couldn't recount. It was like staring into a mirror. A distorted fun house mirror, but a mirror nonetheless.

A crushing realization came down on him. His mom had been forced to look at his face every day and had managed to do so without any resentment or grudge. Only love and devotion.

"I've always liked a girl with fire in her blood. You know what I'm talking about, don't you? Hayley got that same untamed fire. I should have kept her for myself instead of giving her to Carter. He doesn't know how to handle a biter—"

His phone went off, interrupting his speech. He must've been expecting urgent news because he had the nerve to put Jameson *on hold* and pull it out. He gave the screen a glance, then slid it back into his pocket. Satisfaction crossed his face.

Hayley! They have her.

Roy refocused on him, tipping his head at an angle. "I want you to know that I will take great pleasure in breaking her in myself."

Jameson went nuclear. The heat of the rage flooded his tense muscles, and his forearms flexed under the pressure of his fists. He couldn't change the past, but he would protect Hayley from these monsters at all costs…

…even if he had to risk a concussion to do it.

He clutched the lapels of Roy's suit jacket, then ripped his head toward his own skull, bracing himself for the impact.

CRACK!

The high-pitched ringing that resonated in his ears told him that it had been a good one before Roy stumbled off-balance. The cell dropped to the floor. Jameson didn't hesitate. Through the momentary brain fog, he drew his right fist back and punched his knuckles into the asshole's perfect jaw.

The sting shot through the nerves of his hand, vibrating his forearm. It was exhilarating. He watched with satisfaction how the second blow sent Roy spinning face-first into the island. Hands splayed out to catch his fall, his breath exploded out of him, and red speckles of blood sprayed onto the white marble.

More sharp pain darted up his entire arm to his shoulder, but Jameson ignored it. He kept his focus on Roy and reacted quickly when he reached for the rifle in front of him. Leading with the buttstock, he swung around, aiming for Jameson's temple.

He didn't get that far, though; Jameson caught him mid-sweep. He yanked the weapon out of the man's weakened grasp and brought it down on his forehead, dead center. It rendered an imprint of the shape as Roy's body went limp underneath him.

Unconscious, Jameson left him where he dropped.

"It was something Roy said when he looked back at the Bishop's house that morning. It didn't sit right with me."

"What did he say, Dad?"

"He said, 'Always go out with a bang, Tommy'. I thought he was referring to me breaking Liz's heart."

It all made sense now. His best friend had raped Beth the last night at the camp. That was why she hadn't shown up for departure. All these years, Hayley's father had been oblivious to the truth, worked alongside the man, and trusted him…

And she hadn't seen it either. She'd refused to acknowledge the similarities in the grown man in front of her, blinded by seeing the charming boy he used to be. Jamie and Carter looked nothing alike because Carter looked more like his mom. Jamie, on the other hand, was the spitting image of his father—of Roy.

But Jamie was a better man than either of them. He wasn't cruel. Wasn't ruthless. It was a classic case of 'nature versus nurture'. Carter had never stood a chance under Roy, he'd shaped his son into another version of himself. He could've been better, too.

Hayley arranged for the charter jet at the same small airfield she'd used only a day ago instead of leaving out of Sacramento International. She gave the spare iPhone her father had insisted on another glance, then turned it off and stuffed it into her bag. Her Galaxy S22 was still in her bedroom at the mansion, where she'd left it a week ago.

Sam, her father's driver, took the car straight up to the plane inside the hangar, and someone she couldn't see through the tinted glass was already standing by to open the door for her. She grabbed her bag off the seat beside her and stepped out.

"Thank y—"

The words caught in her throat when her eyes darted up… way up, and landed on Mateo's hard features.

Hayley felt her knees go soft. Her hand shot to the top of the open car door as she teetered, and her mouth formed a *no*, but the sound didn't reach her ears.

"Hello, darling," Carter's voice called from the direction of the Learjet.

Her head snapped around to the top of the stairs, where he loomed. He was wearing only his black suit pants and matching shirt, with two buttons popped. No tie or jacket. *Dressed for comfort*, she figured. Hands braced at the top of the doorway, he looked so proud of himself.

The sound of the door behind her slamming shut made her jump. The echo inside the metal tunnel ramped up the speed of her pulse. The pressure thrummed at her temples with every rapid beat of her heart.

"I hope you don't mind me hijacking your plane and redirecting your flight plan?" he asked blithely, as though he hadn't already cleared everything with the crew and pilot.

Her body gave a sudden jerk at the thought of getting on the jet with him. Mateo gripped her upper arm, his cold expression reminding her that she had nowhere to run.

Carter grinned, then nudged his head toward the cabin behind him. "Move it. I'm taking you home."

Hayley's feet refused to move at his command. "Today!" his voice hollered through the hangar in exasperation. "I got a schedule to keep."

He pushed off and disappeared inside. Mateo's grip jostled her forward, half pushing, half dragging her toward the plane.

57

Did they really have her? He couldn't be sure.

As the Bluetooth adapter in the Aux jack connected to his S22, he stared down at the screen and wavered. In his head, he'd dialed the numbers so many times… even keyed them in without his thumb following through on pressing the call button. What were the odds of her still having the same phone number?

"Fuck it." Jameson punched the digits into his cell from memory and held his breath, listening for the dial tone—

Click. "It's Hayley. Leave a message."

He hung up.

Damn. There was a bad feeling churning in his gut when the call went straight to voicemail. It had been her on the recorded message, though, so at least he'd gotten the number right.

He quickly scrolled through his contacts, placing another call, and this time the line connected on the first ring.

"What?"

"I know I'm all out of favors from you, but I need to ask for one more," he implored Paul. "I need an address."

This one wasn't for himself, so Jameson hoped for the best. He also mentioned the break-in and the unconscious man in his kitchen, even providing the sheriff with the intruder's name. To his surprise, Dad's old friend was already familiar with the governor. Before going on his last tour, Ben had asked Paul to keep an eye out for the guy without elaborating on why, but the sheriff had never forgotten about his promise.

Unfortunately, thirty minutes later, Paul called him back with the bad news: they didn't find the governor or his fancy ride at the park.

Great. So there was no proof that he'd ever even been there, and Jameson was about to pull a B and E on the guy's private estate under the mere suspicion of a hostage situation.

He wished he'd taken the keys to the Escalade. He didn't know how much of a head start he had on Roy. He could make it on a full tank, but it would still take him five hours, whereas the governor probably had a jet waiting on standby at the nearest airfield.

Jameson put more weight on the gas pedal, glancing at the *Savage* on the passenger seat. It wasn't the kind of weapon you'd want in close quarters, and he had no idea what he was walking into. He felt a lot better having swiped his Springfield Hellcat from the hidden drop-shelf by the back door before leaving the house. It was a strong but lightweight sub-compact 9mm pistol, outfitted with a low-profile, micro-red dot for instant target acquisition. The reduced muzzle rise of the newer configuration and enhanced trigger offered better control, plus rapid, accurate follow-up shots—if needed.

He dialed Hayley's number again. Still no answer.

She was roused by a voice whisper-shouting her name. "Hayley! Hayley, wake up. Please, wake up."

Blinking herself awake, she recognized the familiar hazel-green eyes staring back at her from a low angle beside her head. It was Aaron. He was kneeling by her head, giving her shoulder a gentle shake. His face showed a flicker of relief once her vision focused.

What was he doing here… in her bedroom… at the mansion?—she quickly identified her surroundings with a shift in view by lifting her head off the pillow. To her knowledge, he was happily married and living somewhere in Colorado.

Sitting all the way up, she raised a weak hand to her temple. Her throat was dry. She tried to swallow but got nowhere.

"Wha—" Her voice croaked, and Aaron shushed her by pressing a finger to his lips while shaking his head apprehensively.

The uncomfortable expression twisting his handsome features told her that he didn't want to be here anymore than she did. He looked terrified. Beneath a faint stubble, his jaw was under tension.

Carter was making him do this. Again. "What does he have on you?" she wondered.

Aaron's warm eyes cut away from her, unfocused, and his lips twitched before they parted to answer. "I… I did something. Something bad."

He appeared guilt-stricken, and it couldn't be from what he and his former roommate did to her. They'd been over that. So Hayley pressed, "What did you do?"

His chestnut-colored hair wasn't as shaggy as it used to be. He ran a hand over the top of the neat, clean cut. "Melissa," he blurted, as if that explained everything.

"Who?"

"Melissa Jenkins."

The girl who cried rape right before they had gone to summer camp that first year?

She remembered that Melissa had been in her and Aaron's grade but had not returned to school the following year, and no one had heard from her ever again. She'd been fourteen. Hayley hardly remembered her at all.

"She was hanging out with Carter in our room while I was out. When I came back, she was in my bed. He had slipped something into her drink and said she was a gift for me."

Yeah, Hayley could imagine him pulling that kind of trick to rope Aaron into unopposed servitude. She scoffed. "And you fell for that?"

"He said if I didn't do it, then he would. I didn't want him to hurt her." Aaron's eyes teared up as he bit his lower lip. "He recorded it to blackmail me."

So Aaron had been Carter's muppet all along? Their entire friendship had been a lie? Hayley couldn't believe it.

"You bastard." Her palms clenched around her thighs, nails digging into bare skin. If she wasn't so sure they were both going to die tonight, she'd happily strangle him for Melissa.

"I was just a kid… I was scared."

"So was she," Hayley stressed. Carter had learned from his father at a young age, hadn't he? She never realized how young.

"I know you hate me, Hayley. But I'm truly sorry," he mumbled with remorse.

"I don't hate you. I pity you," she clarified the distinction. "You rolled over. At least I fought back." Her voice took on a quiver as her hands curled into fists. Her fingers were ice-cold and numb.

"As you can see, I invited an old friend." Carter announced himself from the door to their shared bathroom at her back. "I'm glad you two are getting reacquainted. It's been too long, I thought we should get together again."

Hayley's eyes shifted right as far as they could without turning her head. The mobility of her neck was blocked by the fear creeping up her spine. Over her shoulder, she watched Carter saunter closer with a casual stride, hands clasped behind his back and out of her view.

"For old time's sake," he tacked on.

Aaron panicked, shooting to his feet. "I'm sorry, Hayley. I'm so fucking sorry." His eyes were wide, and his splayed palms went up as he backed away, trembling. "I swear I didn't want to go along with it—"

BOOM!

The bullet between the eyes shut him up. And that was when shit got real.

58

The address from Paul took him to a property east of Salt Lake City, along the other side of the Wasatch Mountains. From what he could tell, the old Nolan family estate sat on a foothill and held a little more than an acre of land. Wild brush and weeds cluttered the range, but there were taller trees too, and now that it was dark, he could sneak up close on foot.

The mansion itself was huge. A castle. Complete with a stone exterior and an eight-foot wall to keep uninvited guests like him out.

What kind of security could he expect? Jameson didn't see any cameras mounted besides the one above the impregnable front gate at the top of the driveway.

He circled the property once, then steered the Silverado toward the rear of the house, where it was somewhat hidden in the vegetation. At least as much as you *could* hide a fully blacked-out Chevy truck with a 6-inch lift kit. He kept it at a less suspicious distance.

Ghosting toward the impressive wall enclosing the mansion, he watched for traffic at the gate. A set of headlights flashed, then a white Lincoln Continental made its way up the driveway.

Is it Roy?

Had he made it this close only for the bastard to beat him by minutes?

A jolt of adrenaline put him into gear. Jameson pushed speed from his legs and charged the 8-foot obstacle in front of him. Thrusting the sole of his combat boots into the stone, he ran up and reached for the ledge. The stone scraped against his chest, his hands burned, but he gripped it tight and pulled up.

He heaved himself to the flat top in time to see two men exiting the vehicle, neither of them Roy. The big one moved like a bodyguard, but the shorter of the two appeared to be in a state of intimidation rather than protection. He was directed to the front door, a forceful grip under his arm making sure he didn't stray.

Jameson squatted briefly on the 12-inch width of the wall to get the layout. A dim light was on in a second-floor bedroom, but there was no sign of movement. The rest of the house was dark and quiet.

No staff?

He turned over and lowered himself on the other side, landing quietly in the grass. His eyes scanned the dark perimeter, and he decided to go in through the kitchen.

Jameson sneaked up to the door, peeking inside to verify the lack of household personnel again. It was late. Maybe they had already taken off—

He ducked. His heart punched him in the throat at the start. There was movement. Through the window, he caught the shape of the large man crossing the foyer and leaving through the front door. No alarm was set, but he did turn the lock from the outside.

Jameson listened for the rustling of keys, footsteps down the stairs, crunching gravel, then the car door…

Before the sound of the engine kicked in, he pulled his gun from the holster inside his right back pocket. Under the noise of the throttle, he used the pistol's grip to shatter one of the 5-by-5-inch panes beside the lock. Keeping a lookout over his shoulder, he waited for the car to pull away, then reached inside and flipped the switch to let himself in.

The *Hellcat* remained drawn as he stepped around the broken glass. Muzzle leading the way, the textured grip felt secure despite his sweaty palms.

He was almost at the archway to the foyer when there was movement upstairs: a door opened, then shut, footsteps, and a familiar voice sweeping the length of the banister—Carter's. "No. The Feds started snooping around… How the hell should I know? It wasn't my fault the handover went sideways."

Another door slammed shut, and Jameson didn't catch any more of the conversation. It sounded as though he'd botched some kind of deal. *Bummer*.

A shadow crossed the foyer's space.

He ducked back behind the cabinets and dropped into a crouch. *Who else is in the house? Where's the other guy?*

Keeping the gun low and his arms straight down between his knees, he heard what he thought were soft paws on tile and a faint jingling sound caused by motion. His eyes shifted to a set of dog bowls against the far wall ahead of him. He wondered what kind of breed fit Carter's personality.

"Please be a Chihuahua," he whispered to himself. *Or some kind of Pomeranian.*

The deep growl that answered his prayer sounded too beefy for that.

Fuck.

Jameson held his breath and slowly angled his head to peep around the cabinet's corner. Directing his field of vision to the open doorway, his eyes opened wide to a robust pit bull. Its lips curled away to flaunt pearly white fangs. It wanted him to know who was in charge.

He swallowed. Forcing his breathing steady, Jameson adjusted his palm around the pistol's grip, slipping his forefinger to the trigger. He didn't want to shoot the dog. It was kind of cute. Minus the razor blades.

Letting out another growl, the canine abruptly sheathed its fangs and stuck its nose up, sniffing the air. It gave a little whine, then began ambling toward him. Muzzle low to the ground, it followed the foreign trail with curiosity, not alarm.

Jameson relaxed his grip on the weapon. The dog kept sniffing him, then, on a weak yap of approval, all but climbed into his lap. It nudged him with its nose as if expecting him to pet it…

So he obliged, taking his right hand off the gun and stroking the white fur on its chest.

Did it welcome every intruder like this? 'The fuck kind of guard dog was this?

"Why you acting like you know me"—Jameson reached for the tag around its muscled neck to get its name—"Smokey? Your name is *Smokey*?" he repeated, suppressing a grin before a large tongue darted toward him in confirmation.

The puppy's paws were white, too, the rest a charcoal gray. *The name, though?* It struck a chord.

"You're Hayley's, aren't you?" Jameson asked, raking his fingers through the fur at the side of his neck.

Smokey chuffed a soft bark.

"She once called me that, too."

The crunching of gravel beneath tires made them both jerk on alert. The beam of headlights shifted through the room as the vehicle approached.

Jameson returned both hands to his gun, and Smokey dropped back into his animus growl before Roy even entered the house. *Interesting*, he thought. The dog had the right instincts.

He had no idea how he'd beaten the governor here, but Jameson wasn't going to argue. He wouldn't let him go upstairs.

"Don't fucking move," he ordered, charging through the archway into the foyer, the barrel of the *Hellcat* level with the bastard's face.

Roy didn't bother raising his hands. He looked unimpressed. "My-my, Mr. Davis. Breaking and entering, holding the governor at gunpoint... you got yourself in quite the pickle there." Hands in his pockets, Roy took a slow step closer. And then another one. "How do you think this is going to play out?"

"I said don't fucking move!" He felt his shoulders flex. Every muscle in his body was under tension.

"Are you going to shoot me in my own house? On what grounds? You are the one breaking the law," he pointed out, brows cocked in a challenge.

Jameson glared at the red dot in the small space between them... and then he didn't. A gunshot went off on the second floor, drawing his attention away.

When his view swung back, Roy had his own gun drawn less than four feet from him.

Both of them fired and dodged out of the way simultaneously, each lunging to their left—Roy in the direction of the front door and Jameson toward the stairs.

Pain flared as he crushed his arm beneath his weight, the edges of two steps digging in.

Wasting no time on the minor injury, he spun around, hitting the stairs again, in four places down his back this time. His legs kicked out, searching for traction on the slick flooring, and his hands shot up, pointing the gun at Roy, who was already back on his feet, doing the same.

Jameson had nowhere to go. He saw the red dot and fired again, unsure where the bullet hit because, out of nowhere, Smokey leaped into his vision. The pit bull's vicious teeth clamped down on Roy's extended forearm, changing the trajectory of his gun and saving Jameson from getting shot.

Fucking hell. He'd felt the slug zip past his left cheek right before it smashed into the step beside him, pulverizing the mahogany.

Roy cried out and went down.

Then something else shattered. Upstairs. Piercing through the sounds of the man's agonizing pain.

Jameson pushed himself to his feet, charging up the steps two at a time. He prayed he wasn't too late. He still heard Roy wrestling with the dog when another gunshot behind him was followed by Smokey's plaintive howl.

Hayley's hands flew up on a spasm, slamming over her mouth to hold in a scream. As she finally turned, slowly rotating her head, large eyes leading the motion, she found herself at the wrong end of a gun. Smoke still emanated from the barrel.

Behind it, Carter tilted his head to one side. "Don't move, bitch."

Right. Hayley gave his suggestion a mental middle finger and lunged for the balcony. He'd have to shoot her in the back if he wanted to.

On her first step, her vision blurred, and she tripped.

"What did I just say?" His hand ripped her backwards, swinging her in such a violent motion that she would've fallen had she not slammed into his chest first.

"You *really* should stop mixing Valium with alcohol. You can hardly walk straight," he rasped mockingly in her ear, as if he hadn't forced the laced champagne on her prior to landing. "And you're not as much fun to play with when you're passed out." The hand that was still holding the gun skated lazily down the front of her stomach, going lower in between her thighs.

He'd also made her change into the little black dress. *Like this is a fucking celebration for him.* The steel scraped against her skin, and her muscles twitched with a whimper. The barrel was still warm from shooting Aaron.

"But you're even less fun when you're sober," he reminded himself, his tone turning annoyed. "It's so tricky to find that sweet spot with you, baby girl."

Ugh. That twisted term of endearment made the bile rise up her throat. He only used it when things were about to get bad. Really bad. She could smell whiskey on his breath. He hardly drank. Was she the cause, or was there something else?

He gave her no time to mull it over. The fingers of Carter's left hand tensed around her upper arm right before he flung her across the room.

Hayley stumbled again in her stilettos when his grip released, sending her crashing into the little table by the window. Her eyes couldn't focus. She tried to block her fall, but the clear top came at her too fast, and the glass shattered in her face. A scream of pain detonated in her head.

Panic took over. Choking on a sob, she scrambled through the shards. Her hair draped over her vision like a sheer curtain, trapping her in a haze.

Disoriented, she braced herself off the plush rug in an attempt to push onto her knees. Her palms stung from a thousand cuts, her forearms too, with splinters of glass everywhere, slicing her open as she moved.

The shag underneath her was no longer pristine white but had a dark pink hue. Still, more blood streaked her skin anywhere she looked. She didn't know how badly she was hurt; the adrenaline kept her numb to most of the pain. All she knew was the fear racing through her veins.

Beyond the tears, her eyes caught the small object amidst the debris that she'd hidden in the gap between the table's glass top and frame. Extending her hand, she tried to reach it right as Carter yanked her head back by her hair.

"You were supposed to be the cherry on top of our arrangement. A toy. But all you are to me is a fucking headache."

She was close to hyperventilating. Her breath tore up and down her lungs, and her chest heaved. She could barely hear his voice.

In her last remaining seconds, Hayley's mind became clear. She was going to die here tonight. Just like Aaron. Carter didn't need her anymore and wouldn't let her walk away; he'd made that clear. This was the end. Even if she fought back, he'd still kill her.

It was time to go. To give up. It would be so easy. She'd fought him for so long… she felt exhausted… she wanted it to end.

He pressed the steel to her temple.

One move… only one move. Then he'll pull the trigger. She let the comfort of her resolve wash over her.

The gun clicked as he cocked it, his arrogance always drawing out the satisfaction in the act. She knew him so well.

"Goodbye, baby girl."

59

The second-story landing formed the shape of an L, with the short side as the first stretch. Jameson saw two doors along each wall, the last part ending at a second staircase leading to a third floor.

He burst through the first door on his left, which looked like the old man's bedroom—not a master's. A set of doors stood open to an adjoining study or home office.

Jameson went on, skipping over the second door on the landing and making his way around the bend. He followed the incoherent sounds of a struggle and glass breaking nearby when he came up to the next bedroom. It was another single. Carter's.

Hayley and he don't share a room? Somehow, that made him feel relieved.

Across from him was a long balcony that he'd noticed in Roy's room as well. He assumed it stretched around the corner of the house, passing by all the rooms.

Jameson swung his weapon right and closed the distance to another door. His heart rate spiked. It went through a bathroom into a third bedroom. Hayley's—

His feet halted. There was a dead man on the ground. It was the guy he'd seen arrive with the big fella earlier, only now he had a gaping bullet hole in his forehead.

Jameson kept his gag reflex in check. It wasn't his first dead body. And the close-range wound looked too familiar as well.

He gave the room another quick sweep but still found no sign of Hayley. What *was* there, however, was a pool of blood, a shattered glass table, and a trail of dark red drops leading out to the balcony, the right side of the French doors open.

Hellcat at the ready, he inched forward, stepping with caution. His boot came down on something nestled in between the high pile of the shaggy rug. He looked down beneath his sole. A metallic gleam within the long fibers caught his eye.

Keeping the gun out in his dominant hand, Jameson lowered himself onto his haunches to pick it up. Confused, he stared at what he thought for a second was a corkscrew. Then he realized it was a cyclone dagger with a T-shaped push handle. The spiraling, tri-edged blade was almost six inches long, and its entire razor-sharp length was coated in blood.

He knew how dangerous these were—from research, not experience. The wounds they caused tended to be lethal. The question was, who got ventilated?

Jameson turned it in the dim light when Hayley's scream erupted on the landing. She must've fled across the balcony and run into Roy outside of his room.

He darted out of Carter's bedroom, rounding the corner of the banister. Gun out in his right hand, he angled his body sideways. Roy was standing at the top of the stairs, using Hayley as a human shield, his left arm hooked around her throat in a headlock.

He swung her around, forcing a shriek from her. She was in bad shape, but there was no indication that she'd caught the business end of the cyclone.

Jameson stalked gradually down the short side of the landing, keeping a vigilant eye on Roy.

"You're still alive," he noted with little surprise. "Did you kill him then? Did you kill your own *brother*?"

The comment was meant to rattle Hayley as he breathed down her neck, but judging by her unfazed expression, she already knew. *How'd she figure it out?*

"Haven't seen him." Jameson raised the little dagger in his left hand into Roy's view. "But something tells me her husband is no longer in the picture. I'm keeping this as a souvenir, by the way." Without taking his sight off his target, he stuffed the blade into the empty gun holster in his back pocket, then returned his palm to the butt of his pistol.

Roy's demeanor didn't reveal any grief. He nudged Hayley's chin up with the muzzle of his gun. "Then you've done me a favor. You got rid of my useless son without implicating me. And in return, I get to keep you all to myself. Unlike him, I won't tolerate your insolence, though. I have no moral dilemma when it comes to hurting you. You only serve one purpose, sweetheart. You'll never see daylight again. I'll keep you in a cage. Heck, I already got the cage. That damn dog of yours won't need it any longer."

Her nails clawed at Roy's forearm collared around the front of her throat. Jameson could see the pain crashing through her as her eyes filled with tears. He clenched his jaw and steadied his gun, trying to get a shot. He was less than ten feet from them now, but most of his target's head remained tucked behind her.

"Are you really going to shoot your father?" he taunted.

"You're not my father. My dad was a hero. And you're going to pay for what you did to my mother."

"Is that why you're here? You want revenge? If it weren't for what I did, you wouldn't be here right now, boy. You should be grateful. You're the son I should've raised. Your mother made a good breeder. She tried to protect you from me, but in the end, she raised a killer, too."

"I've never killed anyone."

"Oh, really?" He angled his chin toward Hayley, his eye remaining on Jameson. "Did you know your lover boy has a criminal record? I had a friend of mine do a little digging. Turns out he killed someone in California. Was never charged, though. He must have some powerful contacts somewhere. Do you want to give her the skinny, or shall I?"

Jameson gave no reply, watching the shock unfold on Hayley's face. Her eyes shifted frantically back and forth between him and Roy.

"See, from what I heard, there was this girl in college that he liked. Unfortunately she was already fucking another guy, so Jameson here got him out of the way. Shot him point blank."

Yeah, there was a lot more to it than that. He remembered Amber always showing up with bruises. Black eyes, cracked ribs... no one cared. Her boyfriend was an abusive asshole when he drank too much. She couldn't get away from him. Had restraining orders, too. It didn't matter. She didn't see another way out. She waited for him to get wasted and then provoked him on purpose, knowing he'd come after her. She knew where he hid his gun. He didn't get one hit in. Amber was the one who killed him, but technically not in self-defense.

Jameson wanted to protect her. He didn't care about going down for it. He came up with a story, gave his confession, and the cops were happy to buy it. But that one detective figured it out. He let him go and didn't charge Amber, either. Her boyfriend was a known piece of shit, and apparently, they'd done them a favor.

"Open your eyes, Hayley. He's a cold-blooded murderer. You sure know how to pick 'em. Guess it runs in the family."

"I'm nothing like you," Jameson shouted in his defense. Hayley knew better than to believe his lies, didn't she? But he'd snapped at her, too. Hurt her…

He hated the way she was looking at him now. She knew what was in his blood; he couldn't explain that away. If he killed Roy, would that prove the man's point?

Hiding behind her, he shuffled closer to the edge of the stairs, ready to drag her down with him. Jameson couldn't get a clear shot.

"Oh, I know you would've made me proud." He scoffed. "Carter has always been a disappointment to me. Couldn't even manage to knock her up. But you did, didn't you?"

A fist clenched around his throat.

Hayley is pregnant? PREGNANT?

By me?

Now it was his eyes darting rapidly back and forth, looking for the truth in theirs. It was Hayley's that confirmed it.

"She didn't tell you? Well, Carter quickly put an end to that, so no need to dwell on it. I'll take over from here."

Jameson felt a crushing sensation in his chest. *A baby! MY baby!* That was why the asshole had beaten her.

"I should've let him drown," he growled as his rage unhinged.

He wasn't going to repeat that mistake. His mind was made up. Roy was going to die. Jameson took two determined steps toward them.

"Back off!" Roy jostled Hayley around, readjusting his gun below her chin, and pressing her up close to his front. "Do I have to remind you that I'm the one with the leverage?"

The high heels of her shoes dragged on the ground for a second before she recovered her footing. She stood almost as tall as him.

"You're going to let me walk out of here," he proposed. "And I'm taking her with me."

"No dice. She stays with me." Jameson watched the small red dot against the dark wall beside her head. It wasn't even trembling.

"Kid, you don't know who you're dealing with. I'm untouchable. Walk away."

Jameson shook his head slowly, calling the man's bluff. He wasn't going to shoot her.

"I'll drain the fight out of her," Roy threatened. "Once she watches you die, she'll be a lot more compliant. She won't have anything to live for."

Then his gun's muzzle kicked out from under her chin, pointing straight at Jameson. He could see clear down the barrel—

All three of them acted at the same time, as if on Hayley's cue. Her body went limp, turning into dead weight and knocking her captor off balance. A burst of fire ignited the inside of the barrel in front of him. Jameson didn't flinch. He aimed above her right shoulder at the man's now exposed torso and squeezed the trigger.

The jolt of the recoil registered in every cell of his body, more forceful than when he'd pulled the trigger earlier. He watched Roy stumble backward into the wall behind him from the impact of the bullet, teetering right at the cusp of the first step. His left hand clutched his chest, and blood seeped through his white shirt.

Jameson's eyes locked with Hayley's. It was over. She was safe, her face carrying a mask of shock, but she was safe.

No. He needed to make sure… had to take a second shot…

White-hot pain flared in his chest. His arms dropped as his left leg gave out, and he went down, the banister crashing into his shoulder.

60

There was so much blood soaking his navy blue shirt. Hayley couldn't tell where he was hit. His gun was no longer in his hand.

She knew she had to give him an opening. Roy had kept his gun pressed to her after she'd rammed her elbow into the bottom of his chin. That had really pissed him off, and he didn't want to take that chance again, but he had no desire to shoot her. He had other plans.

She even had a feeling that Roy wasn't involved in Carter's attempt to take her out. His insecure son had had enough of being ridiculed by her, Roy was different. She was more afraid of him pulling the trigger by accident if she managed to aim her heel at the inside of his knee.

At last, he'd taken his gun off her, and that had been her chance.

Why didn't he fire sooner?

Roy had urged Jamie to walk away. Now that Carter was dead, he was the only son he had left. Maybe a part of him really was proud of the man Beth's son had become.

Hayley pushed onto her hands and swung her head around to see Roy slumped against the wall, one foot on the landing, the other down on the first step. But he wasn't dead. In a last effort to get them both, he leveled his weapon at her face.

MOVE! a voice in her head screamed over the noise of rushing blood.

She threw herself in Jamie's direction, reaching out with her right hand. Her fingers closed around the coarse grip, and she flipped onto her back, aiming the red dot.

She didn't waver. Controlling her breath, she squeezed the trigger twice, firing two rounds back-to-back in between his eyes.

Hayley watched Roy's face freeze in a mix of agony and panic. Then gravity took hold, hauling him down the steps.

Through the space between the dark wood balusters, she followed the flailing motion of his body as it tumbled lower and lower in the curve of the staircase.

He came to a stop on his back, spread-eagle in the middle of the foyer. That was when she heard the sirens outside.

The sound ripped her out of her stun. Hayley scrambled to reach Jamie as blue lights flashed through the windows of the entryway. His back was braced against the banister, chin tucked toward his chest. His eyes were closed now, but they had been open a moment ago.

"Jamie!" His name left her lips in a frantic pitch while she fumbled with the folds of his shirt. She felt for the wound to put pressure on it, but everything was wet... and dark...

His heavy lids opened barely enough to give a glimpse of blue that was dulled by a hazy sheen. His breathing strained, then his lashes fluttered like he was a hair away from passing out.

There! Off to the left side of his chest, she found the hole of the bullet.

440

Hayley stacked both hands on top of one another, feeling his heartbeat against her palms. Outside, car doors slammed shut, footsteps rushed up, the door burst open, and before she knew it, the foyer was filled with people: police officers and men in suits all spilling through, gathering around Roy's body on the ground.

"HELP!" she hollered down to the mass of men to get their attention, then turned back to him. "Stay with me, Jamie."

Seconds felt like minutes. *Why's nobody coming? What's taking them so long?*

His head bobbed weakly. She called for help over his shoulder a second time, her voice shaking. Tears ran down her cheeks and dripped from her chin, but she refused to take her hands off Jamie to wipe them. They landed in her lap, while his blood pooled between her fingers. She was afraid to change his position. Didn't want to risk moving him.

He raised a weak left hand to her face, cupping her cheek. A crooked smile pulled at the corner of his lips as his thumb traced the shape. Then his eyes fell shut, and he slipped out of consciousness again.

"I said stay with me," she repeated with emphasis, shaking him while pressing down on his wound. "Don't you dare—"

His lips parted, and he mumbled something under shallow breaths.

"What?" Hayley leaned in closer.

"…six… oh… two… one…"

Huh? "What is that? What does that… Wait! Is that—"

Jamie's eyes flew open, alert, and focused on her face.

Hayley frowned. "Was that my phone number?"

"Yeah," he wheezed, then grinned. "I memorized it before dropping it into the lake."

"You jerk! You had my number this whole time and never once called?" She squeezed her fingers around his large left pec, pushing him further into the balusters. The wood creaked.

"Ow! Quit wringing me out like a sponge, woman. I'm leaking over here."

She wasn't sorry. And he appeared to have regained his sense of humor along with his consciousness. *What a relief.*

Two paramedics finally came up behind her, taking over his wound and starting an IV in his right arm.

Hayley inched back to give them space, but Jamie's eyes remained fixed on her while one of the men cut away his shirt.

"I need to ask you something," he said, tipping his head around the guy.

"What's that?"

"Did you name your dog after me?"

She sucked in a breath. "Smokey!" She'd forgotten about him.

The sound of a weak bark erupted somewhere downstairs.

"It's gonna be a minute, ma'am," the police officer approaching them said. "The four-legged hero needs a medic too, but he'll pull through. He's a toughie."

The uniformed man crouched down beside them. Hayley was glad that it wasn't the cop she'd seen with Roy. Maybe this would all finally end.

"How's this one looking?" he asked the paramedic working on Jamie.

"BP is steady. Breathing, too. Lungs don't seem to be hit. The X-rays will show where the slug ended up. My best guess is that it ricocheted off a rib but missed any vital organs."

The officer nudged his chin up, turning his next question on them. "You're Jameson Davis, I presume."

Jamie gave a short nod, and he went on. "I received a call from a sheriff in some small town up in Montana a couple of hours ago. We didn't take him seriously at first, but then the FBI knocked on our door, and we put things together from there. Glad you're both okay. I wouldn't mind hearing the entire story once you're all patched up."

After they both agreed, he rose to his feet and returned to his entourage, which was still crowding the entryway of the esteemed Nolan residence. Hayley gloated inwardly. Their legacy would die with them.

"So, you really do have friends in high places," she mused with a chuckle, sliding her palm into his.

Jameson sighed and dropped his eyes. "Hayley…"

He let her name drift and didn't go on, as if he wanted to explain himself but wasn't sure how to start. Stroking his thumb across the back of her hand, he pressed his lips together.

"Amber mentioned an abusive ex," she told him to get the ball rolling.

"I didn't shoot him." His stare cut back to her. "I've never shot anyone before."

"I wouldn't blame you if you had. I know what it's like to be in her situation."

Amber had freed herself, and so had she now. Carter was dead on the balcony, a gaping hole in his thigh near the femoral artery. He hadn't made it three steps outside.

The space between Jamie's brows crinkled as he brought them together and gave her hand a squeeze. The gleaming hint of a tear followed the words he chose. "He killed our baby."

"He tried," she said with a sheepish grin.

She'd been to the clinic in Sacramento to discover that their miracle had managed to hang on.

"You serious?"

Hayley confirmed with a nod, and his face lit up with joy. Yep, there was definitely something sparkling in his eyes. "It's a survivor like you," he noted.

She jostled her head. "You have no idea." Between the IUD, the beating she'd taken, and being drugged twice, their little guy was truly a fighter.

444

Epilogue

Clasping the side of her neck, Jameson pulled her in for another kiss.

"You look stunning," he whispered against her lips.

"Really? You don't think white is kinda… you know…" Hayley scrunched her nose, struggling to find the right words.

"Unfitting for another man's widow?" He arched his brows as he filled in the blank.

And not just any other man's widow, but the groom's half-brother's, who was expecting *his* child instead of her late husband's?

"Nah." He chuckled. "You wear white for me, Virgin." *As if anyone cares about her virtue.* Then he dipped his forehead to remind her, "You were mine first."

Jameson wound his left arm around the small of her back, squishing her glorious breasts into his chest. The way they bubbled out of the top would have him pitching a tent if her body wasn't already fused to his.

The sight of her walking up to him standing beneath the arch had taken his breath away. He still couldn't keep his hands off her, and honestly, he didn't care if anyone was watching as he pinned her against the old barn. It was impossible to get some privacy around here.

But he made due with what little they had. *So what if her dress is getting dirty?* It wasn't going to make it through the night anyway. It would hopefully be in shreds on the floor within the hour.

Five days he'd spent in the hospital post-surgery to remove the bullet. It had zigzagged through his chest before going south past his liver and then stopping just above his kidney. He'd been taking things easy for the last three weeks, but he didn't want to put things off any longer. The weather was supposed to shift into colder temperatures any day now.

He glanced over his shoulder at the crowd. The entire former staff was here, thanks to Carl and Summer's secret planning. He was blown away by the turnout, but he'd been happy to do this in a much smaller circle. It felt undeserved. All the people he'd grown up around had come. Even Paul. Marcus, Emily, and the rest of the guys had flown in, too.

Summer stood next to Eileen and her husband. Jameson also recognized Kate, their youngest daughter, whose wedding he'd skipped, and assumed the man beside her was her own husband. She was only a few years older than Jameson himself. Her son was eight now, from what Summer had told him. Their lives had moved on, bypassing him. He had missed out on all that.

But they had come.

He stared in awe at how much his family had grown. He felt so blessed.

In his periphery, Hayley tipped her head to trace the direction of his eyes. "I never expected him to remember me."

"Who, Carl?" He turned back toward his lovely bride. "I guess my mom talked about you a lot. I never knew you two were so close."

"And he really has no idea, huh?"

"About what?"

"You and Summer."

"Me and Summer?" The air in his lungs grew a little thin. She couldn't possibly be referring to what he was thinking.

"You know…" she left the insinuation hanging in the air.

His pulse spiked with a subtle blow to his chest. "How the fuck do *you* know?" Summer swore to take it to her grave. If Carl ever found out, he was a dead man.

"You told me."

"I did? When?"

"At the lake that night."

"Oh shit!" He remembered now. *That whole rape allegation…* that had been hilarious considering *he* was the one who'd seduced *her*. Honestly, he'd been proud of it too and maybe wanted to show off a little.

He'd never thought Carl and Summer would end up together; otherwise, he wouldn't have touched her. Now the stunt could come back to bite him in the ass. "Well, you better keep that to yourself unless you want to become a widow again real quick."

"You don't think he'd laugh about the fact that his wife took your virginity?"

"Technically, that wasn't his wife. That was our new manager… who just happens to be his wife now."

"But you don't think he'll agree with your reasoning?"

"Nah, he'll kill me," he assured her with a bob of his head.

Hayley snorted a laugh, then nudged his attention back toward the crowd. "He looks pretty good with a baby on one arm."

"He does." *Like a pro.*

Jameson couldn't fight the smile that stretched across his face watching the big man with his two-week-old baby boy. His five-year-old daughter was twirling in circles around him, her pale green flower-girl dress clutched in her little fists. Her dark ringlet curls bounced around her head, and her bright eyes sparkled with the purest joy. She was the perfect mix of Summer and him.

"Not quite as nervous as your friend over there," she hinted.

Yeah, Marcus still had that typical new parent look on his face every time Leah started crying: panicked, overwhelmed, and not to mention tired. But she had him wrapped around her tiny finger.

How was *he* going to fare with the challenge? No one was ever really prepared for this. With Ben and Carl, he had two incredible dads to look up to. Jameson wasn't sure he could fill the shoes. He was nervous as shit.

"I like your friends," Hayley said, the sound of her voice reeling his mind back. "They're good people. I'm glad you had them."

His hand brushed over the bump under her loose-fitting dress, and a sudden weight came down on his shoulders. He dropped them with a heavy sigh. "Tell me the truth." He was afraid of the answer, but he had to ask. "Doesn't it bother you at all that you're still carrying on *his* bloodline?"

She stared at him with those calm gray and green eyes that no longer hid anything from him. "No." She raised her hand to his cheek, her lips hovering mere inches from his. "Because you're not your father's son," she said, her thumb grazing through his beard. "You're your mother's."

Jameson melted into her kiss. Her words were just as powerful as the gesture that affirmed them. The hold she had on his very essence was irrevocable. He loved this woman with everything he had, and he was willing to lose himself in her.

Hayley broke away first. She cracked a wry grin, then rolled her eyes. "If anything, you should be worried about *my* blood. I've killed two people."

"In self-defense. Your blood is pure in my eyes."

'Untouchable' my ass. Roy's empire had gone up in flames after the FBI raids. Carter had brought that on.

She drew up her left hand and placed it on his chest. His eyes flicked to Mom's ring on her finger. He had a feeling she would've approved. Her necklace also looped around Hayley's throat, and since he wasn't wearing his shitkickers today, Dad's dog tags were momentarily tucked into his right vest pocket. The two of them were here with them, too.

Her finger still teasing through his facial hair, Hayley sucked in her bottom lip, teeth raking over the plump flesh. "I love the way it feels when you kiss me."

"Bearded for your pleasure," he muttered, kissing a trail along the edge of her jaw.

She gave a short laugh laced with false skepticism. "Is that so?"

"You know it is." He moved down the column of her neck, letting his rough chin scrape against her to call her bluff. "But I'll be happy to prove it again… and again… and again."

His hands roamed the curves of her waist and hips. The heat of her skin radiated through the thin cotton everywhere he touched. He was aching to feel more. Dying to devour her. He wanted her to ride his face until she came undone. No one would hear her in the woods.

"Time to ditch," he proposed, his voice a hoarse rasp thick with lust. "Sun's getting low, and there's something I want to show you before it gets dark."

Tugging her along by her hand, he led her away from the park's public trails and deeper into the trees. To keep her from getting an early glimpse, he prompted her to close her eyes and carried her the rest of the way in his arms.

Hayley dragged a lazy fingernail down the back of his neck above the stiff, white shirt collar that made him want to drop her where they were and take her against a tree. Her seductive purr let him know she was well aware of what she was doing, too. The blood supply to his brain was running low.

He resisted the urge to go all animal on her. "Keep your eyes closed," he cued. "It's not much further."

And thank fuck for that. No more taking it easy. He was so goddamn hungry for her.

What's she going to say? The wild ambiance of the environment wasn't exactly up to her standards. He had seen the manor she'd called home for six years. *Will she like it?* He was sweating more from the anxiety than from carrying her featherweight.

"Don't peek." Jameson set her feet down, her back toward him, and slid his hands over her eyes.

There it was, less than ten feet above their heads. And no longer with a flimsy ladder to get up, either. They were now facing the staircase that went up and right to the spacious deck. From their angle, they could see straight up to the narrow landing on the front side.

His heart gave another flutter. He'd thought of her every time he'd made an addition to the structure, all while knowing she would never see the finished construct.

He'd built it for her, though—for them—a place for his soul and its shadow to haunt in secret. He'd dreamed of her here… made love to her in his head so many nights under the stars…

Yes, she'd been there for him too. Every time he'd needed her.

Jameson looked up at the strings of solar lights he'd wrapped around the rails. They twinkled in the advancing dusk. Everything was exactly as he'd imagined it. With her here now, it was a dream come true.

"You're making me nervous," she chirped impatiently.

He inhaled slowly, then held his breath as he uncovered her eyes. "What do you say to honeymooning in a tree house?"

Her jaw dropped, and her hands sprang to her mouth on a gasp. "Holy shit!"—*Okay, not the answer I expected*—"This is a small castle," she exclaimed.

"I appreciate the flattery, but I know for someone who grew up in mansions, you're vastly exaggerating."

Nonetheless, his chest swelled with her praise. He reveled in it. The glints of light reflected in her large eyes as she stared up. Her gaze darted back and forth in wonder.

The entire structure consisted of three parts that spread out over six trees and were connected via suspension bridges. The main house in the middle was an 18-by-9-foot cabin with sealed doors and windows to stay warm. The basic two-level design didn't deviate much from his original plan, but the rest had changed over the twelve-year period as his skills had grown. He'd integrated a full bathroom with a shower beneath the lofted queen-size bed. On the opposite side was an L-shaped kitchen that utilized a four-burner electric cooktop. It had lots of counter space and a movable island that converted into a dining table.

But, of course, his imagination hadn't been content with that. The project had blown up from there. The longer of the two suspension bridges went left of the tiny house's entry landing to a cozy seating pit with a built-in couch. It was enclosed by glass on all sides and had a matching tin roof, as well as its own ground access and an attached half-bathroom. The 10-foot-square space even had a stocked bar.

Jameson's favorite addition, though, sat to the right with an elevation of another eight feet. *The Watch Tower*. From the cabin's side deck, a short bridge led to a platform with a ladder to reach the eagle's nest. It had a glass roof, but was open on the sides, so they could be out there in the rain.

"Can it withstand heavy rocking?" Hayley asked, her tone inciting an innuendo.

"Oh, it will hold in a tornado."

Or at least he was pretty sure that it would. The field test for that was pending. But it could definitely hold anything his imagination was going to cook up with her.

"It might not be my best work, but it was my first. It means a lot to me."

"Well, you know what they say about firsts," she prompted, turning around to face him.

"What's that?"

Hayley drew him to her mouth by his tie. "They make a lasting impression."

Bonus Material

Find the official SPOTIFY PLAYLIST for this book at www.runikpress.com/renaterowlandbooks

Subscribe to my newsletter for exclusive sneak peeks and details on upcoming releases like Book Two in the *Bound by A WEB OF WYRD Trilogy* coming this fall.

Thank you for reading

Please consider leaving a review however long. Any review is always appreciated.

Follow me on social media:

Instagram & Threads: @renaterowland

Facebook: @renate.rowland.books

Acknowledgments

I keep this short.

I'm thankful to my steadily growing pack of ARC readers and the friends I have made along the way. Your support means so much to me.

And a big thank you to my beta readers: Jenelle Jenniges, and Sarah Reed, as well as my final proofreader Kelsey Stone. Your fantastic feedback made this possible, and I'm so grateful you took the time to help me out.

Author Bio

Renate Rowland is an author of suspenseful Paranormal and Contemporary Romance. After being fortunate to have called three different continents her home, she has settled with her family in the US. She is an artist at heart, and although she expresses that in various ways, she held on to her stories until she felt it was time to give them air and let them breathe on their own. Finding much inspiration in music lyrics, she is driven by the desire to create something as powerful and moving as the artists she admires.

9 798988 340614